Doyle's Disciples

DOYLE'S DISCIPLES

a novel by

Bob Leuci

Freundlich Books
New York

Copyright © Bob Leuci 1984

Library of Congress Cataloging in Publication Data
Leuci, Bob, 1940–
Doyle's disciples.
I. Title.
PS3562.E857D6   1984   813'.54   84-4184
ISBN 0-88191-006-6

Published by Freundlich Books
80 Madison Avenue
New York, New York 10016

Distributed to the trade by
The Scribner Book Companies, Inc.

Manufactured in the United States of America

10 9 8 7 6 5 4 3 2 1

To James, Lucy and Regina Leuci

I am deeply grateful to a number of people whose encouragement and aid were crucial to me during the past few years. I want them all to know how much they mean to me.

Jay Presson Allen
Roberta Arrigo
Robert Blecker
Laura Harrington
Kathy Pohl
Margaret Shaw
John Soroko

A special thanks to my agent and friend, Esther Newberg and my editor, Larry Freundlich.

If I must continue this cliché
of violence
it should be for police
who also drink coffee all night
and wear their griefs on their hips,
instead of you.

> *from* Confessional For Police
> by WILLIAM KIT HATHAWAY

More whiskey to burn out the feather tickling in the throat
to ease the violence of the night,
to celebrate the loneliness of being men.

> *from* The Poet Hunts Doves With the Natchitoches Police
> by WILLIAM KIT HATHAWAY

DOYLE'S DISCIPLES

I.

Victoria stood motionless on the roof landing, legs apart, bent over, his chin resting on hands that cupped the banister. A long neck on a small, skinny head with shallow cheeks. He looked like a vulture perched on a dead and rotting tree. He was thirty-eight years old and looked a worn fifty. At the end of the month he'd have seventeen years in the department.

Seventeen years is a goddamn long time, he thought, most of 'em spent on tenement roof landings, and here he was again.

Inching forward, he glanced down between the banisters to the first floor. It was the middle of the day. Even so, the tenement was dark. The only windows were those on the floor landings. They were filthy, letting in small streams of beige light that stained the walls and dripped to the floor.

An apartment door opened beneath him. He tiptoed to the rear of the landing. It was easy to merge with the darkness up here. He felt a tingle at his groin and pulled at his pants. He could see them. He could see them all, but even if they looked, they couldn't see him.

Georgia Boy was late . . . what else was new? Six flights below he saw a hand grab the banister and move up the stairs.

In times past, he would lie in wait on roof landings just like this one, hiding in dark corners, ambushing unsuspecting heroin addicts as they shot up. Moving to the rear of the landing, he made sure the hook in the roof door was secure.

To watch as a junkie tied a belt around his arm, then injected himself with a mixture of heroin and water, was fascinating. Crouched, he'd stare transfixed, leering as the sick scene was played.

A door opened two floors below him. Music and laughter rose from the apartment like escaping gas. He remembered the junkies. They, too, were happy, if only for a moment. The moment it took for the heroin-mixed blood to stream toward their hearts. Junkies always seemed like a band of dreamers. Each would be somewhere north of Venus, scratching his balls and nodding as the white lady sailed through his veins, when, screaming like a banshee, Victoria would kick open the landing door and bring down the curtain. There were times when a hypodermic would be jutting from the back of a hand or stuck in an arm like a dart. He giggled when he remembered their surprised expressions as he swung his nightstick and grabbed their dope.

This afternoon was different. He was hanging out on another landing, to be sure, but today someone knew he was there.

Dropping a cigarette to the floor and crushing it, Detective Victoria thought about his friends. He had, as best he could figure it, none.

There was Georgia Boy, but Georgia Boy was business—not a friend. Forget Georgia Boy. There was his partner, Billy Price, but Price was a shine. A white man couldn't really be friends with a shine. All things considered, though, Price was the ideal partner. Price left him alone, allowing him to do his thing. He in turn left Price alone, which was the way Price wanted it and the way he needed it. Who wanted to be friends with a shine anyway? Nobody but another shine.

A test: like a flash he pulled his gun from the ankle holster and spun toward the roof door. "Bang, bang . . . Gotcha, you smelly mother." The door was locked. No one was there. The weight of the gun felt good in his hand. His passport, his guarantee of safety. He was king of the hill. The landing was all his.

Waiting was always the worst. Watching and listening as the assholes went about the business of sharing their lives with one another. Another apartment door opened, more laughter, more music, the sounds of bongos and a guitar. The smell of frying Latin condiments drifted up the stairs toward the roof.

The street door opened and slammed shut. This time a hand he recognized grabbed the banister around the fourth step. Three diamond rings that glittered five floors below told him this hand belonged to Georgia Boy.

From the hallway he heard a shout, then a scream, then again a shout. What the hell was going on? He couldn't see. He moved to get a better look and slid on some sort of goo. Running feet were coming up toward his landing. He reached for his gun. The hammer hung up, caught on his trousers; he tugged at it and cut himself. Bending over to free the gun, he heard a wheezing, gushing sound. When he looked up, four steps below him stood a bare-chested Puerto Rican in sandals and shorts, gasping for air. Around the Puerto Rican's neck was the largest gold medallion he had ever seen. Pointing his gun right at Christ's head, he hissed, "One more step, you pigskin-eating motherfucker, and I'll blow you into . . ." The Puerto Rican didn't wait for him to finish. He yelped, did a pirouette, and headed back down the stairs a lot faster than he had come up. He dodged past Georgia Boy, who stood like a statue against the fifth-floor hallway wall.

"Hey, Georgia Boy, what happened down there?" he yelled.

"I don't wanna look," Georgia Boy called back, standing dead still against the wall as if he were part of the molding.

Someone had kicked an anthill. The tenement exploded with people screaming, shouting, and cursing. Victoria hunched up and stepped back, sliding on the goo. Georgia Boy moved away from the wall and fled up the last flight of stairs. Victoria snapped open the door latch and both men moved out onto the roof.

After the darkness of the landing, the bright afternoon sun made him sneeze and rub his eyes. When he was able to see again he looked into a sneering black face. "What the hell are we doing up here?" asked Georgia Boy, a look of revulsion on his face.

The roof was littered with sable-colored dog shit. Off to one side was a pigeon coop built by a blind man. In the center of the roof, four half-burnt and soggy mattresses stood piled up. Green wine bottles in the hundreds lay scattered about. One, full of urine, stood upright against a chimney. The chimney had a television antenna tied to it with rope, its two metal arms twisted to form a heart.

"Georgia Boy, what's happening, my man?" Shines liked loud friendly greetings, he thought. He also wanted Georgia Boy to forget the incident with the Puerto Rican. Besides, even classy shines loved that voodoo hand-slapping bullshit. With a grin that accented his buck teeth, Victoria stuck out his hand, waiting for a slap as if he'd just caught a down-and-out in the end zone. As it was with most things, he was wrong.

"Fuck you, Sal. Don't talk that jitterbug shit to me. Whaddaya think I am, one of those street niggers?" Georgia Boy snapped as he walked to the edge of the roof and looked down. "You're a cop," he yelled, "don't you know this block is dangerous?" Screams echoed through the street. Victoria joined Georgia Boy at the parapet. The Puerto Rican, gold necklace and all, was hightailing it along a sidewalk thick with people. A domino game at the corner scattered as the Puerto Rican skipped past, a black woman with a machete two strides behind and closing. "Cut the mother," Victoria yelled. As if she heard him, the black woman wildly swung the machete, narrowly missing a teenager on a three-hundred-dollar ten-speed, sending him careening through the scattering crowd.

"This is the last time I'm coming into this hole. The place is a sewer," Georgia Boy said, dusting himself off with long manicured fingers. He was beardless. A scar, like a worm just under the skin, ran along his jaw to his upper lip. He was no youngster, though you'd be hard pressed to guess his age. Processed and pulled back, his oiled black hair gave him a striking Indian appearance. His clothes, silk and linen and custom-made, fit perfectly on a lean six-foot frame. On the hottest of days Georgia Boy wore a jacket. A red silk handkerchief was tucked in the breast pocket of his white linen blazer.

Impressed as he was by Georgia Boy's appearance, Victoria was more interested in the package Georgia Boy pulled out of his inside pocket: four thousand dollars in fresh neat fifties and hundreds, Georgia Boy's monthly payment to the Sixth Division vice and gambling squad.

The son of a bitch could go for twice that and not notice, Victoria thought, snapping up the envelope with a smooth, experienced move.

"Do me a favor. Next month pick a place where human beings go," said Georgia Boy, tiptoeing to avoid a mound of human shit that had solidified, exposing a bit of the *Daily News* at the peak. "Damn, Sal, why do you seem so at home up here?"

"Better be safe than sorry," quipped Victoria, pissed that he felt the need to explain himself to this shine.

"Next time let's be safe and avoid hepatitis," said Georgia Boy with a slight smile, sensing that he had offended Victoria. Keeping his hands in his pockets so as not to touch anything, Georgia Boy moved to the roof door. "By the way," he said, "there's a new captain up at the Twenty-eighth. He busted up three of my spots. Will ya talk to him for me?"

Victoria feigned surprise. "What fuckin' captain busted up your spots?" He knew who the new captain was all right. He also understood that this shine expected more than a bit of concern for the four grand he deposited with him each month. Wanting to make Georgia Boy at least think he got what he paid for, he grunted, "Just tell me his name. I'll have him outta the fuckin' precinct in a day."

Georgia Boy smiled and threw an arm around him. "He just got there. Give the man a week. If he doesn't get the word in a week, then transfer his ass." Georgia Boy's smile faded as screams could again be heard coming from the street.

"It's Aaron Meyer, the Hebe," said Victoria. "He's new up here. I'll have somebody pull his coat. Don't worry; you'll be able to go with those spots in a week."

Georgia Boy opened the roof door and went back into the landing.

"Ya know, I got stoned one night and fucked one of the broads off this block. When I sobered up I washed my prick in Clorox. I suggest you do the same with your feet."

Apparently, whoever used the roof for a toilet had utilized the landing as well, and Victoria had been shuffling around in it. He bent his head slowly, afraid to look. When he glanced up, Georgia Boy was grinning ear to ear.

"I gotta run. Them gangbusters downstairs will be all over me like stink on shit if I'm not careful." Looking back over his shoulder at Victoria's shoes, he moved down the stairs. Halfway down he called back, "I need a fuckin' machine gun to come into this street. Next month a different spot, O.K.?"

Victoria, concerned with the goo on his shoe, kept scraping it along the top step of the landing. It was tough to sound important with shit all over your feet, but he tried. "There ain't been a Jew born that won't bend for a few bucks," he yelled. "I'll take care of this captain for ya. Count on it," he barked at the disappearing figure of Georgia Boy, who was three flights down and fading fast. Honest cops made him sick, especially bosses, he thought, as he kicked open the landing door and moved out onto the roof.

Victoria made for the corner building. As he crossed from one roof to the other, he noticed a supermarket shopping cart. The cart had a wheel missing and stood on edge next to a pile of finished brick. Before going down, he looked over the parapet to the street. To judge from appearances it was midnight, New Year's Eve, in San Juan. He cackled when he thought of the expressions on the faces of the spics below as the cart, neatly stacked with bricks, sailed over the roof, falling silently, swiftly, exploding into the middle of the active domino game seven floors straight down.

Paddy Sheridan loved to listen to country music and gape at black women's asses. "Turkey asses," he called them. Johnny Cash would break into "Ring of Fire," and Paddy would catch a glimpse of a mulatto ass crossing 115th Street and Pleasant Avenue. What better way to spend a hot July afternoon in Harlem?

There was a time when Paddy had other options. A week after the explosion he could easily have been granted a line-of-duty injury pension. Three quarters of his salary tax-free for life. That translated into more take-home pay than he received when he worked. He didn't want it.

As he regained consciousness, when the burning in his cheek, hand, and shoulder was at its worst, the only thought that passed through his mind was: Now I've done it. I've blown the job. A piece of his face blown off, a piece of his hand gone, not to mention a fair-sized chunk of shoulder blown away, and Detective Second Grade Paddy Sheridan's only thought was: Fuck, I don't wanna be an insurance man.

But it all worked out for Paddy. Chief Doyle went to bat for him. He was able to stay on the job, though not in the bomb squad, his first love. He would be Doyle's chauffeur. Not work with wall-to-wall excitement but he was still "on the job," and what the hell, sitting in Harlem looking at asses and listening to Johnny Cash was a lot better than checking dented fenders.

Live and let live, a cliché for most people, was a lifestyle for Paddy. He hated few people and fewer things. He hated poor blacks who threw bricks off rooftops and fucked up his police car. He hated businessmen who thought they could buy him for a chicken. Of course he hated the British. His strong dislike of Sal Victoria was swiftly deteriorating into revulsion. He'd never, not for a minute, understand the Chief's relationship with the greasy son of a bitch. How could this dirt bag rate to be one of Doyle's bagmen? There were at least fifty guys in the unit that would love that assignment. Of the fifty, Paddy would rather be sitting and waiting for anyone—anyone other than this creep.

Pleasant Avenue is as far east as you can go. Fifty yards further is the FDR Drive, then the river. Paddy backed his department car to the curb. He looked north up Pleasant Avenue toward St. Mary's Church. "Our Lady of the Three Kilos," he called it. The church faced out onto a street that supported more drug transactions than the Camino del Rey in Bogotá. All the big-time dago dope dealers contributed heavily to the church and lived in Fort Lee, New Jersey.

Paddy tried not to look in the direction of Victoria's car as it pulled to the curb.

If Victoria would just give him the envelope and leave, that would be bearable, but no such luck. It seemed that Victoria always had a need to jabber. Paddy had nothing in common with him; nothing at all. During fifteen years in the department, Paddy had worked with a ton of partners. Some he liked more than others. He couldn't imagine what it would be like to have to work with this numb-nuts every day. If he wasn't so loyal to the Chief, he'd question Doyle's sanity.

"Hey, buddy, how you doing?" Paddy smiled as Victoria slipped into the department car and shut the radio off.

Victoria hated country music, and never failed to let Paddy know it. "How can you stand that shit-kicking crap?" he said, slamming the door. Paddy let that go. The less said, the better.

"Ya know, Paddy, I'm not feeling too great," Victoria moaned.

"I don't blame you. Have you been listening to the radio? You look at the *Times* today?"

"*The New York Times*! Who gives a shit what those Jews think, and the radio in my car is busted," Victoria blurted.

"I have a copy of the *Times* in the back seat. Take it. You might be front page tomorrow." Paddy's smile had faded. He reached into the back seat and handed him the paper. As Victoria scanned the headline, Paddy turned the radio on.

The New York Times announced that it was preparing to run a series of articles on police corruption. They had reliable inside information, they said.

"Inside information? What bullshit is that?" Victoria scowled and threw part of the paper back over the seat. He kept the sports section, glanced at a few pages, then turned to Paddy. "Do you think they might really have something?"

Victoria's question had an anxious edge. Paddy thought he'd play with this jerk a while. "Hey, look, I don't think the *Times* would announce anything like this unless they had something to go on. So if I were you, I'd dig out my uniform. You just might be dodging trucks on Canal Street in a week." He had a pin under Victoria's nail he could push or pull. Right now he felt like pushing. "Sal, times are changing. There are plenty of people interested in what's going on in the department. If we don't change with the times we could be in a gang of trouble."

"What the fuck are you talking about, times are changing? There are all kinds of people out here doing all kinds of bull-shit. If they want to keep on doing it, they're going to have to pay the fare. No matter what some Jew in *The New York Times* says, I'm the fucking toll taker. If they want to cross my bridge, they'll have to go for it. If not, the bridge is going up and these fuckers are out of business." Victoria was storming. Little white bubbles of saliva rolled out from the corners of his mouth. This

[10]

prick's a mad dog, thought Paddy, as Victoria lurched out of the car and slammed the door behind him.

"Take it easy, buddy, I'm not the *Times*'s informant," Paddy said.

"Fuck the *Times*, fuck the informant, and fuck you, Sheridan." A wino stepped off the curb near Victoria's car. "Right. Fuck everybody, especially that nigger up the street who stole my quarter." The wino wore a military jacket with a hundred nameless stains. He grabbed Victoria by the shoulders, then spit in the street. Paddy thought: Christ, he's gonna kiss him. Victoria twisted away and threw a kick at the wino's groin. His gun snapped loose from its holster, bounced once, then slid into a sewer.

"Damn, Sal. Now you've done it," Paddy yelled.

"Just get this thing off me," Victoria screamed. The wino had him by the collar. Victoria tried to scream again, but it came out a whisper, the rancid smell of the wino taking his breath away. Paddy grabbed hold of the wino and pulled him free. "Here, here, Sergeant. I have a dollar for ya." Taking a dollar from his pocket, Paddy shoved it into the wino's hand.

"I was with Patton in the Pacific," the wino mumbled as he ricocheted off two garbage cans.

Paddy turned to Victoria, who had gotten into his car. It was beginning to rain. A summer shower to clean the streets.

"Buddy, don't you have something for me?" Paddy asked.

"No. I haven't seen anyone yet," Victoria lied. "I'll call you soon as I do." Victoria threw his car in gear and drove off. As he turned the corner into 116th Street, Paddy sensed he'd be waiting a long time for that call. He turned just as the wino reached the middle of the intersection, screaming, "Fuck 'em. Fuck 'em all." The rain began falling in quarter-sized drops.

2.

As summers go in New York, the summer of 1970 was not unusually hot. On July 1, at about four o'clock in the afternoon, five hundred Puerto Ricans began their annual demonstration in front of the South Bronx's 41st Precinct. By four-thirty they were chanting in a language not even the Puerto Rican cops could understand. At six o'clock they began throwing balloons filled with urine and pea soup at the station house. By seven o'clock two or three bricks sailed through the captain's open window, and by nine o'clock, just after the sun went down, salsa music could be heard. Ten-thirty brought dancing in the street. The attack on Fort Apache was over for another year.

July 3, midnight: the sanitation union struck the city. Garbage men let a mountain of trash stand through the glorious Fourth, supplying a smelly harvest for the already gorged rats of Manhattan, while they lounged round their aboveground swimming pools in suburban Massapequa.

During the last week in July the teachers' union announced that both grammar and high school teachers would not return in September unless they were given armed guards. On the morning of the thirty-first some joker climbed the World Trade Center, and at 5:05 p.m. the subways quit working.

In August the police department was preoccupied with a psychopathic killer who stalked lovers' lanes blowing away anyone who resembled his sixth-grade homeroom teacher. A male member of the City Council was caught in leotards and ballet slippers playing doctor with a group of ten-year-olds.

As the maple trees in Central Park began changing from green to gold to brown, as landlords en masse began curtailing oil deliveries north of Ninety-sixth Street, just about the time the first schoolteacher was mugged, raped, and stuck naked in the trunk of her Volkswagen, things began getting a bit tense.

The New York Times, it turned out, did have inside information concerning rampant institutionalized corruption within the police department. They began running a series of very specific articles, naming names, locations, and in some cases amounts. The police commissioner was fired. His first deputy, while sitting in the recently vacated commissioner's chair, was given thirty days to resign. The mayor, shocked and bewildered, appointed an "independent" commission. To head the commission he chose John W. Roxbury, a partner in one of New York's most prestigious law firms and the mayor's college roommate at Yale.

Roxbury took to the task like an avenging angel. He immediately hired forty investigators at two hundred dollars per diem. He would have nothing but the best to investigate the finest. Given subpoena power, he began dropping cops from Staten Island to the South Bronx. Midday local television was all but turned over to Roxbury's dilettantes. The commission named itself "The Mayor's Council for Honest Government." Their logo was a big red apple with an even bigger worm curling out from the center. Superimposed over the apple was a little blond boy in a blue blazer, a scissors in his little pink hand. He stood poised and ready to clip off the head of the worm.

A presidential election received little more attention from the media. The hearings, televised locally, were a midday event. Local newspapers ran outrageous stories of policemen shaking down everyone from tow-truck operators to major drug dealers. The investigation and the hearings lasted eighteen months. The impact on the police department in New York was staggering: wholesale firings, forced retirements, in some cases prison terms. Toward the end of the eighteenth month, Roxbury asked his old roommate if his powers could be expanded to include members of the judiciary, the Bar, and, in some areas, politicians. The mayor fired him. This was a police investigation. "Let's not complicate it." It would be ten years before cops in New York could feel somewhat recovered from the attack. Ten years later, in June 1980, Bobby Porterfield graduated from the University of Massachusetts.

3.

Tom Moran had real difficulty disguising his anger, or his love, for that matter. By his own lights he was what patriotism was all about. William Bendix's death scene in the movie *Wake Island* so depressed him he didn't jerk off for a week. Lloyd Nolan's heroic final transmission in *Burma Calling* (a movie he watched at 2 a.m. on TV) made his gut twist and twirl to such an extent that he had slammed the TV off, grabbed hold of his son's baseball bat, and searched his neighborhood for a half hour. Finding a Datsun Z parked near a streetlight, he parried, stuck, and smashed the windshield, hood, and right front fender of the sneaky Nip car.

Here in the Northeast the enemy was everywhere. He piloted his eighteen-wheel Mack truck through the New England highways and turnpikes as if General Patton were riding shotgun and they were racing the Russians to the Rhine.

Moran thought of the growling hood ornament on his truck as an avenging laser. With it, he destroyed Tiger tanks masquerading as Volkswagens, Mercedes,' and BMWs. Datsuns, Toyotas, and Hondas were Zeros. "Blast the mothers!" he'd scream as he caught the tiny cars in his back draft, whipping their tail ends, scaring the shit out of the drivers.

On this June afternoon in 1980, Tom Moran was trucking south from Boston. He had a stop in Philly, then it was a straight shot on to Atlanta. He popped two bennies and washed them down with a black-and-white thick shake. He was wired and ready, but he had a problem. A glop of thick shake had

[15]

solidified at the bottom of the container. He couldn't get it through the straw. Now he was wired and pissed. Ol' Tom was banging the container off his steering wheel, shaking loose the thick mass, when he saw the hippie. The creep was sitting on the shoulder of the interstate holding a sign. As he pulled closer Moran could make out something about a Willow and he saw a number. But what Tom Moran zeroed in on, what caught his sniper's eye, was the blue peace symbol in the sign's center. Calculating the distance and contact time, he put down his black-and-white, adjusted his baseball cap (decorated with pins of American flags), and turned the volume up on the radio, where Marty Robbins was into the last verse of "Ballad of the Alamo." Lining up his right front wheel on the sliver of road that separated the highway from the shoulder, Tom put the pedal to the metal. He was gonna give this hippie a blow job that would go down in truckers' folklore. He was gonna blast this sucker to Rhode Island.

The truck was about a hundred yards off when Bobby heard the air horn. This guy could be on his way to the Bush Terminal Market, he hoped. It seemed to be slowing, the driver was reading the sign. Good, good. Bobby crossed his fingers and bent his head, a quick prayer to the great hitchhiking sky pilot.

All at once the truck picked up speed and flew past, shooting stones like shotgun pellets from its rear tires. The stones rapped off the sign, then the speeding truck sent a second blast of wind that rolled Bobby right off his knapsack into the milkweed.

As the last bars of "The Alamo" filled Moran's padded cab, his eyes welled with tears. The picture of John Wayne, torch in hand, nailed to a door by a Mexican spear, well, it just tore him up.

Bobby threw the speeding truck the finger, then he looked for a rock, *then* he saw the poison ivy and scrambled back to the shoulder of the road. Pulling his sign from the brambles, he plopped back down. With hands trembling, he searched his pack for the roach his roomie had given him. Finding it, he lit up. Just a little luck, Lord, that's all I'm asking. He took one great pull on the joint and flipped it toward the weeds. After a while a Volkswagen came over the rise and Bobby once more lifted his sign and crossed his fingers. The car slowed and

Bobby mouthed the word "please." The little gold car pulled off the interstate and stopped.

With his sign in one hand and his pack over his shoulder Bobby could barely manage the car door. When it finally opened he gasped.

The girl took one hand off the steering wheel and poked her thumb in the air. He couldn't believe his luck. She was *beautiful*.

"Hi, I'm Cathy Doyle, you can put that in the back seat."

Still shaking from Tom Moran's "blow job," Bobby moved his rucksack onto his lap. His "Help" sign had stuck in the door. Dislodging it and moving the pack became a major undertaking, which he was handling badly. The pack slid from his lap to the floor; grabbing for it, he bumped his head on the dash, then he caught his index finger in the tiny Volkswagen door handle and yelped.

"Take it easy." She laughed, then pointed with her chin. "Just throw it over the seat." He liked the way she pointed with her chin. A great chin it was, too, round and dimpled with a golden freckle just beneath her lip. But it wasn't the chin that made him thankful he'd taken the extra fifteen minutes to shower and comb the unruly mess that sat on his head. It was those long, long legs. The way the muscle firmed and tightened when she shifted.

The sun, reflecting off the hood of the Volkswagen, danced through the windshield, softly dusting her face. What a knock-out.

"My name's Bobby Porterfield," he finally managed. She was wearing white running shorts—an ally—that rode up as she twisted what must be a superior bottom into the VW's seat. Her arms were long and lean, she had the look of the American gentry. Bobby was sure she was from Smith. I don't have a shot, he thought, then he wondered if she could tell he was leering.

"I've been driving home for two years and this is the first time I've picked someone up. But I couldn't pass that sign. Would you believe I'm on my way to visit a friend that lives at 120 Willow Street?" Bobby pinched the back of his hand so hard he almost drew blood. I'm hallucinating, that's it. The toke I took from my roommate's joint must have been laced with PCP. In a second she'll turn into a gargoyle. His sign read: "Help. Must get to 115 Willow Street by 4 o'clock."

"That's Willow Street in Brooklyn?" he asked.

"Same place. Amazing, isn't it?"

"Amazing? More like the intervention of a wonderfully benevolent spirit, I'd say."

He'd never seen such thick brown hair. As she turned to look back at oncoming traffic, blond highlights flashed. She's perfect, he thought. What can I do to screw this up?

Deciding to keep his mouth shut till he had something bright to say, he settled back in the seat, took a quick look at his fingernails, and waited. Nothing happened. She wasn't saying a word, and he was getting no help from the traffic; it was light. The VW buzzed along ten miles above the speed limit. "What kind of perfume are you wearing? The car smells like orange blossoms," he finally said.

"I don't wear perfume," she said with sensuality, a bit of coyness, and more than a trace of "I could like you."

"Then we'd better check under the car. You must have run over a small person carrying a basket of fruit. *Nobody* smells that good."

There was a glimmer of a laugh, muffled, but a laugh just the same. Suddenly she cheerfully announced, "Bobby Porterfield. I'm going to call you Robert. Bobby's a child's name like Bubber or Skip."

Uh-oh, he thought, what do we have here, a Muffin girl? He couldn't begin to deal with Muffin girls. Their fathers were always six foot four and sailed the Atlantic in record time— alone.

"That would be super," he mimicked, "except that my name's Bobby, not Robert."

"That can't be. There's no St. Bobby." (It occurred to him that Muffin girls don't really know from saints.) "Your name is Robert, Bobby's a nickname, isn't it?"

"No, but I didn't know there wasn't a St. Bobby. My parents probably didn't know that either. We're Methodists and we don't have a whole lot of saints. Hoagie Carmichael wasn't sainted, was he?"

She was laughing, he was on a roll, and she wasn't a Muffin girl. His prospects were brightening. He wanted to say, "Do you eat, sleep, burp, fart, and maybe fuck?" Bobby Porterfield was sure that women who looked like this did none of these things. They were somehow excused from such worldly irritants.

Another eighteen-wheeler sounding like an avalanche roared past them, then slowed in front of her; Cathy moved the VW first into the center lane, then over into the slow right lane. She glanced in the rearview, then, like a shot, she was back in the center lane cutting off a pickup with a hand signal and a smile. The truck pulled alongside. The driver, ready to bark, smiled as Cathy showed him three fingers in the air and the circle sign for O.K. or thank you. The pickup slowed and fell into traffic behind her.

"That was a nice gesture."

"What was?"

"Your telling that kid thanks a lot." Bobby repeated the signal.

"That means asshole. He didn't have to ride up on me like that. Guys in trucks like pushing Volkswagens around. It makes them feel good to watch little cars get blown all over the road, the schmucks."

It was Bobby's turn to smile. "Schmuck" is not exactly the normal parlance for a Smithie. She's something special. Suddenly the VW cut off the eighteen-wheeler and Bobby felt the need for a cigarette or a joint or maybe a Valium. Putting his knee up against the dash, he slunk down in his seat. Give it a shot, he thought.

"Do you have any plans for dinner tonight?" What's the worst she can say? Yes.

She turned to him, smiled, then said, "Are you kidding?"

Bobby blinked his eyes, broadened his smile, and said, "Why would I be kidding?" She didn't answer.

The Volkswagen flew south at record speed, south away from Smith College, Mount Holyoke College, Amherst College, and the University of Massachusetts. Bobby's alma mater. She offered no further conversation. He was afraid even to try. He did mention that he had been a sociology major and would be entering Columbia graduate school with hopes for a M.S.W. come fall. That seemed to really turn her on. There was absolutely no response!

An hour and a half later the Volkswagen climbed the upper roadway of the Bruckner Expressway. The South Bronx filled the window to his right. "Not much like Northampton, is it?" he said, moving his now aching knee from the dashboard and pointing with his thumb.

"You're the sociologist. Whose fault is that mess? Yours, mine, or just maybe theirs?" She pointed with her chin . . . again.

"Maybe it's nobody's fault. Then again, maybe we're all at fault." Bobby wanted to develop the idea, expand it a bit, show this brunette vision that he might be a touch raunchy. After all, he had on his "it's a hot day and a long trip" outfit, but he was bright, and bright counts.

"Of course that's what you'd say," she snapped. "You're going to love Columbia. It's full of pinko wimps like you."

"Excuse me?" he said, hoping to regain lost ground. "That's a bit aggressive, don't you think?" Change your approach, he thought, fall back to funny. "What the hell do you have in the trunk of this car—a brown uniform and jack boots?" He tried a grin. She scowled. So that wasn't funny. He'd try again. They weren't in Brooklyn yet. Back off, this was not a day to talk politics. He didn't care if she was Himmler's daughter, those legs must go right up to her shoulders.

"I get real irritated at the woes of the world being laid at the feet of everyone but the woe makers. Do you understand what I mean?" she said quietly. "That doesn't make me a fascist or a sheet wearer or a moron. Does it?"

"No, that simply makes you a member of the privileged class, that's all."

"Privileged? Privileged? Do you know what my dad does for a living?"

"He owns Du Pont."

"Very funny. I wish he did. No, he's a New York City policeman. A cop. Well, now he's an inspector, but a cop nevertheless. Privileged class, my buns."

"And great buns they are, I bet." He grinned. That brought a smile. "Look, let's put the political swords away, O.K.? Especially on our first date, especially since you've been so incredibly kind picking me up and all."

She was laughing again, lighting up the car, giving her circle finger sign to the whole Bronx, and maybe him too.

"You're almost home," she said. That may have ended the conversation, sealed the trip, and kicked his fantasy in the knee.

"Are you sure you won't consider dinner?" She didn't answer, didn't say a word till they crossed from the East River Drive onto the Brooklyn Bridge.

"Do you live with your family?" she finally said.

"No, I live with me."

"In the Heights?"

"Uh-huh."

"Do you rent?"

"Is this a test?"

She laughed again.

"No, I own a floor of a brownstone. Bought it from a friend last year."

"Talk about the privileged class."

"Don't let that turn your head. I bought it from a friend for a giveaway price. With money I was left after my parents were killed in a car wreck."

"God, that's awful." He thought he saw her cross herself.

"Awful. I guess 'awful' is a good word. The driver of the other car was from Queens. Stoned on modeling glue. No license, no insurance, and he ended up with a broken hand. 'Awful' is a good word."

"How you must hate him."

"Well"—Bobby paused a moment—"I did hate him. I used to fantasize about tying a wire to his penis, tying the other end to a girder on this bridge, and then throwing him off."

"I don't blame you. No one would blame you." There was fire in her eyes. She *meant* it.

"He was fifteen and brain damaged. He stole a cab and was going the wrong way down Third Avenue. He hit my folks head on." The Volkswagen had pulled to the curb. They were in front of 115 Willow Street. It was exactly four o'clock. "Cathy"—from his bag of grins he shot her his best—"I can't thank you enough. No kidding, this is great. Forget the political stuff. Smile at me again and I'll meet you tonight with a burning cross if you like."

She smiled and handed him his rucksack, lifting it from the back seat with one hand. She was strong, too. "O.K. I'll meet you here at exactly seven o'clock. And I'll be hungry, so pick a good restaurant."

"Sweet lady, you got it."

"Cut that sweet-lady crap. I'm not so sweet. But I *am* a lady. See ya later." The Volkswagen skipped off and Bobby Porterfield threw his rucksack about twenty feet in the air. Two guys walking three poodles heard him say something like "Sky pilot, you came through again."

The Yemen House on Atlantic Avenue was Bobby's choice. They served mounds of babaganouj and hummus, warm pita bread and shish kebab. The restaurant had no liquor license, so Bobby brought along two bottles of cold, fresh northern Italian wine. They ate an enormous salad that was much more Greek than Yemeni, and the music grated on their ears.

By the last glass of the second bottle, Bobby had gone tone deaf. He noticed a red blush forming at the nape of Cathy's neck. After they had put the second bottle on the floor, Bobby left the resturant. He ran to a nearby liquor store. The third bottle should do it, he thought. *His* teeth were beginning to feel soft; she must be a half glass away from being blasted. When he returned he found Cathy up and folk-dancing with an Arab. Opening the wine, he poured her a full tumbler glass and smiled. When the music ended she returned to her seat, waving a hand in front of her face. She appeared to be overheated and out of breath. Bobby knew better: this girl didn't sweat . . . at all.

"Where did you learn to dance like that?" He tried sounding smooth and under control. But the grin that had etched itself on his face was locked in place by the smooth Frescati. Cathy swallowed a half glass more of the wine and explained, "The dance was simply a jig with a Middle Eastern tempo."

She finished her glass of wine, poured another, ran her fingers through that rolling thick brown hair, and said, "This is just what I needed. I feel great."

Bobby continued to smile, but the tips of his fingers were beginning to burn and the music was starting to sound good. They left the restaurant. There had not been one word about the disenfranchised or the John Birch Society or the ACLU. As they made their way back into the Heights, music was the topic of conversation. She loved the Beatles and classical guitar. He loved everything from Eddie Arnold to Ella Fitzgerald, from Vivaldi to Wagner. He even sort of liked Mohammed on the wood saw. *He was stoned.* Cathy held him by the elbow and Bobby continued to smile all the way back to his building.

Without any discussion that he could remember, they were up the stoop of his brownstone and into his apartment. Bobby flopped onto the bed and waited for Cathy to fall, high and hangup-free, next to him. "Thank you, sky pilot, thank you," he kept mumbling. After a while he realized that the bed was doing about a Mach 1 in circles. As for Cathy, she was singing "Hey, Jude" and brushing her teeth with his toothbrush. She was stone sober.

Sometime in the middle of the night Bobby came slightly awake. He felt those terrific buns nestled against his stomach and the backs of great thighs were resting against his own. They were both naked and slept like spoons in a drawer. Just when and how they had gotten naked was a mystery.

The next morning Cathy delivered two bikes borrowed from the friend who lived nearby. They scaled the Brooklyn Bridge and pedaled to Central Park. Prospect Park, in Brooklyn, was a lot closer but Cathy wanted to go to Central Park. Hell, it was only a twelve-mile bike trip. At Fourteenth Street, Bobby's legs began to cramp. He looked at the bronze-and-white streak in front of him and found a part of his lungs he hadn't drawn from. Clenching his teeth, he sped past her, smiling and waving as he went by. Then like a shot she was by him. Oh, shit, he didn't want to race, but she was off now, all bronze and white with that brown mane flowing, her shoulders moving from side to side. They entered the park at Fifty-ninth Street and Cathy didn't slow till they reached the lake. Settling in the grass,

Bobby was ready for a three-hour nap, when all at once Cathy was back up on the bike.

"O.K., let's get going. There's three things I want to do." She smiled. At that moment he knew he'd follow her right off the top of the World Trade Center if that's what she wanted. "First I wanted to pick up some wine and bread. Then I want to return my friend's bikes." She reached over and grabbed at the top of his head. "Then I want to screw." Bobby fell back onto the grass and looked skyward. Sky pilot, I'm yours for life, lead me to the leper colony. I'm at your command. Just give me another week with this woman.

On their way back home they picked up a loaf of French sourdough bread, some mozzarella cheese and prosciutto. Bobby, sticking the food in his bike bag, couldn't take his eyes from Cathy's long pumping legs. The smell of orange blossoms and Irish mist like a green velvet cloud surrounded them both as they flew over the Brooklyn Bridge.

By nine o'clock they were spoons again, clinging tight to each other as if they were part of the same thing.

That first summer together was a blur of loving, laughing, and, for Bobby, an understanding of what a full-time commitment in a relationship meant. Exclusivity and personal space when needed, but most important, friendship. Completely in love with Cathy, Bobby felt he was ready for commitment. Cathy told him that in her mind there was no doubt. He was *her* sweetheart, she wanted him. Everyone else she had met or thought she loved paled when compared with him. My Marxist Lover, she called him. Right-Wing Wino, he called her.

It was late summer on a rainy Sunday morning after lovemaking. A pot of espresso bubbled, filling the apartment. With crumbs of warm croissants sticking to the pages of the *Times* they had their "serious talk."

"You look *at* things and I watch *out* for things," she said. "Why don't we try to work together, alter our perspectives just a tiny bit."

There was the taste of fresh strawberry jam in his mouth. Still, a sense of dread began to ease through him. After the holding, touching, exploring, and experiencing had been put to rest, the cursed brain shook itself free of all the cashmere emotion and the day-by-day, week-by-week, year-by-year reality of life came into focus. Two lives once separate now joined together, trying to move forward. Visions of their life together began to crystallize. Bobby became a seer. Two people; no longer boy and girl, man and woman. Just two people, with totally different views of the same world. They could become runaway locomotives on one track, soon to come together face to face, out of control, bent on mutual destruction.

Bobby could already see her slipping away. Recently there were biweekly lunches with her father. Essentially that wasn't a problem, a daughter should see her father. Bobby had met the great cop, as he called him, twice. The second meeting was worse than the first, and the first was a disaster. The guy wore a handcuff tiepin. Bobby was swept away, totally in love with Cathy, and she—she said—loved him. But Cathy adored her father.

At their second meeting, a lunch near his office in China-town, the great cop spewed forth the most sophomoric reaction-ary political crap Bobby had ever heard. Cathy was young, politically naïve, but certainly retrievable. There existed in her a wide, sweet spring of kindness. He couldn't hurt her and, more important, he didn't want to lose her.

Now, at summer's end, Bobby felt that many of his feelings were no longer his own. They were being yanked and pulled about. After long talks with Cathy on beaches and in quiet restaurants and in bed he felt he had been beaten black and blue. Christ, what a lawyer she was going to make! She was trying to convince him to postpone graduate school for a year or two.

"Leave the sterility of the classroom for a while. Go into the real world. See the wild and ugly faces. Stand by the spreading pool of a victim's blood. First be a *cop*, then become a social worker if that's what you want."

"A cop? Me?"

"Who better than you? Do your graduate research from inside the police department."

He had been thinking about it since she first mentioned it in passing a month before, and had already made his decision.

"O.K., I'm ready. Where do I get my stick?"

Cathy seemed staggered. She had no idea that he had been playing with the possibility for over a month.

"Are you serious? You'll try it?"

"It might be a good idea."

All in all, it wasn't much of a discussion. He loved her too much. He could always go back to school, and urban social work was what he most wanted to do. In a couple of years he could probably learn a great deal, do a terrific paper.

"Does this mean I can't smoke a joint once in a while?" he asked.

"I'll get you as high as you'll ever need to be." She smiled. "And my father really does like you," she added. "He could be a big help."

4.

Bobby Porterfield pumped his brakes as he made the turn off the Broad Channel Bridge onto Rockaway Beach Boulevard. The Volkswagen felt strange, light, out of control. He was losing it but he didn't know why. Then he saw the water. The puddle sucked at his wheels and flung him through the intersection. The car spun a 360-degree turn, sending water four feet in the air and bringing him to a stop right in front of the station house. He sat still, not wanting to let go of the wheel. That was close. He knew it and now he was playing it back. Where did all that water come from? He never saw it. Kissing the dashboard of his bug, he looked up at the 100th Precinct station house.

It was past midnight. Even so, it was easy to see that the storm had done considerable damage to the beachfront community. Power lines were down and water ran like a river along the curb. An Italian restaurant directly across from the station house looked as though it had been hit by a bomb. Yawning holes took the place of windows and a door. Hurricane Albert, as they called it, was now out to sea, though not before leaving its mark on the New York beaches and totally ruining Bobby's Friday night.

The station house looked abandoned. Not a light shone. If not for the two green lanterns on either side of the front door, the place would have been in total darkness.

Bobby grabbed hold of the knob. His hand slipped and he bruised his shoulder leaning into the massive door. It was locked. It can't be locked, he thought. He pushed again. This time he tried to turn the knob with two hands. It was locked all right. Two years in the department and this was the first time he'd been to a police station with a locked front door. Burke, you son of a bitch, he thought. I'll get even with you. Sending me out on a night like this to a precinct in the middle of nowhere, to a place where you could fire a cannon down the main drag and not hit a thing. He kicked the door. It barely made a sound.

Bobby looked for a bell. Seeing none, he kicked again—this time at the brass-plated bottom of the door. Nothing. Taking a step back, he looked at the windows on the second floor. Not a sign of life anywhere. What if he just left, just said "fuck it" and went home. He laughed to himself as he played with the idea. What if all the cops everywhere just said "fuck it" and went home? He kicked the brass plate again. The door, bathed in the light from the green lanterns, seemed impregnable. It was then he heard the clatter of a teletype machine. There must be cops around somewhere. Shit! He was only a half hour late and this *was* a fucking police station. Grabbing hold of his black-jack, he made ready to really whack the brass plate when the door opened. A beefy, unkempt sergeant with a huge head appeared in the doorway.

"Patrolman Porterfield, from the two-oh. I'm sorry. I guess I'm a little late," Bobby said, smiling.

"You're not a little late; you're a lot late. We thought you drowned. Where the hell were you?" A piece of mozzarella cheese dangled from the sergeant's unshaved chin.

"We really thought you drowned." The sergeant burped. Two buttons of his uniform shirt had popped just above his midriff, allowing a white gash of undershirt to peep through.

"Sarge, it's rough out there. My VW damn near disappeared in a lake right in front of the station house." Bobby thought he'd better entertain this Neanderthal. He *was* late, after all.

The sergeant waddled to the sign-in book and waved Bobby over. Running a nightstick-sized finger down the page, he said, "You'll be working with Manning. He's been out there a hour waitin' for ya."

Bobby turned to the sergeant and smelled pizza. He had the

smile of a giant friendly bear. Flipping the blackjack he had in his hand back into his pocket and nearly running to the door, he quipped, "Okay, Sarge, I'm off."

"Ya know just where the post is, do ya?" asked the bear, still smiling. The sergeant's shirt collar was undone. He'd left the top button open, covering it with a Windsor knot the size of his hand.

"The post?" Bobby shook his head. "No."

"It's 116th Street and the beach, bright boy, right on the boardwalk, or what's left of it."

"Okay," Bobby said. He looked around. The precinct was empty but the teletype kept chattering.

"And by the way"—the smile from the bear had faded—"I want one of you out of the car all night, got me?"

Bobby shook his head. "Yes."

"Any questions?"

"Just one, Sarge. Are you really serious about one of us being out of the car *all* night?" The bear smiled but gave no response.

"Burke, you bastard!" Bobby screamed as he jumped over a puddle to his car.

Captain Arthur Burke was Bobby's commanding officer at the 20th Precinct in Manhattan. He had personally informed Bobby that he had the storm-damage detail. Burke didn't just throw it out, an order to be taken and obeyed. He let the bad news roll from his mouth, savoring every grimace and the "Oh, shit" of Bobby's response. Burke's smile was not unlike the one on the face of the Neanderthal sergeant Bobby had just left.

In order to get to his post and find the patrol car, Bobby had to skirt, then ford, several small rivers. Running salt water was depositing big chunks of sandy beach on the street.

The police car stood like a blue-and-white sentinel at the end of the block. Throwing on his raincoat, he ran to it. The car was locked and empty. Now where the hell is this guy? Bobby thought. What, is somebody kidnapping all the cops around here? Getting back in the VW, he noticed a figure on the boardwalk. He blew his horn once, then again, then three long blasts. A flashlight snapped on and began moving along the boardwalk toward him. As it got closer Bobby gawked at the biggest cop he'd ever seen. Wearing an old-fashioned caped raincoat that flowed like a great black shroud behind him, the cop was massive. Planting himself in the middle of the wrecked boardwalk and waving the flashlight, he resembled a lighthouse, all aglow in the center of a storm.

Bobby had to crane his neck in order to look in the face of this cop.

"Where have you been?" asked the cop, opening the door of the police car for Bobby.

"I got stuck in the storm," he answered simply.

"What's wrong? What's the matter?" the cop asked.

Bobby felt foolish, self-conscious. He was staring. "I'm sorry." He laughed. "It's just that I've met two cops since I've been here. One looked like Paul Bunyan and now you, you look like his big brother."

"You don't know how right you are." The cop smiled. "You must have run into my brother at the station house. The fat sergeant behind the desk," he said, trying to maneuver his enormous mass into the car. Bobby noticed the seat was pushed as far back as it could go; still, the cop's knees were snug against the steering wheel. Dangling from the shield on his raincoat was a leather thong, strung through an ax handle.

"He wasn't behind the desk when I got there," Bobby said. "The front door was locked. Would you believe that the front door of the station house was locked? I've never seen anything like it."

"They were probably eating. Once in a while on a late tour they'll send out for pizza."

"You're right. I saw a piece of cheese hanging from your brother's chin." Bobby smiled. The giant cop burst into laughter.

"He is a slob, isn't he? Christ, the guy eats three whole pizzas by himself for dinner."

Bobby thought that he might have touched a sensitive spot. "Hey, I'm sorry, I don't mean to insult your brother." The comment brought a second wave of laughter, more robust, fuller than the first.

"Insult him? Are you kidding? If you'd stand still long enough the fat prick would eat you." The cop was roaring with laughter. Bobby threw his hat onto the back seat. I like this guy, he thought. It's not going to be a bad night after all. The giant beside him pulled a half-smoked cigar from his coat. Putting a match to it, he inhaled. The cigar threw off a warm orange glow that lit the inside of the patrol car and reminded Bobby that the truth was, he loved being a cop. Sitting in a police car, in the middle of nowhere, with a man he just met, watching a broken-down amusement park.

The hours between midnight and 8 a.m. are the hours when most honest people are asleep. For others it's sporting-life time. The city shudders and comes fully awake, giving itself over to the real New Yorkers, from glossy after-hours clubs in Harlem to S&M playgrounds in the West Village. These are the hours of the yellow-eyed night people, the time that interested Bobby most, the time he felt most alive.

"Hey, maybe one of us should get out and check the beach." The urgency of his suggestion had little effect on Brian Manning, who was awkwardly trying to keep a six-foot-six frame on a five-foot seat.

"What for?"

"Your brother said one of us should be out of the car all night. He said it with a smile but that's what he said."

"Fuck him. He's asleep in the captain's office dreaming about breakfast," said Manning, holding the cigar and staring at it as if it were a jeweled ring.

The police radio cracked on. "In the 100, car 524, 5-2-4, call your command." Manning grabbed the receiver. "Ten-four, Central Read Direct."

"What the hell do you think that's about?" Bobby asked.

Manning drew on his cigar and smiled. "My brother probably wants us to pick up a small dessert."

"You're kidding," Bobby replied as Manning started up the patrol car and moved slowly down the street.

"We'll see. There's a public phone at the gas station on the corner. I called the old lady earlier. I know it's working."

Curious, Bobby couldn't think of Manning in terms of a woman, especially a wife. He wondered what it was like waiting in the half light of a marriage bedroom as three hundred pounds of Brian Manning rolled beneath the covers. He watched Manning intently as he walked to the phone, spoke for a minute, and returned, getting into the back seat.

"Your sister's on her way here. She's bringing coffee and sandwiches. My brother took one. You shouldn't be upset."

"Terrific!" Bobby said as he spun the car out of the station and sloshed back down the street toward the boardwalk. He had no sister, but he knew who the pretender was.

"Brian, listen, I got something to tell you." Bobby glanced in the rearview mirror. He could see Brian Manning sitting upright in the center of the back seat with his outstretched arms easily touching both sides of the car. His hat was perched on the back of his head and he continued to play with the stub of his unlit cigar.

"Ya see, Brian," Bobby went on, "this woman that's on her way here, well, she's not my sister." He practically whispered the last three words.

"No shit." Manning smiled, flipping Bobby's hat off with his ax handle. "If she was, my brother said he wouldn't have taken the sandwich." Bobby shut the car off just as the white El Dorado turned into the street. He exchanged a look with Manning as the Caddy pulled alongside. He could not have been more ill at ease. The electric window slid down. "Hi, Bea, fancy meeting you here."

"Brian, meet Bea. Bea, this is Brian Manning, my partner for the night." Neither Manning nor Bea acknowledged each other. Her gaze never left Bobby.

"Gotcha," she said, slapping her hands together. "I'd find you on the moon, sweet thing." Bea reached through the open window and stroked Bobby's cheek.

Manning's face broke into a full smile. "Well, just another night off the street. Go ahead, Bobby, go sit with your sister a while."

He should have cut this off at the very beginning. As if he were playing a part in her fantasy soap opera, Bobby had allowed Bea to run this play too long.

Bea moved the El Dorado away from the boardwalk further down the block, to the darker side of the street.

"You better hustle; she seems impatient."

Bea, waving out the car window, seemed a bit frantic. Bobby

signaled back with an outstretched hand. 'She can wait. Are you sure you don't mind?"

Manning, please say you mind, he thought. Bobby *really* didn't want to join Bea. Was that a smile or a sneer on Brian's face?

"Okay, I'm going." But he didn't move.

"Go, go already." Bobby sat still. A hint of orange blossoms had eased into his senses, accompanied by a picture of Cathy, sitting cross-legged on a massive pillow popping out answers as he prepped her for a test. He floated off; Manning brought him quickly back.

"Look, I'm not that old. I've had my share since I've been on the job. What is this, a blow job?" Bobby didn't answer. "What the hell are you still doing here?" Manning gently pushed Bobby, if you can do anything gently with an ax handle. Bobby rolled away and was now leaning against the door. But he was still in the patrol car. Manning spun the ax handle around in his hand. "Well," he said. "She doesn't bite, does she?" Bobby studied Brian; a grin was starting to spread.

"I don't want to go. I don't need this," Bobby blurted to the big cop in the back seat, but he was really screaming at himself.

Manning gave off a giant sigh. "Bobby, if you don't get moving, you can stay here and eat the sandwich and I'll go. If I do that, you'll never see her again."

"Brian, let me tell you about this woman."

"I hope it's a short story, that lady is about ready to throw a fit of some kind." All four headlights of the Caddy were flashing; it looked like a spacecraft had landed at the end of the street.

"Look, Brian, I'm going, but I'll be right back."

Bobby jumped into the gaudy and plush front seat of the car.

"I thought we were friends," Bea said as Bobby turned to face her.

"Of course we are." He smiled.

"Then why didn't you tell me you were coming out here? You know I look forward to seeing you on Friday nights."

"No reason. I just didn't think you would want to come and meet me here." Bobby gestured at the broken-down amusement park and the storm-swept street.

"You know I'd go anywhere to spend some time with you." Bobby shook his head and they exchanged smiles.

"Bea . . ." Bobby held still for a moment. He didn't want to hurt her. It was all too obvious how strongly she felt about him. But this Friday-night lunacy had to stop.

"Bea," he began again, "I do appreciate the way you look me up on Fridays. You know I love the sandwiches and the coffee. I even loved the jade plant you left in my radio car with my partner. I even sort of like getting the cards you send to the precinct." That was a barefaced lie, the cards embarrassed the hell out of him. "The Rod McKuen books of poetry and all."

"Bobby, you know how I feel," she said as demurely as she knew how.

"*See,* you're doing it again," Bobby almost screamed. Bea was running her tongue across her upper lip.

"What?" She smiled.

"Bea, I have a woman."

"So."

"I love her."

"So."

"So, so. She trusts me, Bea, we trust each other," he whispered. Bobby could feel the clang of an oncoming crashing headache.

"You didn't complain the first time."

"That was different. That was, was . . ." He was losing it, he started to mumble. "That was freaky," he burst.

"Freaky!" she screamed.

"Oh, Bea, put on a tape. I need a minute to think." What more could he say? Bea shrugged and threw a tape into the cassette. Bobby pushed some buttons on the dash and the car seat lifted and reclined. Johnny Mathis sang "Wonderful, Wonderful" in Dolby sound.

Bobby had been in the precinct for less than a month when he met Bea. On the 4 p.m. to midnight tour he was assigned a foot post on Amsterdam Avenue between Sixty-ninth and Seventy-fifth streets. Bea owned a small restaurant on the corner of Seventy-second and Amsterdam. Bobby took his meal there. This small bouncy blonde with thin penciled eyebrows treated him as if he were the prodigal son returned. It was not possible for Bobby to do anything for himself. Though she employed a waitress, she served Bobby his dinner herself. He couldn't help but enjoy all the attention. When his coffee cup was half empty Bea refilled it. As soon as he'd cut and finished his last piece of pepper steak, his place was cleared and his table wiped, not the usual state of affairs in Bea's West Side restaurant. When it came time to pay there was no charge, though Bobby tried. Bea wouldn't hear of it. All this service was accompanied by Bea's warm, enamored purr. That night, when Bobby was nearing the end of his tour, the Haitian dishwasher who worked for Bea found him in the street and told him to hurry. Bea was in trouble.

Arriving at the restaurant, Bobby found Bea nose to nose with a five-foot, three-hundred-pound dissatisfied customer. The remnants of his dinner of bacon and eggs dripped from the ceiling and he smelled as if he'd been showering in Thunderbird wine.

"O.K., chubby, beat it," Bobby remembered saying, and that's all he remembered. He did sort of remember a shoulder to the solar plexus and a knee to the chin. Later the Haitian would gleefully tell him how Bea had teed off on the guy with a sixteen-ounce bottle of Pepsi, sending him wailing into the street. That night Bea took his police jacket into the bathroom and scrubbed it clean with a damp cloth. Bobby was so touched by Bea's display of concern and affection that he playfully walked up behind her, lifted her lacquered hair, and kissed her neck. Putting his jacket down, not saying a word, Bea knelt in front of him. Opening his pants, she took him fully in her mouth, lifting him clear out of his Florsheims. It all happened so quickly Bobby had not objected or resisted. He did nothing but enjoy it. The following day he did all he could to avoid Cathy's eyes. It had not been easy. Bobby was sure that one of her saints would do him in, deliver the entire Bea scenario to his Cathy in a dream.

It all happened on a Friday night one year ago. Every Friday night since the great event, when Bobby was working, little Bea would seek him out. She'd bring him tea or coffee and sandwiches, watch him eat, and run that pointy little tongue of hers over her upper lip. On Friday nights when Bobby was off, as the clock neared midnight, guilt would do a little soft-shoe in the area of his groin. He would think of Bea and mothballs in a urinal.

Bea's unconditional warmth always ambushed Bobby. Tonight was no different. Fighting her way through a storm, she delivered to him a roast beef on rye with Russian dressing, three sliced chickens with lettuce and mayo, a wedge of cheesecake wrapped in tinfoil, and a thermos of iced tea. But tonight the sky pilot, or maybe a green-eyed demon, might have brought him the answer to the persistent Bea.

"Could we spare a sandwich for Brian?" Bobby asked.

Bea reached into her sack and handed him a neatly wrapped package. "Here; it's sliced chicken. There are two more in there but save those for yourself. It's going to be a long night and it's miserable out here."

This woman was like a mother and a step better. For the right guy she would be a godsend . . . it was just not him. "I think three sandwiches will hold me." He laughed. Bobby grabbed hold of the door handle, then turned to Bea. He'd ask her. She might go bonkers. She just might slap his face and drive off. He doubted it. What the hell. He'd come right out and ask her. All she could say was no. "Bea, would you do me a favor?"

"Sure." She beamed without hearing the request.

"Would you do for Brian what you did for me? The man's depressed, and I think it would be a wonderful gesture." He wondered if he had not gone a mite too far. Then she smiled at him as he hoped she would. Bobby ran back to the patrol car. Brian was close to dozing off on the back seat when Bobby handed him the sandwich and cup of tea.

"Hey, thanks a lot. I was just wondering where we were going to eat. This is great!" Manning put the tea on the seat and began to undo the foil wrapping, the cigar stub still in his mouth.

"Brian, how'd you like a blow job?"

Manning dropped the sandwich, struck a match for the cigar stub. The whole book went up. "Are you kidding? Sandwich, tea, and a blow job; what are you looking for—a new partner?" Manning beamed.

"Just another night off the street." Bobby smiled, but suddenly he was unsure if Bea would really go through with it. What the hell was he doing this for? His partner, Mark, was right. He acted on impulse, and was ruled by his emotions. Not great attributes for a cop. A man ruled by emotion is a man ruled. How would it help if Bea were to give Brian a blow job? How would that stop Bea from continuing to be his Friday-night shadow? Bobby didn't know. It was just a feeling.

He ran back to the Caddy, didn't say a word, but opened Bea's door. The wind and rain had increased in intensity. "You're not making me very happy," she said, but she got out of the car and sloshed over to the blue-and-white.

Bobby sat adjusting his gun belt as Bea entered the patrol car. She was silhouetted in the glow of Brian's cigar. When Bea bent her head Brian took a pretty good pull on the cigar and the patrol car lit up.

The rain was falling now with a steady cadence. What's it like to be you, Bea? Bobby thought. Who are you? Florence Nightingale with a velvet mouth? Like me. Care for me. I deliver chopped liver on rye and head. Suddenly the patrol car was ablaze. Manning had taken an enormous drag on the cigar. Bobby could see him throw his arms in the air. The patrol car seemed to rock. A blast of orange light, brighter than the first, brought Manning into full view. He seemed to push his hands right up through the roof. Bobby turned up the volume of the tape player. From the corner of his mouth his tongue flicked and tasted something salty—sea mist. They were, after all, right on the sea. Johnny Mathis continued with "Wonderful, Wonderful" and Bobby thought: Shit, this is police work?

5.

Bobby felt the poke like a stab in the side. He wasn't sleeping. He couldn't imagine how anyone could ever sleep in a damn police car, but Mark thought he was. Another poke. This one did hurt. He jerked up and faced Mark.

"What the hell did you poke me for?" he said, rubbing his side and stretching. Maybe he had been asleep. He felt groggy, overtired.

"You're damn lucky I don't blackjack ya. Your snoring is giving me a headache." Mark moved his swivel holster off the seat up onto his thigh. Bobby felt his eyelids droop, then drop.

"Will you stay up, goddamnit! The sergeant could come up on us."

Bobby managed to open one eye.

"First of all, I don't snore. As for the sergeant, what time is it, six-thirty? He's having coffee and a crumb bun, getting white powder all over his uniform." Bobby returned his head to that special soft spot between the door and the seat. His eye fluttered, then opened, not wide, just a bit.

"Will you get the hell up?" Mark was shouting.

He couldn't really be angry, could he? Bobby thought as he inhaled a full gurgling pig-in-the-mud snore.

"Ya know, partner, I worked this entire set of twelve-to-eights by myself. You're a real pleasure to be with. When you're not sleeping you're looking for a place to sleep."

"Calm down, Mark, I'm having a dynamite dream; ya wanna hear it?"

"No, thanks," Mark said. "I'll pass. I was thinking we could run over to Seventy-ninth and First, maybe grab a mover at the stop sign. It's just about the end of the month and what do we have, two or three movers and four parkers between us."

Bobby rolled his chin onto his shoulder and opened his eyes.

"I think, ya know what I think," he faltered. He wanted this speech to come out just right. "I think that riding around in circles on these late tours has affected your mind. What do I look like, one of those brown-uniformed retards with a whistle and a flashlight? Jeez, a fucking stop sign? You wanna work? You're gonna hear my dream and like it."

Mark exhaled a long sigh.

"O.K., I'll listen to your perverted story. But I'm telling you this: tonight when we get to work, we're going to spend as long as it takes on that stop sign. We need at least four more movers apiece. If we don't give out some summonses, you can bet your ass the mad hatter will have us walking next month."

Bobby marveled at the way Mark could get so serious over the most insignificant crap. The Ol' Mad Hatter, Captain Burke, knew they were one of the best teams in the precinct. He wasn't about to take them out of their car and put them on foot patrol. If Mark didn't have something to worry about and stew over, he'd read the *News* and find something.

"Mark, you make me crazy," Bobby yelled, grabbing Mark's cap and throwing it out the open car window.

"Oh, that's cute. That's smart. Whaddaya do for your next trick?" Mark moved back against the door. He'd been here before.

"I'll show you what I do." Bobby leapt across the seat and grabbed Mark's leg. He now had him by the ankle, tugging at his shoe.

"I'm gonna give this ugly goddamn ten-dollar shoe to that needy bag lady across the street."

"No, you don't, you son of a bitch." Mark couldn't control himself any longer; he burst into laughter. Grabbing Bobby's cap from the dashboard, he threw it so it spun to the feet of the now-shocked bag lady. She watched slack-jawed as the two uniformed cops tussled about in the patrol car. Bobby somehow was able to remove Mark's shoe. He threw it, a perfect spiral that hit the poor old lady right in the shoulder. She lunged right, then left, dropped her worldly belongings, and began running.

Bobby continued the attack, now reaching for the other shoe.

The police radio cracked on, suspending in mid-tussle the carousing in the police car.

"In the two-oh, sector David, K."

"Sector David," Mark responded, holding the receiver to his ear, letting go of the transmitter button, afraid the operator would hear his gulps of laughter.

"220 East Seventy-fifth Street. A prowler. Meet the woman."

Mark depressed the sender. "Ten-four, Central, we're on our way." He hung up the radio, hit the switch for the roof light, and spun a U-turn. The surge of the car threw Bobby at once against Mark, then banged him off the passenger door.

"Hold it, hold it. Jesus Christ, Mark, our caps; your shoe."

Mark jammed on the brakes. "C'mon, hurry up."

"Don't make me laugh. We got a husband sneaking home is what we got," Bobby shot back. He was out, then back into the car.

Siren off but roof lights flashing, Mark sped the police car through the barely awake East Side streets. As they pulled into Seventy-fifth Street, Bobby threw off the lights and grabbed his nightstick.

The street was tree-lined, with brownstones and walk-ups. A morning mist rose from the already hot pavement.

Mark leapt from the patrol car and sprinted into the alley.

Christ, he's fast, Bobby thought as he followed Mark out of the car and made for the brownstone.

As he hit the first step, the building door flew open. He was met by the frantic screams of a pretty young woman.

"On my fire escape! Mine! He jumped into the back yard," she hurriedly added. Bobby didn't slow down. He sped past her and entered the building.

She yelled at Bobby's back, "Officer, where are you going? You can't get to the back yard that way."

Bobby heard "can't get to the back yard that way," thought, "Oh, shit," turned, and ran back past the woman, who stamped her foot and continued to scream.

"Your partner went through the alley. That's the only way back. Hurry! You'll get him. He's back there."

Bobby stopped and turned to face the woman. She was more than pretty. She was beautiful.

"Calm down," he said with a smile. "He didn't get in, did he?"

"Will you hurry? Your partner's alone back there!"

"Miss, did you see the size of my partner?" Bobby smiled the smile that was as much a tool of his trade as his pistol. It was a pity more cops didn't use it. It had the expected effect. The woman smiled back. Somehow the tension of the moment was relieved.

"Be careful; that creep probably has a knife or something," she called out as Bobby ran into the alley, joining Mark in the rear yard.

Fire escapes lashed to the rear of the buildings ran the length of the block. Neat, clean, cared-for yards were separated by a series of cement and wooden fences. The yard they were in had a cement-block wall around it that was close to seven feet high. Bobby noticed that a landlord from one of the buildings had taken the trouble to jam broken glass along the top of one fence: broken Pepsi bottles to stop a burglar. Bobby grinned to himself. He jumped up and pulled down the fire-escape ladder. Mark was on the ladder before it hit the ground. From this vantage point Mark could see most of the yards on the block.

"Nothing's moving. He's probably across town by now," Mark called down.

"You mean uptown," Bobby replied, moving to the side as Mark jumped from the fire escape, narrowly missing him.

"Ya know, you're a damned racist."

Bobby noticed a pair of sneakers sticking out from behind a half dozen garbage cans in a corner of the yard. He kept up the chatter with Mark.

"Right; so are you." Bobby grinned and pointed to the sneakers. Undoing his nightstick, which he had hung over his pistol, he moved toward the cans. This is what they pay me for, he thought as he inched forward, half expecting a black revolutionary to leap up shouting some political epithet, exploding a

.357 in his face, blowing a searing hole the size of a fist through his chest. Why couldn't he get used to that fucking bullet-proof vest? It was doing him a lot of good right now hanging in his locker. With his stick in his left hand, he reached to touch the grip of his pistol. Suddenly the sneakers were up, no gun, no explosion. He was relieved and agitated at the same instant. The sneakers were attached to a heavy young blond man who ran to the cement-block wall and jumped. He didn't get over.

Hanging from the wall, the young man looked nine feet tall. His head back and straining, he tried without success to throw a leg up and over.

"Get off there. Come down here before you hurt yourself," Mark called out.

The young man tried again. Grunting and puffing, his knee rubbing against the rough cement, he got his leg up to the top of the wall, almost over but not quite.

His leg fell back, almost a surrender. Still he refused to release his grip.

"Schmuck," Bobby screamed. "Get off the wall."

The young man hung spread-eagled on the cement blocks, a picture from the Spanish Inquisition. Suddenly he dropped to the ground. He stood still, facing the wall. A reptilian hiss was coming from somewhere deep inside him. Bobby turned to Mark, who had taken a step backward, holding his nightstick in a half salute.

"Oh, this is great," Bobby said. "Just what I need before breakfast."

"Watch your ass, partner. This guy's a psycho," Mark whispered, and moved for a better angle.

With a frightening scream, the young man spun around and took up a karate stance.

"Fuck you guys. I'm a marine, and marines never surrender," he snarled. Throwing a clenched fist in the air, he did a full spin and shot out his leg, all the while yelling, "EEEEaaaaaaa . . ."

Bobby kicked him in the balls.

"Fuck us, whaddaya mean fuck us? Fuck you," Bobby snapped as the young man fell to his knees grabbing his groin.

The fat man must have come through the alley. Bobby

caught a glimpse of him as he rounded the building line into the back yard. He pushed past Mark and ran over to the young man, who was now stretched flat out on the ground flip-flopping like a salmon on a riverbank.

"Dan, Dan, what happened to you?" the fat man gushed.

The outburst surprised Bobby. He waved Mark back. They might as well let the fat man tend to the kid, he thought.

"The cops, Dad, the cops beat me," the kid wailed.

Terrific, he's the kid's father. Now what? This is really liable to ruin my morning, Bobby thought.

A window shade on the first floor snapped up with an unbelievably loud crack and flutter. A wrinkled old lady with a painted puppet face popped into the opening.

"Mr. Swanson, Mr. Swanson"—the words came through her nose as if her tongue were stuck to her palate. "It was the colored one. I saw him. He hit Danny with a big stick. I saw it, Mr. Swanson."

Mark's three-year college career absented itself. "Say what?" he yelled.

The puppet in the window disappeared. The fat man grabbed the kid by the shoulders and tried to lift him to his feet.

The old wrinkled puppet appeared once again in the window.

"The nigger did it. He did it, Mr. Swanson. I saw him."

"Shut up, you old bitch," the fat man screamed at the empty window. Bobby turned and looked toward the roof, trying to disguise a laugh. He loudly cleared his throat.

"Swanson, you live here?" Bobby could barely get the words out.

The fat man turned from the kid and faced Mark. "I'm the super of the building," he said through clenched teeth.

The puppet was there again. "Danny was pissing on the flowers again, Mr. Swanson, and the nigger cop hit him right on the pee-pee with his stick. I saw him, Mr. Swanson, pissing right on the marigolds."

Bobby looked around the yard for flowers. He saw none. He did see fat Swanson pick up a stone the size of a baseball. He was going to ding the puppet the next appearance she made.

"Mark, grab him, he's got a rock." Bobby didn't like sounding frantic, but he was. Up popped the puppet, back went Swanson's arm, and Mark was on him just in time.

"Hee, hee, hee, hee!" The puppet was laughing.

Mark pushed Swanson to the ground, grabbing the rock from his hand.

"Sit there. Don't move." There was no break in Mark's voice, not the shrill frantic sound that came from Bobby a moment ago. He was in charge. Everyone was still. Even the puppet pulled down her shade.

Bobby looked past Mark to old man Swanson. Danny's father sat, his back against the cement-block wall, a thick heavy arm draped around his son. The boy's head lay flat against his father's shoulder, eyes locked shut, his mouth agape, a mind obviously swept away.

Bobby first heard the footfalls, then the voice of the woman who had made the call to the police.

"Oh, no! It wasn't Danny, was it?" she said as she ran past Mark and joined the pair against the wall. Swanson put his finger to his lips, asking the woman to be quiet lest she disturb his now sleeping son.

"Mark, let me talk to you for a minute," Bobby whispered, then turned and walked into the alley.

Bobby knew that this woman was not about to press any charges against Danny. Without her as a complainant, what could they do? Mark agreed, it would be best to break this off and get out of there. They were twenty minutes past the end of their tour already.

"Look, you're right. We don't have anything here. Nobody wants this kid locked up, except maybe that old witch on the first floor," Mark said, pointing back to the group. The woman stood stroking Danny's chin, getting a ten-year-old's smile in return.

"Fine, we can go, but I hit the kid. I don't want any problems from the old man if we just leave." The rule for all cops was "You hit somebody, you lock 'em up." Handle it any other way and you were sure to end up with a civilian complaint. "Damn, I don't want to lock this kid up," muttered Bobby. But how to avoid it? he thought.

"Officer, can I take Danny home now? I'm sorry for the trouble, but ya know my boy's not well, and"—Swanson paused—"well, I'm sorry. I know he didn't mean to scare Miss Grimes." He filled up. Tears would flow if he uttered one more word.

"Ya see, Mr. Swanson, a complaint was made; it's not up to us; it's really out of our hands." Suddenly the woman was there, too. They were all in the alley now.

"If I had known it was Danny, I wouldn't have called." The woman was twisting a small white handkerchief, pleading with her eyes for the cops to understand, asking them to leave.

"I think we should see what Danny's up to," Mark said as he walked through the group and glanced into the back yard.

"Oh, shit." His voice was filled with real pain. Bobby ran into the yard. What he saw should have simply made him angry. It didn't. Instead it sent a shiver of fear careening through him. Bobby saw Danny step off the fire escape and onto the roof. He turned to grab the ladder, but Danny had secured it to the fire escape with his belt. There was no way to reach it from the yard.

"Get to the roof from inside the building," he heard himself yell to Mark. "I'll call for help." Bobby ran through the alley to the patrol car. His heart was pounding. He felt nauseated. He knew what was going to happen. He just knew. Opening the door on the driver's side, he realized he didn't have the key. "The ignition key, Mark, where's the key?" he yelled.

"Under the mat," Mark called back as he ran into the building. Switching on the car, Bobby grabbed the radio.

"Sector David of the two-oh to Central . . . K." He spoke hoping somehow that the operator at Central Communications would be able to reach a godlike hand through the radio and put a halt to the nightmare. "Sector David to Central K," he repeated.

"Central K." The voice was soothing, professional, totally under control, almost syrupy in its response.

"220 East Seventy-fifth Street." He heard himself whimper, a childlike sound. He had no control over his emotions as he had no control over the unfolding tragedy.

The syrupy voice came through, "What do you have, David?"

Bobby looked up. What he saw would follow him to his grave, and beyond.

"Central," he was able to say, "we have a leaper at 220 East Seventy-fifth Street." As Bobby placed the receiver back on its cradle he heard the disembodied voices responding. "Emergency Service 12, Central . . . on the way . . . Sector Adam on the way . . . Sector Charles . . ."

Danny stood perched on the edge of the roof, both arms straight in the air. He smiled down at Bobby. His cherry-red face and blond hair, a picture slowly branding itself deeply into Bobby's memory. He should say something, do something. Where was Mark? Where was that fucking Emergency Service Unit?

"No!" he screamed. "Danny, no!"

Danny, smiling, sailed toward him. No scream, no arms flailing, no comic attempt at flight, arms outstretched, fists clenched, his eyes wide, so wide. It was the eyes he'd remember. Not a sound when he hit.

Bobby sat on the curb as the Emergency Service Unit sped into the street, sectors Charles and Adam following close behind. He noticed that sector Adam was a sparkling new blue-and-white. Paul Rizzo of sector Adam walked over to Bobby, grabbed him by the elbow, and tried to lift him up from the curb.

"C'mon, get up, give your partner a hand."

"What?"

"Mark! He'll need a hand. You guys are gonna have a ton of paperwork with this thing."

"What?" Bobby was breathing deeply, searching for orange blossoms.

"Porterfield, ain't you learned yet that's all police work is in the end?"

"What?"

"Paperwork, police work is picking up pieces and paperwork."

6.

"Miller, you hear me?" Police Officer Miller didn't look up, nodded yes, and continued to file summonses.

"A week, Miller, seven fuckin' days before the Roxbury Commission kicks off their bullshit, I get first grade." Dolan grabbed the Coke bottle and took a nip. "Fucking numero uno, a gold tin in the old Sixth Division bank squad. Ya know what that meant, Miller?"

Miller nodded no.

Dolan ran the back of his hand across his mouth. "Well, I'll tell ya what that meant. I was all set to put a fucking down payment on a motherfucking hotel, that's what that meant."

Dolan and Miller were 20th Precinct clerical men. Ensconced in a hole of an office just off the muster room, they filed summonses and typed reports. When he was seated at his desk Dolan was too near for Miller to ignore, yet Dolan was far enough away so that he apparently felt the need to shout his reminiscences over and over and over again. It was maddening.

"Miller!" His voice rose a full octave. "You ever see a thousand bucks in tens and twenties? You ever see 'em like Tootsie Rolls tied with fucking rubber bands? Hah, Miller, you ever see that?"

Miller made no response, just peered across his desk at Dolan, who was again sucking on the Coke bottle.

"Of course you ain't never seen it. That's 'cause"—Dolan inhaled a hiccup—"you're a fucking zip, Miller, a zero. A fucking typist is what you are, not a cop." He affected a convincing feminine tone. "With your little bottles of white-out and your hot plate, you make me wanna puke."

"But you're a real cop, right, hero?" Miller whispered. He had a problem with Dolan when Dolan was sober. On a day like today, when Dolan was in his cups, he was impossible to deal with. Blotto though he was, Dolan had bionic ears.

"What did you say? You have the balls to compare yourself to me? You shit, I was ducking bricks on Lenox Avenue when you was in grade school."

Miller dropped his head, submission, surrender, disgust. "Give me a fuckin' break, will ya, Dolan, and let me do my work."

"Work, you prick ya, you call this work?" Dolan tore a report from the typewriter and threw it into a basket. "We got a cunt's job, Miller, face it . . ."

"Dolan, shut up!" Miller hadn't said it. The phrase walked around the corner from the direction of the muster room and landed—plop—on Dolan's desk. "You are a bigmouth turd. You know that, Dolan? You got a big mouth and all that comes out of it is shit." Bobby stood in the doorway and glared at him. Dolan's voice alone had made his skin crawl. Watching him now as his head bobbed from side to side like an arcade target made him all the more angry. He felt his stomach tighten, he wanted to reach over Dolan's desk, grab him, pull him out of the office, drag him through the precinct, down past the captain's office, and toss him into the street. Wouldn't everyone applaud, wouldn't they shout encouragement? Miller, here, most likely would jump up on his desk and cheer.

"What's a matter, Porterfield? What're you so pissed about?" Dolan asked the question without looking up. Bobby didn't answer. Miller was a friend from academy days, but that wasn't it. It was Dolan's tone, his style, the ugly way he spoke his mind. It enraged Bobby to think that he and this foulmouthed drunk had the same job. Dolan was an oiled-up old-timer who drank rye from a Coke bottle and attacked anyone and everyone he came into contact with. He loved to brag about being a crook. Maybe that's what it was, the pride he took at having been on the take and getting away with it. It was degrading to be associated with cops like him.

Dolan took a swig from the Coke bottle, pushed his chair back from the desk, and looked up. Bobby returned his stare.

"What's your problem? You got a problem, Porterfield?"

"You suck," Bobby hissed.

With what seemed to be a tremendous effort, Dolan drew himself up from the desk.

"I'd sit right there if I were you." Bobby's tone was serious.

Dolan smiled and bent his head back in the manner of a prizefighter before the opening bell. Miller continued to file summonses.

"Whaddaya think, you're a tough kid?" Dolan slurred.

Drunk or not, Bobby decided, if Dolan came out from behind his desk he'd lay the souse flat out. Dolan didn't come out from behind his desk. He looked past Bobby to Mark, who stood in the doorway grinning.

"Uh-hah, what do we have here, a one-on-one in blue?" said Mark cheerily.

"Your partner came in looking for trouble," Dolan snapped, then flopped into his chair. Miller, the target of Dolan's tirade, put a fresh report into his typewriter and banged away.

"Looking for trouble? I wasn't looking for trouble. I came in here to drop off the report when I heard this jackass ranting about how much money he stole." Bobby felt Mark grab his elbow, he felt a slight squeeze. Cool it, the grip said.

"Ya see, ya see what I mean, Spencer? Your partner's looking to get his ass kicked." Dolan finished off the Coke bottle and slammed it on his desk.

Bobby pulled his arm free from Mark's grasp and pointed a righteous finger in the drunk's face. "You better learn to watch your mouth before somebody shoves a fist in it."

"And you better learn to control your temper, hero," Miller chimed in, never missing a beat at the typewriter. All three turned in Miller's direction. "O.K., enough; you two get the hell outta here, me and Dolan got work to do," Miller said, rolling his eyes, pleading with Bobby and Mark to leave.

"Give 'em the report and let's go, we got a sector to protect," Mark said, and pushed Bobby toward the door.

Dolan wasn't through. "You oughta take him out and break his cherry, Spencer, maybe grow him up a bit."

"Christ, Dolan, what does it take to shut you up?" A muscle in Mark's cheek tightened, then began to quiver. For the first time in a long while Bobby heard a slight break in Mark's control. Miller stopped typing.

"O.K., O.K.," Dolan was smiling a silly, toothy drunk's grin. The grin faded and he turned away from Mark and returned to his desk. Bobby could hear Miller's typewriter bang away as Mark joined him and they walked to the muster room.

The activity board in the 20th Precinct muster room was a four-by-four-foot chunk of cardboard. Tacked to the board were pictures of the FBI's ten most wanted, a stack of TOPs and SOPs, along with daily messages. Two items jumped out at Bobby and Mark as they scanned the board. The first message brought a questioning, eyebrows-raised glance exchange. "Patrolman Porterfield to report to Captain Burke forthwith." Forthwith in the police department meant immediately or sooner. The second message brought an exclamation in harmony. "Shit!" Sector David was down with a broken shock; they were on foot assigned to special post no. 1.

Like his mind, the door to Captain Burke's office was mostly closed. Bobby knocked once, then again. There was no response; the captain was out. He tried the handle, the door opened. Mark reached around him and pulled the door closed.

"I wouldn't go parading into Burke's office if I were you."

Bobby opened the door again.

"The message said 'forthwith.' I'm here forthwith. Where is *he?*"

"Ya know, partner, there are times you have more balls than brains. Cops don't go barging into captains' offices, ya know what I mean, smart ass?"

"Screw Burke," he said, grabbing Mark by the wrist and pushing his arm away. Dolan's words gnawed at him. The guy was a malicious son of a bitch. It was his maliciousness that he fed off. It was the shocked hurt in others' faces that he enjoyed. The guy was a piss can. Period. And Bobby was angry that he hadn't smacked him down once and for all. The exchange with Dolan continued to bother Bobby. "Break his cherry," Dolan had said. That was not the first time Dolan had used that phrase.

"Hey, partner, you gonna break my cherry?" Bobby said. He

could feel the arrogant edges of his smile, and he knew Mark could see it. He hadn't meant to embarrass Mark.

Mark turned to leave, then called back over his shoulder, "You get into an idiotic conversation with the likes of Dolan, then I have to listen to your shit for the next eight hours. It's boring, Bobby, you should be smarter than that."

"I'm not going to take his crap anymore," Bobby snapped. "The next time that jerk opens his mouth to me, I'm going to belt him." Bobby knew he sounded foolish, so when Mark walked back to him and gently shoved him, then shoved him again, he laughed and felt better.

"Look," Mark said soothingly, "Dolan's got nothing to say. When someone, anyone, has nothing to say, only assholes listen."

"Fuck Dolan," Bobby said.

"Right." Mark grinned.

"Tell me, was he as big a crook as he says he was?" Bobby whispered.

"Whoa, partner, whoa. What the hell do you know about crooks and cops?" Mark said slowly, quietly. There were cops everywhere in the muster room; they could easily be overheard.

"I know the difference," Bobby said, much too loudly.

"Do you know what a Charlotte Russe is?"

"No."

"Of course you don't. You're from fucking Omaha," Mark almost yelled.

"What the hell are you talking about?"

"I'll see ya later on post. Let's drop this conversation." Mark stuck his thumb in the air and headed for the door.

Bobby called after him, "Mark, did you ever . . . ?"

"What?"

"Nothing, forget it, I'll see ya later." Bobby looked around the muster room; four cops, two coming and two going, may have overheard their conversation. Bobby felt even more foolish. He cleared his throat and waved goodbye to Mark, who simply shook his head and walked out the station-house doors.

Captain Arthur Burke, or Hoover Burke, as he was not too fondly called by the precinct old-timers, had survived thirty years in the police department. From the pictures on his office wall it seemed that most of those years were spent on uniform patrol. Well, the Ol' Mad Hatter couldn't be all that bad, Bobby thought.

"See anyone you know?" Bobby spun around as a lumbering Captain Burke pushed past him and took a seat behind his desk.

His bathroom at home and his office at the precinct were the only rooms that Arthur Burke entered with a sense of purpose. The captain shat with authority in Bay Ridge, and his word was law at the precinct house in Manhattan.

"That's the Chief with the ex-P.C., isn't it?" Bobby said.

"Everyone in those pictures is an ex, 'cept me and Doyle. Take a seat. Want a Miller?"

The offer jolted Bobby. A beer he wants to give me. This captain, who has said maybe three friendly words to me in a year, wants me to sit and share a drink with him. I must be in a whole lot of trouble, Bobby thought. But Burke was wearing a faint smile. Maybe he was just trying to be friendly. Good luck, Bobby thought. His problem was that he didn't know how to answer. He hated beer.

"No, thanks, Captain," he answered. What the hell. He can't jump on me for not wanting a beer.

"What's a matter, Porterfield, you don't like Miller?"

"I just don't like beer." Damn, that was a mistake.

"You what?" Burke pushed back in his chair, cocked his head, and looked at Bobby as if he'd called the Virgin Mother a transvestite.

Bobby knew he'd better come up with a better excuse.

"I have weak kidneys, boss. One beer and I'll be pissing all night." Good; Burke was a foot cop once. That he should understand. "And there's not too many places to piss on special one," Bobby added. Might as well let him know that he'd been assigned that dung heap of a post again.

"You work with Sergeant Moresco, don't you?" Burke finally said.

Ah-ha, that's it, he thought. Frank's been a bit strange lately. I told Mark something's been bothering the sarge. What did he do? Forget to turn in his monthlies or something? The Ol' Mad Hatter here wants me to say that Frank Moresco, just the best sergeant in the precinct, is not a good supervisor. He wants to zing Moresco. That's it! Well, it'll take more than an offer of Miller, that old snake.

"Sergeant Moresco is tops, boss, a terrific sergeant. You want my opinion, Captain, he's the best you have." *Fuck you and your Miller.*

"I'm not interested in your opinion. That's not what I asked you."

You mean you're not interested in my opinion if I have something good to say. Who're you kidding? Bobby smiled to himself.

Burke was up now, walking around his desk to the bathroom. Bobby heard a refrigerator door open, then close.

"Something happened, and before the precinct rumormongers get hold of it, I want you and some of the others to know the truth," Burke called from the bathroom. Water was running now. Burke was washing his face. Bobby could hear the grunting and the splashing, then he heard the roar.

"Porterfield, will you tell that fucking broom to bring me some towels. I'm good and fucking tired of drying my face with toilet paper."

Bobby moved to the office door and called out to Police Officer Ruiz, who was busy sweeping around the front desk, "Benny, the captain's out of towels."

Police Officer Ruiz put down his broom, didn't reply, and walked off. Bobby assumed he went for a towel, though you could never tell with a guy assigned to light duty. He and his rubber gun might be on their way to Cleveland. Burke was back behind his desk now. Little specks of toilet tissue stuck to his beard.

"Well, Porterfield, what did you think of Moresco?"

"Excuse me, Captain, you said what *did* I think of Moresco?"

Burke lifted his beer, took a sip, stifled a belch, and stared straight ahead. Bobby felt invisible. Burke was looking right past him.

"He killed himself. Took his service revolver, put it up against one side of his head, then took his off-duty and put it up against the other, then wham! It was like a bolt of lightning hit him in the fucking head. What a thing for his brother to find."

Bobby's mind exploded. Images of Frank Moresco laughing,

doing his Humphrey Bogart number, flew past. Mark, hysterical, as Moresco mimicked the Reverend Ike. Faces and images everywhere. He felt dizzy. He saw Danny Swanson smile just before he splashed against the pavement, sending brain tissue, teeth, and bone splattering into the gutter.

"Why, why, Cap? Why do you think . . . ?"

"You're asking me?" Burke flushed away the bottle of Miller. "Look, I don't know why he did it. Nobody knows anything yet. I just want to make sure that when the news hits, I don't have half the precinct running out to Brooklyn to help solve a homicide that wasn't."

"You mean he may not have killed himself? It may have been a homicide, you're saying?"

"I'm not saying anything of the kind. Nobody knows why he did it, but he did it. The story that will be released to the press will be open-ended; maybe a suicide, maybe a homicide. The Internal Affairs Division is talking to his brother right now over in Brooklyn. His brother is on the job, did you know that?"

"Sure, he works in the seven-six."

"Well, his brother found him and called it in. They weren't able to find his guns. His brother's statement is that when he got there and found him, there were no guns. We think the brother threw the guns in the ocean or something. Make it look like a murder for the mother's sake, or insurance or something, I don't know. There is no doubt that it was a suicide. There are powder burns on his hands and what's left of his head. I know how everyone here felt about him. I don't want a caravan of cops heading over to Brooklyn interfering with the investigation. So I want you and a few of the others to spread the word: no murder, no robbery, a plain and simple cop's suicide. It happens all the time." Burke got up quickly from his desk and walked to the door. Opening it, he called for Officer Ruiz.

"Dolan," he yelled. "You see Ruiz?"

Bobby reached over and took an unopened bottle of beer, unscrewed the cap, and took a long draw.

"Find that space shot for me, will ya, Dolan? And tell him I need some towels. Will ya do that, Dolan? Can you handle that?"

"Sure, right now, Cap," Bobby heard Dolan reply. He was feeling light-headed. He took another gulp and finished the beer.

Returning to his desk, Burke looked worn, tired, brooding. "Dolan's quite a character, isn't he, Captain?"

"Whaddaya mean, a character?" Burke demanded.

"Well, I don't know. He sometimes gets to me," Bobby said.

"He does, does he? That's too bad." Burke rose from his chair slowly. His face started to pale. Cold blue eyes locked on Bobby. Clearly it had been a mistake to mention Dolan.

"Maybe somebody that knows will tell you what kind of a cop Dolan was in his day. Maybe if you listen, you'll learn that this job was a bit more complex a few years ago. Maybe if you listen, you'll learn something. Maybe, but I doubt it. You're part of the new breed, know-it-all, half-assed, educated cops. You couldn't carry Dolan's stick in the old days. Now get going. Tell your partner what I told you about Moresco."

Burke sat down again, turned from Bobby, and was gazing at the eight-by-ten glossies when Dolan knocked on the door. He was holding two white towels.

"Ahh, excuse me, Captain, I got the towels."

"Where's Ruiz?" Burke asked, not looking up.

"Ah, he, ah, he, ah."

"Okay, Dolan. Put the towels in my bathroom. And keep Ruiz hidden. Some brass will be coming by later to go into Moresco's locker. I don't need my attendant bumping into doors and pissing on the floor when the Chief comes by."

"Sure, Cap," Dolan was whispering. "He's asleep upstairs."

"I don't want to know, you asshole! Just keep him out of my way."

Bobby eased past Dolan into the muster room. Dolan tugged at his sleeve and gave him a friendly grin. Bobby pulled free and practically ran from the precinct.

7.

The news that followed the death of Sergeant Moresco was bizarre. The *New York Post* ran a red-banner headline, "Police Sergeant Robbed and Murdered." The *Daily News* piece was very much the same. "Hero Cop Dies Alone, Murdered." The *Times,* on page two of its metropolitan section, simply reported, "Police Brass Investigate Suspicious Death of Police Officer in Brooklyn."

The Grimaldi funeral parlor stands among a row of deteriorating gray and brown walk-ups on Clinton Street in South Brooklyn. Vito Grimaldi and his sons keep the wood frame building's sparkling white exterior freshly painted and the black trim reflects headlights from as far as a block away.

Bobby and Cathy had made it in early. Even so, the funeral parlor was packed, cops were coming from everywhere. Arriving in a steady stream, the guests shouldered their way into the main sitting room. Sergeant Moresco, it seemed, had hundreds of friends.

The latecomers, forced to stand, pushed and edged their way closer and closer to the casket. For what reason Bobby could not imagine. The box, after all, was closed; even the acknowledged artistry of Vito Grimaldi could not make Sergeant Frank Moresco presentable.

Sixty long minutes Bobby sat and watched unfamiliar faces file past. Then he saw Phil Moresco sitting at the end of a row of wooden folding chairs. Frank's brother caught Bobby's stare, shuddered a recognition, and gave a slight grin. He then turned away to accept a hand from yet another guest. This person, too, was a stranger to Bobby and most likely a stranger to Phil Moresco as well. Bobby turned and looked in the direction of the empty chair reserved for Frank's mother. She was, as Dolan had said earlier, throwing a "wop fit" in the adjoining room. The old lady's heartbreaking gasps and sobs could easily be heard through the wall.

Bobby felt Cathy's head roll onto his shoulder.

"Why don't they give her some medication?" Cathy whispered.

"I'm sure they have," Bobby said, attempting a shrug.

"Oh, Jesus." Cathy squeezed his shoulder as an eerie wail floated into the room.

"C'mon, let's get out of here," Bobby said, grabbing Cathy's hand and jerking her to her feet. They moved through the crowd out the back door to the parking lot.

Bobby couldn't rid his nostrils of the heavy, suffocating aroma of hundreds of chrysanthemums. He felt queasy, and the hot, humid July night offered no relief. Suddenly he stopped walking and put his hands on Cathy's shoulders. She looked awful. "Are you O.K.?" he asked, tracing a finger along her chin. She was pale and clammy, her face the color of wet beach sand.

"O.K.? Are you kidding?" Cathy groaned. "That stage show in there made me sick. There was no air in that room, and Frank's mother . . ."

Bobby looked around for Mark's car. It wasn't there. Then he looked up and saw Phil Moresco standing in the doorway of the funeral home lighting a cigarette. Bobby raised a hand and Phil waved him over.

The moment he and Cathy reached Frank's brother, Bobby cleared his throat. What to say? I'm sorry your brother blew himself away? How's your mom taking it? You look great? All the damned lines sounded ridiculous.

"We're real sorry, Phil." It was Cathy's turn. "Please accept my condolences. Your brother was a sweet, sweet man."

"Don't I know you?" Phil said, taking Cathy's hand.

"We've met but I'm sure you don't remember." There was a warm smile on her lips.

"You're Chief Doyle's daughter. We met last year at Captain Ryan's retirement party. You were there with your dad. I remember. But I don't remember seeing you there, Bobby."

"You weren't looking. I was there." Bobby understood all too well why Phil hadn't remembered him. When Cathy was in a room all eyes were on her.

"You know, Phil, when I was a little girl your brother would come out to our house every Sunday morning to see my dad," Cathy said quietly.

"Is that so?" Phil seemed surprised. "I wonder what for."

Cathy stared at Phil for a moment. When she began, she turned toward Bobby. "Frank used to bring us the most delicious pastries. When he stopped coming, Sunday morning was never the same."

"My brother was a thoughtful guy. He knew your father loved Italian pastry, and since he probably didn't have much to do on Sunday morning . . . Well," Phil continued, "I guess you could say he was a bit of an apple polisher." Phil Moresco was now smiling. He winked at Bobby, turned away, and began walking back toward the funeral home. Suddenly he stopped and turned back. "You know, walking out here to light my cigarette I realized my brother was quite a guy. There must be three hundred people here. And you know something else, I don't know half of them. Thanks for coming, you two. Frank talked a lot about you, Porterfield. He said you were gonna make a hell of a cop." Phil then lit another cigarette, took one drag, and threw it down. Turning, he went into the building.

Bobby felt there was more to say but then thought better of it. He smiled a sort of thank-you to Frank's brother, put his arm through Cathy's, and began walking to his car. Opening the Volkswagen door, he looked at Cathy. "Frank Moresco really drove out to your house every Sunday morning?" he asked.

Cathy seemed surprised by the question. "What's the big deal?" Cathy had reached across the seat and pulled the button that released the door lock.

"Cathy, it's a hundred miles round trip from South Brooklyn to your father's house." Bobby didn't know what he was implying; nevertheless, he was beginning to sound like an inquisitor.

"A bit of a long way to drop off a few rum baba, don't you think?"

Bobby pulled the car from the parking lot out onto Clinton Street. As they turned the corner, Dolan stepped from the curb and almost impaled himself on the Volkswagen's hood. Bobby slammed the brakes and the horn simultaneously. "Drunken asshole!" he screamed. "He's on another planet, that jerk."

Cathy threw her hand against the windshield to brace herself, then bounced back into the seat.

"Jesus, you almost hit him." Cathy stuck her head out the passenger window. "Be careful, why don't you!" she yelled. Dolan gave her the finger.

"Isn't that Artie Dolan?" Cathy asked, now laughing at Dolan's response.

"Sure is. You're probably gonna tell me that he came out to see your father, too."

"He did. Sometimes he'd come with Frank and sometimes he'd come alone."

"Bringing pastry?" Bobby's question had a snide quality to it and so did the smirk that had set itself on his face.

"No, as a matter of fact, he'd bring Irish soda bread. Fact is, the men who worked for my dad loved him. Simple as that."

"How lucky for your father. I'm surprised he doesn't weigh three hundred pounds," Bobby said. He slammed the VW into second, then third, leaving South Brooklyn's tenements, heading for the high-priced beauty of Brooklyn Heights and maybe a cooling walk along the promenade.

8.

Richard Smalls was a mess. His life was a toilet.

The killing would be the crowning event of the worst day Sweet Dick had spent in a month. Every month Dick had anywhere from seven to ten worst days, but this one, this one was gonna be a motherfucker.

His jones woke him early. It tingled at his insides, made him nauseated, goaded him.

"C'mon, get up, give me a little," it whispered. Half asleep, he let his hand fall from the bed down into his shoe. It was gone! He came fully awake in an instant, the whisper now a scream. His morning shot was gone; not taped, not short, gone.

"Chocolate. Where is she?"

Dick didn't move; he couldn't move. He turned his head toward the bed. Then he remembered. Chocolate didn't come home with him. That crazy bitch. She had stayed in the street.

Maybe, in last night's stupor, he'd hidden it somewhere else. Under the mattress! He lifted it: nothing. Again, he looked in his shoe. Grabbing it by the toe, he banged it. He held it up and just about pushed his face into it. Maybe it was stuck, hung up near the toe.

Not in his shoe, not under the mattress. His shirt pocket— that's where. He grabbed his shirt from the foot of the bed, scissoring his fingers through the pockets. Zip. "Mother," he moaned. Lorraine, he thought.

Sweet Dick moved from his bedroom into the adjoining room. A half dozen mattresses were scattered about three rooms. Three table lamps and one floor lamp, all with red bulbs, made up the rest of the furnishings. The place looked like the deck of a submarine. The tricks loved it.

There was one real bed in the apartment and that was Sweet Dick and Chocolate's. The other girls turned their tricks and slept on the floor.

Dick found Lorraine unconscious on the mattress nearest the bathroom. She wasn't sleeping, she was zonked, off somewhere lounging in the vestibule of death. Her orange Little Annie wig was off, propped on top of her knee-high white plastic boots. If he weren't so sick, the scene would be funny. Lorraine wiped out on the mattress with an albino midget wearing an orange Afro standing guard. She had gone to sleep in her street clothes. Her white "I Love New York" T-shirt had rolled up and met her red micro-miniskirt at the waist. Without panties her triangular shock of jet-black frizz gleamed as if it had been misted.

Obviously she had crawled into the crib sometime after he did, snatched his wake-up from his shoe, and shot it up. Her own cure, some slow-moving stuff from the street, wasn't going to do it for her. Lorraine had panicked. Afraid she'd wake up sick. She took Dick's heroin, mixed it with her own, and OD'ed. The hypo and cooker wrapped in tissue paper lay next to her wigged boots.

"Fuck it, I hope the bitch dies," Dick mumbled as he threw on his clothes. Taking the apartment's one pillow from his bed, Dick walked back to the sleeping girl, moved her, and made sure she was breathing. Then he placed her head gently on the pillow. He stared at Lorraine for a long moment, then turned to go.

"Dick."

The voice made him jump.

"I'm sorry. I was so sick. I copped some garbage from over on the avenue . . . I was afraid . . . I . . ."

Dick looked down at the rumpled mess that was Lorraine. All of his anger and some of his sickness subsided.

"I know, babe. Lay still. I'll be right back."

Dick grabbed hold of the doorknob. He had to get into the street. Find Chocolate. He had to score, and soon.

"Dick," Lorraine called again. "I'm gonna be real sick."

So began Sweet Dick's day of days. The morning was the high point.

Dick slammed the steel gate that opened to the street. He and the girls had a basement apartment on St. John's Place, a street with a hundred SROs and imploding brownstones. Park Slope was one of the oldest residential neighborhoods in Brooklyn. Ghetto spillage from Bedford Stuyvesant to the north had infected many of the Slope's gracious old brownstones and town houses. The stone and wood façades remained intact— winos, junkies, and other ill-starred citizens allowed the interiors to fall into decay, decreasing the real-estate value of some very valuable property.

Dick reached the corner of St. John's Place and Fifth Avenue and looked around. Not a soul there. Different from other street criminals, junkies were very visible people. Constantly on the prowl, street junkies moved in herds, always looking for a pusher or a score.

They must be down on Fourth, Dick thought as he turned the corner and moved off.

If I were a connection, I'd give it away, he thought. Ease people's pain, be their momma and daddy. No human should leave another human sick.

Dick walked, more quickly now, another block west to Fourth Avenue and Warren Street. When he hit the avenue he turned north. Now he was practically running, heading for Pacific Street. He didn't notice the unmarked police car parked near the corner. Head down, hands stuffed deep into his pockets, he buzzed along, a junkie on a mission.

As he neared Pacific Street he noticed the crowd. Fourth Avenue and Pacific Street was the gathering place, the watering hole for South Brooklyn's junkies. There were people every-where. White, black, Hispanic junkies—all waiting for the man. It looked like half of Brooklyn's addicts woke up sick. Heroin is a bit more expensive in Brooklyn than in Manhattan, but it's a lot safer to buy there. You can save a dollar or two on a bag of dope in Harlem or on the Lower East Side, but after you buy it you have to run a gauntlet of street gorillas to get it home. The take-off artists lurk everywhere, waiting to rip you off. If you're not from the neighborhood, they steal your cure and leave you for dead. No joke for someone like Dick. He had a serious habit, spending one hundred and fifty dollars a day for his cure. Getting high was a thing of the past, a memory, an experience he'd just about forgotten. Nowadays he'd be forced to spend two hundred dollars before he could lay back and enjoy the soothing strokes and warm pink glow of the white lady.

This morning getting high never entered his mind. He needed a wake-up. It had been ten hours since his last shot. He was late getting off and the beast that was his habit was wide awake and running free. He was sweating and nauseated. He'd have to beg something from somebody soon. Failing that, somebody was gonna get robbed. He'd play gorilla. He'd grab somebody else's dope and run off.

The thought of having to get physical made Sweet Dick's sickness increase fourfold. He was no thief, no gorilla. Street anger and motherfucker screams were an act with Dick. He was a pimp. A junkie street pimp. He needed his ladies to earn. He was no smooth, slick uptown dude. No big car, high-heeled shoes, and blue sky for him; not for him, not yet. Someday, he thought, when he cleaned up, someday when he kicked his jones he'd buy some clothes and get some real earners. Young women with cherry asses and smooth mouths would make him some real folding money. He'd have Chocolate and Lorraine to keep the girls in line. Then he'd lay back big and fat and shoot coke all day. He'd wear silk pants and socks and drive a red LD. He'd give money to his old junkie friends so that they wouldn't have to be sick in the morning.

On the corner of Fourth Avenue and Pacific Street he saw B'Back talking with a couple of white guys and Big Lloyd.

"Here's my man now," B'Back said to the white guys. He then turned quickly and walked to meet Dick. Out of the corner of his eye Dick noticed Big Lloyd walk off.

"You see Chocolate?" Dick asked.

B'Back wore a smile like everyone's favorite uncle, genuine

and warm. For some reason, even though he had a raging habit, B'Back never lost weight. To Dick he looked round, healthy; what he was was swollen. Water pushed up just beneath his skin. If you'd stick him with a pin he'd burst and wash himself down a sewer.

"Chocolate got picked up and busted by the pussy posse right after you left the set last night." B'Back moved away a step or two. "Man, you look fuckin' terrible."

Dick let out a shout, more like a wail. "Busted? That dumb nigger! That stupid nigger!" Dick was afraid for Chocolate. He knew she couldn't make a day in the joint. She couldn't take care of business without him around.

"Why didn't that dumb bitch come home with me?" Dick ranted. "No, not her, she had to turn one more trick, suck one more prick, cop one more bag." Dick spun on his heel, his arms flailing. He didn't notice one of the white guys grin and then turn away.

B'Back bent forward at the waist, his hands on his hips. "Calm, my man, calm. Ya know they only hold her overnight. She be in court this morning and be home this afternoon." He then turned to face the white guys and motioned for them to stay put.

"Yeah, well, now I'm gonna have to go and score for both of us. She's gonna come home sick as hell."

"Where's your other woman, Lorraine? Get her ass out here. Put her to work."

"Lorraine came home and shot my wake-up. She'd nodded out at the crib."

"Shot your wake-up, your own wake-up? Damn, man. Ya know what I mean? I mean, you're the man. You is the boss. You gotta whup them bitches, man, you gotta fuck 'em up." B'Back did a half turn. The water under his skin seemed to slosh, causing his belly to slide across his belt.

"Yeah, well, I'll take out my bat on 'em as soon as I get straight." Dick grinned.

"No, you won't, man." B'Back was smiling now, sweat rivulets were running down alongside his ear, on his throat, and into his shirt. "Them bitches don't call you Sweet Dick for nothing."

Dick noticed for the first time that the day was going to be one hot son of a bitch. The temperature must be near eighty-five degrees already and it wasn't 10 a.m. yet.

"Never mind this shit," Dick said. "You got anything?"

"Got anything?! I'm sicker than you."

"I don't wanna hear this."

"See those two white dudes on the corner?" B'Back pointed with his chin.

"Yeah. They look like cops." Dick turned toward the corner. He wanted the white guys to look his way so he could see their eyes.

"Dick, they ain't cops. Lloyd brought 'em. I've seen 'em around."

The white guys glanced toward the pair. Then, as if by a signal, their eyes turned away.

"Well, what about 'em?" Dick asked.

"They got twenty-five bucks, and they want five bags."

"That's cool. Let's go get it for 'em."

B'Back took hold of Dick's elbow and walked him to the corner. When they were in a box, B'Back and Dick would run a game on outsiders. Only strangers would fall. Regulars on the corner knew better. After introducing Dick as a runner for the chief dealer in the neighborhood, B'Back would try to get money in his hand. Getting an addict to surrender money was near impossible. But B'Back was a magician.

"Hey! Me and my man here are on this set ev-er-ry dayyyy. Ya understand what I mean? Ev-er-ry dayyyy. Now how we gonna run off with your bread? Ask the people here. G'head, ask 'em. They'll tell ya. Ain't we here ev-er-ry dayyyy, Lloyd?"

"Uh-huh, ev-er-ry day. They here, umm-hum, dat right."

B'Back would whisper, "Now if'n you'll give me your bread, I'll be right back with the best stuff in Brooklyn."

Dick's role was to stand by and exude "I don't really give a fuck what you do."

Cash in hand, the duo would search out the nearest pusher, score, then scoot to a roof landing. Then they'd open a bag and tap a small amount of the drug. They were able to scratch together and inject enough heroin to take off the edge. B'Back would return to the corner and deliver what was ordered. The strangers, trembling, almost hysterical, fearing that the two had run off, would be so relieved they would ask nothing.

The white dudes moved nervously from the corner into the street, then back to the sidewalk. Heads on swivels, they took exaggerated looks up and down the avenue. When Dick held their eyes with his own, they turned away. If Lloyd had not vouched for them, there would be no question. They looked like narcs. They were too healthy to be junkies.

The one with sandy hair and a ripe pink-and-white pimple crowning his nose walked over to Dick.

"Ya got something decent?"

He had a raspy voice and when he spoke it was almost a hiss. Dick turned away from him. B'Back was with the other guy. He was taller than the first, with a shoulder-length Afro and the arms of a wrestler. Veins like thin snakes pushed up from beneath his skin. Dick noticed there wasn't a mark on them.

"They want our money, T.J. They want our bread." The Afro's voice was friendly but he was wearing a disbelieving grin. This guy is a fuckin' monster, Dick thought, and he stinks like the jailhouse. Grabbing B'Back's shoulder, Dick whispered loud enough so the white dudes could hear. "C'mon, let's go, these guys don't wanna do anything." B'Back didnt' move.

"Man, it's simple as this." B'Back spoke in an unemotional tone, passing on a fact. There was no room for discussion. "You can't come with us. We don't got nothing, nothing here. We gotta go get it. Is that hard to understand? We go, you stay. You don't wanna go for it? Then fuck it. Stay sick."

B'Back's rap sounded good to Dick.

The pimple-nose wheeled on his heel and waved to someone out of Dick's line of sight. Immediately Dick was filled with unaccustomed panic. He felt his heart jump into his throat. Expecting gorilla types, Dick braced and checked for his K-Bar. But he was too sick. He calculated the distance to the subway. That far he could run. B'Back would have to take care of himself. When he saw to whom the pimple-nose waved, there was instant relief.

The girl turned into the street with a delicate gliding motion.

As she moved diagonally across the corner, heads turned. She slow-danced up to Dick like a kitten to a plate of milk. The way she moved made Dick smile. As long as he could remember, an invisible silver thread tied him instantly to a sensual woman. Eight to eighty, women were special to Dick, and this one was world class.

She was small, thin on top, with muscular dancer's legs that pulled tight against cutoff jeans. Long straight hair, so black that blue highlights flashed, fell to the center of her back. Pear-shaped breasts danced freely under a white T-shirt. She looked seventeen.

Now this child could make me a fortune, Dick thought.

The girl took a stance at an angle to Dick and faced B'Back. The curve of her leg and the swell of an exquisite ass were not lost in the fog of Dick's oncoming withdrawal. But it was there: alive and moving, tightening his ass, shriveling his balls.

"Are we going to be able to do something here?" she purred, a voice like a child's.

T.J., the one with the pimple, hissed, "They want us to front our bread. 'Stay here,' he says, 'lay here and wait.' The man thinks we're dufuses."

Dick reached a hand to the girl's elbow. The white guys tensed. They looked as though they'd jump through their skins. The girl turned to face Dick directly. She smiled and the white guys seemed to relax. Dick felt life flow into his prick. He tightened his grip on her elbow. Turning on his practiced, gentle, and all-knowing pimp's smile, he murmured, "Here— listen to me. Why we making such a big thing outta this? We said we'd make the run."

The girl cocked her head, a smile spreading across her baby face, her eyes twinkling. "So make it," she said, and gently pulled her elbow free.

B'Back bent at the waist, put two swollen hands on his hips, and pushed his face a bit too close to the girl's. "We need the bread, pretty thing. Talk to your friends."

Her grin remained etched. Dick noticed that she pushed her thumb between her forefinger and index finger. What would happen if this child blew?

"Who are you?" she asked, looking at Dick.

Dick shot a glance at B'Back, then looked over to the subway entrance.

B'Back motioned to Dick. "Everyone around here knows us. They call him Sweet Dick."

"I bet they do."

"O.K., get us five spoons."

"They're tens," Dick shot back.

The girl turned to the guy with the Afro and tugged at his beard.

"Jimmy, give 'em what you got. These guys aren't going to beat us." The Afro just shook his head and handed Dick a crumpled ball of money.

Dick couldn't help but smile. The monster's pussy-whipped, he thought as he counted out the twenty-five dollars. The girl pushed a finger into her shorts and came out with another crumpled ball.

"Here's another twenty-five, sweetness," she said.

"Not sweetness, Sweet Dick," he said, forming a grin to match hers.

"Uh-huh," she said, closing her hand on Dick's as the money passed between them. Dick grabbed hold of B'Back's arm and the two walked off. Suddenly B'Back stopped in his tracks and turned around.

"Now don't move. Hang right there," he yelled. "We'll be right back."

The girl and the Afro, both with arms folded, broke into wide grins. "Don't worry, and don't get lost." The Afro spoke clearly now. No anxiety. There was almost a sporty ring to his tone.

The motherfucker could be a cop, Dick thought, but the girl: who is she? She certainly can't be a cop. Nah, not her; too young. What am I thinking? None of 'em can be cops. Besides, he saw marks on the girl's arm. It was a small track, but he knew a needle mark when he saw it.

Dick saw the reflection of his own fear in B'Back's eyes. Who were these three people? No matter. They were both too sick to care. B'Back's nose was running, a river gushing from inside him, the sickness pushing up and out through his nose. With

Dick it was cramps and nausea. For some reason, his nose never ran, a small favor in a world of pain and anxiety. The short quick snorts of the junkie experiencing the onset of withdrawal were an irritant to Dick. He marveled at the way a trick could stay hard when Chocolate, snorting, with mucus dropping down her face, lay back with her heels in the air.

Now, with fifty dollars in his pocket and B'Back at his side, Dick flew along the South Brooklyn streets. Five blocks south to Union Street and Fourth Avenue. Up five flights of stairs. A light tap-tap. Pause. Then tap-tap on a steel reinforced door. The hawklike face of Charlie Nose behind a chain and a Fox lock.

"I'm out. Been out for a day. Come back later."

Instant depression. Five flights down, four more blocks further south. Anna Chipi Chipi. Her fortresslike basement apartment was empty; Anna in the wind.

As long as they had the bread it was only a matter of time. A few more streets, across two or three more avenues, they'd run into someone they knew. That had been their history. A junkie on a mission.

Carolina Slim: out. Nicky the Greek: out. Tommy Eyes: killed by take-off artists the day before.

They zipped back to Dick's apartment. Maybe Chocolate was home. Maybe Lorraine was up. Maybe their luck would change.

The apartment was empty but there was a note, "Me an' L are gonna TCB. Where the hell are you? Stay put. Luv. Me."

Dick decided they should keep looking. The girls were out turning tricks. They'd be O.K. Right now he was worried about one person: himself. If he got any sicker he'd be no use to anyone. He was sweating freely and had the runs. In the toilet when he bent his head to lift his trousers, his nose ran a flood. His jones was far worse than he thought. If he didn't get straight soon, it'd be all over.

They tried four more street dealers, heard four more "I'm out"s but the line they heard from Razor, the last dealer they spoke to, crushed them. "It's a fuckin' panic. Everyone's out."

Real or imagined, any excuse would make a street panic very real for an addict. A big arrest at the airport or a longshoreman's strike in Marseilles. It didn't matter. A ten-dollar spoon would be fifty dollars by eight o'clock. That's if you could find a spoon, that's if you could find a connection. Dick and B'Back sat perfectly still on the curb. There had to be an answer. Dick searched his memory for a connection he hadn't tried. The only people with dope in the last panic were the Guineas. The Guineas and people that dealt directly with them—they'd have something. But you could bet they weren't gonna move it, not till the panic really took hold. Dick slid from the curb into the gutter. B'Back had stopped talking an hour before. Dick was frantic. Then he remembered. And for the first time in four hours he smiled.

Chino Feo, the dude from Columbia Street. He lived with that Italian broad. Her brother was a big-time connection. He'd be straight, and what's better, he'd be fair.

Dick patted B'Back's shoulder. "Let's go, bro. We'll be all right. I know someone who has to have something."

As Dick and B'Back moved west toward Columbia Street they began to notice real signs of the panic. Junkies were assembling and moving off in groups. At Third Avenue and Dean Street a group of ten or twelve stood around and seemed to be waiting. All of them were strangers to Dick. Junkies from Queens and Manhattan were coming up out of the subways.

South Brooklyn and the Brooklyn waterfront, where numerous organized crime operations flourished, was the shepherd's horn. As natural as it was in the junkies' minds that death followed addiction, so it was that when your local pusher went dry you got as near the source as possible. For them it was the Brooklyn piers.

The pair walked more quickly now, Dick carrying the fifty dollars, B'Back locked somewhere in suspended animation. Water popped from B'Back's hairline and ran down the front of his face in rivulets. His trousers, too, were soaking wet. A white handkerchief, in a hand the size of a loaf of bread, mopped his face every few steps. He was a walking puddle.

They avoided the questioning stares of friends and strangers alike. Sharing was not plausible. By ten o'clock tonight, Dick thought, junkies would be breaking into drugstores and doctors' offices. Hospital attendants would turn a fortune with legit dope and GBs. Forged prescriptions that usually sold for a dollar apiece would bring fifteen and twenty dollars a copy. Some Mafia connection doling out heroin would become an instant millionaire. A fuckin' panic. Who would have thought it yesterday? One hundred and seventy-five thousand heroin addicts in New York City were in the process of going crazy. Every junkie that Sweet Dick and B'Back passed looked accusingly at them.

At the corner of Atlantic Avenue and Columbia Street they took a left and passed a playground. About thirty junkies were sitting on benches and swings and leaning agaist monkey bars. Dick glanced in their direction and recognized most of them. He extended his hand in a peace sign, then turned to B'Back. "Bro, I hope you got your shank with ya. Gettin' outta here is gonna be a motherfucker."

They crossed Kane Street and were on Chino's block. His apartment building lay straight ahead. There must have been ten people sitting on his stoop. Dick came to a sudden halt, causing B'Back to splash into him.

Chino's apartment was located on the top floor of a six-story brown-and-gray tenement. Dick remembered that both the door to the street and the interior door were locked. Three long and two short rings would buzz them in. Two short and three long rings opened the interior door, allowing access to the building. Chino, from six floors above, was able to identify friend or foe, cop or customer, by looking down between the banisters.

"I ain't goin' through that group of hyenas," Dick said, and moved toward the corner building. B'Back's jaw was still locked. He simply followed quietly.

Dick watched the group in front of Chino's building all the way to the door of the corner tenement. No one looked in their direction. He tried the street door, found it open, and entered the foyer. They were in 136 Columbia and had to get to 148. No big deal—they just had to cross eight roofs.

Dick pushed all the bells on the right side of the hallway. He and B'Back stood still, then a buzz, one push on the door, and they were inside. The interior door continued to buzz as they climbed the first flight of stairs. Two or three heads popped from apartments, then disappeared behind slammed doors, dead bolts slipping back, chains returned, and Fox locks bracing.

By the time Dick stepped onto the fourth floor the commotion below, caused by the ringing bells, had subsided. As he and B'Back moved up the last flight of stairs to the roof, the building was absolutely quiet.

Out on the roof, Dick looked closely at B'Back, who was leaning against the landing door, his head like a giant black pumpkin floating in sweat. B'Back had been completely silent ever since they left the curb an hour before. Dick wanted to reassure his friend. He wanted B'Back to know everything was under control. Sweet Dick was here and he was gonna take care of business.

"Brother, we're gonna be all right." Dick knew a silly smile was crossing his face as he jumped to the second roof.

B'Back didn't answer; he just nodded yes.

"Why can't you talk?" Dick asked, then turned quickly to look across the stretch of rooftops leading to Chino's building.

B'Back rolled over the first parapet and joined Dick on the second roof.

"I can talk, I just don't wanna."

"C'mon, four more roofs we be there." Dick whispered so softly he wondered if B'Back could hear.

They moved across the rooftops like children panting with pleasure and anticipation on Christmas morning. Dick was flying, his feet light. He barely touched the hot tar roof. Soon, he told the beast, soon.

B'Back was fading fast. He was half a roof behind Dick when he called out. "Whyn't ya see if those fools are still on Chino's stoop."

Dick moved over to the roof's edge and stared down. "I'll be a motherfucking, cocksucking, flat-broke trick. C'mere! Look at this, will ya?"

B'Back flopped down next to Dick.

The junkies sitting on and standing near Chino's stoop had multiplied. There were at least twenty-five of them now. All were pulling at their balls, scratching, yawning, and rubbing their noses.

"So what? After we score we'll cut back over the roofs is all."
As B'Back spoke a bead of sweat spilled from the bridge of his
nose, ran along his cheek, circled around his mouth, somehow
doubled in size at his chin, then splashed onto the parapet.

Dick, mesmerized by the rolling ball of sweat, finally brought
himself around enough to tell B'Back, "Now all sorts of people
know that Chino got stuff." But he wasn't getting through.
B'Back was a "no show," his jaws had slammed shut again.

"C'mon," Dick continued, "let's move. We gotta get to
Chino before them people break his fuckin' door down."

Dick sprinted across the remaining rooftops to Chino's building. He found the flush metal door locked. Dick already had his
K-Bar out and open when B'Back rolled up.

"Man, it's fuckin' locked. We can't get in."

"Bullshit!" Dick said, and shoved the blade of his knife between the door and the frame. He slid the blade of the K-Bar
up till he felt resistance from the hook, then he tapped the hasp
once and slammed down at the handle. The hook popped free.

They went from the bright, late-afternoon sunlight into the
uneven gray light of the landing, then into the black stillness of
the building. For a second Dick knew what it would feel and
smell like in his coffin. He shook the sensation. He was, after
all, almost there: soon he would feed the beast.

Chino's apartment lay a flight below. One more set of stairs,
a turn to the left, a knock on a door, and it would be cure time.
Chino was a terrific connection. His stuff was always top quality. Dick felt giddy; the expectancy was almost too much. He
was like a virginal teenager on his way to his first soft, wet pussy.

An erection bulged against his light summer pants. He
pushed it down with the heel of his hand. A weird feeling was
overtaking him. In the past, he could never get it up when he
was sick. He hunched his shoulders and pushed his prick down
with both hands. B'Back almost fell over him. Two marble-sized
drops of sweat dripped onto Dick's back. The sudden wetness
made Dick shudder; it chilled him.

The muffled, whispered conversation exploded in Dick's ears.
He listened to the voices for a second, then motioned for B'Back
to get down. Not this motherfucker, he thought, anybody but
this motherfucker. Dick crouched, then duckwalked down the

last two steps. Now almost lying flat behind the banister, Dick gulped and his erection vanished. He slow-crawled back up the steps till he was less than a foot from B'Back.

"It's that red-eyed, kill-crazy nigger motherfucker—Dutch Krile and two other chumps. They're gonna take Chino off."

Great gusts of air and congestion rattled from deep inside B'Back, then rolled from his mouth in a terrible wheeze. Dick clapped his hands to his friend's cheeks and began to rub, first up and down, then in a circular motion, his hands sliding along B'Back's wet skin.

"Look, you ol' whale, don't blow on me now. I can handle this fool Krile." B'Back made no reply. He just sat deathlike, his teeth grinding, his fists clenched, his chin boring a hole into his chest.

Dick heard the bar of the Fox lock slide. Then he heard the chain slip from the latch. "Don't tell me that Chino is gonna open his door to that fuckin' ape, don't tell me that."

Then he heard Chino's voice from behind the door. "You're alone, right, Frank?"

Dick crept quickly down the stairs. Craning his head around the post he saw that Frank was anything but alone. The most feared gorilla in South Brooklyn and Bedford Stuyvesant stood crouched, ready to spring.

Frank put his hand up against the peep sight of the door and shouted, "Man, you can see I'm alone. C'mon, open up! Let me in." The door opened.

Krile's voice roared through the hallway. "GET HIM! GET THE MOTHERFUCKER! CUT THE MOTHERFUCKER! CUT HIM!"

B'Back slid down the stairs past Dick and onto the landing. Faster than Dick had ever seen him move. B'Back was up and running. He fled past the open apartment door. Suddenly Krile was in the hallway. He reached an arm over the banister and pressed a gun to B'Back's neck.

"Stay put, heavy, or I'll bust a cap in your head."

A woman screamed in the apartment. "We'll give it up! You can have it! Just don't hurt him! PLEASE!"

A male voice responded in a distinctly feminine squeal. "Please," it said. Then a slap like the crack of a whip, another "please," the phony feminine squeal even more exaggerated this time, another slap, then a series of slaps: crack, crack, crack. A blood-chilling moan, a woman's voice rising, screaming, a sickening, outrageously loud "PLEASE!" The shrill scream filled the hallway, followed by what must have been a thundering kick or punch. Dick heard the gorilla grunt as the blow was thrown, "Uh-huh." Finally a whimpering little-girl cry, "Oh, please."

Dick could make out the sound of a shoe skipping along linoleum before it slammed into a belly or more likely against a head. He heard the foot get dragged back, then slide once more between ribs or lips.

Dick looked over his shoulder up the stairs to the roof. Get out of here, he told himself. He turned to look back toward the apartment. Dutch Krile stood in the hallway pointing his gun right at him. Krile had hold of B'Back and was guiding him toward the apartment door.

May as well smile at this chump, Dick thought, ain't no way I can spit at him, not now, not yet. Dick held his smile. Then Krile grinned, his psychopath's mouth agape.

"Well, if it ain't O. J. Simpson, standing there looking like the fool he is," Krile growled.

Dick took a step back. Krile had a handful of B'Back's shirt, the other hand was filled with a pistol. He looked a bit unsteady. Now go for the roof, Dick thought. As fucked up as Krile is, he probably couldn't hit himself in the ass with that cannon. But what about B'Back? Fuck it, he'd sit tight.

"Hi, Dutch. What's happenin'? You look terrific." Dick broke out his best smile, then reached for a cigarette.

"Don't talk that pimp shit to me, scumbag. Get over here."

"I'm coming. Cool it with that piece, man. You know you don't need that with me." Dick joined B'Back and Krile in front of the apartment door. He didn't want to look inside. Then Krile shoved him through the doorway. Dick kept his feet even though he was forced to jump over Chino's woman, who was lying balled up in the center of the kitchen floor. Blood, vomit, and what appeared to be teeth circled her head like a halo. Dick tried to remember her name; then he saw Chino.

A two-handed shove from Krile sent a wobbly B'Back tumbling, tripping, then crashing into the kitchen table. Laughter erupted from the two gorillas in the adjoining room. They were simultaneously pulling a ring from Chino's finger and going through his pants pockets.

Helen, that's her name, Dick remembered.

Shoving his gun in Dick's face, Krile called out, "Larry, Frank, look at this faggot pimp. Don't he look like O. J. Simpson?"

"Who?" a voice from the bedroom called out.

"O. J. Simpson. You know, the brother that flies through airports and shit. C'mon, Sweet Dick, show us how you fly." Krile walked over to Dick and grabbed his arm. Dick held his ground.

"If'n we throw the motherfucker out the window he'll fly, Dutch. Hah, Dutch? Can I throw the motherfuckin' faggot pimp out the window—watch him fly an' bounce?" Frank called out as he tried to push Chino's ring onto his little finger.

Dick's sickness vanished. He felt sore, his joints ached a bit, he had a slight headache, but the beast inside him had been frightened right back into its cave.

This rat Frank is a real comedian, he thought. His mind was racing. He watched as B'Back crawled over to Chino's woman. The girl was trying to move away from her vomit. She lifted her head, then let it drop on B'Back's swollen knee.

Krile bolted the apartment door. He moved from the kitchen into the bedroom. There sat Chino, tied and taped to a kitchen chair. The blood from his throat ran a dull red and it caked along his shoulder line. Chino's tanned skin had already begun to turn a musky gray. Clothesline ran around his chest over his upper arms and was tied to the chair. His hands were taped together with white adhesive tape; another piece of tape ran across his mouth and stuck to his trimmed mustache.

Krile strutted from the bedroom and tossed a roll of the tape to the rat Larry.

"Tape the faggot." The psycho smile returned to his face.

"Krile, why you messin' with me? I ain't goin' nowhere."

Dick didn't want his hands taped, but the real fear came from the thought that these three crazies would tape his mouth. They didn't. Krile, apparently enjoying his dialogue with Dick, wrapped tape around and across Dick's wrists and ankles but left his mouth free. Still, Dick protested.

"Faggot, I can kill you now, right now, mother, if you want."

"Whatcha wanna kill me for, Dutch? You and me, we been O.K., ain't we?"

"I wanna cut your heart out and drink your blood, faggot, then my prick will grow big and sweet like yours," Krile howled. From incisor to molar his teeth were gone. Rotten jawbones hinged inside his head.

Terrific, Dick thought, the junk has disintegrated this maniac's brain. Taking a chair with the tips of his fingers, Dick sat next to poor dead Chino. He heaved an enormous sigh and stared at B'Back. Somehow while sitting on the floor B'Back had managed to cross his legs and he now sat with his great pumpkin head resting against the kitchen cabinet, Helen's shattered face in his lap.

This shooting dope ain't what it used to be, Dick thought. I gotta kick this jones before it kills me.

It was four o'clock, the temperature had climbed to ninety degrees. Ten blocks away, the porter at the Grimaldi funeral parlor was setting up wooden folding chairs. He had been told to expect a large crowd. It was five-thirty when Krile lined the three of them up on the sofa in the parlor and began to search the apartment. It was one half hour before Police Officer Bobby Porterfield and Cathy Doyle entered the Grimaldi funeral parlor. At the very moment Frank the rat ran a razor across Chino's throat, Police Officer Mark Anthony Spencer stepped into a shower in his apartment in Brooklyn Heights. When Dutch Krile checked the tape around Dick's wrists, narcotics detectives Jackie Lerner, Tom Jacobs, and Fred Ramos sat in an unmarked police car sipping iced tea from a container. They were waiting for B'Back and Dick to return to the corner of Fourth Avenue and Pacific Street, so they could add two more felony arrests to a division-leading arrest record.

Jackie Lerner had forty-eight street buys of heroin for the month and not one was from a woman. As she saw it, there was no such thing as a woman dealer. Sure, there were women out there selling dope, but everyone she met had been put there by some smelly, hairy, macho prick. All of the women dealers she met were users. Unable to distinguish right from wrong.

Typical of the men she met in the street were these two today. This B'Back character and that smooth son of a bitch, Sweet Dick.

This month Jackie was shooting for a hundred street buys. A number no one in the history of the Narcotics Division had ever reached. Since she began wearing cutoff jeans and had come up with a way to create very real-looking tracks she was knocking 'em dead. The marks took a minute of sucking the skin on her forearm, a little mascara, and a touch of eyebrow pencil. Then it was just a matter of letting the pusher get a glimpse, and she was home free.

Soon as she hit a set, dope pushers would come running. Fighting over who would sell her dope, they pushed the junk at her with one hand while they tried to stroke her tit or rub her ass with the other.

If the wimp judges would keep these germs in jail, she'd clean up the city. Most judges wouldn't keep Hitler in jail. No room, they'd say; no room or some other phony bullshit reason, she thought. Send 'em out, that's fine by me. I'll send them back. More numbers for my arrest record.

Jackie never dreamed she could get it on with a cop—talk about a club of macho assholes. Mark was a surprise. He was brown sugar—sweet, thick, and warm. Her father must be doing handstands in his grave: she was living with a cop, and a black one to boot.

Mark—she had forgotten about Mark. She'd promised she'd be home by four. It was now five-thirty.

"Are you perfumed with lilac and smooth with cream?" she crooned into the phone. There was no reply. "I know you're there, I can hear your mind hum. It's going doo-be-doo-be-doo. You people are so talented."

Mark Spencer lay naked, stretched full out on the bed, the phone stuck up under his chin and held by his shoulder.

"I hate the smell of lilac and so do you. Where the hell are you, doo-be-doo?"

"I got stuck over in the seven-eight. I'll be home as soon as I can. Don't do anything till I get there."

"C'mon, Jackie, move it. I was supposed to meet my partner at the funeral parlor. Or did you forget?"

"Damn, Mark, I'm sorry; I did forget. Look, I'll be home in ten minutes."

"Hurry, babe, we'll be waiting."

Mark heard Jackie whisper into the receiver before she hung up the phone, "Daddy, will you show me the right way to do it? Nobody's going to be home except you and me. Will you show me, Daddy?"

"I'm going to whup your ass if you don't get moving."

"Fantastic, Daddy, I'll be just a little late then," Jackie giggled.

Mark gently placed the receiver back in the cradle. He let his head sink deeply into the down pillow. Only the purr of the air conditioner disturbed the exquisite silence of the room.

It was six o'clock when Mark heard a car door slam. As Jackie's key slid into the lock, Mark rolled onto his back and pulled the sheet tightly up under his chin. He shut his eyes and tried to conjure up every erotic dream he'd ever had. He entwined his fingers across his chest and willed his prick super strength.

He was pretending to drift off when he felt Jackie's tiny fingers undo his hands and spread his arms. When he felt her roll the sheet back he bit the inside of his cheek. His throbbing prick filled him with an odd pride.

"It's pretty," Jackie whispered.

He loved the little-girl tone Jackie affected when they made love. He opened his eyes and Jackie quickly covered then closed them one at a time with her hand.

"Rest, sleep, let me play."

Jackie was standing next to the bed. Mark reached a hand out and felt her leg muscle tighten, then relax. She was bending now, her hair dancing on his belly and thighs. No erotic dream could match the reality of Jackie now softly covering a little then all of his prick with her mouth. Mark crossed his hands over his forehead and pushed his head deeper into the down.

Reaching a hand to the inside of his knees, Jackie spread his legs as far as they could go. Getting up on the bed, she sat Indian style between them, cupping his balls in the palms of her hands. Gently stroking and squeezing, she softly moaned, licked, and sucked. Mark twirled free as she brushed her hair across him.

It cannot get better than this, he thought. He felt his toes tighten and curl, reaching for the balls of his feet. One tiny hand was gone, a small disappointment; then it was back again, stroking the underside of his balls. She slid a tiny finger into him. He didn't gasp, he barely moved; her entering him was not a surprise.

Jackie pumped and pushed her hand, now quickly circling her finger. Mark moaned, "Yes, fuck me, Jackie, fuck me." He began to empty himself, not in a burst, but in a smooth, steady stream. Jackie seemed to hum and swallowed all of him.

Krile dropped the two clear plastic bags of white powder onto the coffee table.

"Frank tol' me one's pure and one's been stepped on. Which is what, Helen?"

A feeble "I don't know" came out of Helen's shattered mouth.

"O.K. then, we'll just have ta test some of it, won't we? Uh-huh, that's what we'll do; we'll test some of this shit now."

Helen pointed to the smaller bag on the left side of the table. "I think that's pure."

"How are we gonna know for sure? We need a fuckin' tester."

It was 8 p.m. when Krile tied a belt around B'Back's muscle and rubbed his popping vein, and Artie Dolan had come very close to being leveled by Bobby Porterfield's Volkswagen.

"Krile, c'mon, you don't wanna do this shit. Whatcha doin' this shit for?" Dick was pleading—not that Krile would relent, maybe reconsider, not this pain-giving motherfucker; but maybe, just maybe, B'Back would wake up and come back from the no–man's–land he had drifted into.

"Shut the fuck up, faggot. Heavy here, he wanna get high. Right, heavy?"

The wrench in B'Back's mind gave the bolt on his jaw one

more turn. His mouth would be sealed forever. Krile moved the hypo next to the swollen vein behind his hand. B'Back brushed Krile's hand aside and sent the spike home. In an instant his great pumpkin head slumped to his shoulder. Dick noticed all the sweat was gone. B'Back was stone dry. Dick reached his taped hands to B'Back. Stroking his friend's cheek, he said, "It's O.K., you'll be O.K. Krile!" he called out. "He's OD'ed. Get him a salt shot. Krile! You're gonna kill him!"

"Yup, Helen, you was co-rect; that's pure, all right." He laughed.

"Krile! You motherfucker, Krile!" Dick screamed.

Krile stood, gnawing on a knuckle. Great white balls of saliva popped from the sides of his mouth. "Faggot, I got something for you, too!" he yelled.

Helen let out a wail and fell to her knees alongside the couch. When she came up from the floor she had a chrome-plated .357 magnum.

While Dick was wondering where the gun came from, it slipped and fell from Helen's taped and battered hands. Dick lunged and grabbed it before it hit the floor. None of the others moved. Krile spun around, apparently looking for his gun.

"It's on the kitchen table, fool." Dick didn't recognize his own voice. The beast inside him had become the beast on the outside and its claws grasped the handle of a Colt Python .357 magnum.

Krile stood still, a look of disbelief and amazement drifted across his face. Larry was asleep and Frank the rat was in the middle of his last piss.

Up to this moment in his life, Sweet Dick had never hurt another person. He was amazed to find just how easy it was. The Python exploded a thundering boom four feet from Dutch Krile's face. The steel-jacket bullet entered his mouth where his teeth had been and exited behind and to the right of his left ear. The rat Frank slammed the bathroom door. Dick hopped into the bedroom. He banged the gun against the bottom of Larry's foot. The chump was still asleep. Dick cracked him again. Larry opened his eyes wide, wider. He grabbed for a pillow. A pillow? Dick thought. Boom.

Dick hopped past Helen, who had wet a towel and was

rubbing poor Chino's gray face. At the bathroom Dick yelled, "Frank, you gonna come out?"

"Oh, man" was the reply.

Helen walked over to the bathrom door and turned the handle. The door opened. The lock was broken.

"Oh, man."

Helen grabbed the Python from Dick. Frank tried to climb into the shower head. Boom. Boom. Two .357s busted up the rat Frank and all the plumbing in poor Chino's apartment.

B'Back slid from the couch to the floor.

"I love the way the water hits your hair and nothing happens," Jackie said, turning off the shower and throwing Mark his terry-cloth robe.

"That's so when I run through the jungle my hair don't get tangled up in them hanging vines. Understand what I mean, whitey?" Mark wrapped his robe around himself like a towel. Moving into the kitchen, he lit the stove and filled the kettle by running water into the snout instead of removing the lid. That particular move never failed to get a rise out of Jackie. He held still for a moment. The sound of Jackie's singing was drifting into the kitchen from the bathroom, filling him with a warm, settling emotion. Life with Jackie thrived on love, and love was what Jackie was all about. On this hot, humid July night with the air as thick and heavy as wet cotton, Mark knew that he would not want to live a day longer than the day she would leave him.

Taking two mugs and a jar of honey down from the cupboard, he stood and watched the kettle. The pot whistled, drowning out Jackie's version of a Country song. Mark stuck his head into the bathroom. What he saw quickly turned his warm, contented feeling around. With one leg crossed over the other, Jackie sat on the edge of the tub dabbing mascara onto the crease of her arm.

"What are you doing?"

She put the mascara brush down and began darkening the spot with her eyebrow pencil. She looked up, an impish grin crossing her face.

"I'm not shooting dope, if that's what you think." Her eyes sparkled and danced. She puckered her lips and kissed the air in his direction. It was this that made her a child. It was these things that made him love her.

The kettle screamed for attention.

"Go ahead, pour us some tea." Her tone was quiet and sweet. She could see that Mark was disappointed and angry.

"Forget the tea. I want to know what you're doing."

The singing pot changed pitch, then wailed. Mark spun, turning his back on Jackie. He walked into the kitchen and snapped off the gas.

"What time is it?" Jackie said, following him.

"It's eight-thirty," he said sharply, underlining his anger. "Ya know I never called my partner. I just stood him up. I didn't go to Moresco's wake so that we could spend some time together. Now I see you putting that crap on your arm, which tells me you're going out. Excuse me if I'm a bit pissed."

Jackie's voice said, "I'm sorry," but Mark could hear the excitement and he didn't like it. She had slipped back into her cutoffs and T-shirt. Soon that seductive fucking street, his only real competition, would have her back.

Jackie sat on the edge of the bed stirring honey into her tea. In a blink she was off the bed, joining him at the counter, touching his cheek in a gesture to reassure him. It didn't help.

"I made a buy from a guy today that I want to collar as soon as possible. T.J. and Fred are going to come by. They'll pick me up and we'll buzz Fourth Avenue and Pacific Street. If we spot the creep we'll collar him. The whole thing shouldn't take an hour. I won't have to do any of the paperwork. T.J. and Fred will handle it. I may have to run to the lab for a minute or so but I'll be home before you know it."

As Jackie chattered away Mark dressed and flicked on the TV. The Yanks were playing Boston.

"Can't you do this tomorrow?"

"No, the creeps think they beat me. I want them tonight."

"Jackie, you say this guy, or these guys, think they beat you?"

"Uh-huh."

"Then how did you make the buy?"

Mark sucked on the sweet tea.

"If I see the creep I'll make the buy tonight. It'll be a buy and bust."

"Jackie, let me see if I'm getting this straight. You gave a street connection money for some junk today. You were out all day. What time did you give him the bread?"

The mark on Jackie's arm and the circles under her eyes flashed at Mark. For a terrible second he felt as though he was interrogating a junkie. Junkies don't know how to tell the truth, he thought. They're incapable of it. To survive, they lie.

Jackie didn't answer. She took Mark's tea and sipped.

"You're going to burn this guy, aren't you?"

Jackie took another sip of tea; the impish smile returned to her face.

"Are you shocked?" It was a question shaded with disbelief.

Mark was furious, but he didn't want her to know—at least not right now. Instead he chided her.

"Me? Shocked? Are you kidding? With all kinds of intelligent men and women, people of good will, framing people all the time in this fucking police department, why should you be any different?"

Jackie walked over to the refrigerator and took her twenty-five caliber automatic off the top. She jacked a round into the chamber, checked the safety, then stuck the tiny gun into her back pocket.

"He's a fucking connection, Mark, a dope pusher. He took my money and smiled a greasy 'I'll take care of you' smile. You know what his name is? It's Sweet Dick."

"So? He did his thing while you were trying to do yours."

"Sweet Dick," Jackie continued, "do you believe that name? He's not only a pusher, he's a pimp, too."

"So?" Mark repeated.

"So . . . so, I'm gonna burn him. Right. That's exactly what I'm going to do. His bad luck. Sweet Dick's met a woman that'll use him for a change."

"Jackie, there's not a case or a collar worth getting in a jam over."

"The only one getting jammed up is Sweet Dick. And fuck him. I won't lose a minute's sleep over that leech."

Mark could feel his jaw tighten. He wanted to yell at her, scream at her. The fear and anxiety he was experiencing for Jackie reminded him that he really knew so little about her. She was his life's blood, all his fantasies realized. Affectionate pity filled him with a searing hatred of her job. He felt like a loving parent lecturing into the deaf ears of a smart-aleck adolescent.

"Jackie," he said, "Jackie, you don't need this."

Three rapid beeps of a car horn ripped into the apartment. Jackie was up now, all aglow. Mark cringed as she rubbed her arm across a nose that never ran. The street was calling and Jackie was fine-tuning her act. She sniffed two or three times, then she jumped and threw an arm around Mark's neck, pulling him to her. Jackie kissed his cheek, her tongue drawing a crescent to his mouth.

"Be cool, Mark. I'll be right back. When I get home, remember, you owe me one."

Mark dissolved. He grabbed her hand, then her thumb, a loving street gesture.

"Tell T.J. he's backing up my life. Tell him that for me," was all he could manage to say.

"Relax, babe, it's just another street buy. That's all it is. I've made hundreds of them." Jackie stood at the apartment door, her thumbs tucked into the front of her jeans. "Scratch two more street pushers." She was smiling now. Even her made-up junkie's face was beautiful. Jackie turned to leave, then spun back. "Damn, I almost forgot. Yesterday I dropped off some evidence at the lab. While I was there I ran into one of the chemists; you know him, Jake Levine."

"Sure, 'Get out of my way, I'm gonna be a captain' Levine. What about him?"

"Well, he said your Sergeant Moresco didn't kill himself."

"Levine's an asshole. Was an asshole cop, was a bigger one as a sergeant, and now is world class as a lieutenant."

"Mark, he worked on part of the analysis. He said he saw a report that the second bullet entered Moresco's head half an hour after the first. So unless your friend killed himself twice in half an hour, something's not right."

Mark sat back down on the bed. He glanced over at the TV.

[85]

"I gotta stop watching these fucking Yankees." Mark moved to the TV and slammed it off. "Look, go do whatever it is you have to do. I'm going to give Bobby and Cathy a call. Maybe I'll run over to their place for an hour or so."

"That's a great idea. Ask your partner if he and White Bread would like to go to dinner tomorrow."

Mark grinned at Jackie's description of Cathy. Three more sharp blasts from the car horn broke the momentary silence that had settled between them.

"Your public awaits."

"Well, it's show time. I'll see you in a couple of hours. Leave me a note if you go out. And by the way, I love you, ya know."

"Forget this Sweet Dick character, will you?"

Jackie didn't answer him. It was obvious that her mind was set. She was going to jackpot this guy and nothing he could say would change her mind. Sergeant Moresco, though, that was something else again.

"Levine said a half hour between the first and the second shot?" Mark was thinking out loud.

"Amazing, isn't it?" Jackie said, opening the apartment door.

"Not so amazing. I never believed the guy killed himself."

"If he didn't, then somebody murdered him."

"That's a brilliant deduction, Detective Lerner."

The horn blurted three more times. Jackie closed the door and came back into the apartment, her policeman's curiosity piqued.

"Who, then? And what for?"

"Got me. Maybe you can convince yourself that Sweet Dick had something to do with it." Mark rolled off the bed, stretched himself to the full extent of his six-foot-three-inch frame, put both his hands on Jackie's hips, and lifted her till her head touched the ceiling.

"Now that, my little junkie, would be a great reason to frame his ass. Anything else is bullshit."

"Put me down or I'll blackjack ya, so help me."

Mark tossed her on the bed. As soon as she hit she was up and to the door. Now she *was* pissed.

"I tell you about a friend of yours being murdered, you don't say a thing. But you come down on me for some goddamned dope pusher. I think your priorities are twisted."

"My priorities aren't twisted. Frank Moresco is dead. Stone, cold dead. You're still alive. I can't help him."

"Fuck Sweet Dick," Jackie snapped.

Sweet Dick moved with the speed of a man who had shot dice with death and had crapped out. There was a boiling in his chest and his legs were going, but fear ignited his afterburners.

What the fuck have I done? he thought. I've offed Krile. Murder . . . the joint . . a white judge with big teeth is gonna take my freedom away. I know it. Poor B'Back, poor Chocolate poor Lorraine, poor Helen, poor fucking Chino, poor me. One hundred yards from the corner he sighed. Fuck it. I think I kicked my jones. I don't feel a thing. I'm numb. Then he turned the corner from Dean Street into Fourth Avenue.

Even though it was early, the corner was jammed with night people. A parade of washed, powdered, and painted hookers vied with junkies on the prowl for superiority in numbers. Tricks circled the corner in cars and on foot. Bands of junkies stood in groups of twos and threes all up and down the avenue. There wasn't a uniformed cop in sight.

Dick scanned the street looking for Chocolate or Lorraine. Surprise! All the junkies looked stoned. The panic was bullshit. Dick saw Lloyd bent at the knees, stroking a nonexistent beard. Nodding heads and ever-so-slowly collapsing bodies were everywhere. Half-closed eyes, the battle to stay awake, spoke of the availability of good dope. Anna Chipi Chipi, her left hand pulling down on an earlobe and her right holding a cigarette which was burning through her fingers, silly-smiled. "Hi, Sweet Dick. What's happenin'? Ya want some pussy?" Anna had a way with words.

"Thanks, Anna. Maybe later. Ya see my Chocolate or Lorraine?"

"Uh-huh, they wuz wiff ahhh, ahhh." Anna was gone. She sailed behind the moon, then returned, almost squatting on the curb. "Ahhh, a white girl."

Dick felt a real urge to smile. He had little trouble suppressing the urge when he saw the white child getting out of a car with the two dudes from that morning.

Dick didn't hesitate for a second. Keeping his eyes fixed on the trio, he scooted into the subway. Paying his fare, Dick walked quickly into the station. He needed time to think. He could lie here for an hour or so, then peek into the street. He could send word with someone, anyone, for Chocolate or Lorraine. Let the girls know he was hiding out down here. Sooner or later he'd have to know somebody coming off the train.

When he first saw them he couldn't be sure they were cops. Now, up close, there was no doubt. The short dumpy one was so blasted that he twisted and twirled, his handcuffs clinking. The tall one hung tight on to the other. The bulge at his side confirmed what Dick already knew, two drunken cops out for a night on the town.

At first he thought they were looking for him. Now he realized they were just waiting for the train. He stood behind a pole. He didn't need to make eye contact with these two.

The train entered the station with a scraping metal-on-metal squeal. Dick glanced for a second at the two cops, who were wrestling, hugging, and generally making a spectacle of themselves. Dick looked around. He and the two cops were alone. Suddenly the tall one with the bulge grabbed the short dumpy one and screamed, "Dolan, I love ya. Ya motherfucker, I love ya." Then he kissed him on the lips. The train whizzed by. A fucking express, Dick thought. The tall one shoved the dumpy one onto the tracks. A white and red flash followed, a scream from the bowels of hell. The lights on the platform flickered and went off, and so did Dick.

Jumping the turnstile, he fled toward the dimly lit street-exit sign. He didn't look back. Taking the steps two at a time, he came up and out onto Pacific Street and Atlantic Avenue and literally ran right into Chocolate.

"Momma, take me home," was all he could say. Then he felt the tap.

"Hi, Sweet Dick; remember us? You're busted."

Not the child! She can't be a cop! Fuck, I saw her marks!

9.

Bobby Porterfield and Cathy had an argument over the death of Artie Dolan.

"I'm not a hypocrite," he snapped at her. "I couldn't stand the creep."

"You barely knew him," she shot back.

"Right. I only worked with him for a year and a half, but I had to listen to him vent his spleen every damn day." Bobby moved into the kitchen, pulled the cork from a half-empty bottle of wine, and poured himself a glass.

Cathy followed, stood behind him, and poked him in the center of the back. "I don't believe you! His death was gruesome. You're an unfeeling son of a bitch."

"He was a drunken fool," Bobby said quietly. "And what's more, I don't understand your defending him the way you do."

Bobby took a sip of the wine, walked into the bedroom, and flopped onto the bed. Cathy watched him closely. She banged her fists together the way her father did when he was angry, or when he was thinking, or when he was happy. The Doyles were forever banging their fists together. Bobby couldn't tell if Cathy was more angry than hurt, All at once she seemed to shake herself free of a shudder, then crossed over to a large window that faced out onto Willow Street. Standing still and erect, with hands on her hips, she stared out into the street. She was fighting her temper. In a moment she would turn and lash out at him. That was her way. First quietly gather her thoughts, then prepare her argument, then, as though throwing spears, turn and fire. In the future, drowsy jurors would jump in their seats when she performed. Cathy didn't turn, she kept her back to him, her hands squeezing her hips. Taking another sip of wine, Bobby sensed this argument was at best silly, it was getting out of hand. He had no idea that she felt so strongly about Dolan. She might stand by that window till fall, he thought. Softly he called to her, chided her, "C'mon, let's end this." No reply. He began to whistle "Hey, Jude." Cathy stood transfixed at the window. "I never thought that you felt that close to Artie Dolan."

"I felt close to Frank Moresco as well," she finally answered. "Both dead the same week." Cathy was now kneeling on a neatly folded quilt that lay just beneath the window. When she turned, her cheeks were running with tears. "Don't you understand? I never knew my mother, I have no uncles, no aunts, no brothers, no sisters. These men, my father's friends, are all the family I know. I grew up in a world of gruff men who sometimes lack a certain amount of sophistication but who all have great dignity."

Bobby felt the wine massage his innards, and thought of Dolan with the dignity Cathy imagined he had had. He really didn't understand what she was talking about. He did know that this conversation was hurting her. Sitting on her heels with hands folded at her waist, she sighed, "Dolan and Moresco were close friends of my father."

"All right, I understand, I'm sorry."

"No, you don't understand."

"O.K., I'm dead from the waist up. I have no feelings."

"I'm going to tell you something." No more tears. The prosecutor was at work. Bobby grabbed a pillow. Soon he figured he'd be dodging spears. "Dolan used to call my father every New Year's Eve. My father would put his hand over the mouthpiece of the phone, then hold it out at arm's length so that I could hear." She now got up off the quilt and began pacing around the bedroom. Every once in a while she'd shake her head in that special way, causing her hair to jump from her shoulders and cascade down her back.

Bobby wanted to make love, not hear a summation. She turned on him, pointed a finger at him. Bobby stretched flat out on the bed and reached for the edge of the mattress. Quietly, so that she couldn't hear, he whispered, "Irishmen."

"You know what I heard on that phone?" She didn't expect an answer but he nodded his head no anyway. "Well, I didn't *hear* that nasty, foolish, fumbling drunk *you* describe. I didn't *hear* a man who would fall or—God forbid—jump in front of a train." Cathy had a way of biting her bottom lip between phrases when she wanted to make a point. She also bit her lip when she made love, or rode her bike. The times when she needed a little more energy, when she called on some inner strength, her bottom lip paid the price. She was biting it right now. "All I remember about Artie Dolan is that he had a beautiful Irish tenor's voice and he sang 'Danny Boy' to my dad every New Year's Eve." Bobby began softly humming the song, then he covered his head with the pillow. Suddenly Cathy's voice rose and Bobby knew her index finger was pointing straight in the air. "Dolan sang a 'Danny Boy' that would push your heart right out through your chest. He could pull out the kind of emotion, the kind of feelings, that you . . ." She paused. Now he knew the index finger was pointed right at his pillow-covered head. "That you, Wasp, can't begin to understand." Bobby sighed loudly. Cathy turned slowly and went on. "I began New Year's filled with tears listening to that sad, beautiful song."

Bobby threw his pillow into the air, jumped from the bed, and applauded. He smiled broadly, and Cathy, startled at first, wiped a tear from her cheek. Then a faint smile played at her lip. "Guilty, guilty," he screamed, "hang the son of a bitch, take his children out to the marsh and drown the little fuckers." He made ready to chase her.

Quickly she bent from the waist; Cathy wasn't about to run. Suddenly she dove at him, hitting him chest high. They both sailed back onto the bed. She was up on top of him, now playfully punching at his chest. "You still think this is funny. You still think this is some kind of macabre joke."

"Oh, Christ, honey. I don't think this is funny," he said, grabbing her hands, banging them together, and pulling her face up close to his own. "I love you, Cathy, I really love you."

Tears were rolling down her cheeks again. "What happened to those men, Bobby, what happened to them?"

He kissed her eyes, her nose, he licked the tears from her

cheeks, all the while whispering, "I don't know, honey, I don't know."

Cathy and Bobby made love. As the lovemaking went on, a strange sensation crept into him. As Cathy turned, then bent toward him, as she spun above him, moved astride him, and finally pushed up from beneath him, Bobby sensed that he somehow was participating in the last spin of the last game on the last night of Las Vegas gaming. It was a decathlon, a marathon of touches, tastes, strokes, and smells. When the wheel began to slow, when the finish line approached, they held their mutual breaths. Gasping and exhausted, he longed for the marvelous pain to end. Finally they sailed with such intensity it frightened them both. Cathy let out a scream, not of pleasure, but of relief.

In that light floating time just before one falls into a deep, restful sleep, Bobby thought of the coincidence. Artie Dolan and Frank Moresco had both worked in the same precinct as he did. Both men died in ways best described as bizarre. Both men were friends of Chief Doyle, Cathy's father. When Bobby rolled onto his side, when he pulled the down pillow out from under his head, dice kicked back from a cushion and came up sevens.

10.

The trick was to tear from the container lid a tiny half-moon, then you could suck the coffee like a ripe fruit. That bit of work taken care of, Bobby wedged the container between the windshield and the dash. He turned up the volume of the Pachelbel Canon and settled back to enjoy breakfast cop's style. Now if sector David was called he could hold the container in one hand and drive with the other.

Mark's container stood perched on the dash, lid off, the steaming brew sat just above his lap. Bobby watched as Mark used his pinky finger like a spoon. Sliding the jam from the corners of the plastic square, Mark built a round purple hill. He studied his construction for a moment, then zip, he licked it clean. "Ya know, partner, I don't think Moresco killed himself," Mark said, popping his finger from between puckered lips. Bobby agreed, yes, he agreed. Frank Moresco was just not the suicide type. The guy was always in good spirits, he didn't seem to have a care in the world. Weariness, lines that pound out deep ridges, the kind that speak of depression and hopelessness, were not to be seen on Sergeant Moresco's face. Nor was a breaking voice or bent and burdened head. The creases in the sergeant's face were smile lines. And there was no note, no cry for help, no hand reaching to a ledge. What kind of irretrievable circumstance could have possibly swept over him? Forced him to say, "Fuck it, pull the trigger"? Bobby agreed. He didn't know what happened to Moresco, but suicide? Suicide was bullshit.

Mark rubbed the back of his neck, then lifted his coffee with both hands. After taking in a mouthful he told Bobby of his conversation with Jackie. A second shot, maybe as long as thirty minutes after the first, had crashed through Moresco's head. "Ya know," Mark said, "unless we didn't know Frank Moresco at all, something is really strange." Bobby didn't answer. He reached for his container of coffee and stared at Mark. No, through Mark. He was thinking about Dolan and Moresco and "Danny Boy" on New Year's Eve. He noticed that the steam from the coffee had formed a wet circle on the windshield. He ran his finger through the center and formed two half-moons. "Well?" Mark asked.

"Well what?"

"C'mon, what do you think?"

"About what?"

"C'mon, be serious. You don't think Moresco killed himself, do you?"

"Ya know something, partner? I can't tell you why. But not only do I not think Moresco killed himself, I don't think Dolan jumped or fell to the tracks. I figure if someone is going to kill himself he jumps in front of a train, not behind it. How does that grab ya?" Suddenly, like a bass fiddle, the dispatcher's voice filled the patrol car. "In the two-oh, sector David—K."

"David K." Mark reached across to the radio. Now as he spoke into the transmitter, he threw his Styrofoam cup out the car window. The cup smashed against the curb and sent coffee running a brown stream in the gutter.

"On the street. Front of 1444 First Avenue, reports of shots fired." Bobby felt his stomach muscles spin into a ball, then knot.

The once sweet, now sour coffee was somehow making its way back up into his throat .Then just as quickly as it began, the tremor passed. He was calm, almost relaxed.

"We're a block and a half from that location." As he spoke Bobby grabbed his container of coffee. It followed Mark's into the street. Fear, spiked feet and all, had jumped onto him, then ran off a short way. As he touched the grip on his pistol he wondered how long it would be before it was back. Mark snapped on the roof light, its whooshing and red strobe-like reflections danced off storefronts as the patrol car flew along the avenue.

"God-damn!" is what Bobby heard Mark say. It happened so quickly. They were there in the middle of it. Standing right in front of them, not fifty feet away, were three men, all carrying what appeared to be shotguns. A man and a woman, arms and legs twisted in violent death, formed an X at their feet.

Bobby slammed down on the brake. The car spun and brought Mark broadside to the trio. Like a rock group, they spun around, the one in the middle firing a thunderous blast from the hip, his shotgun recoiling in the air. The blue-and-white shuddered, shards of glass exploded into the car. Bobby could see Mark slide from the seat under the dash. Put the engine between me and those cannons, he thought. Kneeling, he brought his gun up, over the fender. They were running in three different directions. Bobby aimed at the one furthest away. He saw jeans and a red shirt moving fast, heading for a double-parked car. A gold bracelet danced on an arm. Squeeze, wham; squeeze, wham; that's it, use both hands, get a sight picture, see the front sight. Like a puppet with strings snipped. Slide the sight onto the target. Glass exploded, splinters along his neckline, down his shirt. The patrol car groaned and shook. *Don't look at the target. Look at the front sight.* Now squeeze —wham again; squeeze—wham. That was a boy's face, almost babyish, he's throwing up, vomiting scarlet. Fuck that double-action shit, pull the hammer back, cock it, you have time. Behind the light pole a yellow shirt; he's reloading. Squeeze, wham, he's spinning. Cock again, squeeze again. Wham. He's spinning like a top. Squeeze again . . . click. Sirens now, reload, reload. Why doesn't Mark shoot? Mark! Suddenly there wasn't a sound except for Bobby's breathing and the dripping of water from a gaping hole in the car's radiator. "Mark!" Bobby shouted. Screamed. More sirens and more sirens. Cops everywhere, blurs in blue all over the place, yelling, the stench of gas and antifreeze. Bobby flopped back onto his rump and into a puddle. Then he felt himself being lifted to his feet. Bullets were stuck between his fingers, the cylinder of his pistol was open. He was ready to reload. "Mark!!" Fear landed on his back, this time banging out his breath.

"Yeah, tiger, I'm here. You dumped all three; you're fucking amazing, a regular Wyatt Earp." Mark's black face, dripping red, popped out of the shattered car window.

"My pants are wet," was all Bobby could say as bullets fell from between his fingers. Mark made his way out of the car door. Glass like diamonds sparkled in his Afro. "You're bleeding. You're shot," Bobby yelled.

Mark brought his hands up to his face. As if looking for holes, he tapped his cheekbones and around his lips. "I'm cut all right, but I'm not shot. Will ya look at the car."

All the windows, front and back, the windshield and the rear window, were blown clear out. Bobby began to tremble, and though he calmed a bit back at the precinct, he didn't completely stop shaking for two days.

Bobby Porterfield was not indifferent to authority. The police world, after all, was a quasi-military environment. Simply put, Bobby was more social than military. Now he was also a hero.

"Smoke 'Em Porterfield" the guys at the precinct were calling him. "Man, this guy does magic with an S&W," Rizzo from sector Adam yelled. "Pop, pop, smoke 'em, Bobby, smoke 'em. Cover them holes with a dime. And fuck 'em if they can't take a joke. Ya-hoo." Rizzo carried three guns, a switchblade, and a blackjack he lovingly called King Kong's Cock. Ya-hoo, three for us, none for them.

"Wear a tie," Stein had said, "and meet him at Dino's across from headquarters at two o'clock." What the hell did Stein think he was going to wear? Cutoffs and a T-shirt? The Chief was the Chief. Cathy's father or not. Cathy's father, oh shit. Bobby straightened his tie and leaned against the bathroom wall. Why was he always so damn anxious when he was to meet Doyle? This was not a pass-fail test; he was a hero. Smoke 'Em Porterfield. Didn't the grand jurors applaud when they heard his testimony? Didn't Mark lift him straight in the air? Didn't the Ol' Mad Hatter, Burke, throw an arm up when he saw him? The Chief had been out of town. "He's looking for a condominium in Florida," Cathy had said.

It was gray slacks, blue blazer, striped tie, and penny loafers. He looked like a kid. A kid with a gun. What happened to that gospel of peace? Fuck it, he thought, a vigilante lives in all of us. He smiled as he ran down the steps of the brownstone. Smoke 'Em Porterfield.

Bobby scooted around the restaurant in his bug for thirty-five minutes looking for a place to park. He finally gave up and zipped into a parking lot about a block from the place. A Puerto Rican in shiny blue-and-green pants, a gray fishnet shirt, and a straw hat yelled at him from the curb as he buzzed past him into the lot. "Hey, chu! Hey, chu! Chu leave the bucking car in the street! I park it. That's my yob!" Bobby slid the Volkswagen alongside an elegant red Mercedes convertible with its top down. Getting out of the bug, he adjusted the Colt. Then taking his handcuffs from off the passenger's seat, he hung them on his belt near the small of his back. "So chu a bucking cop— big deal!" The Puerto Rican said "big deal" with both his elbows tucked into his side, his palms in the air. "Everybody park over here, big deal. That guy judge; dat guy big lawyer." The Puerto Rican pointed to a Chevrolet sedan, then to an Oldsmobile. When he pointed to the red Mercedes he said, "Dis guy crook; he going jail, big deal." The Puerto Rican threw his head back and laughed so hard his straw hat toppled off. He tore a parking receipt, gave it to Bobby, then stuck his hands out in front of him and swayed his hips side to side. "Big-time *jefe*, big deal, I got gun, too; you want see my gun?" Bobby looked back over his shoulder. The Puerto Rican had both his hands pulled up tight into his crotch. "*Chuleto*, you want my gun? The Puerto Rican was kissing the air as Bobby crossed the street shoving his left fist in the air, giving the Puerto Rican the finger with the other hand. All this bullshit just to park a car, he thought. What a fuckin' city. He loved it.

As Bobby pushed open the door to Dino's Italian Restaurant he could smell the cologne of the serious drinker. The whole damn place smelled like Dolan on a bad day. In the street it was a two o'clock July afternoon. Inside Dino's it was two o'clock at night. The restaurant was dim and still. Solitary figures sat at the bar, a few in booths, everyone was alone. A perfect cop hangout. It was a big room with small booths along one wall and a thirty-foot bar at the other. A few round tables with red checked tablecloths filled the center. No one was eating. After a second or two, when Bobby's eyes became accustomed to the darkness, he could make out several small groups of men sitting in corners and whispering. Dino's had the perfect ambiance for the quiet conversation of the police officers, sergeants, lieutenants, captains, deputy inspectors, and inspectors of the palace guard. They all were deeply immersed in the political shenanigans and Machiavellian plots of headquarters units. Inside cops, Bobby thought. For private parties or secret meetings, Dino provided a room. No one gained entry to the private room without first passing Dino's heavy, sullen, and pockmarked face. Dino's was the kind of place Bobby had avoided at almost any cost. This afternoon he somehow felt at home. He began walking toward the bar, then he thought: Strut, don't walk. Guys in jackets and slacks with a Colt at their side and handcuffs stuck in the small of their back strut, they don't walk. Cops in uniform walk, cops out of uniform, while working, strut. And he was on the city's time. He was working. But something was missing. Then he realized it was Mark. Mark wasn't with him. The security he felt when in the company of his big, handsome partner wasn't there. When he put his hand on the bar someone called out, "Hey, Porterfield, hey, kid," Kid, Bobby thought, then he turned. Chief Doyle's chauffeur was sitting in a booth that was practically in total darkness.

Sheridan sat at a table with a tiny red candle in a bowl at the center. Not a single spray from the bright day found its way into this sanctum sanctorum. Booze and water in the early afternoon brought on the pallor of the midday drinker. And from what Bobby could see, everyone's complexion in this place was the same . . . gray. He looked first at Sheridan, then at the group scattered about the restaurant. There's not a liver in the place smaller than a football, he thought.

"Hiya, Paddy. Nice seeing you here."

"Whaddaya say, killer. Take a seat. I'll be right back." Paddy smiled and the scar tissue on his cheek crinkled like crepe paper. Bobby watched as Paddy sauntered over to the phone. He made a quick call, then walked over to the jukebox. After dropping change into the box he turned to Bobby. "Whatcha drinking, kid?"

Bobby thought for a moment. He was going to ask for white

wine, then thought better of it. "Oh, a gin and tonic would be good."

Paddy pushed the same button twice and called, "One G and T, Dino."

"And you, Paddy?" Dino had a voice that sounded like it came from a cardboard box under his arm.

"Need you ask, my man? I'll have a white wine spritzer. It's too early for booze." Paddy slid into the booth next to Bobby. He was a good two inches shorter than Bobby. That put him at about five feet nine or ten inches, but his shirts must have been custom-made, because although his upper body was bigger than average, his arms were enormous. Through his jacket you could make out the definition of his muscles. "Well, kid. What does it feel like to be a hero?"

"It feels good," Bobby said. "As a matter of fact, Paddy, it feels fuckin' teriffic."

By the time Dino delivered the gin and tonic and the wine spritzer Bobby could see clearly the place wasn't *so* bad.

"Dino, this here is Bobby Porterfield. Remember we saw him on TV the other night?"

"Yeah, yeah, whaddaya know, whaddaya say. You clipped those three scumbags, right?" Bobby just nodded his head. The guy looked like he'd been in a hammer fight without a hammer.

"Yeah, yeah, whaddaya say, fuck 'em, dey wuz scumbags, ya know what I mean . . . scum . . . bags." It was a long two-syllable word for Dino.

Bobby felt as though he had to say something, anything. "Yeah, well . . ." That was about the best he could do.

"Yeah, yeah, derr fatters shoulda jerked 'em off in the fuckin' bay, ya know wha I mean, ya know wha I say? Am I right, here, Paddy? Give me right, Paddy . . . hah? Scum . . . bags. Don't let it bother ya, kid. Ya did the world a fuckin' favor. Am I right, Paddy?"

With his pinky finger Paddy scratched his cheek. Bobby couldn't help but stare at the stumps. "Most people in this world are wrong most of the time, Dino. Not you. You're right most times." Dino had a smile on a face that was attached to a head that resembled a missile with a hundred dents. He turned to face Bobby directly. Bobby gulped the G and T. He suddenly missed Mark terribly. Partner, you should be here; you have to see this character.

"Ya know wha I say, kid? Fuck 'em in der eyes, fuck 'em in der nose, fuck 'em where dey breathe. Scum . . . baaaags. Fuck der kids, fuck der gramutters, fuck der, fuck der . . ."

Bobby stared at the missiled head. There had to be someone else to fuck, he thought. "Thanks for the drink, Dino. Let me get this." Bobby reached into his pocket.

"You pull money out here today, I'll spit on it. You understand wha I mean? You understand wha I say? Your fucking money ain't no good here. Besides, it probably got fucking blood and piss all over it. Their blood, your piss . . . ahah-ha-ha." Dino's monologue finished, he shuffled off.

Bobby got up from the table, glanced down to see if his pants were as outrageously creased as he suspected. When he looked he became ill; they looked like Paddy's cheek. Paddy curled a finger over a shoulder. "Follow me," he said. Paddy was moving behind Dino through the restaurant, heading for the back room. Bobby noticed that others in the restaurant had paused in their conspirings long enough to glance at the threesome.

Dino walked to a wood-paneled door, knocked twice, then moved off to the side. Now he was a watcher, a sentinel, and seemed pleased with his assignment. The door opened. The light that radiated from behind the Chief jarred Bobby's eyes. He had a premonition that when he passed through this door his entire life would be moving in a direction he would not have dreamed just three days before.

With the flourish of a Black Watch bandleader, Chief Doyle waved Bobby in. He took a step back, bent at the waist, sloshing a tiny bit of Miller onto Paddy's stumps. "And now, Paddy, if you will." Sheridan walked over to a table stacked with sandwiches and a rather old-fashioned reel-to-reel tape recorder and flicked the switch. Bobby's eyes latched on to Cathy's. He barely noticed Mark and Jackie standing off to the side. The full rhythm of Glenn Miller's "Danny Boy" filled the room. Cathy, as usual, went awash at the trumpet solo. Chief Tom Doyle put his hands on Bobby's shoulders. "Detective Porterfield," he said. Cathy was covering her mouth. "Welcome into the bureau. The orders were just cut. No more silver shield for you. It's gold from now on." Bobby's eyes drifted to Mark. He had both his thumbs in the air. A gold shield hung from a chain around his neck. "You, too, Mark?" Mark bit into his bottom lip, much the way Cathy did, and smiled a yes. Jackie, in a ponytail, looking like a high school sophomore, raised her hand. The light was good in this room. No sullen faces; smiles all around. "Smoke 'Em Porterfield"—Bobby grinned to himself—shook the Chief's hand, grabbed Paddy's good hand and slid to the thumb, threw his arms around Mark, then shook Jackie's hand, then turned to Cathy. "My husband the detective." Husband, Bobby thought. She kissed him in a way that embarrassed and surprised him, and he sailed with all of it. Coming up for air, he shot a grin at the Chief, who was ear-to-ear smiles, his arm draped over the shoulder of Bobby's now ex-captain, Burke. The Mad Hatter was holding a bottle of Miller with the tips of his fingers. He wasn't smiling.

Bobby was a man for parties and he was having a hell of a time at this one. After his third G and T he had a need to see for himself just what he looked like with the gold badge draped from his jacket pocket. Telling Cathy, Mark, and Jackie that he had to run to the bathroom, he made his way through the crowd, opened the door to the main sitting room, remembered to strut, and entered the large restaurant room. His eyes were less stunned than they had been earlier; it was probably the gin. He immediately picked out the profiles of the Chief and Burke. They were in friendly but animated conversation. Not wanting his eyes to intrude, he turned away from them. They would expect that from a detective. Still, he couldn't help but try to get just a bit of an overhear. And so though his eyes turned away from their table, he bent his head in their direction. Bobby was a fast learner. "Bobby, Bobby, come over here a minute." Shit, they weren't even looking in his direction; how could the Chief see who was passing behind him? Along with everything else, the man has eyes in the back of his head, Bobby thought, as he tried to feign surprise at bumping into the two. Doyle slid over in the booth, making room for him, and pointed at Burke with his cigar. "Artie, here, is upset. He says I'm taking his best radio-car team. The twentieth Precinct is up for grabs. The bad guys are gonna take over in a week." Burke made a pretense at a larger laugh than the joke called for, then took a slug from his Miller. "What do you think of that? Your captain thinks that you and your partner are the best team he has." Doyle stretched his arms across the top of the booth. His fingertips tapped Bobby's shoulder.

"We are," Bobby responded simply.

Burke, his hands wrapped around the beer bottle, his head bent, leveled his eyes. Those cold blues were drilling into the Chief. But there was a slight smile on his face.

"Was he really that good, Artie?"

"He was O.K."

The pair of them seemed warm, friendly. Bobby felt like he belonged.

"Don't forget my partner; he's the best there is," he said.

The Chief looked up from the table. Damn; his eyes were a deeper blue than Burke's. "Yeah, yeah, I know, for a spook he's a helluva cop." Doyle grinned.

Like someone had poured a bucket of ice water down Bobby's sweating back, as if he had been hit just below the knee with a rubber mallet, Bobby's response was involuntary, totally a reflex action. "What!" The suddenness and sharpness of his response had caught them completely off guard. He hadn't intended it, but his response was like the shove of a shoulder or the grabbing of a tie. The "What!" was part of "What did you say, asshole?" Only the last four words were left unsaid. They needn't have been; it was clearly understood.

Burke threw his head back and, as was his manner, flushed away the twelve-ounce Miller in a flash. When Burke returned the bottle to the table he glanced at Bobby and recognized the look that would become Bobby's trademark. The kid had a one-inch fuse. "Tommy, Tommy, Tommy, you never change. You're gonna have your future son-in-law here thinking you're a racist."

Bobby's chest ached, he was so close to the edge, so near sticking his fist in the fire. Doyle turned away from the table, and Bobby's eyes locked on a diamond-shaped freckle the color of rust, pointed like the head of an arrow just above his collar. Bobby couldn't tell how old Doyle was, but his hair was knotted silver wire and so was his body. He was about Paddy's size—that made him a bit shorter than Bobby—but different from Paddy. He was strikingly handsome, with a large chin cleft and smooth skin that was dotted with rust, red, and tan freckles. He seemed to be in perfect physical shape. There wasn't an ounce of flab on him, and his spotted hands were large, with one or two knuckles not exactly in the place they were meant to be. The man was a legend in the Detective Bureau. He was left-handed, and lightning fast. It was the knuckle of his left index finger that had been blasted a half inch up into the back of his hand. Cathy had his slight overbite—next to her legs, Bobby's favorite characteristic. His language was a curious mixture. There were times he sounded educated, using the right words, in the right order, all tenses in place. Other times the snarl of the Tenth Avenue, Hell's Kitchen New Yorker rang clear.

"Hey, Artie, how many years you know me?"

Burke was unscrewing another of the dozen bottles of Miller he would consume. "We came on the job together. That's twenty-three years, my friend."

"Well then, you know I'm not a racist. Have you ever known me to be down on someone because he was a nigger or a wop or, worse, a fuckin' Jew?" Doyle's shoulders were rocking. He was laughing with his mouth closed, his chest bouncing, his eyes locked on Captain Burke's. And his subordinate responded in kind.

Christ, Bobby thought, a pair of steel leprechauns with cement heads. They both had a bit of a glow about them. Bobby inhaled enough oxygen to calm himself, then moved to get up. This was too good a day to mess up. "Well, I have to go off to the bathroom now. I hope you two will excuse me?" He tried to sound as articulate as possible and remain under control. But the time bomb that was his temper was a tick or two from zero.

"No, no, Bobby," Doyle said, "hang on a second. I want to know. What the fuck is a Porterfield?"

Bobby remained immobile, his eyes fixed on the Chief. He had an impulse to just turn and walk away, but he couldn't move. Finally he said, "Didn't Cathy tell you?"

"No. She did say you weren't Irish. After she told me that, I wasn't much interested in the rest."

Bobby debated whether to say "I'm an American," and just

leave it at that. Then he thought it would be just as well to answer him and be done with it. "I'm a bit Irish"—Bobby winked—"just a bit. The rest is a mixture of Welsh, Scotch, and some Dutch." What he wouldn't give for another gin and tonic, he thought. Then the ticking in his head began again. "What's the difference?" he asked accusingly. "I never thought any of that was important. I'm an American, a Yank. Shit, my family is from Omaha."

The Chief reached over to Bobby and tousled his hair. "Look, don't be so defensive. I'm a chief inspector; I can break your chops if I want to." Bobby felt the ticking stop. The Chief was smiling. The tension surrounding the booth ebbed.

Now feeling sure of himself, Bobby decided to ask the question that haunted him. The question that had even penetrated the furor of the shoot-out. He ran his hand through his hair and drew himself up. "I have something to ask both of you."

"As a new detective, I guess you're allowed one question of your bosses." Doyle grinned. "Whaddaya think, Artie? He gets one question, right?" Burke, who knew better, didn't respond. Instead he called over his shoulder to the sentinel at the back-room door, asking for another beer. The Chief slid forward a bit, then brought his eyes up quickly. "Well, what is it?" He was still smiling.

"What do you two think *really* happened to Moresco and Dolan?"

Bobby could tell that the Chief was ambushed by the question. He turned to Burke, then back to Bobby. "What do you mean, really happened?"

Burke, who was obviously going to defer to the Chief, called out again, though louder this time. "Hey, Dino, what do I have to do over here, ring a bell?"

"Well?" the Chief asked with a blunt stare.

Bobby had jammed his foot in the door; now he had to kick it open. "I didn't know Dolan all that well," he began quickly, "but I knew Moresco. He was not the type of guy that would suck on his gun." Bobby paused and looked to Burke, who was doing his bottoms-up number. He marveled at the way it just disappeared. Bobby hadn't even noticed Dino deliver it. When he turned back to the Chief he saw that the smile was gone. He continued: "Two days later, Dolan, a guy from the same precinct, does a swan dive onto the third rail. That's too much of a coincidence for me."

Without asking, the Chief took a sip of Burke's beer, wiped his mouth on the back of his hand, then tapped Bobby gently on the shoulder with his forefinger. "Moresco killed himself, and Dolan either jumped or fell onto the tracks, it's as simple as that."

Captain Burke eyed Bobby; he was saying, "Enough."

Bobby turned to face Burke directly. "There was a second shot, you know. A second shot, thirty minutes or more after the first one." Bobby didn't let loose of Burke's eyes. It was easier, much easier than matching Doyle's stare. But the Chief snapped his head back.

"Look, Sherlock, we're not exactly sure what all the facts are regarding Sergeant Moresco. But I'll tell you this, we are sure beyond a doubt that he killed himself. As far as Dolan is concerned, not a witness has come forward. Therefore we have to assume he either jumped or more likely fell onto the tracks."

Bobby hung in; he'd opened the can, now he had to let the worms dance. "Isn't it possible that someone shot Moresco and made it look like a suicide? As for Dolan, he could have been pushed. Is any of this possible? Or am I totally out in left field?"

Doyle sat, showing the slightest grin. "Question all you want. It won't help you. It certainly can't help them. But we go with what we have. And we have"—Doyle paused and made the three-finger-and-circle sign, Cathy's gesture—"zip. As far as the department's concerned, Dolan's death was an accident." When he finished, the Chief reached to grab Burke's beer bottle again. Burke pulled it away, smiled, and handed it to him.

"And Moresco," Bobby muttered, "he'll be a closed-out suicide?"

"Hey, give it up! I just finished telling you. We know what happened." It was secret information, private information, palace-guard information.

Bobby heard the buzz in his ear go tick . . . boom. "No! Hell no! The guy was my friend." Bobby forced himself to remain seated but he was pushing up against the tabletop with the tips of his fingers. Fortunately for him the table was bolted to the floor.

Doyle, surprised again at the quickness and sharpness of Bobby's response, leaned back in his seat, then came forward, pointing his cigar at the center of Bobby's chest. *"Your* friend? I knew Moresco for fifteen years and Dolan I knew just as long. They both worked for me and with me. I've been a cop for twenty-three years, Bobby. I don't believe in accidents or co-incidences. And I'll tell ya, the words 'I'm sorry' don't make it with me. So if there was anything more to these two tragedies, I'd know. Bodies don't necessarily mean murder. Now do your-self a favor and forget this. When we're ready to make a state-ment you'll be one of the first to know. Even before the P.C. O.K.?"

Feeling dismissed, Bobby got up to leave. "Well, Chief, I felt I had to ask. Somebody had to ask. Nobody has said a word about these two men in over a week."

"We have had other things on our minds, and now you've asked. Are you satisfied?"

Bobby stood, took a deep breath, and shook his head no.

"I have news for you, kid"—the grin was back on Doyle's face—"you're more than a bit Irish. Those balls and temper you have are a product of home. Whaddaya think, Artie, the kid's a harp in his heart, ain't he?"

"Naw, I don't think so, Tommy. Like he said, he's a fuckin' American. But he looks Irish; that's good enough."

Bobby slid from the booth. Now he bolted to the bathroom. He heard Doyle call after him, "Wash your hands and meet me in the kitchen when you're through, Yank." Bobby pushed open the bathroom door and screamed, "Jee-sus!!"

Bobby Porterfield stood for a long minute staring at the reflec-tion that was at first grim and now seemed to be ready to smile. The smell of camphor, mothballs in the urinal, brought a smile to him. Ah, Bea, what are you doing today? he thought. Dino's bathroom mirror sparkled and there were fresh towels and a liquid-soap dispenser that had soap in it and worked. Just like Bea's restaurant. He reached into his back pocket, took out his badge case, folded it, then slid it into his top jacket pocket.

"Detective Porterfield, present, your honor," he announced to the reflection. Unimpressed, he stepped back a pace or two. Now the reflection he saw was from the waist up. He opened the button on his jacket and put his hands in at his sides. His jacket fell back over his wrists, exposing the grip of the three-inch-barrel Colt. God, was it possible that in a few years he could look, sound, and feel like Chief Doyle? Not a chance, he decided. But there was something he'd noticed the first time he met him. He didn't pay it any mind then, but today with his jacket and tie the resemblance was amazing. He looked so much like the Chief he could easily pass for his son. Son, my ass, Bobby thought, I look more like his younger brother.

"Well, partner," Mark said breezily, "what do you plan to do, move in here?"

Bobby, embarrassed, bent his head into the sink, wondering if Mark had noticed his posturing in front of Dino's sparkling mirror. He turned the cold-water faucet much too quickly. Manhattan beige gushed out, splashing over the rim of the sink, wetting Bobby's pale blue shirt and striped tie. Mark pulled some paper towels from a roll on the wall and handed them to him. "Good move, hero." He laughed. "You've been gone for twenty minutes." Mark was wiping nonexistent dust or fallen hair from the back of Bobby's jacket. "What have you been doing, wrestlng on the floor in here? The back of your jacket is full of chalk or something." There was nothing on Bobby's back. The brushing was Mark's way. He was an older brother; unable to bring himself to hug, he groomed Bobby instead. They had had little chance to talk over the past few days. Mark was now telling him, "I'm glad you're all right, partner; that was a close one." He said it with the rub of a hand across Bobby's back. The words that could be said would not come easy to Mark.

"Have I really been gone that long?"

"Longer. Cathy asked me to come and find you." Her father's gone, too. She's afraid that you two would be boozing it up someplace." Bobby finished drying his face and straightened his tie.

"Doyle and Burke buttonholed me in the restaurant. I made a mad dash for the bathroom, otherwise I'd still be out there."

Mark was patting the sides of his Afro. The medication covering the cuts on his face looked like war paint. "Did they pass on some words of wisdom?"

"Some words passed, all right. But not too much wisdom."

"Ya know, we're assigned to work directly for the Chief." Mark grinned.

"I guessed as much. What do you think?"

"I think it could be terrific. You're talking the big time. The Chief's office doesn't work on any bullshit. They're all important cases up there. It could be real good."

"Seeing him and dealing with him every day doesn't sound like summer camp to me."

"Fuck it. As long as we're together, who cares. C'mon, the girls are waiting."

Bobby faced Mark's reflection in the mirror and told him that Doyle was waiting for him in the kitchen. "What for?" Mark asked, gently pushing Bobby aside so as to get a better look in the mirror.

"I don't know. Maybe he wants me to give Dino a hand with the dishes. Or maybe he wants to pass on more wisdom," Bobby said wearily. "The guy makes me crazy; fucking crazy." Bobby suddenly began jumping up and down as if he were on a trampoline. The door to the bathroom opened with a bang.

"What the fuck is going on in here?" Paddy Sheridan stood in the doorway, his hands on his hips, his head bobbing.

"Nothing, Paddy. I'm just so excited that I could crap my pants."

"Well, crap; then get into the kitchen. The Chief's waiting." Paddy then turned to face Mark. "Is your partner always this hyper, or what?"

"Shit, Paddy, this is mild. You should see him give out a ticket. He does handstands, backflips, and ends with a split, handing the summons to the citizen all in the same move."

There was no way that Bobby could have prepared himself for the surprise that greeted him in the kitchen. The Chief, his back to the door, was bent over a four-foot-square butcher-block table. On the table was a large silver-and-black radio, the antenna taped against the side of a beautifully polished copper skillet that hung from Dino's spotless ceiling. The Chief was playing with a dial on the radio. Standing in front of the Chief and therefore directly facing Bobby as he entered the kitchen was the Puerto Rican from the parking lot. They exchanged glances. A wide grin spread across the Puerto Rican's face, and his eyebrows began to dance in his brow. Bobby continued to stare at him. Doyle brought an overhand right down onto the top of the radio with such a resounding slam that Bobby jumped and the antenna pinged off the frying pan. "Ralph, this thing isn't working." It was both a question and a statement.

"Yes, it is, Chief. You just keep missing the frequency." The Puerto Rican was totally without an accent. He still wore the fishnet shirt, the blue-and-green pants, and his straw hat sat perched on the back of his head. Still, he was very different from the guy that Bobby had tangled with in the street. Bobby moved around the table so as to look directly at Doyle and to try and figure out just what the hell was going on. He was now standing shoulder to shoulder with the Puerto Rican, who smiled and extended his hand. "Hi, I'm Ralph Cruz. I work in the Chief's office." Bobby nodded a disbelieving yes and stared now at Doyle, who was ever-so-slowly tuning the radio. The Chief had pulled the radio flat against his ear. His eyes were shut. A low and steady hum came from the speaker.

"Okay," Doyle said blithely, "find the frequency." Then he spun the radio so that it faced Cruz. Cruz glanced down at the set, then over to Bobby, who looked and felt as though he were pirouetting through an early-morning dream. This just couldn't be real—a chief inspector trying to find a station on a radio that was not working at all; a Puerto Rican who earlier sounded like a fishmonger but who now seemed like a graduate student from MIT. Bobby stood with his hands in his pockets, his head moving from side to side like a dime-store parakeet.

Cruz broke the trance. "Chief, that is the right frequency," he whispered.

Doyle, his voice even softer, "Then why don't I hear anything?"

Cruz, even more quietly, so that Bobby had to strain to hear, "That's because no one is near the transmitter."

"Don't you think I should pick up a little street noise, professor?" Doyle's tone had a friendly quality to it. He even had a warm smile on his face. Cruz shook his head no and returned Doyle's grin. "O.K.," Doyle said, "you're the technician." They both began to laugh, a warm, rumbling exchange between expert and novice, the expert not wanting to insult the older and much-higher-ranking man. The Chief, understanding and feeling foolish, threw his arm around Cruz and for the first time spoke directly at Bobby. "This guy is a damn genius, but like all Puerto Ricans, he's a burglar in his heart." Bobby winced and Cruz broke into an uproarious laugh. "If you could have found an Irish detective sober long enough to get into that car and stick the bug in, you would have done it. So the kid from Ponce had to come through for you." Cruz paused for a moment, then he and Doyle shouted in unison, *"Otra vez."* For the first time Bobby felt he had just the inkling of the Doyle charisma, the Doyle charm. Interestingly enough, Bobby felt that it was authentic, real. These two had enormous respect for each other. Suddenly there was the sound of a car door opening, then a shout rang from the radio's speaker, "Where the fuck are the keys?" Now a woman's voice, "Look under the mat." The air in the kitchen grew thick and still. A grunt from the radio speaker. The starting of an engine. Again, the woman's voice, "Did you fix your radio yet?" The man again, "I have an appointment next week." The conversation increased in intensity, began to break, and finally was lost in static. "I'll say you have an appointment next week," Doyle shouted, and clapped his hands. "Ralphie, it works beautifully." Doyle kept slapping Cruz on the back, then he turned to Bobby, who stood wide-eyed, touched with wonder, and just a bit jealous that he was not receiving the great cop's accolades. "You know what this guy did?" Bobby shook his head no. "Well, I'll tell you what he did. Last week he not only gets a job parking cars in that lot across from the court, but he gets into the germ's car and takes the radio apart so that they need an electrical engineer to figure out how to fix it. That was last week. He works the lot for a whole week. The germ shows up for court again this week and he bugs the car. By the way, I didn't tell you, he also bugged the germ's home phone, his office phone, and both the rooms the phones are in. What do you think of that?"

All Bobby could think of to say was, "What did this guy do?"

"It's not what he did; it's what he's planning to do," Doyle snapped.

Bobby watched as, behind the Chief, Detective Ralph Cruz guided the radio antenna down and into the set. He then slid the radio into a plastic shopping bag decorated with green-and-red parakeets and blue palm trees. Neatly folding the top of the bag, Cruz stuck it under his arm and turned to leave by the restaurant's back door.

Doyle paid not the least attention to Cruz, and Cruz—he just left. No "Goodbye," "See ya later," or "Excuse me, Chief, I have to go." He just left. Bobby began to say something, then he looked into Doyle's eyes and dropped his head. Bobby had never felt such a strange mixture of excitement and apprehension. A warm rush began to fill him. He recognized the feeling instantly. It was respect. Such an intense mask was crossing the Chief's face that Bobby took one easy step back. A muscle danced in Doyle's cheek and his left hand squeezed the butcher block with such force that purple veins pushed up and straddled the rust freckles behind his hand. "I've never wanted to jam someone the way I want this guy. He is very special to me. He is evil itself. He is king shit."

Bobby exhaled some nervous air and watched the handsome, serious face, the silver-wire hair, the blue, blue eyes. No one he'd ever met so impressed him. Doyle started to turn away. He was looking for Cruz, but Cruz and his radio and plastic bag were gone. He gazed for a moment at the rear door, then turned back to Bobby.

"Paddy has a copy of the case folder. Take it. Go over it with your partner. Tomorrow morning you'll hook up with Ralph and Paddy and get on this guy."

Bobby was past any kind of surprise now. Still, he had to know something more. "Chief, can I ask one more time? Who is this guy?"

Doyle smiled and grabbed Bobby's shoulder the same way he earlier held Cruz. "He's a lawyer. His specialty is defending radicals and radical causes. From L.A. to Boston he's freed them. He's masterful, he's brilliant, and his bastardizing of the Constitution has made him a very rich man His name is David Allen."

Bobby knew the name. The guy, as far as he knew, was not that big a deal. But now was not the time to express that thought to the Chief. Like a man recalling painful and gruesome pictures, the Chief linked his hands and ran them through his hair. "For years this dirt bag has been skipping through no man's land. About a month ago he crossed over. Now he's one of them. He sits in the lap of killers and gets fucked in the ass by vermin," Doyle hissed, then went on; "Allen defends people that ambush cops, mutilate them, then dance in the street. Right now he and that *cunt* he's running with are planning to break three of these creeps out of the West Street jail. When they make their move we'll cut their arms off at the shoulders. I want him out of the land of the living and shoved into the hole he belongs in. Right along with the rest of his crew."

Bobby knew Allen to be leftist, maybe even a bit radical, but he was shocked to hear that the former law professor had skipped off the edge.

"You want Mark and Paddy and Cruz and me to drop this guy?"

The Chief tightened his grip on Bobby's shoulder and pulled him to himself in a warm, loving gesture. "You don't have to drop him. He's teetering at the edge. You just have to catch him when he falls. Then I want the pleasure of cuffing the shit myself."

Now he grabbed hold of both Bobby's shoulders and turned to face him directly. Bobby could feel the energy of the man rush into him. "Help get this guy for all of us." The Chief put him away with a hug and a smile. All Bobby's fears, anxieties, melted in the glow of Doyle's warm embrace. "You're the future, Bobby. Make me proud, make Cathy proud. Remember, there are only two things that are really important in this job. That's getting home in one piece, and your partner. You take care of those two things, everything else will fall into place. In my office we're all partners."

They were now standing at the kitchen door. Fifties music

from the jukebox filtered into the room and Bobby suddenly realized he hadn't seen or spoken to Cathy in over an hour.

"I was opposed to Cathy's getting serious with a cop. Would you believe it? I was wrong. You're good for her; I can see that. All that's the best in me is in her, and none of the bad."

"I know, Chief. I love Cathy."

"She's easy to love."

"That's true. She's your daughter, isn't she?" The intimacy of the moment had swept Bobby away. He had had more than his quota of gin and more than enough of surprises. The Chief smiled and Bobby felt as though he really was a New York City police detective. The finest of the finest. He could hardly wait until tomorrow. He wanted the creep Allen so bad he could taste it. And within the folds of the emotion Bobby felt terribly ashamed. He felt his judgment of the Chief had been harsh and elitist. He believed that a man so committed to law enforcement and justice could not be a bigoted, racist boor. He didn't think it was possible. Doyle's exchange with Detective Ralph Cruz was a display of warm human interaction. Didn't that prove Doyle's earlier ravings were just an act? Wasn't it a performance choreographed by the Chief and played out in tandem with Captain Burke? But for whose benefit, and for what gain? When Bobby posed these questions to himself he found no rationalization. He decided for the moment to forget it. He'd leave past thoughts behind him. Maybe it was all misconceptions and false illusions. Tomorrow would be his first day as a New York City police detective. Tonight he decided he would enjoy the warm afterglow of the day's adventure with the woman he loved and the friends he cared most about. Doyle had said, "Take care of your partner and everything else will fall into place." This day is probably what being a policeman is all about!

Bobby waited quietly in front of Dino's. The heat and humidity felt somehow comforting, far less horrid than it did earlier. Cathy, Mark, and Jackie were still in the restaurant making their final goodbyes when Captain Burke came out the front door. They nodded at each other and as Burke began to walk off he ran his hand across Bobby's midsection and patted his stomach. "Good luck, kid. I know you're going to be terrific."

Burke moved off a few steps, then turned and called to Bobby. "You know, an intelligent, educated cop, in my humble opinion, is a pain in the ass." Those deep blue eyes were rimmed with red, and his speech slurred and churned like a motor unable to start, almost getting there but not quite. "That kind of cop uses the word 'why' too much. Do you understand what I mean? Rules don't really count for much in the Detective Bureau. Give me a bright, intelligent detective any day over a follower, a member of the herd. You know what I mean?"

"Sure I do, boss. And by the way"—Bobby paused for a moment; it would be better to say something nice to Burke—"I enjoyed working for you. You're a good boss."

Burke threw his head back and gave off one great laugh, then turned to go, stopped, and turned back to Bobby. "As a patrol cop you were a classical pain in the fucking ass. But you're going to make one helluva detective."

Bobby couldn't help but smile. And in a kind of sophomoric, school-rally response, he put both his thumbs in the air, then gave the three fingers in the air and the circle sign for O.K. When Cathy did it, it meant asshole. Now early on this hot July night in lower Manhattan, with Chinese men and women fighting for breath in sweatshops just a couple of blocks from where they stood, and kids in Harlem, their brains boiling and their emotions out of control, a couple of miles north, Bobby's three-finger-and-circle sign meant everything is O.K., Captain Burke. All is fine with the world. I'm a detective. Ya-hoo . . . Smoke 'Em Porterfield.

It had been three hours since Bobby's mind had been bent in the sparkling kitchen of Dino's restaurant. Now he and Cathy, Mark and Jackie, sat with their legs in the pit of a tatami room of a Japanese restaurant in midtown. Bobby sucked on warm sake and extolled the seemingly magical and theatrical talents of Ralph Cruz. At first he was self-conscious and attempted to hide his collegelike enthusiasm, but now the sake melded with the gin and he rolled and rambled. He told them that apparently he had not understood the Chief at all. So sudden was the change that had overtaken him, the three others in the pit sat enthralled. They listened as Bobby described his metamorphosis and his now-rampaging enthusiasm for police work.

Cathy fairly bubbled and shared his fervor. "I knew once you got to know him, I mean really know him, you couldn't help but respect and like him. The old Irishman does have a way about him, doesn't he?" she said with a laugh.

"I'll say," Bobby responded.

Mark was genuinely excited about the prospect of working with both Paddy Sheridan and Cruz. The case sounded fascinating, and as he leafed through the folder his chest seemed to swell with the importance of it all. Jackie put a damper on the festivities.

Bobby was going on endlessly about Cruz, Paddy, Dino, Burke, and the Chief. Then he said something that brought a response from Jackie that Cathy would never forgive. "They all seem so committed, so dedicated, so open. I may have misjudged all of them, Dolan included."

Cathy was smiling a wide toothy grin.

"They are essentially honest and good men." It was the word "honest," the way Bobby said it, he clenched his fist and brought it up to his chin, shook it once, then again. Had he stopped right there things might have turned out differently. But he didn't. He went on. "In their hearts I think these are decent guys."

That did it. Jackie gagged on the cold Kirin and spit a geyser across the pit, staining Bobby already wet light-blue shirt and striped tie. Mark pounded her back, beer rolled from her mouth and dripped from her nose. She coughed and Bobby thought she would spit again. She didn't, she just wiped her face with her napkin and said, "Oh, Bobby, I'm sorry, I really am. Look, I screwed up your jacket." Then Jackie began to choke again. Her attempt to cut off a laugh was causing her to choke. Gagging and choking, she reached across the table and patted Bobby's cheek. "Bobby, you're hysterical." Bobby frowned and looked to Mark, who sat with his napkin over his mouth. Cathy looked like she was ready to take someone's head off. It all passed after a time, but Bobby didn't have to search far into his memory for what it was he said that caused such an outburst from Jackie. When Bobby looked at Cathy she was very close to biting right through her bottom lip.

II.

Burke turned away from Bobby and headed for his department car, his bladder full of Millers, his prick lunging through his jockey shorts. With the first shadows of night drifting down onto the city he had come fully awake and horny. Thoughts of his wife, Mary, sitting at home, crunching on apples and celery, watching *Love Boat* on TV, gave him the horrors and reinforced his will. Mary, dear Mary, with her great white legs and ripply thighs, would wait till long after Johnny Carson before Arthur Burke rolled home again. In part it was the fourteen Millers and in part it was the call of the sporting life that sent Burke wheeling onto the East River Drive, northbound. The beer's residue hung thick and sticky in his mouth. It fogged his brain. The captain was scurrying with pictures of Mary's thighs driving him, convincing him that he desperately needed a roll at Madame Toni's. Dear Mary's snow whites had turned off his key and stifled his engine. It wasn't the sickening whiteness of her legs that did it. It was the way the whiteness contrasted with green and blue lines that resembled Chinese kites, their tails drifting this way and that, their purple crossbow connecting depressingly just above the knee. The captain longed to put his hands on young brown legs and muscular thighs. Arthur Burke loved his Mary, or at least he thought he did. But tonight was a night for Madame Toni's brown thighs and raspberry-colored nipples on mocha-toned skin. He was so fixed on his journey north that he never picked up on the silver Buick falling into a tail position two cars to his rear.

Lightning slashed through the Harlem sky as Burke pulled his car into a spot near the corner of 115th and Fifth Avenue.

When he turned the key to lock the door the tune of an old Latin song ran through his mind, "Rum and Coca-Cola." He glanced at his watch, pulled at his crotch, then felt for his gun. Everything was in place. As he began moving down the street, whistles, like blue-jay barks, rang a warning, "The man's in the street." He took a route down the center of the sidewalk, kept his eyes fixed straight ahead and moved briskly. It was an East Harlem street on a hot July night and it was precisely the way he expected it to be: smelly, sticky, and like a circus.

Some policemen take pride in the fact that they can move and pass anywhere when in civilian clothes. Not Arthur Burke. He wanted anyone looking, considering, wondering, to forget it, lay back in the cut, let this guy pass, he can't be anything but a cop. Burke could always find the nerve to come up to East Harlem. He had been going to Madame Toni's for years and he'd never once been hassled, no matter what the hour.

Toni's building, like no other on the street, was both formidable and attractive: an East Harlem fortress. Totally renovated, the six-story walk-up was a bastion. Its outside walls were braced with brick, steel, and oak. The front door was heavy wood with a four-inch peep sight framed in steel. The building on 115th Street was one of four Madame Toni owned in Harlem. She also had a condominium on a Bahamian out island and a co-op in Madrid. The co-op she rented to a German diplomat, an old friend and customer. The windows on the street level and first floor were decorated with reinforced S-shaped steel bars painted a racing green. All Toni's buildings had steel bars across the windows on the first two floors. But only this one, the one from which she conducted her very lucrative business, had twenty thousand dollars of Sony surveillance equipment built in.

With mischief tickling his balls and fourteen Millers suppressing his better judgment, Captain Arthur Burke leaned into the bell. Instantly he heard the fish-eye sight on the door slide open. He leaned back, hoping that whoever was passing on him would be quick about it and get him in off the street. He waited till he was beginning to feel uncomfortable, then rang the bell again. Suddenly the door buzzed and he pushed it open. Entering a vestibule, he was startled when the outside door slammed and locked behind him. There was a resounding finality to that particular slam, though Captain Burke would not have noticed, not with the fourteen Millers and tingling balls. Now he was in a six-foot-square foyer. Another oak door, this one as massive as the exterior door, continued to bar his way. He heard a click and a whirring sound, looked up and smiled into a TV camera. From a tiny speaker just below the camera he heard Toni's surprised and very sexy voice. "Artie! What are you doing here?" "I'm horny as hell, dear heart, horny as hell." Toni's laugh, that great full roar, rattled the tiny speaker and the interior door buzzed and swung open. Taking the steps two at a time, he hit the second-floor landing just as Toni was opening the door to her office. She ran to him and jumped, throwing her arms around his neck, then ran her hands to his shoulders. Burke lifted her, then twirled her in the air. He could easily twirl her. Compared to Mary, Toni was Lilliputian. She weighed less than a hundred pounds and looked up to everyone over five feet tall.

"What happened to my svelte and passionate Artie?" Toni called out as she pounded his shoulders with tiny hands. He put her down, stepped back, then moved in a tight circle like a rutting peacock. "You are a mess, Artie, look at you. My God, your gut has a gut." Burke's form had changed little over the years. This little game was both a testimonial to his and Toni's longtime friendship and a ritualistic greeting.

Burke slapped both his hands across his stomach. "It gets bigger by the week, dear heart, but you can bet the passion's still there." Burke leaned back against the hallway wall and ran his eyes up and over Toni. It was her turn to perform. "Great, Toni, you look great. You must be spending a whole lot of time with your young Jewish accountant."

"I'm a lot of things, big spender, but I'm not dumb. No one that goes near my books goes near me."

She was genuinely pleased to see him, Burke could tell. Her smile was full and warm, but then it always was. Why should he think it would be any different this night? Her tiny hands disappeared in his and he spread her arms. "You do look damn terrific, lady, but a little tired."

"She works too hard," growled a voice from behind Burke.

Not letting go of Toni's hands, Burke looked back over his shoulder into her office. Sitting in the winged chair next to her desk was Toni's chauffeur and bodyguard. He smiled and waved a greeting to the captain, then bent his head back into his newspaper.

"Trunk, how've you been? Are you taking good care of the princess here?"

Trunk didn't respond, didn't look up. That was a question he needn't answer. It was true that Toni's numerous business ventures weighed heavily on her. But her life was not unpleasant. She lived well, though no one knew where; no one, that is, except Trunk.

In the early sixties Trunk had a walk-on tryout with the Pittsburgh Steelers. Having dropped out of high school, Trunk had no playing experience. One Friday night Trunk carried two guys, both of whom were over two hundred pounds, out of a Harlem bar. He deposited them in the street next to the tire of a Pittsburgh Steeler scout. The scout asked him if he'd ever played football. He was nineteen at the time. The scout convinced him to go for a tryout. Trunk did, but in a week he was let go. During practice he sidelined an all-pro guard, a rookie sensation quarterback, and a world-class hurdler. He sidelined them all—for a year—in one play. While playing defensive nose guard, Trunk came up from the ground with a right cross that popped the screws in the all-pro's face mask and sent his bottom teeth grinding and slashing through his tongue. The blow shattered the guy's incisors and four other front teeth. Not stopping with the all-pro center, Trunk was on the rookie quarterback. He picked the kid up, raised him over his shoulders, and threw him head first at the offensive coordinator. He then loosed a primal scream that froze everyone in the stadium. The offensive coordinator grabbed at his chest and turned dumbstruck to the head coach. The Olympic hurdler, who up until that very moment had never seen a compound fracture, tossed his lunch as the quarterback's elbow shot through his skin, all white and dripping red. Trunk threw his helmet ten rows up into the stands. He then walked off the field and came back to

Harlem. Toni found him and hired him to do general management work, and she taught him to invest his money in Treasury notes. His loyalty and devotion to this princess, though a bit scary, was inspirational.

Toni got up on her toes and the captain bent to meet her. This embrace was more than friendly. Burke felt as though years had been stripped from him. A renewed vitality surged, and the Millers' fog began to lift. He felt a tingling, then a pinch. It was quick and a surprise, then it was gone. It came back again, a painful stab at the head of his prick. He bent and grabbed the front of his pants. "Ow, damn!" he yelped.

"What happened?"

"I don't know." The pain had arrived and then it was gone, then like a dentist's drill it returned, taking a good bit of him this time.

"Son of a bitch!" Burke pulled his pants out from his waist and stuck his hand in. His prick, thick and beating as if it had a heart of its own, had maneuvered its way out of his shorts and was now rubbing its velvet helmet against his coarse zipper. "Damn," he said as he adjusted and soothed himself with his palms.

Toni smiled knowingly, took hold of his arm, and led him down the hallway. She brought him to a bedroom with green walls, green curtains, and a green carpet. The bed was covered with a green bedspread. The bedroom suite had a small bathroom. Like a trainer leading a thoroughbred through the paddock, Toni guided Burke past the bed into the bathroom and told him to wash. "You smell like a camel, wash yourself," she commanded.

By the time Burke stepped out of the bathroom it was evident that Toni the impressario had been at work. The lighting in the room had been dimmed and soft piano music came from a hidden speaker. The green bedspread had disappeared and now sheets of sparkling white contrasted with the green room. And Toni, she looked spectacular. Sitting nude with her legs bent beneath her, yoga fashion, she resembled a cocoa doll engulfed in white, perched on the bed's edge. Easing himself down near her on the bed, Burke suddenly felt foolish. He knew what he looked like naked. And now sober, the effects of the Millers long since gone, a luxurious feeling filled him and a full smile covered his face. He could feel a thousand little tensions fall away.

"Toni, I look like a trick, don't I?" he whispered.

"The whole world's one big trick, Artie." She grinned. "But tricks don't have faces, just pricks." At this moment Burke knew that his resembled a mushroom, a tiny mushroom.

"Dear Toni, all this success has made you philosophical. You're a rich philosophical night lady."

"I don't work anymore, Artie." The sound of a small hurt was in her voice. "I have twenty girls, I don't need to go heels up for anyone."

"Whaddaya mean? You slept with me last month, didn't ya?"

"That wasn't work, Artie"—the small hurt sounded bigger this time—"you're special, very special." She traced a line with a long tapered fingernail across the head of his prick. And he felt special, and he felt better than he had felt in weeks, and he knew he loved her. Not in the way he loved his Mary, of course, but he loved her just the same. And his mushroom grew and stood proudly as he did the day they pinned on his captain's bars.

Toni had ten hands, five mouths, and a hundred tongues. She touched every part of him all at once. Spreading his legs, kissing, licking, probing, a damp finger or was it a nipple in his ear. He couldn't make a sound other than to breathe in sharply when she suddenly rose over him, taking him; all he heard was the sliding of his prick. She squatted above him, feet flat on the bed, her tiny hands clutching his shoulders, her ass bobbing. A scent, at first familiar, had vanished and was back now, clearly recognizable, cocoa butter and scented candles, "a Latin woman."

Toni wasn't black but she also wasn't brown. She was a wonderful shade of cocoa. With her white kimono and jet-black hair pulled tightly back away from her face, she resembled a princess from Bombay. She was a queen in Harlem. And now she walked her knight—that is precisely how she felt about the captain, her knight in blue and gold—as far as the foyer. Opening the door for him, she suddenly seemed terribly concerned.

Toni was part witch. A *bruja* the people from her country called her. The demons gave her plenty of room; they knew she could pick up their stench a mile off.

"You didn't forget your gun or your badge case, did you?" Her voice was a husky whisper. She was concerned. For twenty-three years, whenever Burke got into bed, his gun and badge were left on the nightstand. Mary had long since gotten used to seeing them. Toni was always unsettled by the sight of them. "Painful death lives in that machine," she once told Burke as they lay in bed. "A person shouldn't have to look at that when she makes love." "They're a part of me. They go where I go. When I die, I want them in the box."

Burke kissed her lightly on each cheek and turned to go out the front door.

"Artie, are you O.K.? Do you need some money or anything?" she asked, grabbing hold of his elbow.

The camera was buzzing. Burke knew Trunk was watching. It didn't matter. "Why do you ask?"

"I don't know, nothing special, but you seem more tense than usual."

Burke reached down and picked her up so that her nose touched his. "Old habits are hard to break, even for you, Toni. You don't have to give me money."

"I've never had to do anything. I do it because I want to."

"I'm fine, princess." Christ, what a lady, he thought. "I was just O.K. when I got here; now I feel terrific." He kissed her fully on the mouth this time, then put her down. When he turned to take hold of the doorknob a sudden impulse made him look over his shoulder back at her. Toni's eyes were filled with tears and her cheeks bulged like a hamster's. She seemed ready to sob. "What the hell is the matter with you?"

Her little hands grabbed hold of his lapels. She was forced to hang on tight as he straightened, lifting her off the floor.

"Toni!" He was genuinely surprised. She never in all the years he'd known her behaved anything like this.

"Don't go, Artie. Stay here tonight. You could call Mary."

It was curious the way she used his wife's name, like she was an old friend.

"I can't. But next week I'll pick you up on Thursday and

we'll drive out to Montauk. Eat a lobster or something." He winked and smiled. He wanted out the fucking door. He was beginning to feel creepy. He tapped his side; it was a reflex, he wanted to make sure his gun was there.

"I don't care about next week. I want you to stay here tonight. With me and Trunk." She wasn't backing off. He'd never known her to insist about anything. Even in the old days, when she had to take a bust she did it with a smile.

"Trunk, are you losing your grip or something?" he muttered, and shot a glance up at the camera's eye.

"Don't ask me why, Artie, but I'm afraid."

"Afraid with Trunk here and this castle to protect you? What are you afraid of? Certainly not the police." He paused for a moment. "Is it the police, Toni? Are you afraid you're going to be hit or something crazy like that?"

"If you really want to know, I'm afraid for you—not me. *I* can take care of myself."

"I suppose you think I can't?" he snapped.

"Oh, Artie, just stay. Why don't you stay?"

Burke paused for a moment, considering. He ran his hand across his mouth, then along his cheek. The smell of her lay thick and heavy on his fingers. It made him hungry.

Toni leapt into the opening. "I just had a hot tub installed in the basement. Tomorrow you'll feel like a new man. Believe me, it's better than sex."

"No, I can't tonight. But I'll be back next week." He kissed her quickly on the forehead, turned the knob of the heavy door, and was out in the street, Toni's "O.K." sounding constricted and small.

On the stoop of the building he let air out from deep inside his chest. He was glad to have part of the night behind him. Now to an all-night deli and a slow drive home to Brooklyn.

His gaze drifted across, then down the street. He moved down the stoop, across the sidewalk. When he stepped into the street loaded dice took a billiard bounce off a cushion and came up snake eyes. The engine of the silver Buick turned over and revved up. The thunderstorm had come and gone. The street was quiet, unlike earlier, when the howl and screech of the jungle was everywhere.

Captain Burke heard the engine roar and the tires scream, a sound not uncommon in the middle of a Harlem night. When he turned and looked behind him the bottom of his world fell out and he was slammed away. The first rush of pain was like nothing he could have anticipated. He was smashed, then lifted, then driven down, then smashed again. Sliding and bouncing like a dummy on a movie set tossed off a mountain. His face and chest skimmed across the pavement, shredding his skin, breaking his bones, and puncturing his lungs and spleen. He came to a stop tangled and broken against the curb. Bones, flesh, and water mixed with polyester, teeth, and empty fried-chicken boxes stuffed with last week's newspapers. There was no pain and it was all pain. Mary's face, that beautiful alabaster face framed in lace, smiled down at him from inside what was left of his eyelids. What a beautiful bride she had made. Every man in church had envied him that day. The pain was gone. His nerve endings were numb now, there was nothing more. Acceptance and resignation sucked at his will. In a Harlem gutter; fuck; he always knew he'd end up right here, his lips kissing a wet curb. If he could only reach the hydrant and pull himself out of the street. Then he heard the roar of the engine one more time. Toni, this motherfucker is gonna kill me. It was his very last thought.

Trunk was in the street as the car turned the corner into the avenue. He threw an empty garbage can and howled a scream of frustration. Toni smashed a saint's statue with the flat of her fist. Driving it against the wall, watching as it bounced, first off the wall, then along the floor, bouncing, bouncing, but not breaking. She ran to it, picked it up, and slammed it off the banister. It shattered, then lay in chunks at her feet.

12.

The surprises of the day had been too much for Bobby. He couldn't sleep. There was no use in his staying in bed. His constant twisting and turning could wake Cathy at any moment. He decided to get up. Like a spirit, he moved softly and quietly from the bed into the bathroom. Flicking the switch, he remembered the exhaust fan. It was not working. That was good. There was light but no noise. It was just him, the white tiles, and Cathy's things. He spotted a black water bug running, sliding, and spinning around the sink's drain. He opened the faucet, then shut it quickly. A few drops splashed off the creature, knocking it over onto its back. Bobby gave the faucet a half turn, then waved goodbye as the bug circled round and round, caught in a whirlpool of Brooklyn water.

The sound of Cathy's deep breathing, in harmony with the hum of the air conditioner, gave the entire apartment an air of easy resting. And the smell of her was overpowering. Strong and stubborn, it quickly erased a nagging anxiousness that had been pecking at him, keeping him awake.

Now as he stood in front of the bathroom mirror the pecking returned. He surrendered to it, gave himself over to it; the pecking vanished, replaced by terror. Bobby had buried his feelings for a week. But now, in the bathroom, the terror that he had been able to push away joined him in front of the mirror and put age in his face. Bobby had not taken the shoot-out lightly. Subconsciously he had been dealing with the reality of it. He whispered to his reflection, "Smoke 'Em, Porterfield, kill the mothers, watch the blood splash." He looked over at the nightstand, where his gun and badge rested.

The grand jurors not only found that the shooting was a justified use of "deadly physical force," they had stood and applauded. At the very moment he completed his testimony, when he bent his head, they applauded. Some even cheered. It was at that moment the images began to sail from behind his brain, projecting a monstrous picture on the screen of his eyelids. True, he'd killed killers. Neatly, effectively, he'd smoked a dope dealer's henchman. Instant justice. It had happened a matter of seconds after their killing of the dope dealer himself, along with his wife. Nobody knew why exactly. A deal gone sour, simple jealousy, or parking tickets. These people killed each other for exercise. Rizzo had said it all: "Fuck 'em, three for us, none for them." Maybe it was four or five for us. Dino had underlined Rizzo. "Fuck em, dey wuz scum . . . baaags." A shudder began at Bobby's toes and ran on icy feet up and through his soul. The sociologist had entered graduate school and he had received a doctorate as an executioner. Now he was a detective, his education had really begun.

He wanted out of the bathroom. He wanted Cathy. He wanted to be back in bed feeling those great thighs and classic buns. It was strange how terror, killing, and fear moved him. He was horny. He crept back to bed and was beside her. Cathy pushed back against him. She too had been up. Bobby curled his hands over her shoulders and met her backward thrust midway. Then the athlete came onto the field and took over. She pounded him, but he held on tight. Sliding a hand from her shoulder, he grabbed a mass of her hair. A strange, unearthly stench like a cloud from hell crept into his senses. He turned his head quickly toward the bathroom, then it was gone. Cathy, wide awake now, lunged back with a fury. Pushing and grinding at him, her breath coming in the open-mouth puffs of the sprinter. Then the little girl that was at the center of her being called out to him, "Bobby, your woman is here. Come with me, with me!" It was four in the morning, and Arthur Burke's demons stood around picking their noses, playing with snot and staring down, their triumph secure. Bobby rolled back, away from Cathy, and fell off into a deep dreamless sleep.

* * *

The ring of the telephone startled the lovers' bedroom like a shout in a confessional. They sprang up together, stared blankly at one another, then looked away. The phone's second shout brought full awareness and also a little fear. Bobby reached across Cathy to the phone.

"You up?" came the disconnected voice.

"Uh-huh."

"I'll be by to pick you up in twenty minutes."

Bobby was not up, not really, and he had never heard that voice on the phone before. Then he realized it had to be the Chief.

"You're not up." The voice, now clearly recognizable, sounded clipped, sharp, and irritated.

"Chief?"

"Right, it's the father of the girl you're sleeping with. Get up, get ready, and be in front of your house in twenty minutes."

"Yes, sir, sure, O.K., I'll be there." Bobby hadn't finished the "yes" of the "yes, sir" when the Chief hung up.

"What did my father want?"

Bobby was still holding the phone. He looked over at Cathy. She had skipped out of bed and was pouring him a large glass of orange juice. "How do you know that was your father?"

"He is the only person, other than the President, that can get a 'yes, sir, sure, O.K.,' with no questions asked at six o'clock in the morning."

Bobby, still not fully awake, held tight to the phone. "I wonder if I should call Mark," he thought out loud.

"Did my father ask you to?"

"No."

"Then don't." Exactly like the Chief. This was an order to be taken and obeyed without question. Bobby hung up the phone.

The gleaming Chrysler stopped in the middle of the street. Three antennas jutted from the trunk and the windows were tinted, hiding the identities of the occupants behind a fine curtain of blue.

The Chief exited the car from the driver's side, waved a hello to Cathy, then told Bobby to hurry, they had a long way to go. Bobby barely got the door closed when the car roared off. It was six-thirty on a Saturday morning. The sun felt like it was already coming straight down.

The Chief's car was air-conditioned and was one of the few things moving through the daybreak Brooklyn streets. Paddy sat grim-faced, both hands on the wheel. He appeared so solemn that, after saying good morning and being ignored, Bobby didn't say another word but sat still in the seat. He watched as Paddy moved the car frantically to the highway, past the Brooklyn piers, past Bay Ridge, and onto the Verrazano Bridge Expressway. Once on the expressway Bobby watched as the speedometer jumped from sixty to eighty-five and was approaching ninety before Paddy began to slow. They were coming on the toll plaza. Paddy showed the toll collector the official police department plate, rolled through the plaza, then slowed again so that the collector could jot down the car's license-plate number. He then stepped on the gas, throwing Bobby's head back against the rolled leather seat, and flew into Staten Island. Still no one said a word. The Chief cleared his throat, then lit a cigar. The pungent smell and heavy smoke nauseated Bobby and he rolled the window down an inch, sneaking a glimpse over his shoulder at the Chief. Doyle sat trancelike, his chin on his fist. He was staring out the side window. They could have been three submariners unable to speak because a destroyer sat above them, listening, waiting, ready to deliver a depth charge. Finally the silence was too much for Bobby.

"Chief, I want to thank you for the great time we had yesterday. It was a very special day for me." That wasn't bad, Bobby thought. It certainly didn't call for the cloud of smoke that the Chief had blown in his direction.

"Yeah, Bobby, it was a great day for everybody. Except for Artie Burke. Somebody killed him last night."

An all too familiar numbness spread through Bobby. He turned away from Doyle and looked to Paddy, who nodded his head up and down, then stepped on the accelerator with a vengeance. The car shot over the Outerbridge Crossing; the Garden State Parkway and the flatlands of New Jersey lay straight ahead.

The Chrylser floated smoothly into the parking lot of an

elegant Victorian manor house. The porch was cluttered with white wicker and cane furniture. Long light green stems from a great billowing asparagus plant glowed in the bright early morning.

Bobby stirred in his seat, then he grabbed for the door handle. He was still tired. Keeping his eyes fixed straight ahead, Paddy reached to Bobby's thigh and squeezed. "Sit tight," he whispered. Bobby glanced at him and noticed that Paddy's profile was set. He made it clear Bobby should stay in place. The Chief, meanwhile, was already out the rear door.

Doyle met Red Burke halfway and circled an arm around his waist. He held him close as they turned and walked off. Red Burke and the Chief had first met twenty years ago. They shared many beliefs, many passions. They agreed in almost every way about what was right and what was wrong. Now in a small New Jersey shorefront town they were sharing a mutual anguish. One was dealing with the loss of a twenty-year fellow cop, the other with the loss of his younger brother.

Red Burke walked as if carrying bags of cement, the weight pulling and bending his shoulders. Still he dwarfed the Chief. Different from his brother, his gut was tight and his arms firm. His thick red hair was trimmed and he could outrun, outswim, and outwrestle any of his subordinates. Big Red attended eight o'clock mass every day of his life and took communion three times a week. This morning he had offered endless rosaries for the soul of his murdered brother and damnation for his brother's killer. Christian kindness and forgiveness only went so far. Vengeance was real for Red Burke. Red stopped walking and turned back to the car. He waved for Paddy and Bobby to follow. Bobby looked to Paddy. But Sheridan sat perfectly still, then the Chief nodded and Paddy said, "O.K., let's go."

Paddy Sheridan had a rule. He didn't move till the Chief told him to. He had been the Chief's driver for ten years. Never once during that time had it been necessary for the Chief to tell Paddy to hang back. When something important was taking place Paddy was at his best. A roll of the eyes or a nod of the head, signals from the Chief, moved him; nothing else. It was clear that Bobby came up short in that area. He had little patience for sitting and waiting. He knew better than to question the Chief, but Paddy, Paddy was a detective like himself. And cops and detectives were in a different room than supervisors. Bobby would not be put off by Paddy.

Sea Girt is a town on the Jersey shore that comes alive with blond and red hair and the thunderous laughter of the Irish during the summer months. There is nothing shanty or tacky about the town or the residents. The homes are well kept, and the people expensively, though casually, turned out. Rugby shirts and sailcloth shorts abound. A sight that would bring a warm glow to the heart of L. L. Bean himself.

Bobby put his arm up over Paddy's shoulder, and despite his intentions he snapped, "What the hell is going on? What am I doing here? Why does the Chief want me around when he talks to Captain Burke's brother?" Paddy didn't turn toward him, he just kept moving straight ahead. He was not going to answer any questions. Bobby would learn that although he fancied himself Paddy's friend and colleague, this was the bureau—not a precinct. Loyalty to bosses came first. This was a good time to demonstrate what that meant.

Paddy stopped walking and bumped Bobby's arm with his shoulder. It was a gentle bump, but a bump just the same. "We're not dealing with parking tickets here. When the Chief wants you to know what's happening, he'll tell you. Till then, sit tight." Paddy didn't allow Bobby's attention to drift. There was a sharpness in his manner and Bobby sensed it was best not to answer or question. He nodded his head and began walking toward the hotel. Paddy hung close to his side.

It wasn't Bobby's way just to let things pass, though. He turned to Paddy with a sheepish grin, but there was impatience in his manner. "Whose side are you on?" he asked. Then he said, "What are you, a lance corporal or a cop like me?"

Paddy bumped him again, though a bit less gently this time. "This ain't the precinct, kid. There, it's cops against bosses. This is the bureau. We're all partners here. And the Chief's been my partner a lot longer than you have."

Bobby nodded and picked up the pace. There had to be a reason for him being here, and listening to Paddy's soldier's oath was not it.

Bobby and Paddy took the stairs slowly, one behind the other.

Once on the porch, Red Burke motioned for them to sit down. He seemed genuinely impressed that such a young man as Bobby was already a detective.

"You know, in my twenty years as a state trooper I've seen four officers killed in the line of duty. Our people don't work in a killing ground the way you people do in New York." He bent his head as he spoke so that he could wipe a running nose and a tear-filled eye with one move.

Bobby forced himself to focus on Red's folded hands, which he had extended out onto the table. Every few seconds he'd shoot a glance up and across to Red Burke, then feeling self-conscious about the man's tears, he'd drop his head down and away.

"When Artie and I were kids all we ever talked about was policemen, FBI agents, and troopers. We both wanted to be FBI agents. You know, shoot it out with Dillinger and Ma Barker. We had gunfights with the bad guys every day and never took a bullet."

It was apparent that everyone wanted to be somewhere else, anywhere else, talking about anything else. But they were here to share in Red Burke's grief, and Bobby, for one, felt very uncomfortable. Red, who had been leaning across the table, straightened up. "Now I have to bury my brother. Let me tell you guys, this is special." He looked across at the Chief, who had no reaction. He then dropped his head. There was a short uneasy pause as the big Irishman softly sobbed, "He was a big foolish man, Tom, I know that, but he was my baby brother."

The three dipped their heads as if acknowledging the end of a short prayer. Bobby could see snatches of Captain Burke in his brother, but just snatches. These were very different men.

"I understand how you feel," the Chief said quietly.

Big Red turned to him and his blue eyes flashed. There: that was the captain. That was the shared blood. "Oh no you don't. But I understand how you feel, and I appreciate it, Tom, I truly do."

The Chief got up from the table and took something from his back pocket. Bobby couldn't make it out at first, then it snapped open and Bobby was shocked. The Chief held a pearl-handled switchblade, and he maneuvered it like a pro. He twirled it once, then grabbed some yellowing strands of the asparagus plant and sliced off a handful that had brushed his shoulder. Closing the knife, he sat back down. Everyone's eyes were latched on to him.

"We're all cops, Red. And we were all close to your brother. Bobby here worked for him more than a year." Captain Burke's brother didn't lift his head but kept staring down at his hands, opening and closing them into fists and banging them together. "Paddy, how long did you know the Captain?"

Paddy seemed embarrassed by the Chief's question. A rising tide of emotion had overtaken him and fissures were racing through the tough cop's exterior. "I knew him for ten, eleven years," he whispered. Now it was the Chief's turn. "Red, your brother and I came on the job together. You know that. We were in the same class at the academy. That's twenty-three long years ago." Chief Doyle was a bit smug in his reply to Red Burke. He had no idea what was really eating the state trooper. This was a man who had led an exemplary life. This morning, though, he was deeply wounded and grieving, he was also very angry.

Young and very pretty girls were waitresses at Shenanigan's beach house. They attracted the young men who spent money there as if they didn't have to earn it. Which, in most cases, they didn't. So when the waitress approached, she not only brought a menu, she also was a fresh and lovely distraction. All smiles, scrubbed, with chestnut hair and soft, creamy skin. She resembled a turn-of-the-century housemaid fresh from Kerry.

"Well, gentlemen, I hope you're hungry. We can make any breakfast you'd like." The fresh openness of the girl eased the tense gloom for everyone but Red Burke, whose stomach pulled tighter still and whose hands continued to pump open and close.

At last Paddy said, "I could use a bloody mary."

"Good, good." Red almost smiled. "And you, Tom?"

"That sounds good. I'll have one too."

The pretty girl, totally oblivious to the pall at the table, stood jauntily on tanned legs in white shorts and an emerald-green shirt that had written across it in white script: "The Queen sucks and not well."

"And you, Major? What'll you have?"

"I'll tell you what, Sharon." Red Burke stared at the script. Bobby doubted that it could be anything else: the girl didn't have breasts. "Bring me a stiff pot of tea and a great big tumbler of Hennessy."

"Hennessy and tea, Major?"

When Red didn't respond, the girl smiled, nodded her head approvingly, turned, and walked off.

"Sharon," Burke snapped. His tone had the ring of a man long accustomed to command.

"Something else, Major?" She was still smiling, but Burke's next phrase erased the sparkle.

"Sharon, don't ever wear that shirt when I'm here. It's shameful."

The girl looked down at her shirt and went scarlet.

"If you don't give a hoot about yourself, then think of your parents. They would be furious if they saw that shirt on you."

"My parents don't come in here, Major." Her explanation was mouselike and had the opposite effect from what she'd hoped for.

"But I do. And I'm your father's friend." Red Burke got up from the table and pointed a belligerent finger at the girl. "I know exactly how Michael Flynn would feel. Now bring us our order and take that damn shirt off."

The girl turned on her heel, began to walk, then ran from the porch into the manor house. The Chief pushed his hands through his hair in his special way.

"That was rough, don't you think?" Doyle grinned.

Red didn't answer, but he got up quickly from the table and began to pace. Finally he stopped at a point that brought him directly opposite the Chief. "I appreciate you three coming out here to share my grief."

"That's not why we're here, Red," Doyle answered quickly. And for a second it seemed that he would get up from his seat. But the pretty girl had returned quickly and was setting the orders down. She was wearing a Kelly-green Izod shirt. The one she most likely left her house with that morning. Red Burke smiled at her and she raised violet eyes and returned his smile with one of her own. The Irish, Bobby thought. She didn't say anything to anyone; she delivered the order, turned, and went out, leaving no bill.

Red cleared his throat and turned back to the group. "Well, if you're not here to express your sympathy, I don't know why you came. In any event, I have something to say to the three of you." Bobby noticed the beating in Doyle's cheek. He didn't know if Paddy's response had been involuntary, but his knee slammed against Bobby's thigh.

"Tom, I know you for as long as you knew my brother, true?" The Chief didn't reply but dropped his head once. Then Red turned to Paddy. "Well, Paddy, I guess I met you when you and my brother worked Harlem gambling and pros, right?" Bobby sat still and stared up at the big red-headed man, who was beginning to pace around the table. He looked like a man delivering a lecture. And that was exactly what Red Burke was preparing to do. Bobby's gaze drifted over to the Chief. He was resting his head on his hand and biting his bottom lip.

"Uh-oh," Paddy whispered.

"Bobby, what I have to say may have nothing to do with you." Red Burke faced him directly and memories of his dead captain drifted back. "If that's the case, then I apologize up front." Now Bobby really began to get anxious, because Paddy squirmed and Bobby could hear his teeth grind. He reached past his coffee and took a sip of Paddy's bloody mary. "You guys in New York are perverse," Red Burke said simply. He didn't shout it, it wasn't really even an accusation. The big Irishman was stating what was for him a matter of fact. Chief Doyle took a quick nip of his bloody mary, then pushed himself up from the table, and went nose to nose with Burke.

"Red, there's no need for this." The Chief didn't shout either. Nevertheless, there was a clear warning in his tone.

"Tom, please sit down. Allow"—Red Burke faltered for a second—"allow a hurting brother to tell you how he feels." Burke's eyes were filling, still Doyle didn't move. "Please, Tommy. Sit back down." The freckle-covered veins in Burke's neck were dancing. The Chief breathed out deeply, but he did sit down.

"You're all great cops. I know that. God knows, I know that.

I worked with some of you. I know many of you guys personally. My brother was one of you."

"And he was a hell of a cop," Paddy snapped. Clearly he knew what was coming.

"Yeah, Paddy, he was. But you know what: my brother and all of you allow that miserable New York City street life to rub off."

"Bullshit," Paddy said, but Red Burke went on.

"And none of you seem to notice how it finally gets to you. It makes you foul. All of you."

That did it. The Chief pushed back in his chair and whispered, so that Bobby had to strain to hear. "Red, I've heard this speech from you before. I didn't like it a bit then. I'm liking it less now."

"Well, that's too bad, Tommy, because you're going to have to hear it again. Maybe for the last time, but you're going to hear it again."

The Chief waved a hand as though brushing a fly from in front of his nose.

"You all become reflections of the slime balls that you police."

Bobby couldn't believe that Captain Burke's brother was really going to continue this tirade. But Major Burke of the New Jersey state police was moving into high gear. "You guys in New York adopt the street's morality." The major's voice rose. Soon he was shouting. "The street's language, its values, become part of you." Bobby considered grabbing hold of Paddy's slamming knee. "After a while you're no longer law enforcement people. You become indistinguishable from the sewer rats that climb out of their holes at night to play in that sporting life you all talk about." The major was hammering away at the three of them now and Bobby felt sorry for him. Because it seemed he alone understood that it wasn't them that Major Burke was attacking; it was his own brother. And from what Bobby remembered about Captain Burke there was no way in hell he would have allowed even his older brother to talk to him this way. And the major knew that too. He wanted to scream at his brother, thrash him, say all the things he'd always wanted to say when his brother was alive. The major needed this chance to tell it, and say it and get it done with. Maybe if he'd had the courage to confront his brother years ago Artie would be sitting here on this glorious morning sipping a Miller instead of having his chest cavity sawed open by a medical examiner. Great silver raindrop tears ran down Red Burke's cheeks and he turned his anger and anguish directly on Chief Doyle. "You tell me why it is, Tom Doyle, that man like my brother, once a good family man, ends up a heap in Central Park?" Paddy's leg again began bouncing off Bobby's thigh. But it was the Chief who got up. And it was the Chief who answered the red-headed man, weeping. Chief Doyle brought himself up to his full height; still, he looked up to Red Burke.

"First of all, I didn't come down here to discuss comparative policing. You and I and your brother went round and round on this very subject once before. I told you then and I'm telling you now, and you can bet it's for the last time, there is no fucking comparison between urban police work and some fucking yahoo smokey eating dust on a highway."

Red Burke murmured, "Integrity is integrity, Tom."

As if he didn't hear, Doyle went on. "The pressures are altogether different on a big-city cop than on a state trooper. But you know that, Red. And why you're digging that hole at a time like this is beyond me." Chief Doyle was furious, and though he was holding tight to his temper, Bobby could tell there could be one hell of an explosion if these two bucks locked horns. "Red, you really fucking upset me. You really do."

"You don't have to curse, Tom. You can express yourself without four-letter words, Tom Doyle." Red Burke sipped noisily on the remainder of his tea and brandy.

Chief Doyle sat down in his chair and waited until Red emptied his cup. Then he said with his most affected rolling brogue, "Red Burke, go un fook yerself."

"What happened to my brother, Tom? Tell me what happened!"

"Artie was murdered, Red. Maybe because he was a policeman, or maybe because he was just in the wrong place at the wrong time. I don't know—yet!" The exclamation left no doubt that the Chief meant to find out the answer, and soon. "Paddy and I came out here for two reasons."

"One," Red Burke said.

The Chief was right at the edge of his control again. "One is that we are goddamn sorry and pissed that someone killed your brother and our friend."

"And two." Big Red spoke now in a low whisper.

"I want to go over the specifics of how and in what condition your brother was found." Tears ran down Doyle's cheeks. His temper was out of control. If the Irishman didn't cry he'd hit the red-headed man. Everyone at the table knew that. Bobby so twisted the napkin he held that his elbows burned and his wrists ached. But now, maybe, just maybe, he'd find out why *he* was here.

"Red, you can help us. I was Artie's friend but he didn't share everything with me." The Chief turned to Bobby. "I want *you* to pay close attention to this." Bobby wondered why. The Chief answered his thoughts and the answer excited him like never before, then nauseated him to an equal extent. "You and Spencer are going to work this investigation full-time. Nothing else matters. I don't want Artie Burke's name slandered, but I want his killer. And whatever it takes to get him, or her, or it, I want it done. Now tell me, Red, was there anything going on in Artie's life that I wouldn't know? Something that may point to a motive for the killing?"

Red Burke was now under control and he answered Doyle's question quietly and without emotion.

"My brother played in those New York City streets. He knew how I felt about that filth. So we never discussed it. Even when you had all that heat a few years back, I only knew what I read in the paper. Artie never talked about it."

Heat? Heat? What the hell is he talking about? Bobby thought.

Doyle picked up the questioning look on Bobby's face and changed the subject. But enough had been said. Bobby knew how to find old newspaper stories if he had to. The Chief was pointing at him now.

"Nothing goes on paper. Do you understand?"

Bobby nodded his head and Doyle stared at him and Bobby stared right back. Something was not right here, he'd always suspected it. Now, though he couldn't say why, he was positive.

These deaths were linked somehow. Doyle once told him that he didn't believe in coincidences.

Everyone at the table was aware that there was something not being said. And it was clear that whatever it was, Doyle was not going to drag it out. And Paddy, Paddy was in Doyle's shadow. Bobby would learn nothing from Paddy.

"O.K., you got that? Nothing goes on paper."

Bobby nodded again.

"Homicide will generate enough paper to bury anyone else interested in the case. You and Mark will parallel their investigation. Share nothing with them, but you'll get whatever they have. Chief Weitz understands my interest and he's agreed. You'll have no problem with them.

"Red, I want to ask a favor of you."

"Ask." Red was not warming to the Doyle charm, but his brother had been murdered and he *was* a cop. In the end, Red Burke was a cop.

"This is going to be an official unofficial investigtaion. If you know what I mean?" The big red-headed man nodded his head quickly. "If Bobby were to need a good man or two, can I count on you?"

"To do what?"

"To quietly and unofficially send me someone?" Red Burke took another sip of his tea, but for the first time Bobby noticed a slight smile invade his face.

"Are you crazy, Tom? I can't ask New Jersey state troopers to get involved in a murder investigation in New York City. They can't even carry firearms there."

Doyle seemed to have anticipated Burke's answer; still he seemed disappointed.

"But I'll tell you what I will do." Red Burke turned to Bobby. "Bobby, if you feel you need any help, any help at all, call me directly and I'll be there."

Chief Doyle got up from the table, whipped out his white slasher, and snipped another stem from the asparagus fern. He trimmed the leaves, then cut the stem and used the shortened piece like a toothpick. At last he seemed ready to tell the story.

"Someone"—he looked at Bobby and made a motion that he should begin to take notes—"probably more than one, laid Artie out on a grassy knoll in Central Park."

Red Burke flushed away the tea the same way his brother used to flush away his Miller. "Goddamnit, Tom, you're full of shit," he shouted. "You describe it like he was laid out for a wake. What you mean to say is that someone threw or dropped my brother into the park."

There was a real smile on Doyle's face now. "There's no need to curse, Red," he said quietly. "And when I say laid out, I mean laid out. He wasn't killed in the park. Go ahead, Paddy, fill them in."

Paddy reached his good hand into his jacket pocket and removed a notebook that was thick but only two inches square. Bobby had already taken the pad and pen Cathy had slipped into his jacket and placed them on the table in front of him.

"Ya see, Paddy, a college graduate: he has a real pad." The Chief now had a full grin on his face.

Paddy didn't respond. He just leafed through his little book. "At exactly four o'clock this morning, the Nineteenth Precinct received a call on their direct line that Captain Arthur Burke had been killed and his body could be found on a hill at the entrance to the bramble path in Central Park. The caller then hung up. He was obviously a black male and was puffing as though he'd just been through a vigorous workout. The Nineteenth uses a jeep to patrol in the park; they were there in ten minutes. The call went out over the air as a ten-thirteen, assist patrolman, so cars from all over midtown and Manhattan south responded. One of the officers from the Nineteenth came close to shooting someone or something he described as having the proportions of a gorilla that crashed through the weeds near the body. He didn't shoot because he couldn't make out what or who it was, and there were cops all over the place. The team in the jeep found the body. Now, here comes the part that blows everybody's mind."

"O.K., Paddy, cut the editorializing. Finish the story." Bobby surprised himself as well as everyone else at the table with the quickness of his remark. He then took Paddy's bloody mary without asking and knocked it back. Paddy smiled at him and made no comment.

"The body was wrapped in a green satin sheet, tied with a red cord—the kind you see on old-fashioned drapery. There was a large white candle in a glass dish next to the body. The cops couldn't miss finding the captain: the candle was like a strobe in that part of the park. When they opened the sheet they, of course, found the captain. He'd been dead, we figure, no more than an hour and a half. Someone had covered his body with roses, carnations, and some flowers that no one's been able to identify." Paddy paused for a moment, catching his breath. "The body had been washed and rubbed with some kind of scented oil."

"Christ," Bobby said.

Paddy continued. "A glassine envelope, the kind that stamps and dope come in, was pinned to his shirt. In the envelope were two one-inch-by-one-inch-and-a-quarter chips of silver paint. We're sure it's auto paint."

"He was run down? It was a hit-and-run?" Bobby's remarks were questions and statements. All three men turned toward him and though he felt self-conscious he continued to probe. "Well?"

Paddy didn't reply to him but looked down at his notes. After a moment's pause he told them that a resident at Mount Sinai emergency room likened Burke's wounds to those of a victim of a plane crash. Red Burke finished his tea, then looked around for another drink. He found none; all the glasses were empty.

"Anything else, Paddy?" Red asked.

"His gun and his badge case had been put in a silk purse, tied to his right hand. As of now, that's all we have."

Red Burke got up from the table and walked into the house. After a moment he appeared back at the door. The other three were sitting quietly at the table. Bobby was busily filling in blanks and drawing up questions. Questions whose answers he'd have to find for himself.

"Anyone want another drink?" Burke called out. When no one answered, the major walked into the great old Victorian manor and gently closed the door behind him. Bobby suspected that he would apologize for earlier embarrassing the pretty young girl. He was wrong. Major Burke never apologized.

The tension that was thick and oppressive on the trip to the Jersey shore was absent on the way back to New York. The Chief spoke calmly and without emotion about the Burke brothers. It was obvious that though he cared a great deal for Artie Burke, he had little use for his brother, Red. As the Chrysler mounted the George Washington Bridge, Chief Doyle looked out at the world's greatest city.

"Red Burke's a quiff. He wouldn't last a month in a real police department," he said to no one except himself.

13.

Retired detective Salvatore Victoria watched as the pelican's glide pattern brought the bird up and over the mangrove. Wings tucked close in to its body, the bird held still in the updraft, then like a flash it fell into the water.

If he was in New York Harbor and did that, Sal thought, he'd break his fuckin' head on a floating refrigertaor.

U.S. Route 1 sashays south from Miami to Key West. Seashell stands, motels, and diners that sell Key lime pie rim the route. The sea is always warm there, with pearl-white sandbanks that spread from shore, disappear, then reappear in an ocean of jade. The cream-colored sand seems to be offering a highway to red and yellow sunset horizons, the way to Shangri-La.

South Florida is a fisherman's paradise. Bluefish, red snapper, a wide range of bass, and the feisty bonefish are plentiful. For the sportsman to whom only the struggle has meaning, sailfish, tarpon, sharks, barracuda, and swordfish roam in deep offshore waters. In the shallows, wondrous reefs containing worlds of alabaster, burgundy, sienna, and pink coral create a medley of color. Tributaries and canals flow through and around the keys, spilling into the Gulf and the Atlantic. Causeways link the tiny islands to the mainland; they span wide stretches of water and small bridges dot the highway over canals.

Just south of Key Largo, Sal Victoria stood atop a small bridge. He was waiting, and while he waited he watched the fishermen.

Assholes, he thought, all they do is hang around under some bridge and try to sucker some jerk-off fish into biting a hook.

"Whoopee."

Asshole! Some guy caught a fish, turned and waved to Sal, who stood looking down at him. After a moment Sal decided that they were both assholes: the fish and the fishermen. The fish for going for the obvious setup, and the fishermen for not using nets.

Victoria's mind had been put together by a paranoid street peddler. He had lightless eyes that darted and searched, always on guard against someone who'd steal his apples. He spent a desperate life among a circle of men even worse than himself.

After his retirement from the New York City Police Department, Victoria relocated in Miami. He took to wearing brightly colored jumpsuits and gold chains, and he grew a beard. Nothing helped. The man was ugly, lean as a goat, his face a swarthy hatchet.

I'm in great shape, he told himself. Things are better for me here than they were in New York. When he was a cop in New York, his gun and badge gave him a license to steal. In Florida there was no pretense. He wasn't a crooked cop; he was simply a crook. Arranging deals between Cuban importers in Miami and black drug dealers from New York, he was making money he didn't need. Even his old friend Georgia Boy turned a package once in a while. Though East Harlem lived in his memory, new big bucks kept him counting and sorting and grinning in South Florida. It didn't take much to excite the ex-bagman, so it wasn't a surprise that he skipped in the air like Hitler in Paris when he saw the two black kids jump out of the Volkswagen bus. They walked quickly toward him, glancing at the fishermen as they came. Soon they were greeting him with slaps and pats and "What's happenin', bro?" That same old voodoo; it made him nuts.

"You ready, my man?" the big fat one whose name was Nicky said.

"Everything's everything. Ya got the bread?" Normally Victoria wasn't much of a conversationalist. With Fat Nicky's arm wrapped around his waist he felt more like running than talking.

Fat Nicky smiled, the contented full grin of the successful drug dealer, as he pointed to the van. "Fifty big ones," he said with no little pride.

Then Victoria noticed the other kid, the one whose name he'd forgotten. "Tell me, what the fuck is he doing over there?"

Fat Nicky turned around to see his crime partner balancing on his stomach, hanging from the bridge, his feet kicking circles in the air. He was straining to see something under the bridge.

"Hey, Hole, whatcha doin'?"

The kid flopped back up onto the bridge. His eyes were open wide and his eyebrows ranged up to a place where his hairline would have been if he hadn't shaved his head.

"Dis dude down here caught a buncha red fish. I ain't never seen no fuckin' red fish, man. Only them gray motherfuckers we got up in New York."

"Der ain't no such . . ." Nicky yelled.

"Don't call me a liar, nigger, don't do that. Come over here and look first."

"Hole, ya know, man . . ." Nicky's reply was a whine and he slapped his knee in disgust. "We down here to take care a business and what you doin'? You lookin' at red fish." Nicky's voice trailed off; Hole was hopeless.

As in most successful business transactions, the real business had been taken care of earlier. Now all that remained was the transfer. Nicky had already left Sal and was in the van when Hole joined Sal on the bridge. He was sniffing the air like a rabbit, looking up at a cloudless sky and peering suspiciously at the fishermen on the bank.

"You like living down here, man?" he asked.

"I love it," Victoria answered, totally uninterested.

"Ya gettin' a lotta young pussy? I love young pussy." Hole grinned.

Kids, Victoria thought. I'm tired of dealing with dumb shine kids. But they can turn a dollar. Nicky had removed a gold leather overnight bag from the van and was now placing it in Victoria's car. After taking care to lock the door, Nicky joined Victoria and Hole on the bridge.

"My uncle tole me ta tell ya that the last package was a perfect six. It did just what you said it would. That's what he said, right, Hole?"

Hole didn't answer; he just kept sniffing the air. And Victoria saw no need to reply. He did smile a knowing what-did-you-expect? sort of grin.

"He tole me to tell you that if the skag's the same this time, next time we double up."

Fuckin' kids, Victoria thought. Not even twenty and they're gonna come up with a hundred grand. The shines can turn a dollar, no question. They sure can turn a dollar.

Telling them to be on the bridge the next day at noon and not to worry, the man will find them, Victoria got into his car.

"Yeah, we're hard to miss," Hole shouted.

Victoria said, "Bye," and drove off. He watched through his rearview as Nicky and Hole both spread themselves over the bridge edge to get a good look at the red fish.

When Victoria opened the gold bag he felt all warm inside. Roll upon roll of fifties the size of a man's fist had been stuffed in the bag. Around each roll was a thick rubber band; jutting from under each band was a small piece of paper with the number 1 written on it. Fifty rolls in all, and ten of the little barrels were his. Not bad for a day's work.

As Victoria approached the outskirts of South Miami, he turned up the air conditioner two full clicks. Then he snapped on the radio. A blast of cold air filled the car, pleasantly chilling him. But the blaring sound of Latin music sent Victoria into a rage. He spun the dial, punched the dash, and bit his fist. "Those banana-sucking, pigskin-eating motherfuckers parked my car and changed my station," he complained aloud. He was pissed because it had taken him so long to find the station that played Eddie Fisher and Johnnie Ray. He punched at the padded dash again. His frenzied wail awoke demons that were sleeping peacefully in his back seat. They were comfortable and felt very much at home in his company.

Victoria did not want to be a major drug dealer. At the moment he was content with moving a package of heroin a month. He did nothing but pick up and deliver money. An old trade, the art of which he'd mastered years ago. Victoria received twenty-five thousand dollars a kilo from the black New York dealers. And he delivered twenty of the twenty-five to Santiago, his Cuban connection. He was a middleman. It was no big deal. The white powder never touched his hands. He was simply an expediter of death. Santiago and his band of ex-Batista soldiers took care of the particulars.

Victoria didn't perceive himself as a criminal. After all, he didn't take money or make a profit from innocent people. John Doe citizen never suffered as a result of what he did. Of course, Sal Victoria was deliberately ignorant as to the results of what he didn't do as a policeman and what he was doing as a mover of the deadly white lady. As a policeman he did what policemen had been doing in New York for a hundred years. He convinced himself that he was simply a part of history. Now in Florida he told himself that the drug laws were wrong. Drugs should be legalized like liquor. That's what he said to those who would listen. After he was dead Victoria would be accused of many things; no one would say he was insightful.

Sal Victoria's view of life was simply this: Everybody would like to make easy money. Some people got the balls to do what it takes to make it. Some people don't. Usually it isn't difficult or hard work, it's only illegal. When Victoria was a teenager America's heroes had names like Ruth, Lindbergh, Sergeant York, and Red Grange. Victoria, too, had heroes. One was the former Police Commissioner and ex-President Teddy Roosevelt. Not a bad choice. The man had a strength of character and a rigid moral standard that even his most vocal detractors were forced to admire. He was an adventurer, a sportsman, and an inspiring leader of men. Unlike Victoria's bosses in New York, Roosevelt would never ask a man to do what he wouldn't do himself. Yes, Teddy Roosevelt was a true American hero when the standard for heroism was high. Was it these admirable qualities in the man that made Victoria a rooter? No way . . . As Victoria often put it, Teddy was the last politician we had that knew how to handle these banana-sucking, pot-smoking greasers from south of the border. "Gimme a big stick and some guys from East Harlem; we'll straighten out them Commie faggots." Victoria saw himself as a political wise man. "Ain't none of them spics any good 'cept maybe Santiago." After all, Santiago gave him his heroin for twenty thou a key. And always trusted him with the money. But Santiago was real Spanish. Victoria could tell; the guy had green eyes.

Victoria's other all-American hero made a statement to a woman journalist once. A statement that Victoria read and immortalized in black script on a piece of paper that he tacked to his bathroom wall: "When ya get right down to it, lady, ain't nobody legit." What a saying. It became the linchpin on which Victoria hung his life. Sal Victoria's other hero was Al Capone.

The rain began as nuisance splatterings the size of sea-gull droppings. It now came in sheets, totally obliterating his ability to see. The car's wipers were going full out and the air conditioner blasted. Sal decided to try the radio again. By the time Hank Williams got past the first phrase of "Your Cheating Heart" the shower had passed. Now steam rose from the pavement. Country music reminded him of New York, Paddy Sheridan, and East Harlem. He glanced at the gold bag and remembered the day Sheridan told him that times were changing and they had better change with them. That fucked-up Mick had stayed on the job in New York with the rest of Doyle's assholes. Not him, not ol' Sally boy. As soon as Doyle sent the word that the gambling unit was being disbanded, as soon as the Chief said they would have to become involved in real police work, Sal threw in his retirement papers. When he backed his car into the numbered parking spot behind his high rise, he shut the radio off. Then for the last time he called Paddy Sheridan an asshole for listening to that shit-kicking crap. It was just past the noon hour. The Latins that worked in the lot, the ones he so enjoyed slandering, were of course not to be seen. It was the middle of the day; only fools, killers, and tourists moved about. He pushed the seat back as far as it would go and grabbed for the gold leather bag. As he pulled it toward him he was forced to maneuver it around the steering wheel. He laid it in his lap. The weight felt good. He bent his head and watched as the bag rose slightly. The delicious secure feeling of all that money so turned him on that he had an erection. His bent head made a great target.

The volume of his scream in no way reflected the seriousness of his wounds. He barely made a sound. There was no time to call to the whomever or whatever for absolution. Not that it would have mattered to Sal Victoria. He'd stopped believing at the orphanage, right after the sixth time the nun beat him for snoring while he was in a deep sleep. Sal Victoria didn't believe in anything except what was rolled and secured with red rubber bands in the gold bag on his lap. So in that bright all-knowing time before the lights go out forever, there was no remorse or guilt in him; just bullets.

The first bullet followed a downward trajectory, exploded through the windshield, and penetrated the top of his bent head. His head snapped back, splashing bone and brain off the headrest and across the top of the gold bag. Inexplicably, Victoria, already dead, lifted the bag to his face. The brain, ambushed and shocked, attempted to save itself. The second bullet, following on the heels of the first, came through the windshield, passed through the bottom of the bag, and lodged in a roll of fifty-dollar bills. The bullet had passed through five other rolls before coming to rest. The killer then opened the passenger's door and fired four more times into his chest. If there is such a thing as instant death, Sal Victoria had experienced it. A lot of kids on rooftops in Harlem wouldn't be so lucky. Their death throes would last for years, as the white lady sailed through their veins and brought them on pink fingertips to the moons of Jupiter, then dropped them through cold empty blackness, depositing them in hallways and on rooftops north of Ninety-sixth Street and south of Scarsdale.

14.

Red Burke of the New Jersey state police had given Bobby the clue. When the major talked about "the heat my brother lived through a few years back," he was undoubtedly talking about the material Bobby was reading. And the major had said it all. He may have used other words, but what he said was: "Shame on you, Tom Doyle. Shame on you, and your department. You people, and your way of life, corrupted my brother —you changed him. In the end, it was you that killed him."

Bobby Porterfield was getting a history lesson on the New York City Police Department. He was learning things he would have preferred not to know. He settled back into his seat in the library and glanced at the people around him. Some had their heads bowed into books, others leafed through magazines, and still others, younger and apparently students, took notes.

Bobby rubbed his head and massaged his temples, he was tired. He stretched, and a stack of ten-year-old magazines, along with a folder of photographs, slid from the table and fell to the floor. An avalanche in church. Three people sitting across the table from him raised their heads; two decent sorts smiled, then went back to their work. The third, a sour-faced woman biting on a pencil eraser, just stared. He rearranged his material to give himself more room, then leaned back and closed his eyes.

Paging through these old newspaper stories, magazine articles, and commission reports was exhausting; it was a nightmare. These stories told a tale of a police department out of control, a police department he didn't recognize, a police department gone bat-shit. Finally, he told himself, they're not talking about his police department. This is Tom Doyle's police department. He decided to read through a few of the news stories and maybe one of the reports again.

The Roxbury report was the most interesting. He took the report and turned to the section on the Sixth Division, Chief Doyle's old command. "The Sixth Division is comprised of five precincts: the 28th, 32nd, and 34th in northern Manhattan, and the 23rd and 25th in East Harlem. In one precinct alone, the 28th, there are forty-five policy-drop locations. Each location, we believe, pays the police one hundred dollars per day." He closed the book. That's every day, three hundred and sixty-five days a year, and that's only from one precinct. It was obvious to him that he was an outsider, he didn't relate to any of this. But he *felt* like a cop. But what kind of a cop? Doyle's kind or Red Burke's kind? As he read on, he mumbled and suddenly felt embarrassed. He looked up. The sour-faced woman, still chewing on the eraser, was staring—again.

He wondered whose bright idea it was to have the local police enforce gambling laws anyway. It said here that they had precinct commands, division commands, borough commands, and even citywide commands. All these commands, all these men, doing nothing but enforcing gambling and prostitution laws.

Look at that poor, silly drunk Artie Dolan. Forever talking about the hotel he could have owned. If these figures were to be believed, Dolan's rantings and ravings made sense. If not for Roxbury and his commission, the poor bastard most likely *would have* been able to put a down payment on a hotel. The amount of payoff money described here was enormous. The specifics had remained a secret. Roxbury never made an allegation or a case involving the Sixth Division stick. It seemed that he never got the right information, he never had real proof. The protection of that information sure as hell could be a motive for murder. Policemen killing policemen—every criminal's fantasy.

In the news photographs, the cops looked like they had had a drink too many. Their heads were cocked this way and that, and silly, self-conscious grins covered their faces. With each photograph was a bit of copy, the story of the picture. One photo was of a raid on a policy bank, another was of an arrest of a group of controllers, and still another caught eight whores and a pimp slow-dancing to a paddy wagon. When his eyes fastened on *the* photograph, he shouted. The bowed heads across the table rolled up. He smiled an apologetic grin. The sour-faced woman gave a small, mean look and shook her head.

Taking a red pen, he X'd faces in the photograph. As he completed each X, he muttered, "Shit!" Then finally, as lights and music went on in his head, he practically screamed, "SHIT!" The woman said, "Excuse me?" He had drawn X's through the faces of Frank Moresco, Artie Dolan, and Captain Burke. He was studying the face of a cop he hadn't seen before. Salvatore Victoria—Bobby found the name in the news copy that accompanied the photo. This guy looks like a criminal, he thought. He put a short red line under Victoria's face, then he put a check next to the face of Paddy Sheridan. On Chief Doyle's forehead, he drew a star, a big red star. He didn't know Detective Salvatore Victoria. Never heard of him. When he got Stein on the phone, the clerical man told him that Victoria was a retired detective, and presently the subject of an open homicide.

"He was shot five times in a Miami parking lot, two days ago," Stein said. "Take my word for it, he's no loss."

Bobby used his red-tipped pen to draw an X through the fourth face in the photograph. Four dead people smiled up at him from the photo. The answer was here. Right here, he told himself. He ran his finger under each of the faces in the photograph again. He came to Chief Doyle's face, and held. Of the six men in the photo, only two were still alive. The Chief and Paddy Sheridan. My God, he thought, the Chief's next . . . The X's he had drawn followed a pattern.

First there was Moresco, then Dolan, then Burke. Now Victoria, shot two days ago in Miami. In the picture, Doyle stood with one arm around Victoria, the other draped over Paddy. This is it, he knew it, he could feel it.

He ran to the phone and called Chief Doyle's office. Stein put him on hold. The answer to why these people were being killed, he didn't have. But the Chief would know. It's a pattern, it's clearly a pattern. Right now, he was sure that Chief Doyle was next to be killed.

"Porterfield, what the hell have you been up to?" Doyle screamed through the phone. "Where the hell are you?"

"Chief," Bobby said, trying to cut through the growl. "Chief, you have to hear me out."

"Hear you out? I'll kick you out. Whaddaya think, ya think you're a star? Just because you're living with my Cathy, don't give you the right to disappear for two days. I don't play favorites, Bobby. I'll have your ass shipped so far up in the Bronx you'll be sharing lunch with a Canadian Mountie."

A slow, burning feeling was beginning to take hold in Bobby's stomach, and he could hear the countdown in his head. He should let this bigmouth son of a bitch get killed. The file he was holding fell to the floor. When he bent to pick it up, he moved the phone from his ear; he could still easily hear Doyle's rage.

"You're supposed to call every two hours, goddamnit!"

"Chief"—it was a weak call for attention that got nowhere. Bobby doubted that Doyle even heard him. Then he tried again, but firmer this time. "Chief," he said sharply.

But Doyle's reply quieted him. "Just shut up and listen," the Chief said. Bobby tightened his grip on the folder and listened carefully to what Chief Doyle had to say. "I go out of town for a few days and the office goes on vacation." He went on for about another two minutes or so. He talked about his trip to Florida. How he couldn't trust anyone at the office to keep things straight. Bobby's legs began to shake. When he hung up the phone, he couldn't remember if he'd said "Goodbye, talk to you later," or just said "Yes, sir."

Doyle told him that he and his shadow, Paddy, had been in Florida looking at condominiums. "Southern Florida," he said, "was as hot and as uncomfortable as I thought it would be this time of year." The bastard was the killer! If not him, then he pointed his finger, and Paddy, the good soldier, struck, pushed, shoved, and shot. Bobby stood, paralyzed.

"Why?" he said out loud. "Goddamnit. Why?"

As he dialed Cathy, Bobby thought about the Roxbury report. It was not the corruption that now angered and depressed him. It was the fact that Doyle and company were not only corrupt, they were also killers. No better, and maybe worse, than the three men he'd shot it out with in the street. He'd killed them. And there had been moments of guilt. But only moments. Rizzo from sector Adam was right: "Three for us, none for them, ya-hoo." Us and them, them and us, the good guys and the bad guys, the evil and the fair. Well, he hadn't even smoked a joint after the day he was sworn in as a cop. How do you enforce the law, then break it? Doyle and his crew were a bunch of hypocrites. "We get the job done," was the stock reply. Red Burke was right about these guys, they're reflections of the people they police. But *he* was better than that. "Be a policeman," Cathy had said. "You'll love it." That's exactly what he was, and he did love it. But he was Burke's kind of policeman, not Doyle's.

Now he'd have to tell Cathy what he thought. He'd do what he knew was right, she had to respect him for that. It was her idea to have dinner. "Meet me in an hour at Dino's," she said. "I'm starved."

Bobby put three dimes in the photocopier, pushed the button, took a copy of the photograph, and put it in his folder.

In the cruiser, on the way to the restaurant, his resolve began to wane. He didn't know anything for certain. What proof did he have? He had only the proof that most good detectives ever have. A feeling in his gut and a sense that he was right. He was actually trembling when he parked the car. Maybe you're totally wrong, he thought. Maybe you're wrong! A cop two and a half years, and you're ready to accuse a chief inspector of murder. And the first person you plan on telling is your lover, his daughter. You *are* an asshole, he told himself. Bobby, relieved that Cathy wasn't in the restaurant when he arrived, ordered a double extra-dry vodka martini on the rocks.

"I've been watching you for five minutes from the doorway," she said, sliding into the booth. "You're by far the most handsome man here. Does it embarrass you that I say that?"

"I look like your father." Bobby smiled.

"You've noticed."

"I've noticed; I used to think you were in need of some serious couch time."

"Thanks."

"You're welcome," he said, "Do you want a drink?"

"I'd love a drink," she said, raising her hand to Dino. The strange man quickly stopped what he was doing and shuffled toward them. Cathy flipped open her napkin and waved it like a flag, then placed it on her lap. After smiling and waving a hello to three men standing at the bar, she blew a kiss to the approaching Dino. It seemed that everyone knew her, everyone liked her. She was tough Tommy Doyle's daughter. You could tell she felt good. She looked proud and seemed happy to be with him.

"What's the special, Dino?" she asked, tapping out a beat with her fingertips on the tabletop.

"How do you like your new job, Cathy?" Dino asked, placing a plastic basket of sliced Italian bread on the table. For two months, Cathy had been working as a student assistant in the Manhattan district attorney's office, and she loved it.

"It's great, but right now I'm hungry. What's the special?"

"It's osso buco, with a little pasta and some spinach. I made it myself. Believe me, it's fresh."

Cathy flashed a smile to two more men from headquarters. She was really up.

"Go ahead, Bobby, why don't you order. I want to give my dinner some thought." She was tapping the table with both hands now, beating out the rhythm of "If I Had a Hammer."

"How about spaghetti and meatballs, Dino," Bobby said, with little enthusiasm.

"What?" Dino croaked.

"Spaghetti and meatballs," Bobby said simply.

"No good, have the osso buco."

"I'd rather not."

"We don't have any meatballs. I didn't make any meatballs," "I only make meatballs on Tuesday and Thursday."

Bobby's eyes followed a pair of men from the doorway, through the restaurant, to the bar. They were detectives from the arson and explosion squad. He'd met them at headquarters a week ago. They seemed decent, sensitive men. They wore pins in their jacket lapels that said "Cops for Christ." He looked up at Dino and said, "O.K., forget the meatballs, I'll just have the pasta."

"You want the osso buco on the side, or what?"

"Osso buco is veal, isn't it?" Bobby asked.

"Right, it's veal shank made with a light sauce." Dino kissed his joined fingertips, then opened them as if he were gently letting loose a small bird. The two guys from A and E tipped their beer glasses as a greeting to Bobby.

"I don't eat veal. So just bring me the pasta."

"Git outta here, whaddaya mean, ya don't eat veal?"

The truth, he thought, would not be of any real value to Dino, but he'd risk it. Cathy had paused in her reading of the menu. She sat gazing at him as if he'd just lost his mind.

"I don't eat veal," Bobby repeated, "because I read recently that they put the poor animals in small cages, in a room without light. Then they shoot 'em up with antibiotics and steroids."

"You read that recently?" Cathy asked.

"Yes, I did. I read that yesterday, at the library."

Dino stepped back a foot or two and began to breathe noisily. Bobby continued: "They keep them in the dark in order to deny them vitamin D. That's how they keep down the muscle and keep off the fat. That's why the meat stays so tender. I don't want to eat it."

"Git outta here, they don't do that," Dino whined.

"They do," he said. It was a calm statement of a truth Bobby wasn't sure of.

"Git outta here," Dino said, looking around the restaurant. "What are you gonna have, Cathy?" Dino asked.

Cathy went through the motions of studying the men, then said, "I'll have the osso buco. The one with the tan." She smiled.

Dino threw his head back and laughed and laughed. Then he turned to Bobby. "Ya know what we did to rabbits in the old days? We useta hang 'em by their hind feet," he whispered, "then slit their throats. We did it to bleed 'em. Soon as I useta grab the rope, they'd scream like children. Yaaaaa, yaaaaa, they'd yell, just like kids. My old man said rabbits could tell by the look in your eye that it was bleeding time."

"Dino, would you do me a favor?" Bobby asked.

"Sure, kid, wha?"

"Cancel the spaghetti, and just bring me a glass of the house white wine."

"Ya see, talking all that shit about the veal an' all ruined ya appetite. Ya sure you ain't got too sensitive a stomach ta be a cop, Bobby? Ya gotta be tough to be a cop. Ya gotta have a strong stomach." Bobby mumbled something and Dino walked away, shaking his head.

The "Cops for Christ" winked and smiled at Bobby. They acted together, real partners: one winked, the other smiled. Nice guys, he thought. I wonder where they worked ten years ago. The pair had been pushed along the bar. They were now forced to stand with their backs against the wall by a stream of off-duty cops.

"You haven't told me anything about how your case is going," Cathy said. She wasn't looking at him, her head was bent into a plate of pasta. He didn't have to look into her eyes. This is the opening I need, I can say it now, I could slip it into the dinner conversation. Right now, right before Cathy ordered her tea, black with no sugar. How would it sound? "Cathy, I learned today that your father is a criminal, a killer, masquerading as a policeman."

"Well," she said, "are you going to tell me?"

"Tell you what?" he said, and reached for his glass of wine. Bobby's hand was shaking. Smoke 'Em Porterfield, he thought to himself.

"What's going on with your investigation? You went to the library, did you learn anything you didn't know before?"

"I think it would be fair to say that I learned a few things at the library." Oh, that was good, good; be proud of yourself, you worm.

"So you learned something at the library. About what? Veal?" she said slyly.

"I notice that you haven't touched yours," he said quickly, then drained his glass and poured himself another.

It was true, Cathy hadn't touched her meat. It sat, a chunk of flesh on a bone, in the center of her plate. She raised her head slowly and smiled at him. It was a tight-lipped smile. There was a toughness in her face he hadn't seen before. This truly was a side of her that was new to him. That look was her father's genes, his blood. The giddiness that arrived all shiny and bouncy with her, like a first date, had vanished. She now sat staring at him as if she knew a horrible secret, a secret that she would keep from him.

"My dad came by the office today," she finally said. "Just came by to say hello. It was a nice surprise."

It seemed to Bobby that Dino's restaurant was taking on the appearance of Frank Moresco's wake. More and more cops were filing in, shouldering their way to the bar. And every time Cathy mentioned her father, his mind sprinted off, searching for courage and finding none. He turned away from her, cleared his throat, and sipped his wine.

"There's too many Jews in the D.A.'s office," she whispered.

He almost choked on the wine. "Excuse me?" he asked.

"All politicians, all leftists. No wonder the system stinks. And next week, Roxbury begins his term as interim D.A. They'll be even less concerned about crime. It'll be open season on cops, my dad said."

He'd forgotten! It would have escaped him completely had she not just mentioned it. That's right, Roxbury had been appointed the interim D.A. in New York County. Frank Stilson, the current D.A., was terminally ill and the mayor was going to replace him with Roxbury until the next election. That's the hook: Roxbury was going to get another shot at the police department. Damn, he wished he could figure this out.

Totally oblivious to the Chinese fire drill taking place in Bobby's mind, Cathy poured herself a glass of wine. She wore a faint smile, and her eyes closed to slits. "I hate them," she said. "They're a bunch of lonely people over there. They all run alone and sleep alone. They have no loyalty to each other or anything else for that matter. The miserable bunch of careerists. They stab each other in the back just to make points with their bureau chiefs." She gulped her wine and dropped her head back against the booth. "I hate them all," she said, so softly he had to strain to hear.

He was trying to remember when Cathy had first mentioned the Roxbury appointment. He recalled it was during one of her early tirades, one of her lectures about the liberal conspiracy that was destroying the criminal justice system. It was her first or second day as a student assistant. That was five weeks ago, on a Monday or a Tuesday. Five weeks ago today, he thought, on a Friday, Frank Moresco, they say, killed himself.

Cathy was lecturing again, a familiar hum. Another speech, another summation; she was demanding the death penalty again for the world's liberals.

"Don't you see, Bobby?" she said sharply. "People have to belong to something, believe in something. The jerks at the office I work in belong to nothing but themselves. It's not like the police department. There's loyalty in the police department. These people, like Roxbury, only want to make a name for themselves. Then they can quit being prosecutors, join major firms, and make giant bucks bastardizing the Constitution."

He wondered if she knew anything about her father. She must know. Then again, no one really knows anything for certain until you tell them. There was no guilt without admission. And it didn't strike him that Chief Tom Doyle felt a compulsion to confess to anything.

"Do you agree with me or what, Bobby?" she said, tapping her temple with her index finger. "Do you spend any time thinking about any of this?"

"What?" he said. It was true. He didn't hear her. He could turn her off.

"The fucked-up criminal justice system, that's what."

"No, I mean, sure I do, when I have the time."

She turned away from him and exhaled a great sigh.

"Cathy, who else did you tell about Roxbury getting the D.A.'s job?"

"What are you talking about? You didn't listen to a thing I said. You turned me off"—she paused—"again."

"We can talk more about that later if you like. Right now, I'm curious. Did you tell anyone else besides me that Roxbury was to be appointed interim D.A.?"

"No, I did not."

Bobby looked at her in astonishment. "You didn't tell your father?"

"Of course I told my father."

"Isn't he somebody?"

"Bobby, that was a rumor that I would share with someone who had a need to know. My father is a chief inspector in the police department. He needs to know that the Manhattan D.A.'s office is getting a new D.A., don't you think?"

"Oh, sure, sure," he said.

"Well, don't say it like that," she said abruptly. "He *is* my father."

Cathy smiled nervously at him. He couldn't return the smile. He probably should have. But it would have been a lie, a pretense. Cathy looked around the room, then pointed with her chin, that great aristocratic chin, to the back door. "Well, look who's here." The tense smile she wore faded from her face and she immediately bit into her bottom lip. Mark and Jackie exchanged greetings with the men at the bar and moved toward their booth, grinning as they came; smiling as if they didn't have a care in the world.

"Going to a costume party, Jackie?" Cathy asked as Mark sat beside her and Jackie took a seat next to Bobby.

"I'm going to walk with some greaseball informant over in the Village tonight. You know the type—hair and muscles, mostly hair. The backup said I should dress as if I were this guy's girlfriend."

"Well, I suppose you've done just that." Cathy smiled.

Mark reached a giant hand across the table and patted Bobby's cheek.

"Do I look like a cocker spaniel to you, partner?" He smiled and tried to shove Mark's hand away. He couldn't budge his arm; the guy was like a pillar of steel.

"I've missed you, partner. What've you been up to?" Mark said, bringing his hand up from Bobby's cheek, now tousling his hair.

"I've been working. What the hell have you been doing?"

"Just sitting around at the office waiting for you to call, and, of course, solving the murder."

"You plan on keeping it a secret?" Bobby said quietly.

"I have a meet with an old friend of mine in East Harlem tomorrow or the day after. Who knows, maybe we'll get lucky."

"You plan on telling me about it?"

[159]

"Later, partner, later. As for now, I'd like a drink. How about you, Jackie?"

Jackie was preoccupied with half the men at the bar. They were waving, and smiling, and whistling; even the two "Cops for Christ" blatantly gawked.

"I'd love a drink, but it's almost show time. I have to be across town in a half hour."

While getting up, Jackie's thigh rubbed Bobby's leg, sending a chill through him the likes of which he'd never felt before. It gave him goose bumps and instantly made him feel guilty. He wondered if Mark and Cathy had noticed. He knew that Jackie intended to touch him, she'd done it before.

"Is that dress silk?" he asked. Then suddenly he turned away from her and smiled at Cathy, who sat like a stone in a tomb.

"Silk, are you kidding? This is some kind of fabric made from oil. But it does the job. What do you think, Cathy, do you like it?" Jackie did a slow turn and Bobby couldn't help but stare. The dress did look like it was made of silk. It was black with tiny white polka dots, its hem was right at the knee. When Jackie angled her leg, the dress clung to her thighs and pulled tight across the swell of her ass. There was a slit on one side that ran to the center of her thigh. It was sleeveless and had a Chinese collar. Jackie wore no bra; her nipples, clearly defined, were pointed upward beneath the material. The dress was a cheap, tasteless imitation of a tasteless original. Along with every other man in the restaurant, it took Bobby's breath away. Only Mark didn't seem to notice. But then again, that dress, full of Jackie, would be coming home to *his* bed that night.

"I think it's awful," Cathy said, her head resting on her fist, her eyes latched on to Bobby, her teeth close to drawing blood from her bottom lip.

"I guess 'awful' is a good word. Do you think this dress is awful, Bobby?" she purred.

Bobby shrugged his shoulders, then took a sip of wine, drowning a laugh. Jackie kissed the air one time in the direction of each of them, turned on her heel, and glided toward the door. Everyone at the bar ordered another drink. Mark called out for her to be careful, and Bobby tried another smile on

Cathy, who turned away. The grace and talent of Jackie had long since lost its appeal to Cathy. She barely hid her feelings as she testily cleared her throat. Jackie was a celebrity, but Cathy was tough Tommy Doyle's daughter. Mark laughed at Jackie's performance, and Bobby smiled; Cathy bowed her head and poked at the cold osso buco. This was not the time to tell Cathy about Tom Doyle.

The police cruiser's steering wheel vibrated violently as the car jiggled over the Brooklyn Bridge. Bobby glanced into the rearview mirror. Cathy seemed to be asleep. Her head rested on the seat and her hands were folded in her lap. Mark stared out the passenger window at the vista that was Brooklyn Heights.

"From up here, the city looks peaceful, even gentle," Bobby said, softly so as not to disturb Cathy.

"Yeah," Mark said, "from an airplane, at night, the South Bronx looks like Brussels."

"We always see what we want to see, it's the smell and the sound that we can't deny." Bobby smiled.

"Porterfield, the poet," Cathy announced from the back seat.

"I thought you were sleeping," Bobby said as he expertly maneuvered the cruiser into the exit lane, then off the bridge road. Driving a police cruiser, even an unmarked cruiser, with its three antennas and somber look, was like driving a Bentley or a Rolls-Royce. Other cars gave you plenty of room.

"How do you sleep in the back seat of a police car going fifty miles an hour over the Brooklyn Bridge?" Cathy asked, sitting up and stretching.

Mark turned in his seat and faced her. "Cops do it all the time," he said matter-of-factly.

"Cops do a lot of things normal people can't," she answered.

Cathy asked to be dropped off first. She was tired, she said. She needed a shower, she said. There was some material she needed to read, she said. Bobby knew she was angry with him, that she wanted to be alone. Cathy would be asleep before he got home. Sometimes he preferred her passive-aggressive behavior to her fury. Why she was angry with him, he didn't know. It could be anything. A look, a word, a phrase, or maybe a smile at Jackie. Bobby never forgot that Cathy was Irish, and fury could come from the memory of a battle that had never been fought. Sometimes her fury came from nowhere, it was just there; like her brown eyes and chestnut hair. To be closed out of her life this night was fine by him. He needed this time to spend with Mark.

After letting Cathy out of the car, he drove to a coffee shop. Getting Mark and himself a container of coffee, he drove to a spot near Mark's building. He parked, then moved the seat back as far as it could go, giving his partner some badly needed leg room. It was ten o'clock at night, they were in Brooklyn, and there wasn't a soul in the street.

It'd been a while since he and Mark spent time over a container of coffee. He missed it. Now sitting here, it was easy to remember why. He most enjoyed the down time. The time when night crept slowly to daybreak, the time their car cruised in slow, premeditated patterns at fifteen miles an hour through and around sector David. It was those quiet periods when he felt they were the only people awake, maybe the only people alive, in their ten square blocks of Manhattan. This was the time when minds touched and secrets were shared and fears explored. This was the time when your partner smiled at you and said, "Fuck it, you were right." Better than a wife or lover or parents, partners always said, "You were right" and "Fuck it if you weren't." Bobby believed that as long as they were together, each one looking out after the other's back, they would be fine, they would be safe, they would survive.

"So, partner, tell me about this old informant in East Harlem," Bobby said, putting the container lid from the coffee into a brown paper bag.

Mark sipped his coffee in that way that he did with both hands wrapped around the container and both eyes closed. "I think I know where Captain Burke went the night he was killed. A guy I know in East Harlem will be able to tell me if I'm right."

There was much about Mark that Bobby knew. He knew, for example, how Mark liked his coffee, and what made him angry when they were on patrol. He knew why Mark had become a policeman, and where and when he'd met and fallen in love with Jackie. He knew what words hurt him, what smells he detested, and he knew something that even Jackie didn't: he knew what terrified him. But there was a lot he didn't know. He knew almost nothing about Mark's police career before they had become partners. Mark didn't talk about it and Bobby had not asked.

The light from the moon lit the inside of the cruiser as if it were midday. Mark lifted the container of coffee, then sipped as if he were drinking a wonderful espresso from a tiny gold inlaid cup.

"So, did you learn anything at the library?" he said, a dis-believing half smile on his face. When he'd told Mark what Major Burke had said, about the heat and all, and that he wanted to check into it at the library, Mark hadn't objected. He'd simply said he thought it a waste of time. "You don't solve a week-old murder by reading ten-year-old newspaper stories," he'd said.

"I'll show you what I found. You know me, I made a copy of everything," Bobby said, suddenly feeling good about him-self, feeling like a detective, feeling like he had something im-portant to say. "But first, I want to hear about your friend."

"My friend . . ." Mark paused, then looked out the window, searching the night for something just out of sight. "He's not my friend. He's just someone I knew well a long time ago."

"Can he help?" Bobby said, opening the door, getting out of the cruiser, and moving to the trunk. He took out the attaché case. The weight of it felt good. There was information here that would solve this mystery. "So," he said, sliding back into the seat, "can your friend help?"

"I'll find out tomorrow or the next day. As soon as I talk to him, I'll let you know what he has to say." A surprised look came to Mark's face as Bobby lugged the heavy attaché case into the car.

"Can't I go with you?"

"To Harlem?" Mark asked, staring at the case.

"Yeah."

"No, you'd bring heat to us in about thirty seconds." Mark grinned.

Bobby didn't like the idea of Mark going off on his own. It

was important that they stay together. He opened the attaché case and pointed to the stacked newspaper articles and magazine stories, and he held up the Roxbury report. The photograph, his little piece of magic that he believed held the answer, he had put in a sealed manila envelope. The envelope was at the bottom of the stack of clippings.

"Is this what you went to the library for?" Mark asked, taking hold of the Roxbury report, quickly leafing through it, then putting it on the dashboard.

Mark seemed even less interested than he sounded and he was beginning to sound annoyed. "What *is* all this crap?" he asked, removing one clipping after the other, glancing at the headline, then throwing the articles up on top of the dash. He was showing little respect for Bobby's discoveries, but he hadn't seen the photo, Bobby thought. The photo sat at the bottom of the stack. Mark never got there.

"You wanna tell me what all this shit is, Bobby?" Now he sounded really angry.

"Mark, this is the story of the Sixth Division." He was ambushed by Mark's tone. He expected Mark to be more supportive, maybe even compliment him. He was wrong.

"Bobby, I think you're fucking loose in the head. You never cease to amaze me. Do you want to tell me what this cop-baiting crap has to do with Captain Burke's murder? That's what we're investigating, the killing of Captain Burke, not some corruption shit. We're not in the Internal Affairs Division or is that a surprise to you?"

"Mark, what are you getting so tense about?" He was taken aback, really shocked, and Mark could hear it. But it didn't matter, because when he tried to say something else, bring up the photograph, tell him about Doyle—tell him who the killer was—Mark cut him off. And now, as he spoke to him, he pointed his index finger right at Bobby's heart.

"Look, you and I should have had this conversation a long time ago. But we didn't, so I blame myself."

Bobby began going through the attaché case, looking for the manila envelope; Mark slammed the case shut. Bobby pulled his hand away just in time.

"You know who Chief Doyle is?" Mark said quickly. Bobby grunted. He'd wait, he'd listen first to what Mark had to say.

"Why don't you tell me who *you* think Doyle is?" Bobby said quickly.

"Don't push me, Bobby. I have fifteen more years than you do on this job. There's a fuckin' world of things you know nothing about."

Bobby took Mark's container of coffee from off the dash and took a sip. Then he handed the container to Mark.

"Well, old-timer, you're my partner, educate me," he said.

"Chief Doyle is your rabbi, your hook, the only weight you have. You got less than three years on this job, and you're a detective. You think that's because you're cute and smart? Or maybe you think it's because you wasted three guys in a shoot-out? Don't kid yourself, bright boy, you're a detective because of Cathy, period." Each sentence from Mark was like a slap across the face. The words weren't hard to take, it was the tone of their delivery that rattled him. "You take off for two days . . ."

"What?" Bobby asked.

"You're gone for two days. I knew you were at the fucking library. But did you think to call, let anyone else know? You drive a department car. Your own fucking department car! There are guys with more time on the witness stand than you have on the job that don't get a car."

The comment about the car did it. Up until that statement, Bobby had little to say. Mark was right. His delivery left a lot to be desired, but he was essentially right. Though he never had admitted it to anyone, not even to himself, he knew that Cathy's father had pushed his career. But this nonsense about the car, now that did it.

"We're talking about murder here, Mark," Bobby said angrily. "And we're talking about crooks. Big-time, serious crooks. And those murders and those crooks are directly linked. Don't tell me you don't see that, partner. I have something here that proves the connection." Bobby opened the attaché case a second time. Again he went through the clippings. And again Mark exploded.

"We're not investigating murders, we're investigating *a mur-*

der. The killing of Captain Burke. And who are the big-time crooks you're talking about?"

"The guys in the Sixth Division. That's who I'm talking about. The guys that worked pros and gambling."

"Listen," Mark said, and when he spoke, he touched Bobby's shoulder. "I know Doyle was the C.O. of the Sixth Division. And I know there was a lot of heat up there a few years back."

"I think he killed them all," Bobby said simply.

"What?" Mark roared.

"That's right. I know he was a fucking crook. I know the Sixth Division was full of crooks. Let's put that aside. I think the son of a bitch killed, or had Paddy kill, four people."

"You think Chief Doyle killed his best friends?" Mark said.

"Right."

"Why? For Christ's sake, why?"

"I'm not sure."

"Terrific. Wonderful." He sipped his coffee, choked a bit, then said, "You're fucking crazy."

"Mark, Roxbury is gonna be appointed interim D.A. Did you know that?"

"No. So what?"

"There's no statute of limitations for members of the department. I think Doyle is afraid that Roxbury is going to reopen this investigation." Bobby took the report off the dash, turned to the section on the Sixth, then said, "I think Doyle knows that Roxbury will turn someone and get him this time."

Mark pulled the folder from his hand and threw it on the back seat.

"That means all Doyle has to do is kill about a hundred and fifty cops. You should be committed. You're fucking nuts."

"No, Mark, not a hundred and fifty cops. Just the bagmen. And they're all in a picture I have. You want to see it now?"

"No," Mark shouted. "I don't want to see your fucking picture. I read the pathology report on Moresco. The man killed himself. Read the fucking report, why don't ya. And Dolan, Dolan took a header. He slipped or fell or dived, who gives a shit, he fried himself. The poor guy fried himself. If you're going to kill someone, you throw him in front of a train. You know what the odds are of throwing somebody onto the tracks and hitting the third rail? About as easy as hitting the moon with a rock. What else do you have here?" He glared.

Bobby just held Mark's eyes; he didn't respond, he just stared at his partner, who was sweating, rubbing his head, and talking in half sentences. Finally, Bobby said, "You just made my point. I didn't say Doyle, or Paddy for that matter, was either sane or smart. I just said they're killers."

"And Burke? You think Paddy or maybe the Chief himself ran over his best friend?"

"You got it."

"Have you told anyone else about this fantasy of yours?"

"Who else am I going to tell, partner? I wanted to talk to Cathy about it tonight. But I don't think I have the balls to."

"Balls has nothing to do with it. You're not totally crazy. That's good. That's a good sign. Promise me, now, goddamnit, promise me you'll not say a thing about this; not to Cathy, not to anyone. Not until I talk to my guy in Harlem. Please, promise me that, will you?"

"O.K., O.K. But listen, you've left someone out," Bobby said quietly, trying to soothe, trying to relax his partner.

"Who? What are you talking about?"

"Do you know where the Chief and Paddy were for the past three days?"

"They were out of town. That's all I know."

"Yeah, they were out of town all right. They were in Florida, in Miami, Florida. Did you know a guy named Sal Victoria?"

Mark asked, "What about him?"

"He was shot and killed day before yesterday in Miami. And guess what? He's in the picture I have. He worked for Doyle in the Sixth, too." Now Bobby smiled. It was a smug smile. He felt smug, he felt good, he was one hell of a detective, and he knew it.

"Coincidence, all this is a coincidence."

"Coincidence, shit. Take a look at this picture and tell me this is all fantasy and coincidence," he said sharply.

"Goddamnit, Bobby, I don't want to see your picture. Look, follow me, read my lips if you have to. I have seventeen years in. During those seventeen years, I've been shot at, stabbed, run over, spit on because I'm black, and spit on because I'm blue. I was ready to retire as a cop, a patrolman, but now they've made me a detective. In three years, I'm a retired detective. I can lay in the sun and feel good about myself."

"Mark, there's a bigger issue here."

"What?"

"Murder and a little something called honesty. I know it sounds like bullshit, I know it sounds naïve, but the Sixth Division, where all these guys worked, was a snake pit. It was a sewer of organized criminality. And not you, or anyone else, is going to convince me that these deaths are not directly linked to what went on up there. And the Chief's involved. I know he is."

Mark got out of the car, he closed the door and leaned his elbows on the frame of the open passenger window.

"I want to ask you something," he said. "Forget the murders for a second. Now think before you answer." Bobby nodded. "Assuming that what your hero, Roxbury, says in his little book is true, do you think that we should arrest or fire all the cops that behaved that way?"

"Mark, for Christ's sake, I'm talking about murder." Bobby shouted, Mark was patronizing him and he didn't like it. "But if you want my answer to that question, my answer would be, yeah, maybe we should."

"Well, Bobby, let me tell ya, if we did that, you'd be one hell of a busy guy. Because, partner, there would be about seven cops left in this fucking police department."

For a moment, there was absolute silence. Mark just stared blank-faced at him.

"What does that have to do with these murders?" Bobby said finally. Then he closed the attaché case, leaving the manila envelope, with his magical piece of evidence, buried at the bottom.

"I don't know what that has to do with these deaths. Not a thing, I suppose. I only know that I don't want to be stirring around in some old shit pile. I don't want to embarrass this police department. Because in the end, Bobby, the bottom line is, nobody gives a shit. The only thing people care about is getting from place to place in this city in one piece. And to be safe in their homes. And not worry about some predator climbing in their fucking window and tearing their fucking heart out for a fucking TV or a fucking gold chain. That's what people want from us. They want us to shield them from the fucking animals. And what you're doing, and what Roxbury did, is to make people afraid, more afraid than they already are. You go ahead, continue to conduct this investigation the way you're doing it right now. You'll never find out who killed Burke, but you'll convince a whole lot of people that they can't trust their police."

Bobby tried to say something, but Mark cut him off with a wave of his hand.

"I've been a cop for seventeen years," he said, "Through all kinds of changes, all kinds of bullshit. I don't want to be a part of that, not because I've got something to hide, but because it's not true. One thing has nothing to do with the other. Cops that do things that maybe they shouldn't are, most times, the best street cops around."

"Do you believe that?" Bobby said, now feeling like he was speaking a foreign language. He'd told Mark that he thought the Chief, their C.O., was a killer and Mark was giving him a lecture on corruption.

"You're damn right I believe that," Mark said.

"Well, you're wrong. I may have only two and a half years in, but I know there is no such thing as a good cop that's crooked. And you know what else?"

"What?" Mark whispered.

"You're too smart to believe that shit," Bobby said, and started the cruiser's engine.

"And you're from fucking Omaha. I'm tired. I'll talk to you tomorrow." Mark slammed his hand on the roof of the cruiser, turned, and waved. Bobby watched as he walked toward his building. "Read some history, Mark," he said to himself.

"Doyle's a fucking killer and you should read some goddamn history," he called after Mark. He was surprised at the sound of his voice. It was accusatory, he didn't mean for it to be.

Mark turned, there was a smile on his face.

"Give me your word you'll leave this Doyle business sit for a day or two."

Bobby said he would. Then Mark came back to the car, and again pointed a finger at him.

"I don't have to read any history. I've lived it. And what's more important, I don't have a need to make any."

He then turned and disappeared into the building. Bobby never got the chance to show him the photo. And he hadn't convinced him to take him along to meet his old friend in Harlem. Bobby needed help. He needed an ally. He needed to understand more about this police department's twilight world. Doyle and Burke's world. He thought about Cathy. Then he thought about Jackie and smiled. He didn't think anything of the mint antique silver Buick parked up the street from Mark's building.

15.

On Wednesday mornings in Brooklyn a procession of unlikely-looking cops sneak into the basement of the Supreme Court building on Tillary Street. Squeezing into an elevator reserved for judges, they ride to the sixth floor. Once off the elevator, they move quickly down a narrow hallway and enter the Kings County grand jury room through the back door. Behind closed doors they stand around twitching and turning, scratching and yawning, unlit cigarettes dangling from their mouths. They slap one another's palms and grab each other's thumbs. Loud laughter can be heard coming from the room, but most conversation is conducted in whispers. They say things like "Brooklyn sucks" and "I hope the fucking chemists are here." They sip morning coffee and tell each other big lies; the small ones they save for the grand jury. After a while they queue up on benches in the large, normally sedate room. Assistant district attorneys whose job it is to prepare them are in awe of them, repulsed by them, and in most cases ignored by them. On Wednesday mornings in Brooklyn, undercover narcotics detectives, the police department's heroic crazies, turn the grand jury room into a zoo.

Detective Jackie Lerner sat in the first row. She was wearing her "it's summer and time to testify" outfit. A yellow sundress dotted with white flowers, and sandals. Her face was dusted with just a touch of makeup. Her waist-length black hair was braided and tied with white ribbon. Her attaché case, filled with brown evidence bags, lay open on her lap. A detective's gold badge hung like a religious medal from a chain around her neck. She was a genuine beauty, the real thing, and the only woman in the room.

Having testified hundreds of times, Jackie wasn't at all nervous. No need to be, there is no cross-examination at the grand jury. It's the prosecutor's ball park, his ball, his bat, his rules. The game is played but the final outcome is a foregone conclusion. She sat quietly waiting her turn, checking her appointment book, and smiling every so often as her cohorts turned the room into a day at the beach.

Frank LaRosa, a young man who cheated his way through a second-rate law school, then passed the Bar on his third try, came slowly through the waiting-room door. Dressed in a cheap summer-weight gray suit and black patent-leather shoes, he squeaked when he walked. Assistant District Attorney LaRosa wrinkled his nose when he saw the room full of police department weirdos. But his face lit and he licked his top lip when he saw Jackie. Straightening his tie, he squeaked around the benches and took a seat near her.

"Ya got something for us today, cutie pie?" LaRosa asked.

"No, I come here for the company," Jackie said, but she also smiled; no point getting the D.A. mad. The sound of LaRosa's voice made Jackie twitch. As he sat his leg moved too near hers and she got up. Smiling the meaty grin of the big macher, LaRosa reached a hand as if to touch her. Jackie stepped back, but continued to smile. A strange sensation swept through her. Maybe I'm going gay, she thought, every man I meet lately makes me want to vomit. LaRosa got up from the bench and crowded her. Jackie hated to be crowded by people she *liked*. This guy, with the smell of cheap cologne and garlic jumping out of every hole, was gonna get a knee in the balls if he didn't back off.

"If you're ready I'll get you in first," LaRosa whispered, trying to draw her into an intimate conspiracy. There was something green lodged in his bottom teeth. Jackie held her smile, and her temper.

"That's O.K.," she said, "Wilson was here before me. I'm up second." Jackie was hypnotized by the green fleck; it somehow popped free and now rode on LaRosa's bottom lip.

"Wilson's not here," he said, looking around the room.

"Yes, he is. He went to the bathroom. Magic will be right back," Jackie said, turning to look at the hallway door.

"No sweat. I'm the boss here, kiddo. If I say you go in first, you go in first."

The door to the hallway swung open and Detective Jimmy Wilson sailed into the room waving brown evidence envelopes and white lab reports.

"O.K., LaRosa, let's git it on. It's show time. Stop trying to get laid. Her ol' man'll bite your knees off. Let's get going. I got shit to do, man, people to see, dope to buy. I can't be fucking around in here all morning with this band of do-nothin's."

Wilson moved between Jackie and the D.A. He threw an arm over LaRosa's shoulder and turned him toward the grand jury room. "Whew," he yelled, "what you wearin'? You stink like chump change. Man, you a lawyer! Ya gotta get yourself some Brut or Canoe, spend some of dem bucks." Wilson turned LaRosa around in a circle. The D.A. tried to smile, he made a halfhearted attempt to move away from this madman detective, but he was gripped by the magic. "Whew," Wilson yelled again, rubbing his nose with the palm of his hand. "You're still eatin' them pickles for breakfast, ain't ya? Better stand back and let me do all the talking. Our citizens in there ain't ready for your cloud, man." Detective Wilson was six four and weighed one hundred and fifty pounds. He was a whirlish dervish. Now clucking like a chicken. Magic Willow Wilson brushed LaRosa's lapels with his hands and hustled him to the courtroom door.

Dealing with this D.A. was a piddling thing to Wilson. For years he had been the top-rated undercover narcotics detective in the city. But Jackie was closing the gap. Wilson's preeminence was threatened by this stunning little girl-woman who had the instincts of a street shark. As Jackie watched Wilson work LaRosa over, the style and grace of his moves made her wonder if Magic had ever framed anyone.

In ten minutes Wilson had done his thing with the grand jury. He zipped through the waiting room, waved to Jackie, and was gone like a genie. Now it was her turn to perform.

The grand jury seemed stunned when Jackie entered the room. After all, they had just been held spellbound by Wilson and now act two was a coed. They continued to murmur as Jackie placed her hand on the Bible.

"Do you swear to tell the truth, the whole truth, and nothing but the truth?" the clerk asked.

"I do," Jackie lied. She saw LaRosa slip a folded note to an attractive woman seated in the first row.

"Name, rank, shield, and assignment," LaRosa asked, taking the gorgeous woman's reply, unfolding it, glancing at it, crumbling it, then throwing it into a wastebasket under his chair.

"Jacqueline Lerner, detective, shield 594, Narcotics Division, undercover group."

"How long have you been assigned to your present command, Detective Lerner?"

"Five years."

"Tell the grand jury, if you will, how many purchases of illegal drugs you have made in that time. You don't have to be exactly correct. In round numbers, about how many buys have you made?"

Jackie loved hearing the response from the jury when she answered this question. She answered the same question every week, and every week the same long, rolling "wowwwww" came from the housewives, schoolteachers, engineers, and other good citizens who made up the grand jury.

"About twenty-five hundred," she said, and the expected response filled the room.

"I think we can call you an expert," LaRosa said, and smiled at the pretty woman in the first row. Embarrassed, the woman turned away.

What a schmuck, Jackie thought.

"O.K. Let's begin, shall we? On the twentieth of July of this year, at about eleven p.m., were you at the corner of Fourth Avenue and Pacific Street in Kings County?"

"I was."

"And did you purchase four glassine envelopes containing a white powder you believed to be heroin from a man later identified as one Richard Smalls, but known to you as Sweet Dick?"

The men as well as the women on the jury allowed themselves a giggle at that one. Jackie answered, "Yes, I did."

"Did there come a time when you opened the envelopes in order to field-test their contents?"

"There did."

"Could you tell the jury, Detective Lerner, under what conditions the test was made?"

Jackie turned away from LaRosa and looked directly at a woman seated in the second row. The woman, Jackie guessed, was in her late fifties. And it seemed to Jackie that the woman dabbed at a tear. Jackie smiled at her and the woman bent her head. She *was* crying.

"After I made the purchase, I took the envelopes back to my department car, which was parked at Fourth Avenue and Warren Street. I removed from my attaché case a Marquee Testing Kit. Opening each bag, I took out a bit of the white powder. Then I opened two phials of sulfuric acid and put small amounts of the drug in each. The test was positive. I then resealed the bags and initialed each one. I then placed the bags into a police department evidence envelope. I taped the envelope closed and wrote the time and date, my initials and badge number across the seal, along with the John Doe name of the subject, Sweet Dick."

LaRosa got up from his seat and walked to Jackie. He handed her a police department evidence envelope and asked her if it was the same envelope she just described. Jackie told him it was. LaRosa asked that the envelope be marked and entered as State's exhibit no. 1. He then walked back to his desk and asked the grand jury if there were any questions. The woman in the second row raised her hand.

"You have a question, Mrs. Cohen?" LaRosa asked.

"It's nothing to do with the detective's testimony." Nervously the woman glanced around the room. She smiled at several people and they smiled back sympathetically.

"Are there any questions regarding Detective Lerner's testimony?" LaRosa asked, rubbing the back of his neck as if he had a headache. No one moved. The woman remained standing.

"If there are no questions about this case, you can go right ahead, Mrs. Cohen. Stenographer, this is off the record."

Jackie felt a tingling in her stomach. She felt as if she had to pee.

"Aren't you afraid in the street around those animals you deal with?"

Jackie was relieved, it was a typical question.

"Well, it's my job, Mrs. Cohen. If I were afraid, I'd find other employment."

"You are a very brave young lady." Mrs. Cohen's voice wavered. "I, for one, Detective Lerner, as a mother and as a woman, am very proud of you."

"Thank you," Jackie whispered.

"I had a niece. A beautiful young girl. She resembled you very much. She died at fifteen from a drug overdose."

Anger and pain distorted the woman's face. Jackie hoped for Mrs. Cohen's sake that she had the strength to hold together.

"I'm sorry for that young girl, Mrs. Cohen. Believe me, I understand," Jackie said. And with her smile she tried to give the woman strength. The jury room suddenly was still; everyone reached for Mrs. Cohen. Even LaRosa's dull and one-track mind offered support.

"Most people in this city don't know that police like you exist. More people should know. They should be told about policemen and policewomen like you," Mrs. Cohen said, then sat back down.

"Let's keep it our secret," Jackie said softly.

"Well, if there are no further questions, you can leave, Detective Lerner." LaRosa's face was as bright as Jackie had ever remembered seeing it. Maybe the guy does have a brain, she thought; it's a shame his prick gets in its way. As Jackie got up to leave, Mrs. Cohen began to applaud softly. Suddenly the entire grand jury room broke into a rousing round of clapping and cheering. Jackie waved a little-girl goodbye and left the room.

"Fuck you, Sweet Dick," she whispered to herself as she got on the elevator reserved for judges and rode it down to the underground garage. The cheering and applauding rang in her ears, the picture of Mrs. Cohen's tears and unquestioned support eased her conscience and convinced her that it was right to frame the Sweet Dicks of this world.

* * *

[176]

Fred Johnston looked at the calendar Scotch-taped to the wall behind his desk. Well, it wasn't a desk really, it was an old bridge table stained with paint, and it had an ugly tear that cut a diagonal through the material of the tabletop.

It was September 3. Fred took his Magic Marker and carefully began darkening September 2. A year ago today, his wife Millie left him. Friends said that it would take a year for him to recover. A year had passed, his friends were right, he no longer missed Millie, now he wanted to kill her.

Millie took every cent of his six-thousand-dollar bank account and his Plymouth wagon. She left behind Fred, Jr., and a page from a lined yellow pad. Written in block letters were the words "Don't try and find us." Us? Us? The "us" Millie referred to was her soulmate, her new best friend, and *their* mailman. Last he heard, Millie and the mailman were sipping piña coladas near Orlando. Fred Johnston dove headlong into a bottle of scotch and stayed.

Fred had been a New York State court officer for twenty-two of his fifty-four years. His record was good. He was thought to be reliable and honest. But Millie, the mailman, Fred, Jr., and, finally, the scotch shattered him. Before long, Fred was unable to call the court docket, or enter cases in the ledger, or deliver prisoners from the courtroom to the holding areas. He began misplacing them, like cheap pens. No one escaped, but on one lunch break two of Fred's charges took their meal in a judge's chambers. They were discovered smoking his honor's cigars and calling friends and family in Puerto Rico. Fred could have been fired; he could have forfeited his pension rights. He wasn't; everyone knew his story. He received a thirty-day suspension, enabling him to drink for a solid month without interference. Upon his return to work, Fred found himself relegated to guarding judges' cars in the underground garage.

He spent his days reading girlie magazines and daydreaming about his last screw. He had had Millie three months before she skipped. That was fifteen months ago. Fred was horny as hell, but he had another problem that made the rumbling in his balls academic. One night, on the corner of Fourth Avenue and Dean Street, Fred found a twenty-dollar hooker. In the glare of headlights and streetlights, Fred could see tracks of black lines on the veins behind the woman's hands. And scabs covered holes in the crease of her arm. The marks reminded him of Fred, Jr., who had begun to shoot dope, and the hot night and crowded corner brought thoughts of Millie and the mailman in Florida. Fred couldn't get it up. His chest ached, his balls burned, and Fred felt like strangling someone. There had been a time when he was respected, even judges listened to him. Now hookers pointed dirty fingernails at his limp prick and laughed. The judges, they just told him to make sure no one parked in their numbered spots. But someday, Fred thought, someday soon, his flag and prick would rise back up, and he'd be a man again. He'd go find them and kill the mailman outright. Millie he'd torture first.

Once Jackie found out about the bathroom in the underground garage, it became her personal dressing room. The image delighted her. Like Superwoman, she strolled in Little Miss Sweetness, then sauntered out Street Lady. Part of the mystique was the canvas beach bag. In it, she carried the costume of the day and her Colt .25 automatic. Today it was her "I'm here to score quick" outfit: denim cutoffs, a T-shirt, and tennis shoes. The clothes were rolled and tucked into the beach bag, tucked into the roll was her Colt. The smallish gun fit snugly into a clip-on holster and rode at the hollow of her back.

The .25 was a shock gun, a panic gun, a gun that would be all but useless in a fire fight. But it was easily concealed, and in the right hands, deadly accurate at close range. Since 90 percent of police shootings in New York occured within seven feet, she felt secure. Jackie could drill quarters at that range, she knew she could, she'd done it. But then again, as the instructor said, "Quarters ain't coming at you with a knife, or a gun, or a bat." Jackie told him, "Really," then winked and knocked off three more quarters.

The elevator jerked to a stop at the garage landing, the door opened, and Jackie made for her dressing room. She walked with her head down; no need for street eyes down here. She was in the garage at the Brooklyn Supreme Court building; the only people allowed access were judges and cops.

Mrs. Cohen from the grand jury was right; the people of this city should know about cops like me. We're the dark-siders. She smiled to herself. We don't sit back and wait for the snake to take a piece out of us, we crawl into his hole, we lie down with him, stroke him, then rip out his fangs. She loved this job; even if they didn't pay her, she'd do it. There was a full grin on her face as she opened the door to the bathroom. Bye, Sweet Dick, she thought.

Jackie sat on the edge of the commode with her legs crossed, her head bowed, dabbing eyebrow pencil at her forearm. When she heard the knock at the door, she didn't answer. But she came bolt upright when she saw the doorknob turn. She hadn't locked it.

Jackie relaxed when she saw Fred, in his uniform, come through the door. Fred glanced at the black mark on her arm, he stared at her muscular dancer's legs, and at the beach bag from Florida. Jackie smiled, without meaning to, and something in Fred's head went siss-pop.

"Hello," Jackie said, still smiling.

"Don't hello me, bitch," Fred said, glaring at her. Now they were both smiling. Jackie thought he'd mistaken her smile for fear. She wasn't afraid. This guy didn't know what she was, or who she was. And he looked harmless. At best, an amateur come to play with a pro. Show time, she thought. She got up off the toilet seat, then reached down to pick up the beach bag. For a second, she considered flipping out her badge. Then she thought: What for? I didn't do anything wrong.

She'd made a mistake, she wasn't perfect, maybe she wasn't nearly as good as she thought she was. The blow stung her. She'd taken her eyes off him for a split second and he'd hit her.

Her head banged off the tiled wall. She dropped the bag and brought her hands up to her face; he punched again, this time at the back of her head. Her raised hands acted as a cushion, but she bounced off the wall again. She'd never been hit this hard. Then she saw the billy club, and fell to the floor. Fred swung the club wildly, it sailed over her head.

"Bitch—bitch," he wheezed.

"I'm a cop!" she screamed.

Fred didn't hear her. He couldn't over the sound of rockets doing loop-the-loops in his head. He kicked and sent her rolling into the corner. She was more afraid than she ever remembered being. Jackie felt herself drifting, she could barely breathe. She was on her hands and knees. She reached for the chain around her neck for her badge. He kicked her again, lifting her off the floor, slamming her against the tiled wall. She fell into the corner and pulled her knees up. She reached her hand around her back and felt the butt of the automatic.

"I'm gonna fuck you right where you're sitting. I'm gonna fuck you in the ass, you junkie bitch."

Her breath was panicked and shallow; she was shaking, vibrating like a fevered child. She didn't want this man to hurt her anymore. She thought about Mark and she thought about Bobby Porterfield. She wanted to cry, to sob, then maybe this beast would let her be.

"Pig!" Fred screamed, then brought his head back and spit on her.

From somewhere deep inside, like a rush of warm tropical water washing away her chill and soothing her wounds, strength came to Jackie's legs and rage filled her being. I'm a fucking cop, goddamnit. She was a cornered cat with no escape, nowhere to go, other than over her attacker. Then Fred made a mistake. He reach down and opened his fly. His prick flopped out, limp and flaccid. It lay there against his uniform trousers. He looked at Jackie and saw that she had a hand behind her back. He'd hurt her, he knew it, he didn't care. He wanted to kill her. He bent his head to look at his prick. He pulled at it. He rubbed it with both hands. The unmistakable sound of metal riding along metal and the sharp click of a round locked in place brought control back to Jackie. The panic was now on Fred's face. He couldn't believe his eyes. The little junkie broad had reached into her shirt and pulled out a chain necklace. Dangling on the end of that chain was a gold badge. Fred had been a court officer for twenty-three years, he'd seen hundreds of them. A detective's gold badge.

"You're dead," she screamed. But strangely, the power was ebbing from her. She couldn't stop shaking. She knew she had him. She could kill him and get a damn medal. But her hand was shaking, so much so that she was forced to grab the gun with both hands to steady it. In the street, she was world class; the dumbos out there weren't in her league. She'd never been afraid, she was in control of every situation. She'd thought she was immortal. This fat old man, now blubbering out of control across from her, had done her, and done her good. She'd been lucky. Jackie wanted to cry, she wanted to scream, she wanted to run to strong arms. Fred brought his hands up to his face, and when he did, he moved toward her.

"Get on *your* knees, you son of a bitch," she hissed. But Fred had returned from the insane place he'd earlier jumped to and was now drowning in oceans of humiliation, shame, and running rivers of fear.

"I said get on your knees," Jackie yelled again. She shoved the automatic at the mass that was Fred's chest. He was four feet from her, she could put a bullet in the second buttonhole of his shirt. Fred kept coming. Jackie blinked her eyes and drew in as much air as her lungs could hold, then exhaled slowly. There were muffled sobs coming from behind the hands that Fred had brought up to cover his face.

"Get on your fucking knees or you're dead," she howled.

Like a collapsing tree, and without any attempt to break his fall, Fred dropped to his knees. He hit and rolled off to the side, away from Jackie. Then it came, a scream that had been caught in his throat. Jackie braced herself in the corner. Fred's scream continued with heaves and gulps. He got to his feet, then he vomited with such incredible force that he was thrown back.

Assistant District Attorney Frank LaRosa came into the bathroom and gagged. Then he saw Jackie, squatting in the corner with the gun in her hand. He'd seen his share of guns. He saw them in court and in hallways, always carried by cops. But he'd never seen one pointed in fear and anger. When he saw Fred Johnston, the crazy court clerk, he became nauseated. He put his hands over his stomach, took a deep breath, gagged again, and said, "My God, what happened?"

"This son of a bitch attacked me," Jackie said, pointing the gun at Fred, who had rolled himself into a fetal position. "Outside, Mr. LaRosa. The smell is too much." They stood outside the open bathroom door.

"What did you do to him? You didn't shoot him, did you?"

"No, I didn't shoot him. But I should have. I should have shot his damn prick off. You see it, look at it, Mr. LaRosa."

Jackie pointed at Fred's prick with the automatic. Fred covered himself with his hands, rolled into a tighter ball, and began to twitch in spastic convulsions.

"My God!" LaRosa yelled. "The man is having a nervous breakdown, he's throwing a fit."

Jackie said, "Fuck him."

"I know this man, Jackie. Believe me, he's a decent man. He must have . . . lost his mind, or something."

A gurgle came from deep inside Fred, and he whimpered, "I thought she was a junkie. I thought she was shooting up in here."

"And what were you going to do? Handcuff me to your prick, you bastard!" Jackie screamed.

"There's no need for hysterics, Jackie," LaRosa said. "Remember, you're a professional. Clearly this is a case, an unfortunate case, of a monumental misunderstanding.

"Jackie, I know how you must feel. I know Court Officer Johnston. The man should not be working, but he should not be arrested either. He needs medical attention, he needs psychological attention. Jackie, that's a sick man on that floor in there."

"No shit," Jackie said softly.

"Let me take care of this. Let me see to it that Fred Johnston goes some place where he can't hurt anyone, especially himself."

Jackie had had it with Johnston, with LaRosa, and with the fear that came by to play with her and now seemed to be gone.

"Frank, you're the D.A. Do what you think is right," she said. "If it's all right with you, I just want to go home."

"Jackie, do you have any idea what the press would do with this? I mean, can't you see it? Brooklyn court officer assaults and attempts to rape narcotics detective?"

"Fine, Mr. LaRosa, fine. You take care of it. I'm going home." Jackie threw some water on her face and, from the corner of her eye, she could see LaRosa eyeing her.

"And take my advice, kiddo, maybe you shouldn't walk around real people in that outfit. If you know what I mean."

"Goodbye, Mr. LaRosa." Jackie smiled. Then she picked up her beach bag and walked out of the garage. Out into the bright afternoon Brooklyn sun. She wanted to go home, she wanted to be with Mark. And if Mark wasn't home, she'd call Bobby Porterfield. She had to tell someone this story. Now, as she thought about it, she hoped Mark wouldn't be home. She thought about Sweet Dick and felt guilty.

16.

Bobby awoke slowly. Dreams of Chinese dresses stretched tight across apple asses were doing slow turns on the screens of his eyelids.

He looked past the swell of Cathy's hip to the clock on the dresser. It was just past seven. He rolled onto his stomach and discovered he had a glorious erection. It was a pleasant surprise. He exhaled deeply, laid back, and closed his eyes. But a morning tickle, a nice little stirring, continued to haunt him. He reached over and stroked Cathy's hip. After closing his hand on the part of her that jutted from under the sheet, he pulled. Cathy shrugged, wiggled a bit, then said, "Leave me alone."

"Are you up?" he asked softly. She didn't answer. But she moved a millimeter, and put herself a thousand miles from him. He could still reach her, but only with his fingertips. He tapped a greeting on her hip, then moved his hand toward her thigh. Finally, he stopped at a place where he felt nothing but sheet. Retracing his steps, he moved back to her hip and pulled again. He expected Cathy to reach and take hold of him. In ten seconds, he thought, I'll be resting inside her.

"You don't want to?" The questioning tone of his voice made it clear that he did.

"No!" she said sharply. Clearly she meant it.

Bobby was hurt, he felt horny, and he knew she was wide awake. Cathy made a short "mmmmm" sound, and moved to the very edge of the bed.

"There is something bothering you?"

"You're bothering me. You, the sound of your voice bothers me."

At first he was puzzled and embarrassed, then angry. "Oh, that's terrific," he grumbled. "We're in great shape." He rolled out of bed, took his running shorts out of a drawer, sat on the edge of a chair, and began lacing his shoes.

"Where are you going?" Cathy asked.

"Dancing, I'm going dancing."

"Typical, so typical of your smart-ass remarks."

Bobby was angry, confused, and, he knew, though he fought against the realization, afraid. A run along the Brooklyn Heights promenade might help. Cathy hadn't budged an inch. She lay under the tent of the sheet, her back to him.

"Listen, before I go out, you want to tell me what's typical?"

She picked her head up. There was that tight-lipped look again. Maybe this was the battle she was searching for.

"We have a problem," she said with a half smile. "We should talk. But not you, not the good soul, Bobby Porterfield. Bobby, little Bobby doesn't get what he wants, and he's off running." She turned back into the pillow and pulled the sheet over her head.

"Hey, all I wanted to do was to make love to the woman I live with, that's all," he said.

"You didn't want to make love. You wanted to fuck," she spit.

"Excuse me, dear lady," he said, now dancing excitedly around the bed. "But I seem to remember on more than one occasion your mounting me like I was some kind of sleeping dildo."

She mumbled something he couldn't hear, then she turned and sat up. "I don't trust you," Cathy said slowly, distinctly, and with care. From the way she said it, and from the way she looked, Bobby knew he'd better not answer her.

"I sometimes wonder if you're not just a little boy—a long way from being a man. And you know something else? My father feels the same as I do. He thinks I'm too rough on you. My father likes you, Bobby. He said you're doing fine. He also said you are a little boy. You're doing fine, but you're a little boy, my father said; and he thinks I need a man, not a boy."

Bobby dropped down into the chair. He put his elbow on his knee and cupped his chin in his hand. He was grinding his teeth with such ferocity, he swore she could hear him.

"Do you have anything to say? Or are you just going to sit in that chair and vegetate?"

"Not yet," he said, "I have to get my toy soldiers and run down to the park. I'll see you later." He didn't dare say a word.

Bobby walked to the door, opened it slowly, then closed it. He walked down the steps to the street. Little boy, he thought, and began to trot. Soon he picked up the pace and began running at a steady jog. When he got to the promenade, he opened up and began to run full out. Little boy, he thought. When he reached the end of the promenade, instead of turning back he continued to run. He wasn't tired, not even a little cramped. He ran down Montague to Hicks Street, and then made a right, away from Brooklyn Heights. The world sloped toward Atlantic Avenue, and the running came easy. He dodged a truck and he was across the avenue, heading into South Brooklyn. The brownstoned Heights were behind him now, the gray and tan and the soot-colored tenements of Columbia Street lay ahead. There was a slight burning in his chest; he wondered if little boys got heart attacks. He was running south on Columbia Street, past Kane, toward Sackett. The powerful smells of the summer slums filled his head, he began to slow. By the time he reached Union Street, he was walking. He'd run two miles. But two miles full out, and that was all he could ever do. When he turned into Union Street, the sweet, rich smell of fresh-baked pastry and bread cleared his head, and he suddenly felt hungry.

Sweating as though he'd just dismounted from a six-day bike race, Bobby walked into the bakery. The cool air-conditioned shop was a relief. He'd been in Italian bakeries before, but never this early in the day. The fragrance was wondrous. Anise, cinnamon, powdered sugar, and fresh-baked bread. An espresso pot perked somewhere out of sight.

There were two small round tables off to the side. In the center of each was a shiny metal container that held paper napkins. He looked at his reflection in the mirror behind the counter. His face, which he needed to shave only twice a week, was blotched with red. He smiled. With his hair wet and dripping onto his face, he looked like a college sophomore.

"Yeah?" the girl behind the counter asked.

"How much for a loaf of the semolina bread?" he asked, grinning.

"Seven thousand dollars," the girl said, then pointed to a sign on the wall that read: Semolina bread $1.75, all other bread $1.50. Bobby stuck both his hands in this pockets and shook his head.

"Whasamatta, ya faget ya money?" she asked accusingly.

"I have a quarter." Bobby grinned. He held it up and showed it to her.

"So, go home and get a dollar and I'll give ya the bread." She was beautiful, far more beautiful than even she thought.

"C'mon," Bobby said, "I live miles from here. Can't you give me a quarter's worth?" Sometimes, he thought, a little pleading helps. Once you get past the humiliation, pleading comes easy. And when you're hungry, and there's fresh bread, and the smell of fresh espresso, well, he'd plead.

"Whaddaya think we're doing over here, selling used cars?" The girl's eyes were running up and down; when she bent her head to try to see behind him, he gave her his best smile. It worked before, why not now?

"I only have a quarter," he said.

"We don't talk over price here. And we don't sell bread in pieces."

"C'mon, be nice, just cut me a piece of bread."

"You'll choke to death eatin' a chunk of bread, dry like that." Bobby thought he heard a ring of concern in her voice.

"O.K.," he said, widening his grin. "You lend me two dollars. I'll buy the bread from you. Then I'll go across the street and get myself a container of coffee. How's that?"

The girl put her chin down onto her chest, she looked at her fingernails, then glanced up at him, and said, "Go do yourself a favor and take a jog. Gahead, go do whaya gotta do, and take a jog." Turning away from him, she took three loaves of bread from a wicker basket, then neatly stacked them in the display case.

"Pardon me," he said. "Pardon me, can you give me a minute,

please?" The girl folded her arms in front of her. The body language was interesting, Bobby was really getting into this. Then she began sucking on her bottom lip.

"Listen, I have a terrific idea," he said, now trying to make each word count. "I need to borrow two dollars, right?" The girl moved her hands to her hips. Less protective, more open, a bit aggressive; but, then again, at least she looked like she'd listen.

"I need about two dollars, for coffee and bread, right?" The girl nodded.

"I promise I'm not going to steal your two dollars. I'll come back and pay you later. How's that?"

"Yeah, what other tricks you do?" She crossed her arms in front of her and gave him the finger. He couldn't believe it. The pretty little girl gave him the finger.

"Listen, what's your name?" he asked.

"What are you, a cop or somethin'?"

"As a matter of fact, I am a cop. I'm a detective. My name's Porterfield. Now you know I won't steal your two dollars."

The girl threw her head back and laughed, then clapped her hands and laughed some more. "A cop? Hah." She kept on laughing.

Bobby took a seat at the table and ran his fingers through his hair. The girl had her arms folded again. The bakery was empty, not a customer had come in since he'd been there. It was still early, but the street was busy. A few frowning old ladies in black sleeveless dresses, pulling shopping carts, passed by. No one came in, but they all waved to the girl.

"You don't do a whole lot of business here, do you?" he asked. The girl turned and looked at a large double doorway. There was a white cloth curtain, embroidered with red roses, across it. Behind that curtain was a room; the smell of espresso came from that room.

"You dont' look like no cop," she said.

"Yeah, what does a cop look like?" He'd given up. He decided he'd rest for another minute, then head back home. He'd get coffee and a roll in Brooklyn Heights. It wouldn't be as fresh, but he'd live.

"You haven't told me your name," he said softly.

"My name's Phillie."

"How's that?" he asked her.

"It's short for Filomena," she snapped. And shook her head as if he should have been able to figure that out for himself.

"Of course," Bobby said. "How could I be so stupid?"

Phillie walked through the curtain. Bobby could hear conversation in the espresso room. The curtain opened, and out came Phillie, along with a guy that had to be a relative.

"Detective Porterfield, meet my brother Phil." Phil and Phillie, that's cute, he thought.

Phillie's brother Phil, unlike Phillie, was not nearly as beautiful as Phil thought. He did have a spectacular tan. And the tan was a striking contrast to the white Italian knit shirt and cream-colored linen slacks he wore. On every bare spot of his body he wore gold. A watch, a bracelet, three rings, and a chain that clung to his neck. His face was clean-shaven, and his nails flashed with a high gloss. The cologne he wore hung thick and heavy around him. It spoiled the good smell of fresh-baked bread.

"You tell my sister you're a detective?" There was a real nasty edge in his voice. And the cologne he was wearing, as if it were a match, set fire to the fuse of Bobby's temper. Bobby was embarrassed, he felt awkward, he would have liked to excuse himself and leave.

"That's right," he said, "I'm a cop. But I'm not here officially. I was running . . . listen, forget it."

"Yeah, O.K., I'll forget it. But let me tell ya somethin'. I don't believe you're a cop. You don't look like no cop to me. To me you look like a kid; a college kid or somethin', trying to run a game on us. That's what I think."

Bobby told himself to get going, forget this guy, and get going. But even as he was telling himself, he turned around. He'd had it with this kid, little-boy crap. He'd take it from Cathy, even from Mark, but there was no way he'd take it from this character.

"And you know what I think?" Bobby said sharply. "I think you look and smell more like a fuckin' pimp than a baker."

"Hey," Phil said, and turned toward Phillie. "Watch your mouth, my sister's here."

At first Bobby thought that the voice came from a hidden speaker. He heard it clear and full, and Phil and Phillie heard it as well. The voice said, "Philip, you're a fool." They both turned and looked behind them. Bobby didn't see anyone. Then he heard the voice again, and then he looked down and saw the dwarf. The dwarf came out from behind the counter and pushed himself between the brother and sister. He walked right up to Bobby and reached out his hand.

"Don't pay my nephew no mind. He doesn't mean to be rude. He just doesn't know any better. I'm pleased to meet you, Detective Porterfield, my name's Carl Marx Syracusa. You know, we don't normally get policemen coming in here putting the arm on us for a piece of bread and a cup of coffee," the dwarf said.

He was perched on a large red pillow that had been quickly put on his chair by Phillie. He spoke in a soft, patient whisper, and he had bright, intelligent eyes that clung to whomever he spoke to. He wore gold-rimmed granny glasses, and around his neck was a tiny gold cross on a chain, thin as a strand of hair.

His name was Carl Syracusa; the Marx, he said, was added by neighborhood people who found his politics far left. He loved the name and adopted it. It even appeared on his driver's license. Carl Marx had no problem believing Bobby was a detective. He was warm, and friendly, and disarming. Bobby relaxed with him, and they had a great conversation about life and loves, crime and dwarfs.

"I don't know any," Carl Marx said. "I avoid the circus like the plague. Not that all small people are circus performers. But they're the only ones I've seen. Besides, I only leave the neighborhood when I have to. And I almost never have to."

When Bobby asked him what kind of business he was in, Carl Marx told him that he owned the bakery and one or two other small businesses in the neighborhood. Phil and Phillie disappeared behind the curtain.

"So you like being a cop?" Carl Marx asked.

"I love it," Bobby said, returning the little man's smile. He hoped that Phillie hadn't forgotten the second cup of coffee he'd asked for. He looked at his watch. It was getting late. But this conversation was the most fun he'd had in days.

"Love it? How can anyone love being a cop? You like taking white people's liberty away?"

"What do you mean, white people? I put blacks in jail too, you know."

"Yeah, but they don't count."

"Carl Marx, I thought you were a liberal. Are you telling me you're only concerned about the poor white masses? Don't you agree that socialism is color-blind?" Bobby was smiling.

"Sez who?"

"Karl Marx, I suppose." Bobby laughed.

"Oh, that Jew! Naw, I'm a socialist, like Mussolini was."

"Mussolini was a fascist!"

"Same thing," the dwarf said, then climbed down from his chair. "Big government, big police forces, a lot of cops with clubs and guns. The same crap."

"Well, we have big government. And we have big police forces."

"Like I said, the same crap. Cops every place, you can't live your own life."

"Well, Carl Marx," Bobby said, "your reasoning, even though it's wrong, makes absolutely no sense." Bobby laughed and called for Phillie. He needed that other cup of coffee. Carl Marx walked to the door. He asked Bobby to wait while he ran an errand. "I'll only be gone two minutes," he said.

After Carl Marx left the shop, Bobby went to the pay phone on the wall, dropped in his quarter, and called Cathy. There was no answer. He then dialed Mark and Jackie's number. Phillie flew through the curtain.

"Don't use the phone," she said. "You have to ask my uncle before you use the phone."

Bobby continued dialing. Jackie answered. Mark had gone up to Harlem again, but Jackie would meet him later. She said yes, she'd meet him. She'd said it so quickly, and with such enthusiasm, that the sound of her voice excited him.

Carl Marx looked in horror at the sight of Bobby on the

phone. He began yelling and pointing. He kicked one of the display cases so hard Bobby was sure he must have broken his foot.

"I tried to tell him, I swear to God," Phillie said, "but he wouldn't pay attention to me. Don't blame me, Uncle, I swear on Jesus I tried to tell him."

Carl Marx scooted behind the counter and took a knife from a shelf. He then scooted to the table and grabbed a chair. Bobby watched. He wondered what the hoopla was about. Carl Marx put the chair under the wall phone and climbed up. He then cut the cord and threw the receiver across the room.

"Is this your way of telling me you don't like people using your phone, Carl?" he asked.

"My phone's tapped," Carl Marx said. He was sitting on the edge of the chair and he had his arms folded. His little feet were wrapped around the legs of the chair as if he were sitting on a horse.

Bobby didn't know a great deal about wiretapping. He did know that it was all but impossible to legally tap a public phone. And the phone on the wall was a pay phone, it was public. He decided that Carl Marx was fucking crazy.

"What makes you think your phone's tapped?" he asked.

"Like I said, big, out-of-control government. They tap everything and everybody. They've got no reason to tap my phone, but they tap it anyway."

"How do you know?" Bobby asked.

"I hear clicking and zinging, and I get weather forecasts without calling the weather bureau. That's how." Carl Marx's feet were kicking circles in the air in front of him. A fucking lunatic.

"Well, Carl," he said, "I want to thank you for the coffee and for the bread."

"You're the cheapest cop I ever met," Carl Marx said. "Come back again soon."

"But bring money next time," Phillie called from behind the counter. Phil, her brother, was nowhere to be seen. Bobby didn't miss him.

By the time Bobby got back to Brooklyn Heights, he was

walking. When he turned into Willow Street he began to run just in case Cathy was watching.

He ran up the steps of the brownstone and rang the bell. There was no answer and he didn't have the key. He rang the upstairs neighbor and stepped back so the old lady could see him. The door buzzed, he went inside and found the spare key under the mat along with a note from Cathy that said, "Gone out."

As he stepped into the shower he wondered what "gone out" meant. As he toweled himself and looked in the mirror, he wondered what questions he'd ask Jackie. When he slipped on his loafers, he realized that he was thinking more about meeting Jackie than what "gone out" could mean.

17.

The face that looked back at Jackie from the mirror frightened her. Her cheek was discoloring, and though she'd continued to dab face powder on the bruise, it was becoming darker. She finally decided that the more she studied it, the worse it appeared. She slipped back into her sundress, braided her hair, and looked at the clock. She was to meet Bobby in ten minutes. The phone rang.

She lived by her own rules, and her own sense of timing. Jackie Lerner, undercover agent, was not going to answer that phone. But the ringing persisted. O.K., she'd pick it up, but no matter who it was, or what it was about, the call would not stop her from meeting Bobby. She picked up the phone, looked in the mirror, and thought: I panicked. I should have shot the slime. Her failure both humiliated her and filled her with fear.

"I need another ten minutes," Bobby said, "I had a helluva morning."

"Take all the time you need. We have all day; and as far as I'm concerned, all night." There, she'd said it. Jackie held her breath waiting for Mr. Straight's answer. There was a monstrous pause on the other end of the line.

"I'll meet you in a half hour near the deli on Clark Street," Bobby said finally. "How you feeling?"

She'd love to tell him how she felt. She'd love to tell him about the court officer, about LaRosa, and about Sweet Dick.

"I feel terrific," she lied.

"Good, I need you," he whispered.

"I know, I know you do, Bobby."

Jackie hung up the phone. After she had gone through the closet for the third time, and opened and closed her dresser drawer as often, she sat on the edge of the bed and plotted.

Bobby waited in the car while Jackie picked up sandwiches and beer at the deli. It was a crystal-clear day. The kind of day New York City is blessed with in late summer and early fall. The kind of day that gives birth to memories. As Bobby looked around at the people walking in the street, he had a sense that they all seemed comfortably alive. He, too, felt the surge of excitement that comes when endings roll into new beginnings.

He glanced at the pictures in the folder for the hundredth time. The Chief, with his arms around Paddy Sheridan and that guy Salvatore Victoria, smiled at him. "This is the bureau, we're not dealing with traffic summonses here," that's what Sheridan had said when they visited Captain Burke's brother in Jersey. You're damned right, Paddy, he thought, this is murder, cold-blooded premeditated murder. Bobby's eyes fell on the smiling face of Frank Moresco. Burke was smiling too, and Dolan wore his usual sneer. Bobby let his eyes drift back to Moresco. "I want to know why you killed yourself, Frank. Why a second bullet in your head?" He ran the tips of his fingers across Moresco's face. "Why?" he shouted.

"Why, what?" Jackie said, getting into the car.

"I'll tell you later."

Jackie had a soft, curious smile on her face as Bobby moved the department car out from the curb into traffic.

He parked a block from the Brooklyn Heights promenade and took Jackie's hand. Why was she nervous? he wondered. Her hand was wet and she kept asking to see what he had in the folder. They walked to a magnificent overlook of the river and lower Manhattan. Jackie wanted to talk, and though she continued to tug at the folder, Bobby wasn't ready to get into it just yet. He wanted to enjoy his sandwich, sip his beer, and get off on the world's greatest city. He never tired of this view. Jackie stopped her tugging attack and made herself comfortable next to him on a bench.

"Did I ruin your suit with my beer shower the other night?" she asked.

"Oh, hell no. A good cleaner will get it out." Cathy swore the suit was totally ruined. She wanted to tell Jackie to buy him a new one. "The dumb little bitch," she had called her.

"Jesus, I thought Cathy was going to go into orbit. She really looked pissed."

"She was." Bobby smiled.

"Was she really? Was she really pissed?" Jackie's eyes were wide open and her face was at the same time intense and full of childish glee.

"What's so funny?" he asked. Jackie began to laugh and when she laughed she placed her hand over her mouth so as not to shower him with beer a second time. Bobby put his beer down, the shocked expression on Cathy's face as Jackie gushed beer at the Japanese restaurant flashed back. He joined Jackie in a great laugh, a rousing, roaring, friendly hysteria.

Jackie was still laughing when Bobby moved to the promenade railing. Looking down at Pier 3, he watched for a moment as the freighter *Calle* was being off-loaded. He then looked across the river to the Battery, the World Trade Center, and finally let his eyes drift north to the Manhattan side of the Brooklyn Bridge.

What a magnificent city, he thought, I'm a New York City policeman, a detective, and I feel like an alien. This city has so many faces, so many hearts. The place was a mystery to him. Like a schizophrenic lover, it made him nuts.

He felt Jackie's hand on his shoulder. When he turned, they were so close that her breath splashed off him like a wave against a sea wall.

"You're crying," she said. The fresh breeze rolling up from the river had blown dust from the Brooklyn–Queens Expressway, irritating his eyes, causing them to tear.

"I'm not crying." He laughed. Jackie's hand felt good as she ran it across his cheek. Reminding himself that this was Mark's woman didn't help. He felt an unbearable urge to hold her, to pull her close, so he did. And Jackie responded. She melted into him. He wasn't surprised at how much he enjoyed touching her.

"Ya gotta help me with this, Jackie," Bobby said, slapping the side of the case folder he held. "Ya just gotta."

"Gotta? That's great, two years a cop and four years of college go down the tubes."

"Hey, lady, the last thing I need now is another critic," Bobby said cheerily.

Slowly she moved away from him. The look on her face was familiar, too familiar.

"I'm tired of this patronizing crap," he said. "I get it from the Chief, from Cathy, and even from Mark. I don't need it from you, too, hotshot."

"I'm not such a hotshot," she said with a sad smile.

He reached a hand to the back of her head and pulled her close to him again. She kissed his cheek, turned away, and went back to the bench.

"O.K., Mr. Straight, what gremlins are dancing in that clean-cut head of yours?" As she sat down, Jackie crossed her legs, causing the dress she was wearing to ride up way above her knee. It was Jackie's childlike manner, caught in the most sensual body, that was her claim to beauty. And that body promised hours of pleasure. He toyed with the fantasy. If there was no Cathy for him and no Mark for her . . .

He was thinking that Jackie was tempting him. That smile she showed him now was not a smile between friends. He wondered if she could tell that he was receiving all her signals. But Jackie was an undercover agent, she possessed a finely tuned knowledge of body language. Breaks in voice tone were telling insights and he was having a little trouble breathing. Jackie was rubbing her leg with one hand and her neck with the other. "God, I could use a rubdown," she moaned.

He kept still.

"Bobby, you're so damn good," she said.

"No, I'm not," he said, annoyed at the tone of her voice.

"Oh yes, you are. You should have been a priest or a damn social worker. You weren't meant to be a cop, Bobby. You were a fool for allowing White Bread to talk you into taking this job."

"Look, Jackie, I like this job. Cathy and me, well, I don't really know what's happening with us. I think it's this investigation, it's making me crazy. I've had a crash course in police corruption over the past few days and I gotta tell ya it surprised me, even shocked me."

"Stop being so judgmental and you won't be so shocked," she said with a smile that made him laugh.

"I'm not so straight and I'm not judgmental."

Jackie reached into her bag and came out with a tightly rolled marijuana cigarette. He looked at it, then quickly pulled it from her hand and threw it away. Then he turned to see if anyone was watching. The Brooklyn Heights promenade on a sunny day, at the noon hour, draws many strollers, and cops from the Internal Affairs Division were known to take their lunch there. Their office, located in an old station house right around the corner on Poplar Street, was near enough to give Bobby the horrors. When he mentioned this to Jackie, he got a silly smile for a response.

"You know Doyle's people were crooks, don't you?" he asked. "That's why you damn near choked to death the other night when I made a fool of myself with that dumb little speech."

"Bobby, how would I know if they're crooks, and who cares anyway?" she said softly.

"I care," he said. "Look at this photograph." Bobby reached into the folder he was carrying, then like a lawyer displaying his most damning evidence, he handed her the photo. Jackie took it, but turned it face down.

"Before I look at your big-time evidence, I want to ask you something. Are you some kind of spy for IAD?"

He couldn't tell if she was joking. She sat there tight-jawed, her black eyes trying to read every move, her street sense listening for some tip, some clue. What a weird lady, Bobby thought.

"Oh, you are a real genius. You ask me if I'm a spy for IAD after you show me a joint. Go to hell, Jackie, I'm no spy."

"Then why all this mystery? What's the big deal?"

"Just look at the photograph and tell me what you think."

Jackie glanced at the picture, turned to Bobby, then glanced at the photograph a second time.

"So you've found an old photograph of a bunch of people that we know," she said, handing the photo back to him.

"How old do you think that picture is?" he asked.

"I don't know. Ten years maybe."

"Ten years exactly. And here, read the news copy that accompanied the picture."

Jackie took the copy of the *Daily News* story, skimmed it, then handed it back.

"Doyle was the commanding officer of a group of cops that made a big arrest in Harlem, so what?"

"Doyle wasn't the commanding officer of that particular squad. Burke was. Doyle was the C.O. of the division that the squad worked in."

"So," she said, throwing her cigarette down, searching her bag for another one, finding it and lighting up.

"So! Everyone in that photograph is dead, Jackie, except the Chief and Paddy Sheridan."

"Who is this greasy-looking character next to Doyle?" she asked, tapping the photo with her finger.

"A retired guy by the name of Salvatore Victoria."

"What about him?" She smiled.

"Someone shot the shit out of him two days ago in Miami."

Now she was paying attention. The fear he had felt over the past two days he could see growing in her.

"You're in a big jam, you know that, don't you?" she said, frowning. "This case is a real nightmare."

"Jackie, so you know where I stand, I don't care who is responsible for these murders. I'm going to get him."

She raised her eyes skyward like a parent who'd been asked an unreasonable question. "Doyle's a crazy son of a bitch, but I doubt if he's a killer, Bobby."

He didn't answer her, but smiled instead, then shook his head.

Jackie peered out over the river. After a while she turned back to him. "What is it you want from me?"

"Jackie, I read everything there was to read at the library about the Roxbury Commission. There's no doubt Doyle and his crew were involved in some gambling corruption. But I have a feeling you know more than what was in those clippings."

"Some!" She laughed.

"So you do know something?"

"Bobby, I'm an undercover officer. I look up from the street at the police. I know what's going on out there now, and I know what went on ten years ago. But I'm not as smug as you. I don't make judgments."

"I'm not smug, Jackie, I just know the difference between right and wrong. When a cop is bad, he's bad. He's liable to do anything to protect himself. Even murder."

"Is that what you think?" she said, taking a nervous drag on her cigarette.

Bobby shook his head. "Yeah, that's what I think. And let me tell you something else. These guys in this picture were more than just crooked cops, they were bagmen. Each one was hand-picked by Doyle. Just look at their careers and their relationship with the Chief. These were his special people. Liars, cheats, crooks, the whole nine yards. And now a few years later somebody is killing them. It's connected, all right, these deaths are all connected. And I think there may even be more we don't know about."

Jackie began waving both her hands in the air. "Stop, stop. What are you saying? I don't think you know what the hell you're talking about. There's over a hundred officers in a division gambling unit. You think someone is out to kill a hundred cops?"

"No, just the bagmen."

"Have you talked to Mark about this? I can't believe he didn't try to straighten you out," she said.

"Mark has seventeen years in. He's not about to take a swing at a windmill, best friend or no best friend. I understand that."

"Oh, that's big of you. How about Cathy? Have you told White Bread you know her father was a crook? Have you said your daddy may be a killer? Did you sit down over morning juice and vitamins and fucking Ovaltine and tell her, dear, I'm going to do my best to put your daddy in the slammer."

"I'll deal with Cathy when the time comes."

"Fine, you'll deal with her when the time comes, terrific. I think Cathy can take a joke as well as the next puritan. Make sure you call me before you tell her; I want to be there," she said, moving off the bench and walking to the promenade railing. She was far more tense and upset than Bobby thought she would be. He needed her help and he assumed that when she found out what he and Mark were up against she'd want to help. He was saving his most important piece of information till last. Now looking at her, seeing how anxious she was, he was having second thoughts. He wasn't sure if he should confide in her. Lighting a cigarette, she turned away from the railing and sat down beside him again.

"Jackie, why are you so upset? This case is Mark's and my responsibility. I didn't ask you to join us . . . yet."

"True enough. But I'm afraid that you're losing sight of what you're doing. You're turning this murder investigation into some sort of exposé or something. This department has had enough dirt thrown on it over the past ten years. Too many good people get hurt in those things, Bobby. And in case you don't already know, I happen to love both you and Mark. There are people in this department that would squash you two like a pair of bugs if you bring up this old shit."

Bobby took hold of one of her braids and flipped it. "Not so old," he said. "You know the D.A. in Manhattan has resigned?"

"I heard."

"Did you also hear that the mayor is going to appoint Roxbury as interim D.A. till the next election? And Roxbury said that he has some ten-year-old unfinished business that he's going to make his priority. Did you hear that, too?"

"No, no, I didn't hear that."

"Well, I did. I have inside information. I have a friend that's working part-time at the D.A.'s office while she goes to law school."

"Cathy? Cathy told you that that cop-hating wimp Roxbury is gonna be appointed D.A.?"

"Yup."

"Ya think she told her father?"

"Of course."

"Shit."

"My feelings exactly. Put yourself in Doyle's position. He's the chief inspector. Ten years ago, when he was only a deputy inspector, he escaped being jammed up by the skin of his teeth. Now ten years later, with a lot more to lose, somebody is going to turn over that rock again. Then think of who it is that could hurt him. Who was on the inside of that gambling unit? Then look at this picture again, and tell *me* what you think."

"Christ, Bobby, does this get any better?"

"No, it gets worse. Cathy told me she told her father about the Roxbury appointment five weeks ago. You know how long ago Moresco killed himself?"

"Don't tell me."

"O.K., I won't, but your guess is right on."

"Shit."

"That's the second time you said that."

Jackie reached her hands to Bobby's cheeks and pulled him toward her. "Considering the circumstances, you might think this is a hell of a thing to say, but I don't care what the likes of Roxbury think. I'm more concerned about what it is that you think," she said, kissing his forehead.

"What I think about what?"

"In one way we're all friends, aren't we?"

"Who?"

"Cops." Jackie said "cops" in a gentle, loving way. A way Bobby had never heard the word pronounced before, the way a lover would. She said "cops" the way one would say, "I love you, you can't leave me." From her lips it was a beautiful word and at the same time terribly soulful.

"What do you think of cops who do things they shouldn't? Who, in some cases, commit crimes?" It was obvious to Bobby that Jackie needed some reassurance. She had sad and beautiful eyes, and at this moment they were pleading. But he was what he was, he was not a phony, he'd be honest with her.

"You and I know cops commit small crimes all the time," he said.

She was smiling at him in that patronizing way again. The way the Chief smiled at him, the way Cathy smiled at him, the way Mark had smiled at him the night before.

"Jackie, I don't mean lying about a speeder or taking a free meal—all crap; you and I know that. It's the other things. The things that scream out, 'This is wrong, this is criminal.' The 'I've crossed over, I'm one of them now.' That's what I'm talking about. Outright criminality."

He was sounding more and more like Burke's brother, he knew it, but he also knew that the big red-headed man in Jersey was right. There's right and wrong, there's good and there's evil. The gray area existed only for those cops who needed to rationalize behavior that on the face of it was criminal. The explanations were all bullshit, he knew that, and so did Jackie. The reports and testimony he'd read over the past two days described organized criminality, nothing less. And Doyle, Burke, Sheridan, and the whole crew were involved right up to their blue eyes.

Jackie turned away from him for a moment, then spun her head back. "O.K., Bobby, but don't you think that there are times when a cop makes a mistake, does something he shouldn't? That doesn't make him a criminal, does it?"

"C'mon, Jackie, that's not what I'm saying. I'm talking about taking money, *framing innocent people,* beating the shit out of someone because your wife or your girlfriend is making you crazy."

"It must be terrific to be as secure as you are, Bobby," she said.

Bobby stared sadly into that beautiful childlike face of hers. He wanted to share whatever it was that was passing through her. A dark cloud had entered Jackie, and its shadow covered her face. Then suddenly she was smiling, the cloud passed, and for the first time Bobby noticed the welt rising on Jackie's cheek.

She noticed that he was looking and turned away. He put his hand on her shoulder, but she pulled free.

"What the hell happened to you?" he asked.

Gently he took hold of her chin and turned her jaw toward him. It was worse than he had thought.

"I'll tell you about it later," she said, and moved a step back.

He wouldn't let go. And he was holding her tightly, too tightly.

She yelped and said, "O.K., O.K., let go of me."

She tried pushing him off. She put her hand on his chest and gave a halfhearted shove. She wanted him to hold her, to touch her, still she pushed him away.

"Listen, hotshot, I want to know what happened to you," he

said angrily. "Your face is swollen. Christ, Jackie, your whole cheek is black and blue!"

It didn't seem possible to him that someone could hurt her like that. Bobby held the notion that people he cared about were somehow immune. True, the danger was always there to really get hurt. But it just didn't happen in his world. He took hold of her head with both hands and studied her face. There were other marks and bruises.

He felt disgusted, then furious, and suddenly he was filled with rage. All this anger he focused on himself. He sat down heavily on the bench and dropped his head into his hands. He had been going on and on about this damned investigation, and all the while Jackie was sitting near him. He was, in fact, looking at her. Still, he saw nothing. He hadn't noticed a black-and-blue mark the size of a silver dollar right below her eye. Only his own grief concerned him. He'd behaved . . . just like a kid. Jackie sat down near him on the bench and blew softly on the hands that covered his face.

"I'm sorry, Jackie," he said. She put her head on his shoulder. He tucked her in, with his hand he held her close.

"Why?" she whispered. "Why are you sorry? You didn't hit me."

"I'm so into my own head, I didn't even see that you were hurt."

"Do you want to know what hapepned to me?" she asked.

"Of course."

"Fine, I'll tell you all about it. But not here. Not in the city."

She took his hands and held them to her breasts. It was like touching her through a nightgown. Jackie never wore a bra.

"O.K., then, let's pretend the rest of this day is a fantasy. Let's play," she said, getting up from the bench and pulling him to his feet. "Let's go off into the country. There's an inn. It has rooms that overlook the sound. You know I want you. You've known I wanted you for a long time. Let's go, you and me. Let's go play."

Jackie dropped her hands to his waist and pulled him to her. He almost lost his balance.

"You forget this investigation for a while and I'll try and forget my bruises."

"Oh, I really want you." He knew it was a terrible thing to say. But that's how he felt. And she was right. They'd been playing with each other for a long time. And he did need time away from this case.

"I really *do* want you," he said.

"I know, I can tell." She smiled, and raised her knee gently up between his legs.

"But what about tomorrow, Jackie? What happens tomorrow when . . . ?" Jackie's smile stopped him.

"Life for me, Bobby, is timeless. Tomorrow is just too far off for me to worry about. Let's do this for us. For you and me. We owe this to ourselves."

He felt her hand slide from his waist and take hold of a cheek of his ass.

"I'm gonna tell ya something," Jackie said, "we deserve it." Her words put speed in his blood. He bent and put the folders he was carrying in Jackie's beach bag, took a deep breath, then grabbed hold of her hand. It was a tiny little girl's hand. He smiled at her and they both began running toward the police cruiser.

18.

Mark knew he had better get off the street, and quick. Black or white, in Harlem it didn't matter. A stranger on a high-crime block was either a victim or a cop. And Mark didn't look like he'd be anyone's victim.

Moving like he belonged, he slipped into the corner building on 116th and First Avenue. The street door and the interior door were both open. Without looking behind him he hurried through the hallway. At the door leading to the back yard he stopped and looked at his watch. It was four o'clock; he was already late. He moved down the steps into the yard and the smell hit him, heavy and thick, foul and familiar. He knew the building, he'd been here before. Nothing had changed. It smelled the same. The yard was piled with the biggest mountain of crap he'd seen in years. No, he didn't miss Harlem. He could do without this shit. About a thousand wine bottles and a refrigerator that looked like it had been thrown from the roof filled one corner of the yard. Plastic and paper garbage bags were stacked as high as the rear fence. Thinking about what must be a herd of overweight rats living under the mess, Mark gingerly stepped on the garbage pile, then clambered over the fence. He started into a cavernous passageway under the tenements of 117th Street. He was aware of every sound and smell around him. This was not an alien place, this was his boyhood play-ground. And in those days he didn't have a gun, just Keds on feet that could move like the wind. But Mark Spencer didn't run away from too many things, never from another man.

Once in the building on 117th Street, he took the stairs two at a time, heading for the roof. One flight below the landing he smelled the candle and heard the moans of junkie pleasure. He moved quickly up the last flight of stairs.

Three junkies, two already off and wandering, sat up against the landing wall. Like schoolchildren at nap time, they sat, their heads cradled in arms with collapsed veins. The third sat near the candle, a belt in his teeth, his cooker over the fire. They barely looked at him as he went to the roof door and pulled the hook latch free.

The swift spring snap of a blade cracked like a rifle shot.

"If any of you fuckers wanna die, *go for it.*" There wasn't a sound. He was out, over the roof, and into the next building. He felt marvelous, he wasn't even breathing hard, he was in great shape. He thought about Jackie and the amount of cigarettes she smoked. When he knocked on apartment 14B, a quick, hoarse "Who?" came through the door.

"It's me, Mark."

"Who?"

"Trunk, will you open the fuckin' door, man. This place is crawling with junkies. I could get hurt out here."

"Ah, excuse me," Jackie said, "but I've been waiting a long time for you. I'd prefer that when the time comes, I'll have you all in one piece."

Bobby was certain that if a word passed between them this spell somehow would be broken. The sound of either or both their voices would be enough for them to change their minds. He was running full out now, he didn't want that to happen. So he sat still and quiet behind the wheel, and did some serious driving. But the concern in Jackie's voice forced him to glance at the speedometer. He was ripping off a solid eighty-five. "Oh, shit," he said, then slowed to seventy.

Something had to go wrong. This was too good. He'd managed to block his mind, to focus only on Jackie and nothing else. And strangely, up to this very moment, there was no guilt. It was as if this was totally out of his hands. Nature had taken urgent command. Then he remembered he had no more than twenty-five dollars with him. An inn on Long Island would have to be twice that. He slowed and pulled the cruiser off the highway to the shoulder.

"What are you doing?" she asked. There was that panic again, she could feel it. Like this morning, she squirmed, then he said quickly, "Jackie, I'm embarrassed. I don't think"—he paused —"I don't think I have enough money."

What a relief, she thought. "Just drive this car, Bobby. Nothing is going to spoil our game. I have money, and I have a credit card. What I have little of, is patience. If you don't want me to be all over you right here, step on it. You go north at the next exit. At most we're fifteen minutes away."

The cruiser kicked stones back fifty yards as Bobby flew into the traffic lane. Jackie was sure she'd just imagined it, but it seemed another column of dust lay still in the air on the shoulder of the road behind them. It was a fleeting thought, a street hint, that she paid no attention to. Then again, why should she? They weren't doing anything wrong.

How to talk to Trunk was a problem. On the one hand, Mark had known him since they were kids. They both came up on the same ghetto street. One became a cop, the other famous throughout Harlem for being everything but. There was mutual respect, but no love. Growing up, they gave each other plenty of room. Everyone on the block had waited for the day the two of them would go round and round. They knew it, and that was precisely why it never happened. "He's the baddest motherfucker north of Ninety-sixth Street"; that's what everyone said. They said it about both of them. Odd thing was, no one had ever seen either of them fight. True, they saw Trunk take a billy club from a cop once and break it over his knee. And there was the time Mark lifted Trunk over his head, just playing, just fooling. "The man picked him up like Trunk was Sammy Davis. The dude is Sonny Liston's twin and dat dude Mark Spencer from over on the 117th picked him up like he wuz da Jolly Green Giant fucking with one o' dem little pea motherfuckers."

"Still buying your clothes at the Monster Man shop?" Mark said, grabbing Trunk's hand and smiling.

A patient grin crossed Trunk's face and sort of a laugh came from his throat. "You still dressing like you some kinda faggot college boy? You big-time police, you da man, you steal legal. All that cash and you buy trash threads."

"Good to see ya still got a sense of humor, Trunk, rich as you are. Ya know what they say about people with bucks. The tax man, he takes their smile along with everything else."

"I don't pay no taxes."

"No shit. I never would have guessed."

"You come up here ta take some a my money? Is that what you want, cop?" Trunk leaned back in the kitchen chair. "The cop wants ta cop some o' my bread, that figures." Trunk was smiling; he was coming on big, tough, and bad, but he was smiling.

"Good buddy, if I wanted some a your money I'd just come and take it," Mark said softly, matching Trunk's grin with one of his own.

Trunk raised his eyebrows casually and then turned and opened the refrigerator. "Ya wanna beer?"

"Sure. Can I sit down?"

"Man, you can fuckin' move in for all I give a shit. I don't live here."

The apartment smelled like a slum, but that was not the fault of the tenant. The building was ninety years old and wet with rot. Through the open kitchen window Mark heard the whoosh, then saw a bag of garbage sail past. It crashed against other garbage bags that had found a home in the rear yard. The apartment itself was clean with scrubbed linoleum floors. A pink Formica table and four pink kitchen chairs with matching pink plastic cushions were in the exact center of the tiny room. Mark hadn't been past the kitchen, but he knew that this was a single working woman's flat. Probably one of Trunk's score of aunts. Women who lived alone most of the time. Every so often a guy would show up and stay for a while, like a stray cat, live off the woman for a week or less, then move on to the next block. That's how he remembered it, men coming and going, never staying.

"Who lives here, Trunk?"

"My aunt Lorraine. She cleans office buildings somewhere downtown."

"Any kids?" Mark was sure there were kids, but none at home. This was a woman alone's apartment. The woman had the biggest print of Jack Kennedy he'd ever seen outside a public building. It hung droopy and sad from over the sink.

"She has five. None of them here, though. Two of 'em up in the Bronx and two in Brooklyn." Trunk didn't mention where the fifth was. And Mark didn't ask.

"Your buddy, the stool pigeon Pee Wee, told someone you hadda see me. So whaddaya want?"

"Trunk, I want some information."

Trunk stared impassively into Mark's eyes. He was about to say absolutely nothing.

"I want to know the last time you saw the captain from downtown. You know, Captain Burke?"

"Wha the fuck you talkin' about? Captain from downtown. Whaddaya doin,' takin' dope or somethin'? How am I suppose to know about some downtown Captain Burke?"

"I worked for the man for ten years, Trunk. I know where he went whenever he got high. And he was high last Thursday."

Trunk had a blank look on his face. "So you don't know a police captain named Burke, is that what my boyhood friend is telling me?" Mark said, sounding a little disgusted.

"Your boyhood shit, Mark. You and me, we ain't never been tight. You always thought you wuz too good to be tight with me."

"Well, I guess I have to go and get myself a warrant and go over to the princess's house and break down that big ugly fuckin' door. Is that what you want me to do, Trunk? Cuz if that's what I have to do, then that's what I'm gonna do. Understand what I mean, bodyguard?"

"You'll have to walk over me to do it, nigger."

"I won't walk over you, bodyguard, I'll dance over you. What do you think this is, some kinda street shit? I'll come through that door with fifty cops, man, and take everything apart, including you—nigger."

Mark had enough of Trunk's bad-man act. He got up from the table and pointed a finger right up against Trunk's nose. Trunk blinked once but he wasn't backing down.

"Don't talk that Dodge City cop shit to me. You uptown

now, my man, and that badge you got ain't no fuckin' magic carpet. It can be a long way downtown, college boy."

"Come on, Trunk, talk straight to me. I got a feeling the fuck what killed Burke ain't a friend of yours either."

Trunk finished his beer and lit a long, thin black cigarette.

"I gotta make a call first," Trunk said, and got up from the chair. Mark had forgotten how big Trunk was, six six, two ninety-five. Mark thought: The first place I'd hit this mother would be in the Adam's apple, but I'd need a hammer for it to do any good.

Bobby turned to Jackie and found her watching him. The sign he just passed said Cold Spring Harbor, one mile. She had undone her braids and now the wind through the open car window was billowing her hair up and over the seat. Mark was his best friend. He took another deep breath.

Bobby pulled the car in at the Cold Spring Harbor Inn, turned off the engine, then tried to get out of the door. He couldn't budge, couldn't move. He felt as though his feet were nailed to the floorboards. Jackie opened the passenger door and as straight as you please walked around the front of the car and now stood waving to him. Then, as if walking into a dream, he walked up to the desk clerk and asked for a double room. "With a king-sized bed," he was quick to add.

"We don't have double rooms with king-sized beds. This is a country inn, not the Holiday Inn."

Terrific, just what he needed, a smart-ass desk clerk. The guy probably was an off-duty cop moonlighting as a clerk. He probably knew Jackie, every cop in the state knew Jackie. Her picture, in uniform, appeared on the cover of a national magazine not long ago. Inside the magazine there were pictures of her in an evening gown. The article was great, too. Wonder Woman, they called her. Narcotics detectives called her stupid for allowing her picture to be published. Her bosses went batshit, and Jackie made a hundred more junk buys that month. Shutting everyone up. Numbers. Give the department arrest numbers and you could pirouette naked in front of St. Patrick's. Don't give out summonses and they'll fire you for too much facial hair and wearing white socks on duty.

"Just give us a room with a bed," Jackie said as she slid her credit card to the clerk. "This is going to be on me." She smiled a smile that sent a shiver up Bobby's back, over his shoulder, and right down to a place about four inches below his belly button.

Trunk put down the receiver, lit another of his giant cigarettes, then walked back to the pink kitchen table. Pointing back at the telephone with his thumb, he said, "That woman is the best there is, Mark. How she let herself get wrapped up with the man the way she was, twists my head. The dude was a fat bust-out nothin'. And that princess of a lady, man, she loved that heavy mother."

"Nobody loves like a hooker, Trunk, you should know that," Mark said as Trunk slumped into a chair opposite him.

"She ain't no hooker, don't call her no hooker, man."

"O.K., she's a philanthropist."

"And don't call her none a dem college fuckin' curse words either, man, or I'll get back into my attitude bag and maybe bust your fuckin' head. Ya dig?"

"I'm sorry, I really am. I don't even know the lady."

"Right, you don't know the lady"—Trunk spoke in a low voice—"and if I got anything to say about it you never will. Dat woman ain't never had nothing but grief from you cops."

If not for some cops, that woman would have been in the can a long, long time ago, Mark thought. But leave it alone, he wanted Trunk's help. Mark smiled and nodded, then got up from the table and straightened the Kennedy print.

"The captain came up to the house Thursday night, is that true?" Mark asked.

"Yeah, he came up Thursday, he used ta roll in once a month or so."

"Was the princess still laying bread on him?"

"Fuck you."

"Well, that's an answer, I guess. Tell me, did you see him leave Thursday?"

"I saw him die, bro, and I saw the motherfucker what did it."

A charged silence filled the room. Mark turned from the print. "You saw what?" A wild hope soared in him. Was he going to find out who the killer was this easy? Could he get that lucky? He was trying almost desperately to remain calm.

"The man was blasted right out in front of our spot, Mark. And I mean blasted, that motherfucker hit him 'bout fifty miles an hour, turned around, and did him again. I seen the whole thing. He ran right up on the curb to get him the second time. Then my lady, she cleans him up and tells me to put him down in the park and call ya all. I damn near got snatched by one a your fool cops in a jeep. The man came outta nowhere, scared the shit outta me."

"You telling me you saw the driver of the car?"

"I'm telling you I seen the car, I seen dat da dude were white and had black curly hair. I ain't never seen his face, Mark. No, I ain't never seen his face. But I get that mother I'm gonna tear it off. He ain't gonna have no face, I get him. Doin' a damn police captain right in fronta our spot. Dumb motherfucker."

"What kinda car was it?"

"It was an old silver Buick, a big mother, one a dem old ones with the, ya know, with the bullet taillights. I don't know what year it is, but it's real old."

"Yeah, yeah!" Mark said.

"Yeah, a real old piece a shit. But it'd hit ya like a damn tank if it hit ya, man, and it sure hit your captain."

Mark believed he knew whose car it was, and now genuine fear was beginning to play billiards in his stomach. Unless he was mistaken, which he was sure he was not, there had to be either a ghost driving or someone who had access to a dead man's car. Someone with black curly hair, one crazy son of a bitch. Mark smiled at Trunk, and Trunk smiled back.

"Ya know who it is, don't ya?" Trunk said, and Mark's smile faded. "Looks like I just gave the baddest cop in Harlem a case a da shits. What you so tense about, man? You look real unhappy."

"There ain't a whole lot to be happy about, ya know what I mean, friend?" And there wasn't, *a cop killing cops.*

Trunk took the cigarette out of his mouth and held it under the kitchen faucet, then he threw it dartlike across the room. It landed with a plunk in a plastic-lined trash pail. "This is a true-life police story, ain't it, Mark? That fucker was a cop, wasn't he? And it look like he got you scared, too. C'mon, I don't like seeing you scared. Fuck this guy, Mark. Just tell me where I can find the chump and I'll throw his ass off a bridge."

"Tell ya what, Trunk, that ain't the worst idea you ever had." Mark knew that he had tiptoed around the edge longer than he should have expected to. Now he was sliding, with nothing to grab on to. Taken by itself, Burke's killing made no sense at all. But joined together with the others, just like Bobby said, there was a pattern. But what Bobby didn't know, he, too, was a piece of that pattern.

The more he thought about it, the more he knew his clear-headed partner had come close. Bobby Porterfield, he thought, was wrong, but he sure came close.

Mark managed a smile, which he focused on Trunk.

"Ya know, man," Trunk said, "it's sad you and me ain't been closer over these years." Trunk spoke in a voice as soft as the look on his face was hard. Then he giggled. "You coulda made me your deputy or something. And I coulda made you rich, college boy."

Trunk reached into his jacket and took out a leather-bound red book. He slapped it on the table once, then handed it to Mark.

"What's this?" Mark asked.

"You went to college, you tell me."

Mark turned back the cover and looked at the first page, and said, "Holy shit."

It was the old Sixth Division pad, complete with dates, amounts, and initials. It was a passport-sized book and it was a ticket to prison for a lot of people he knew. This just gets worse. He couldn't believe it, this case just kept on getting worse.

"Where did you get this?" he asked.

"Where you think? The princess, of course. I'm tellin' you, she loved that dude. She thinks that whoever wasted him is in that book. She wants to see the dude dropped as bad as you do. Maybe even more than you do."

"Trunk, do me a favor, will ya?"

"Name it."

"I want you to mail this book to me at this address." Mark wrote his address on a piece of paper and gave it to Trunk. "I don't want to be walking around with this. And it looks like I'm gonna have a busy night."

"Done," Trunk said. "I'll drop it in the mail tonight."

Making ready to leave the apartment, Trunk took Mark's hand. He held it an extra moment, then paused at the doorway. "You can lay here as long as you need to. My aunt's staying with her daughter in the Bronx tonight."

Mark told him that he needed to make one or two calls. Then he would leave. "Thanks a lot, friend." Mark smiled.

Trunk lowered his gaze. "Remember what I said, my man, tell me where I can find this guy and I'll splash him for ya."

Lifting both his hands to Trunk's shoulders, Mark squeezed and could feel the strength of the man. But there was a softness in his face, a softness that Mark remembered from childhood. There was a madness in Trunk, that was for sure. But there was kindness, too, a need to be liked, and a gentleness. As with so many things in Harlem, a sad song played at his center, but boundless strength lived there as well. Mark knew what Trunk was saying with his handshake; it was a connection that sprang from alleyways, rooftops, and basements, and corners jammed with people who smiled more often than they had reason to. And it wasn't false; "they fuck with you, my man, they gonna have to fuck with me, too." That's what his handshake said, and Mark tried to say thank you with a full grin. Then he said, "The man that killed my captain is not in this book, but tell her thanks anyway."

"Don't forget to slam the door when you go," Trunk called back. He stopped for a second and lit another cigarette, then turned back to Mark, who stood waiting for him to hit the stairway before he closed the door.

"The next time you need to see me, call me direct. I left my number by the phone. Stay away from that rat Pee Wee. He'd burn you quicker than he'd burn me. And he'd burn me in a fuckin' flash."

"I'll call ya," Mark said, and closed the door.

[215]

Police Officer Stein answered the phone on the first ring.

"Barry, this is Spencer. Do you have Frank Moresco's file handy?"

"Spencer." There was relief edged with righteous anger in Stein's voice. "Spencer, where the hell are you? The Chief's been looking for you, and I got a message here from Porterfield that he'll call ya later. It came in this morning but he never called back. I got a message here from Detective Lerner. I guess you know who she is. She called this morning, too. Where the hell are you?"

"Hi, Barry, this is Mark Spencer. How've you been? Now can we try again? Could you please pull Frank Moresco's folder?" Clerical men were the same everywhere; in the precinct, in the detective bureau, in special squads. Everything was out of control unless they knew just what was going on. Once they were told, things were fine again; they could go back to crossword puzzles and cleaning their hot plates.

"Look, Spencer, this ain't no shit. I gotta know where you are."

"I'm uptown, Barry, uptown."

"Oh, that's a help. I expect the Chief any minute now. When he comes in looking for you, I'll say you're uptown. He'll say thanks a lot and send me back to patrol. I don't wanna go back to patrol, Spencer, I got a top vacation pick here and I go to meals whenever I want. I get sick and throw up on late tours. So if you want any help from me, you'll have to give me the number where you are and I'll call ya back. If not, then you'll have to drag your ass down here and look through the file yourself. Those are my instructions. Get the number and I'll call back. Your smart-ass partner gave me a fuckin' Alaska area code when he called in. A real smart-ass, your partner."

Mark gave Stein the number and hung up. Before he could get a can of beer from the refrigerator the phone rang.

"Ya see how easy that is, Spencer? Just give me the number and I get right back to ya. Now we're all covered. What did you want?"

"Pull Frank Moresco's folder for me."

"I have it right here. You said you wanted it and I got it

right here. See, Spencer, that's why I'm gonna make boss someday. I pay attention, I listen, I follow instructions."

"O.K., pull his ten card."

"Got it."

"Well, read it to me."

"The whole thing?"

"It should only have four or five lines on it. You'll be able to get back to your sergeant's study book in a minute. Just read me the fucking card, Stein, before I do come down there and throw you, your book, and your hot plate right out the fucking window."

"Calm down, Spencer, I thought you people exuded patience."

"STEIN!" Mark screamed into the phone.

"O.K., O.K., just trying to break up the night with a little patter, Spencer, no need to get tense."

Night? Was it night? Christ.

"Well, Stein, I'm waiting."

"Got a pen?"

"Yeah, I got a pen."

"Frank Moresco, sergeant, 20th Precinct. Born February 26, 1930, Brooklyn, New York. Male, white, Roman Catholic, five feet nine inches, one hundred and eighty pounds. He lived at 1444 Ocean Parkway, apartment 17A. He had one dependent, his mother. He was fluent in Italian and Spanish. He was a butcher before he came on the job. Now here's a surprise."

"What?"

"The guy was a collector of classic cars."

"Yeah, I know," Mark whispered.

"He had three cars registered in his name. A 1979 Volvo sedan, a 1957 Chevrolet coupe, and a 1958 Buick coupe."

"What color was the Buick?" Mark asked, already knowing the answer.

"Silver. A 1958 silver Buick. If they're in good shape, they gotta be worth big bucks, don't you think?"

"Stein, do me a favor, will ya?"

"Sure. Why else am I here? I do people favors all the time. Ya think when I need a favor I'll get it? Bullshit I will."

Mark took a sip of beer. When Stein finished he said, "Leave a message for Porterfield. I'll meet him at the seven-six as soon as he can get there. And if Lerner calls back, tell her I'll call her at home later."

"Sure, I'm working till midnight, got nothing else to do. I'm not investigating big-time murders like you two. I just sit here and take messages and file cards. A degree in criminal justice from John Jay and I take messages and file cards."

Mark had barely hung up from Stein when the phone rang. He answered it and was ready to tell Stein to fuck off, then he heard Doyle's voice. He instantly began running through cover stories for Bobby. He settled on the public library. If the Chief asked, Bobby was at the public library.

"Where are you, Spencer?"

"In Harlem."

"I know that. Where in Harlem?"

"226 East 117th Street."

Doyle repeated the address in a way that made it clear he was writing it down, or more likely having Paddy write it down.

"What's going on?" Mark asked.

"We know who the killer is," Doyle said disgustedly.

"You know who killed Captain Burke?"

"Yes," Doyle said, and paused. "We know who killed them all."

"Phil Moresco," Mark said softly.

"Right! Goddamnit! Right! How'd you know?"

"I found out that the car that ran down the captain was Frank Moresco's old Buick. And the description of the driver sounded like it could be Phil. It was a guess. Just a shot."

"Pretty good fucking guess." Doyle laughed. "We've known for a few days. But we didn't have enough for an arrest warrant till this afternoon."

It would have been nice if you told us, Mark thought. Fucking Doyle never changes. Nobody knows what he's doing, except Paddy.

"Me and Paddy hit his apartment this afternoon. The crazy bastard got out the window on us."

Doyle had to be the only chief in the history of the department to execute a warrant by himself.

"He's crazy, Mark, the man's fucking nuts. He found Frank after he blew himself away, and his mind went south. Can you imagine a guy shooting his brother after his brother is already dead? Just to cover up a suicide the man shoots his own brother. Tell me the man's not psycho."

"I only met Phil once or twice, Chief. I know he was real close to his brother, but . . ."

"The prick's a fucking nut, Mark, a fucking psycho." Doyle was screaming so loud that Mark held the phone a foot from his ear and heard every word.

"He blamed me! Would you believe it? He blamed me and my people from the old Sixth Division bank squad. He's out to knock everyone off," Doyle shouted. "I guess he's saving me and Paddy for last."

This sounds familiar, Mark thought, my rosy-cheeked partner wasn't so crazy.

"The son of a bitch even went to Florida to get Sal Victoria. I went to Miami myself and saw the ballistics reports. He killed Victoria with his brother Frank's gun." Now the Chief was laughing, it was a strange laugh, a drunk's laugh. The laugh of a man with one leg over the edge. "He thinks we drove his brother to suicide."

"How do you know that?" Mark asked.

"Every crazy I've ever known's kept a diary."

"Then it's over," Mark said.

"What's over? The silly prick is running loose out there. I have something else to tell ya."

Mark heard the anxiousness in Doyle's voice and panicked. Bobby was in trouble.

"Is it Bobby?" he asked quickly.

He heard that crazy snicker on the other end of the line again. "Porterfield is a whole other story," Doyle said.

Mark smiled to himself, but didn't answer.

Doyle cleared his throat, then began again. "Porterfield is a fucking loser. I'll tell you all about *him* when I see you." The Chief paused again, now there was serious concern in his voice when he began. "Mark, I have to tell you, we found a list at Phil Moresco's apartment. Burke was on the list, Artie Dolan was on the list, and so was Victoria. And guess what?"

"I'm on the list," Mark said matter-of-factly.

"I told you years ago that you'd make a great detective." Doyle snickered and continued to talk. Soon he was rambling, then he was shouting, and every so often Mark heard a snide laugh. But Mark had stopped listening, his mind was sidestepping, shooting off in nine directions at once.

What could have happened to Bobby? he thought. What could Doyle have on him? Whatever it was, Mark could tell it was serious. He was tempted to ask Doyle straight out, but that just might set him off.

"Has Cathy heard from my partner today, Chief?" he asked casually.

There was silence on the other end of the line. Then Mark heard a muffled self-conscious laugh.

"I warned her," Doyle said sharply, "and now, finally, she's found out for herself. Bobby Porterfield is a fucking stupid kid. A fart in a blizzard. Artie Burke and I asked you to look out for him and you did. You almost made the quiff a cop. Now I'm done with him, Cathy is finished with him, and when I see you, and can talk to you face to face, you'll write him off too."

Damn, Bobby, what the hell did you get yourself into? Mark thought.

"Chief, I have my car here, I'll come right down to the office."

Mark's voice trailed off as he hung up the phone. As soon as he hung up he dialed Bobby's number. There was no answer. Then he tried home; again, no answer.

Suddenly depressed, Mark rose to his feet and headed for the door. He knew that when Doyle said he had you, he had you. And from the tone of his voice he had his partner right by the short hairs.

Mark felt himself dissolving into a cold sweat when he thought about Bobby. He couldn't imagine what the Chief could have on him. Shit, he thought, I'm too old for this damn intrigue.

They'd arrived at three o'clock. And though Jackie insisted they head straight to the room, Bobby wanted a drink. He said he wanted to know about the marks on her face. It was true, but he needed a drink. So they took drinks to an open deck that sat above the water. Bobby listened like a family lawyer. Jackie described the confrontation with Fred. At first she warned, "You'll only get five minutes of details," but then, with her eyes wide and brilliant, she talked, nonstop, for an hour. At the end of the hour Bobby wanted to kill Court Officer Johnston, he wanted to arrest Assistant District Attorney LaRosa, and he wanted Jackie, more than he'd wanted any woman . . . ever.

He got up from the table, took Jackie's hand, and they walked to the bar. He paid cash for a bottle of wine, then asked the bartender to open it. The bartender smiled, and handed the uncorked bottle to Jackie. She put it in her beach bag. Then Jackie asked the bartender for a container of ice cubes. The bartender told her he didn't have a container, and besides, the wine was already cool. Jackie smiled at him, then told him to put the ice cubes in a tall glass.

The room they were in was elegant. Sparsely furnished, with a green leather, gold-embossed Federal writing table, a floral-pattern love seat, and a Colonial Williamsburg cherrywood four-poster covered with a spotless but well-worn patchwork counterpane.

Jackie told him to make himself comfortable. She told him she had a surprise for him. Dragging her beach bag, she went into the bathroom.

Bobby half filled a water glass with wine. A raging battle was taking place on the well-lit field of his psyche. This was no guerrilla attack at night. Another voice screamed at him, "What the hell are you doing?" He tried a rationalization, a small one. "If no one knows, who can I be hurting?" he told himself.

"Mark's your best friend."

"No one will know! I need her. I deserve her. She needs me."

He couldn't tell what Jackie was doing, but he could hear her."

If the slightest chance existed for Bobby, to call time-out, if by some happenstance he'd decided to ask for asylum, Jackie eliminated it when she stepped from the bathroom wearing her tasteless polka dot dress, the one with the slit up the side. The one that clung to her thighs and buttocks.

"I know you like this," she said, standing like a street-corner hooker.

"I do."

"Well, then, let's play."

There was no more conversation. She walked slowly to him, that little girl's smile on her lips. She put her hands up to his cheeks, then ran her hands down across his chest. She arranged his legs so they stood open and apart. He felt her tiny hand caress him, touch him so lightly that a sound, which he at first tried to suppress, jumped from his throat. He was afraid to move.

Jackie's eyes never left his. Everything was still. Not a hint of movement. Then suddenly he was up on his toes. She had undone his slacks. He was in awe of her. A hand moved material aside and she held him. She stroked him, rhythmically, gently. She brought him to the very edge, then allowed him to peek over, just a bit, just a tiny bit. Then she brought him back, with a gentle squeeze, she brought him back to safety.

He looked down, stared at that face as it receded.

Expressionless, she fell away, her eyes fastened to his own. Then he saw just the top of her head, then he closed his eyes.

Sounds of laughter and music filled the tenement. Children running and jumping, scaling whole flights of stairs. A basketball bounced in the hallway right outside his door. It was almost eleven-thirty at night and the tenement sounded like a playground in the afternoon. Women's voices, full-bodied and firm, called out children's names. "Billy, get in here, you know what time it is? Child, ain't you tired?" "Alberta, you come down from that roof, ya hear." Doors slammed shut and more doors opened and more women yelled and other children screamed and more doors banged. It was time for Mark to leave. But he sat still listening, breathing in deeply, hearing and smelling his childhood. Harlem was alive with laughter. Almost no one smiled in Brooklyn Heights. There was always so much goddamn noise in Harlem—on the sidewalks, in the street, on stoops, and in the hallways. So much noise, so much life, and so much poverty. But Mark didn't remember feeling poor. How do you feel poor? he thought. He always had sneakers, he always had a basketball, and he always had plenty to eat. He was an only child; he got an abundance of love from a devoted mother and a kind, always laughing maiden aunt. There were no men. Men didn't come and stay for a short time, then leave, like Trunk's relatives. There simply were no men, men never came into his house, and he didn't much care, never thought a whole lot about it. He'd have to call his mother this week for sure. Christ, he hadn't spoken to her in over a month. Maybe this weekend he'd bring Jackie. He knew his mother missed him terribly, but he also knew that she couldn't deal with Jackie, and Jackie, right now, was his life. There was a quick ominous shift in his mood. Doyle, that slick son of a bitch, was no dummy, but, he smiled to himself, neither was his partner.

Mark heard the lock snap shut, tried the knob just to be sure, and turned to leave. Then he heard the phone ring. There was no way to get back in, but he stood in the hallway till the ringing stopped.

The tenement had grown still, as tenements will; it was sort of a half-time pause. The early evening begins with men coming home to women who make a pretense of anger, who shout and yell and curse, but who in reality are glad to see a man's face come through the door. Mark remembered that he'd always thought some man would come through his door, then announce, "Daddy's home." The fucker never did.

It made no sense to go back through the yards and over the roof, not at this hour. No one would notice him coming out of the building, and Trunk was long gone. No way to connect the two. He was wrong about Trunk. Trunk had waited, he had mailed the package to the address Mark had given him and now he waited. He sat on a stoop, drinking soda from a bottle in a paper bag, directly across the street. When Trunk had walked out of the building, a street kid, a twelve-year-old extortionist, anxious to please, told Trunk that he saw a white guy go in the building two doors from his aunt's. Trunk told the kid, "Go over and peek, see if the guy is still here. Maybe he's hanging in the cut." The kid, with just the hint of a strut, danced across the street and up the steps of the building, then disappeared inside. In a minute he was back, kneeling next to Trunk, whispering in his ear. Trunk gave the kid a five.

The kid's wrong, the guy's not gone, Trunk thought; he's laying up somewhere, probably one of Mark's cop friends. Then again, maybe not. One thing was for certain. If the sucker had curly black hair, he was gonna get his face torn right the fuck off. So Trunk sat still while his ten- and twelve-year-old peepers searched the street for the white guy. One named Ivory brought him a Pepsi in a paper bag and a sack of chips. He sipped and munched, but his eyes never left the door to his aunt's building.

Accompanied by a teenager with a four-foot silver radio slung over a shoulder, Mark stepped through the building door and now stood on the very top of the stoop. He had that melancholy sense of being home and not feeling good about it. The night air was cool, it was like autumn, still the street was packed. There always were too many people in the Harlem streets. When fall and winter arrived the numbers dwindled. More people than warm jackets, Mark remembered. He watched as the teenager strode off, Motown in stereo blaring in his wake.

A half dozen guys stood beneath a streetlamp. One bent and threw dice against the curb. Battered and empty garbage cans blocked the sidewalk in front of the building. Like Latin American soldiers, they stood around, each one out of place, each one a hazard. A woman's voice rose from across the street. She was yelling for a child. The woman sounded so much like his maiden aunt, Nan, that he caught himself looking for Nan's face in the crowd. His aunt had been dead for three years. A picture of himself, a recollection of his childhood, flashed. Surrounded by admirers, he swaggered down the center of the street. He was bouncing a basketball, shooting it from hand to hand. Every second bounce he snapped between his legs, then brought the ball up to his index finger, spinning it. He cut a princely figure in those days. Younger boys, smaller and less talented, mimicked his moves. Bouncing invisible balls, they strutted like he did and acknowledged his greatness. "That one's special," someone said. For a second Mark experienced the worst kind of pain. It was real and it jolted him; it was the memory of innocence now long gone.

The night people had taken control of the street. Mark knew all their brown eyes were on him. What the hell made him wear a suit to this meeting? He looked like a damn FBI agent, or worse, a local precinct detective. Still, he was in no rush to move off the stoop. From his vantage point he could see the whole street and he enjoyed playing with his memories. He looked at the sad faces of the men under the lamppost. What was understood by outsiders as faces full of violence were in reality faces full of desperation. He understood the desperation; that didn't mean he liked being around it. Harlem had been his home. It fascinated him. Still, black as he was, strong as he was, there were times his own people frightened him. Things he remembered that were good about Harlem lived in his heart and sang songs in his memory. What was evil played in its nighttime streets. He suddenly felt like he didn't belong. This was no longer his home. He wanted to leave this place, as nicely and as quickly as possible. Like so many who had jumped clear of the ghetto, there was no way he'd come back.

Another woman's voice rang out. It sang words in a tone eerie and alien. She didn't sound black. The scream sent him flying from the stoop. "HELP—POLICE—HELP." Now in the street he looked into the building next to the one he'd come from. Trunk's voice, loud, frantic, and closing, came from behind him.

"Mark, watch, that bitch ain't no bitch," he screamed, "don't move, stay where you at."

The woman stepped from the darkness of the doorway. She was wearing a tan trench coat that brushed the top of running shoes. Long, straight red hair rested on large shoulders. Big, hairy hands were wrapped around a leather shoulder bag. Mark went for his gun. It was Phil Moresco. Moresco's hand went in, then came out of the bag like lightning. It held a heavy-barrel Smith & Wesson police special. The heavy-barrel S&W was distinctive; it was a cop's gun. It roared before he touched his own. A lead-tipped hollow point exploded in his chest. It lifted and flung him into the squad of garbage cans. He had his gun now, but Trunk, charging like a bull elephant, was between him and the shooter. Three more shots, so rapid they could have been one, bangbangbanged. Mark remembered falling from a tree once and landing flat on his back. He was fourteen, and wanted to scream. But the pain was so intense, there was no breath in him, he couldn't yell, couldn't even murmur.

That pain had passed quickly. The fire now boiling yellow-red in his chest was here to stay.

Trunk lifted Moresco above his head. The red wig dropped off. He turned toward the street, toward Mark. Black curly hair sat atop a man's head with a painted face now contorted in terror. Moresco's fists clawed at the air. The front of Trunk's golden silk shirt ran streams of scarlet. Trunk brought the swinging, flailing, clawing body down and brought his knee up. Even in his world of searing pain Mark heard a sharp crack, like the breaking of a dry, rotten branch. Mark tried to get to his feet. He stumbled and coughed, blood sprayed onto his jacket and splashed off the garbage cans. He flopped onto the curb, his hands crossing his chest, his back resting against the light pole. Trunk screamed his name as he brought Moresco above his head once again. This time Trunk slid his hands to the ankles and slammed the body off the stoop, like a child in a rage smashing the head of a doll.

Mark heard the sirens; the fire in his chest hadn't cooled, he felt as tired as he'd ever been, he felt tipsy, then he felt himself being lifted and carried. Carried the way his mother had carried him when he fell from the tree. Cradled like a child, Trunk had him, and was running, stumbling, and kicking empty garbage cans. Red lights swung, lighting the street. There were more sirens and yelling. He heard, "Where's the cop? Which one's the cop?"

"Fuck the ambulance; put him in the car."

"Put them both in the car."

He heard Trunk say, "I got him, man, I got him." Then he heard someone yell, "Christ, that's Mark Spencer. Look for his partner. His partner's probably here, too." He felt a hand push down so hard on his chest that the air he was able to get was shoved out of his mouth. He heard a terrified voice say, "Fuck," as a hand was pressed even harder this time. He heard the muffled whimper of a cop that knelt above him. He felt the cop pry his mouth open, he could see him, his hat was off, then he tasted stale breath and he tasted coffee and he felt the cop's lips cover his own. He saw Bobby Porterfield's smiling face and he heard Jackie's voice. She was singing a sad, country, down-home song.

19.

Like a princess of whores, she played with him. At first exploring, she'd reach across the bed and touch him with the tips of her fingers, but then she'd pull her hand away as if she'd been scalded. Soon she began tracking a course with her finger from the top of his head, across his forehead, around the curve of his nose, she held at his mouth.

He kissed and licked her fingertips, the smell of her own sweet musk was fresh there. He felt her fingers move from his mouth and travel along his neck to his chest.

"I've wanted you for so long," she whispered. Then she pinched his nipple, lightly first, then tighter, and tighter still. It hurt, he hunched his shoulders and moved her hand.

He looked at her as if for the first time. Jackie smiled, those brilliant eyes were dancing, then her hand ran off. Holding tight to his cock, she pulled herself to him. She kissed him with such hunger that for a second he was frightened. He pulled away, and put her head to his shoulder. He looked at the polka dot dress, it lay with her tiny black panties, draped over the foot of the bed.

He rolled over, he wanted to be above her. She took him easily, smoothly, then she frightened him again. Jackie slapped the cheeks of his ass with the sides of her feet. Sweat was pouring from him now, it dripped down onto her chest, and ran circles around her breasts. The slapping of her feet, easy at first, became harder. Then ferociously she kicked at his ass with her heels. Her eyes became wide and held his. How silent she was. He only heard her sounds of breathing slowly, deep and firm.

Then the sound increased in intensity. He wanted to put his head down between her legs. He took himself from her.

"Turn me over. Please, Bobby, turn me over," she gasped. He did, and she arched her back, and jutted up her ass at an unbelievable angle. He put his hands on her hips and pulled her to him. He could feel the firmness of her thighs and buttocks. He could tell she was caressing and touching herself. In the end, this spectacular little girl-woman had to masturbate. Jackie had to fight for her orgasm. She had to earn it, work for it. Nothing came easy for Jackie. She worked hard, then harder still. Finally, she cried, "It's good, it's good, I'm here."

Bobby felt that one more push, one more thrust would kill him.

Then the phone rang.

He lurched.

And Jackie screamed, it was a terrible scream, a scream much more of terror than one of pleasure . . . she'd frightened him . . . again.

There were lists of things Ralph Cruz hated. But *the* thing that won the gold medal on Detective First Grade Ralph Cruz's hate list was the telephone.

Ralph hated criminals. He hated all kinds of criminals. Little shit heelers to big-time connected assholes. They were all the same to Ralph; puke bags, he called them.

He also hated judges, meter maids, poets, panhandlers, Russian cabdrivers, French waiters, and ex-wives. Detective First Grade Ralph Cruz had a never-ending list of people he hated. That's why Ralph Cruz always worked alone.

For fourteen years Detective Cruz had been tapping telephones for Tom Doyle. He tapped them for Lieutenant Tom Doyle, Captain Tom Doyle, Deputy Inspector Tom Doyle, Inspector Tom Doyle, Assistant Chief Inspector Tom Doyle, and now for Chief Inspector Tom Doyle. Doyle kept on getting promoted, and Ralph, he kept on connecting pairs and dropping bugs.

Ralph had never seen it fail, the instrument of doom and destruction, that's what he called the telephone. Sooner or later it brought everyone down. Friends, lovers, killers, and kidnappers, everyone talked too often, and too long, on the telephone. That's why Detective Cruz's number one rule was: if it's important, you never use the telephone. Ralph Cruz had another rule: there were no conditions, and there were no circumstances, that made it O.K. to hurt another cop. Bobby Porterfield had broken *both* those rules. Still, Detective Ralph Cruz felt a terrible pain for him.

Ralph walked around the parking lot of the Cold Spring Harbor Inn like he didn't belong. He hated the water, he hated the traffic, he hated Long Island. He hated the assholes that lived out here and put their grass clippings in plastic bags. But most of all he hated what he was doing here. The Chief had turned him into a private detective, and he hated private detectives.

Ralph threw stones toward the water. Little round flat stones. He was still pissed, so he picked up rocks, big rocks, and tossed them as far as he could.

Bobby held still for a minute. The last time he and Ralph Cruz met it was in a parking lot the day of his promotion. The memory of the Chief and Cruz in Dino's kitchen playing with the receiver was still fresh.

"What's going on, Ralph?" Bobby asked. "What the hell are you doing here? Your call scared the shit outta me. How did you know what room I was in? How the hell did you find me?" Ralph Cruz kept his back to Bobby. He bent and picked up, then threw a giant stone that landed "splat," about a foot from the water.

"Until I finish," Ralph said in a cool voice, "I don't want you to ask another question. O.K.? First, let me ask you, do you have any dope?"

"What?" Bobby asked.

"I said, do you have any dope? Ya know, smoke, some speed, or a whole lot of Valium?"

Ralph Cruz continued to look out in the direction of the water. He had yet to look at Bobby.

"I don't use dope," Bobby said smartly.

"That's admirable, let me tell ya." Ralph turned and looked straight into Bobby's eyes. "By the time I'm finished you'll wish you did."

Bobby was very near feeling sick.

Ralph Cruz stood and looked out into blackness, and he seemed to Bobby to be the saddest person he'd ever seen. Bobby was frightened, now he *really* was frightened.

"What was the worst day you ever had?" Ralph asked, tossing a softball-sized rock up and down in his hand.

Bobby turned away.

"C'mon, I asked you what the worst day in your life was."

Ralph threw the stone out into the darkness. It must have landed far out, for it barely made a sound.

"I guess it was the day my parents were killed in a car wreck," Bobby said quietly.

"How long ago was that?"

"Five years."

There was no emotion in Bobby, he was meeting with Ralph Cruz somehow in a nightmare. He had been snagged in Doyle's net.

"I didn't know that. I'm sorry to hear it," Ralph said. "Are you over it?" Ralph was kicking at the ground, trying to loosen another rock.

"No," Bobby said.

"That's too bad, because I got another one for ya. It's not quite as bad as the day your parents were killed, but I'll bet it's a close second."

"Goddamnit, Ralph, you're getting me angry. Tell me what the hell is going on."

"Don't waste your energy," he said. Then looking at Bobby's face, he added quickly, "I don't know where to begin. I thought it would be easier than this. At this moment, *chuleto*, you're not my favorite cop." But you are a cop and I feel sorry for you, he wanted to add.

"Try the beginning," Bobby said, looking at Cruz's calm face.

"Yeah, the beginning would be fine, a good place to start. The problem is, I'm sure the ending is more appropriate. But if I tell you the ending, you'll leave. And I'll be standing here alone, throwing rocks at the fucking water."

"The beginning, Ralph, the beginning is always easiest."

Cruz made a harsh, tired sound. "You had breakfast this morning with a Mafia guy, a connected Shylock, the dwarf, Syracusa. Ya know why they called him Carl Marx?" Ralph asked. "Because he collects his debts with a hammer and sickle. A real cute little prick. I've been on his phone for a month." Bobby crouched and sat on the heels of his feet.

"You used that phone to call Jackie. Then, on department time, and in a department vehicle, without permission, you left the city. You've been shacked up all day out here, when you were supposed to be working. The Chief knows, of course, and I'm pretty sure he told Cathy. How's that for a beginning?"

"So this is why you called me, to warn me?"

"I wish that's all it was," Cruz said with a quick mocking sound.

Bobby straightened up, he put his hands on his hips.

"Don't tell me that son of a bitch Doyle told my partner. That's it, isn't it? Doyle told Mark that I'm out here with Jackie."

Detective First Grade Ralph Cruz took a few steps down the path toward the beach. He reached down and pulled a giant stone from the sand and mud. He ran a couple of steps and flung it. The rock landed with a clear, loud "splaaashhhh."

"Doyle didn't tell your partner anything," Ralph Cruz yelled from the water's edge.

Bobby began walking toward the sound of Ralph's voice. The water smelled, and not like the smell of a rolling ocean, more like a swamp, with mud and muck and gnats that flew into the corners of his eyes. The place stunk to high heaven.

"How do you know? Why wouldn't he tell him? Doyle has no love for Mark. And he sure as hell hates me."

"Mark's dead, goddamnit! Mark Spencer died an hour ago in Harlem Hospital. That psycho prick Phil Moresco shot him up on 117th Street. He's dead, *chuleto*, your partner is DOA at H. and H. And I'm here to get your gun and your badge. You've been suspended. How's that for an ending?"

A monstrous scream came from the darkness of the path behind him, then a moan. It sounded like the whimpering of a child, giving birth.

"Mark, oh my God, not Mark."

He could see Jackie, backlighted from the lights of the inn's parking lot.

"I'm going to the hospital," Bobby yelled, then turned and began heading up the path. Cruz ran up and grabbed his elbow. He pulled himself free, then turned on Cruz. At that moment Bobby knew he would never be frightened again.

"Take your hands off me. I'm warning you, Ralph, don't touch me again."

"I have to take your gun and shield," Ralph said, but he looked in Bobby's face and took a step back.

"Take my word for it, Ralph. You don't want to try and take my gun and shield. You think you know me? You think because you snuck around behind me all day you know me. You think because you heard me on a telephone you know something about me. You knew my partner was in the hospital and you waited to tell me. Come and try, you come and try and take my shield."

"I don't have to take your gun and shield, Doyle will."

"He'll try, *niño.*"

"Don't call me *niño*, Bobby, I don't like the sound of it," Detective First Grade Ralph Cruz said.

"Maybe you like the sound of rat better?" Bobby said, and he took a step toward Detective Cruz. Ralph turned away and walked down the path. You should have known better, he told himself, you see what happens when you feel sorry for somebody? He took a rock and threw it as far as he could. Ralph heard a soft "plunk" when it hit the water. He was alone again, but that's exactly the way he liked it.

Bobby's entire being was ripped and torn, he was shot through with agony. He drove the car with Jackie curled in the corner of the passenger seat. There was no fear in him, just confusion and anger.

Anger, anger, and more anger; Doyle had Cruz follow him, report on him. Doyle was like a criminal; he was a criminal. Then came a picture of Mark's face. It evoked pain, pain, and more pain. What am I? he thought. What am I? He tried to shake himself free of the pain. He looked for something, anything, some kind of help. But all he saw was more pain.

"Why Mark?" he asked out loud.

Jackie sat in the corner, her hand on her cheek, her face resting against the window. She began to say something, then stopped. Her head dropped back against the headrest, and she sobbed.

"My God, my God, he's gone, Bobby, Mark's gone."

"But why him? I don't understand. Why did Moresco kill Mark?"

"Mark worked in the Sixth Division, Bobby. Mark worked for Doyle. It was years ago, but he worked prostitution and gambling in the Sixth. I don't know"—Jackie was weeping—"maybe . . ." Her voice trailed off. "I don't know."

"Why didn't Mark tell me he worked in the Sixth?" He asked the question. But he already knew the answer. He'd certainly made it clear how he felt about cops who worked that unit. How Mark must have suffered listening to his righteous bullshit.

Then he yelled, he screamed at Jackie, who was no longer listening. She was off somewhere, looking out the window, staring out at the lights of Harlem.

"No! No! No!" Bobby yelled. "He should have trusted me. He should have known I'd understand."

Bobby paused by the door to the emergency room. He took hold of Jackie's elbow. "Are you O.K.?" he asked.

Jackie closed her eyes, took a deep breath, and pushed open the door. Then she stopped and turned to face him.

"I'm not ashamed," she said, "I'm not afraid to face anyone here. The only eyes I couldn't deal with can't see me. The rest of them"—she paused—"can go and . . ."

He smiled at her, she put her thumb in the air, and Jackie Lerner, undercover agent, walked through the door, and with her head up, she walked toward the crowd of cops.

Bobby didn't usually remember his nightmares, or his dreams for that matter. But as he watched the Chief stride toward him, he sensed that he'd been here before. He knew exactly what Doyle would say. It was his own response he wasn't sure of. As Doyle closed the distance between them, Bobby knew that tomorrow, and maybe thousands of tomorrows, he'd have to deal with his guilt. Tonight, though, he'd deal with his anger.

Doyle smiled as though he were pleased to see him. "I don't know where you found the balls to show up, but I'm glad you did," Doyle said, stopping two strides from him.

Doyle looked more like someone from the corner near the Syracusa bakery than he did a chief inspector of the police department. With his tan, his blue-sapphire pinky ring, and his two-dollar cigar.

"I came to see my partner," Bobby said simply. Doyle stared at him.

"You're too late. The M.E. has him." Bobby felt nauseated, his legs began to shake.

"I gave you a direct order, through Cruz, to turn in your gun and shield."

"I don't give my gun and shield to another detective. Only to my C.O. And tell me, Chief, don't you get tired of sending people out to do your dirty work?" Bobby asked softly. Doyle looked at him as if his ear were missing.

"Porterfield, you're an idiot."

"Chief," Bobby said, "you're a *crook*; a hypocrite, and a *crook*." More silence from Doyle, then he screamed.

"You've run your string, smart-ass. You're played out. I have enough charges against you now to keep the Department Advocate busy for a month." Doyle was mumbling, there was plenty of fire, but he was mumbling. There was something of the drunk Dolan in his face. And at that moment, Bobby knew Doyle was a coward.

"Look at you," Bobby said, "you're a fake."

"And you're a faggot social worker, an extremist, the scum of the earth. Your partner is dead, getting sawed open right now. And you're out trying to make a case against me. Cathy told me. Cathy saw your notes."

"My partner's dead because he worked for you. They're all dead because they worked for you. Chief Inspector, you're a joke."

"O.K., smart-ass, I want your gun and shield." Doyle took a step, then he reached a hand to Bobby's side. Bobby grabbed his wrist.

"No one's taking anything from me," Bobby said calmly.

Doyle smiled, then he tried to move his hand. Bobby squeezed tighter.

The green and gray walls of the emergency room seemed to be closing in on him, and the dirty white ceiling began flowing in and out. Bobby began thinking of the M.E. and Mark. He stood with his legs spread, his feet firmly planted, and he squeezed Doyle's wrist harder still. If he wanted to, he could bring Doyle to his knees. He knew it, and Doyle knew it too, because he stopped resisting, and the smug smile he wore faded.

As if catapulted, Paddy sprang from the center of a group of uniformed cops. In a flash he was at the Chief's side.

"Chief?" he asked.

Bobby noticed that Patrolman Rizzo, from sector Adam, along with three or four other cops from his precinct, began to move toward them. But they stopped when they saw the Chief and the look on Bobby's face.

"I'm O.K., Paddy. It's O.K.," the Chief said.

"No, I don't think it's O.K. You let go of him, Bobby; if you don't do the right thing we're gonna have a bad scene here."

"The right thing?" Doyle mocked. "This kid don't know the meaning of the words."

"I'll give you my gun and my badge. Just don't try and take them," Bobby said evenly.

He released Doyle's wrist. Then he handed him his revolver and his shield.

"You creep, you smart-ass. When I get through with you . . ."

"What's the matter with you, Chief? What are you so afraid of?" Bobby smiled.

"You're dead!"

"No, I'm not dead. Frank Moresco's dead, Artie Dolan's dead, Burke's dead, that guy in Florida is dead, and my partner's dead. Your disciples, Chief, they're all dead. I'm still alive, you hypocritical bastard. And we both know you're responsible, you're responsible for all this."

Bobby turned and walked out the door. Doyle was screaming, screaming something that he barely heard. Something about Cathy. Something about "the right thing." Bobby had dealt with his anger, now it was time to find a place to roll up and deal with his guilt.

Over the next four days Bobby ingested more booze than he had during the previous twenty-five years of his life. Now in the night of the fourth day, his liver was in a panic, and it seemed his intestines and colon were gone. Water fell from him, first in great slow waves, then in sudden bursts.

Sleep was the greatest of all horrors. The M.E., with his tiny saber saw, and his oilcloth apron, and rubber gloves, was the honored guest of his never-ending nightmares.

He'd left the apartment the first night of Mark's wake. Walked all the way to the Grimaldi funeral parlor. Saw the herds and herds of cops, saw Jackie and Mark's mother, saw Mark's flag-draped coffin, walked into the parking lot, vomited, then walked home. He'd stopped only for another bottle of bourbon.

He'd heard nothing, not one word, from Cathy. He had no idea where she'd gone off to. If she cared at all, she'd call, he thought. She never did. So he sucked on his bourbon, with visions of the Swanson kid sailing through the air, the M.E. waving his saw like a baton, and Mark with his legs draped over a marble table. He knew the drink was only making matters worse. But the bourbon had become his friend, and considering the way the cops at the wake looked at him, it may have been his only friend.

The doorbell rang, and rang some more. He sat up, looked at the clock. It was eleven o'clock, and it was night, he could tell, the streetlight lit the corner of the room. The bell rang again. He lay back down. Then thought maybe it was Cathy. He got up and walked to the window. Jackie stood on the stoop. She rang the bell, took a step back, and stared at his window. He moved back into the darkness, then crawled back to bed. Back to the M.E., the Swanson kid, and Mark's brown body on the white table.

When Bobby awoke, rain whipped horizontally by the window. He felt chilled. Wasn't it still summer? he thought. In September, New York played games with you.

Controlling the urge to succumb to major panic, Bobby quickly opened his eyes. It sounded like the M.E. was trying to get into his room. There was banging, and screaming, and kicking. The door to his apartment was vibrating. He looked to the dresser for his gun, it wasn't there, he panicked. Where's the damn gun? The door was about ready to come off its hinges. He jumped out of bed, the room did a full loop, and he flopped back down.

"Open this damn door or I'll shoot the fucking lock off."

Doyle had his gun, he remembered. Doyle also had his shield.

"I know you're in there, Bobby, open this door."

It was Jackie. She stood in the hallway sopping wet.

"How ya doing, hotshot?" he said.

"How am I doing?"

Bobby stood in the middle of the room. "I had to be alone. I couldn't deal with any of it," he said, looking around the apartment. It was a wreck. "Go away," he whispered.

Jackie eyed him as if he were saying something she couldn't understand. "Mark, Mark's mother, and half the police department. I had to deal with them all." Jackie brushed wet hair out of her eyes. "While you lay up here getting loaded. You're terrific."

He wished she'd get out, leave him and go. Suddenly he was having trouble staying on his feet.

"You look terrible," she said flatly, then pushed him aside. And though Bobby protested, she moved through the apartment, picking up, throwing bottles in the garbage—trying to set things straight.

"Get into the shower," she said quickly, and shoved him with her hand.

When Jackie poured sour milk into the sink, his stomach charged toward his throat and he ran into the bathroom.

"Jesus," he yelled as water exploded from him, pouring from every orifice.

"Die, you son of a bitch. I hope you die." Jackie sounded like she meant it.

He rolled from the commode into the tub, then lay on his back. He couldn't move.

Jackie walked into the bathroom, reached down and pulled off his shorts, then turned on the shower.

"Some hero you are," she said.

"Yeah, I know, a real certified hero, that's me."

"You were Mark's hero, and no one was a better judge of people than he was." Jackie turned on the water. It was ice cold, Bobby felt as though he could jump right from his lying position clear out of the tub. Then the water suddenly felt warm. It ran over him, comforting him, it felt wonderful.

Jackie said, "And you're my hero." He opened his eyes and saw the tears, she tried a smile, but more tears came, then he felt his own, burning under the warm spray of the shower.

An hour later he stretched and opened his eyes. Jackie was watching him, again. The water in the tub was somehow still warm, and he could smell coffee, and bacon, and toast. And the sound of Vivaldi's "Spring" filled the apartment.

At the kitchen table she told him how Doyle tried to jam her up with the Narcotics Division. But the detectives in her office had covered her.

"When he asked if I was on duty, they figured something was up and told him I'd been off duty since eleven o'clock that morning. They said the son of a bitch sounded disappointed."

Then she showed him the book. "It came in the mail," she said.

He flipped through the pages, and asked her what it was.

"Look at it again," she said.

"What is it? It looks like some kid's paper route."

"It's the Sixth Division pad, is what it is. If Roxbury got his hands on that, Doyle, Paddy, and a whole lot of other people would be in one helluva jam."

He smiled.

"They'd get locked up," Jackie said simply. "Sure as hell, Roxbury would lock 'em all up."

"Is Cruz in here?" he asked.

"What do you think 'R.C. two hundred' means?"

He smiled again.

"Look," she said, "that book is yours now. Do whatever you want with it. O.K., hero?"

After a while they sat on the couch and Jackie circled herself in the corner. She was playing with a handkerchief, twisting and curling it, her expression was empty. She shrugged her shoulders and sighed.

"I miss him, you know," she said with that little-girl smile. She murmured something he couldn't hear.

"What?" he asked.

"I asked you if you've ever been afraid."

He didn't answer.

"I mean, really afraid."

He was trying to remember.

"So afraid that you think that any moment you'll pee," she said quickly. "So afraid that you can't catch your breath. That you blubber and moan, and you don't care who's watching. Have you ever been that afraid?"

No, he'd never been that afraid. To be that afraid must be like dying. No he'd never been that afraid.

"The other morning I was that afraid. I acted like a schoolgirl, a rookie . . . me . . . the hotshot . . . the queen of the street, taken off by an old man with a belly."

"The nightmares. Yes. They've made me that terrified."

"So, you've been having nightmares?" Jackie understood, with barely suppressed rage, that anything she wanted to share with him about her own terror and humiliation would fall on deaf ears. Self-pity. She saw it in his whole being. And it ripped her apart with compassion for his suffering, and contempt for his weakness.

Bobby nodded.

"You make me sick. You know that? Lord hear me, Jesus. You men are babies. Self-centered, egotistical babies." She wanted Bobby to speak of their time together. But in his maudlin self-loathing, he seemed to have forgotten their shared love.

"Go easy, Jackie, it was horrible," he said softly.

"Bobby, Mark and I had a time. There was a time for us. But that time was over, it had passed. If that weren't true, I wouldn't have gone with you."

He had an uneasy sensation that he wouldn't be able to look at her now. So he walked over to the window and looked out into the street.

"I have no guilt, Bobby. I know what I am. I'm not a witch. I'm not a seer. I didn't know that some crazy would kill him. My life has been, is, and will be, an adventure. Mark knew that. He knew me and he loved me. And I loved him in my way. I thank God I had the chance to know him. And you know what, hero?" Jackie was sobbing now. The words were coming in starts and stops and gasps. "Look at me!" she screamed.

He wanted to. He wanted to hold her, but he couldn't. Mark was looking. He stood staring out the window, his back to her.

"I was good for him. I made him feel like the man he was. But goddamnit, he knew it wouldn't last forever. There is no forever for me. I don't know why . . . but there is no forever." Jackie wept openly, fully, like a child.

He yearned to turn around, he tried to force himself to look at her, he couldn't.

"Mark was glad he knew me," she said. "I'm a damn special lady."

He heard her go to the door.

"Go ahead, hero, go do whatever it is you have to do. But when this passes, and it's gonna pass, you better call me."

The door slammed, and Jackie, the police department's main event, was gone.

He watched as she flew down the street, skipping between steps as she went. A car horn blasted. He looked, and Jackie stood in the center of the street, her hands on her hips. A taxi had rolled into the crosswalk. Jackie pointed a finger at the cabdriver, then pointed to the traffic light. When the cab started to go she kicked the fender.

20.

Chief Assistant District Attorney Frank LaRosa sat in his burgundy imitation-leather chair. He had just changed from his patent-leather narcotics grand jury loafers to his hole-in-the-center-of-the-sole tassel tops. He'd cross his legs when that Legal Aid whiz kid showed up. Right now he sat more comfortably with his feet flat on the floor. LaRosa concluded long ago that a hole in a shoe, better than a liquid-plastic-covered diploma, was somehow a window to the intellect. Instead of tattered law books, his shelves were lined with tropical-fish tanks, ceramic pots, and pieces of imitation African sculpture. He told visitors about his year and a half of Peace Corps experience. Further evidence that he was bright and sensitive. He'd never been in the Peace Corps, but what the hell, who would ask him to prove it. Behind his desk was an American flag; its tip touched a place where his law books should have been. LaRosa leaned back in his chair and closed his eyes. He was thinking of that day in the distant future when he would go into private practice. When that day came he would get a real office with real leather chairs, a receptionist who could speak English, and a secretary he could screw at will and who typed with both hands. For the present, he was content. He had his American flag, his tropical fish, and his power that made cops listen when he spoke.

The intercom button on his phone buzzed.

"Mr. Jaeger to see you, sir."

"Send him in." LaRosa took out the Richard Smalls file and spread it out on his desk.

"Frank, you wanted to see me?"

"I'm afraid I have some bad news for you, Ivan," he said shrewdly, wondering which way he should sit in order to get his hole-in-the-sole foot up.

"You're resigning from the D.A.'s office?" Jaeger appeared shocked.

"That would bother you, would it?"

"Are you serious? This place is a real drag with you here. If you left, I'd never get a laugh." Ivan Jaeger was twenty-six years old. He made Law Review, and graduated second in his class from New York Law School. When he walked into a courtroom everyone stopped what they were doing, all heads turned to watch the young lawyer whose resemblance to Robert Redford was startling. Ivan found a place on LaRosa's burgundy vinyl couch and flopped. It had been a normal day in the courtroom wars. He was exhausted.

LaRosa turned his chair so he could face Ivan. He crossed his legs and stuck his hole about three inches from Ivan's knee.

"I'm afraid," LaRosa began slowly, "we were premature with our offer to Richard Smalls."

"Well, I guess that's your problem, Frank, isn't it? You offered Smalls an S.S. for a guilty plea and you got it. He promised his testimony in that cop killing; I know, I was there. You put it on the record."

LaRosa shrugged his shoulders. He drooped his lips into a knowing, understanding sort of smile. "There have been some rather drastic changes in that case. The suspect was killed after he killed another cop. The case is closed. We don't need your client's testimony. Tell him we're rescinding our offer. It's as simple as that. The district attorney's office owes nothing to Mr. Smalls."

Jaeger, his hands rubbing the tops of his knees, his body rocking, looked as if he were ready to come across the room and physically attack Frank. Frank stopped grinning. Jaeger cocked his head, pointed his index at Frank, shook it, started to say something, swallowed, then said, "You really are amazing. I convinced my guy to come forward and behave like a good citizen, what does the state do? It goes back on its word. And you wonder why your courtroom is full of pissed-off people?"

Jaeger looked at his hands, then rubbed them together. "You're fucking amazing, is what you are," he said softly.

LaRosa began going through the file on his desk. Jaeger's eyes followed his.

"A good citizen? The guy's a dope pusher, a pimp, a thief, and God knows what else."

"He told me he's innocent, Frank; he told me he didn't sell Lerner the dope. The point here, Counselor, is that the sale was never consummated. Your officer perjured herself."

"Then why did he plead guilty?"

"Because you offered him a deal. I told him that trials are chancy. He's just concerned about doing time, not keeping his record clean, for Christ's sake. The guy is what he is, but I gave him my word. And that was based on what *you* put on the record."

"Innocent people don't plead guilty, you know that, Ivan."

"I'll tell ya what I know, Frank. I know that Richard is going to withdraw his guilty plea. If he'll listen to me, he'll take you to bat on this one. The guy says he's innocent and I believe him. Nobody sells dope five minutes after he witnesses one cop killing another one."

"Ivan, I got another deal for you. You interested?"

Ivan Jaeger was studying his fingertips.

"You tell Sweet Dick—you know that's what his name is, don't you, Ivan? Sweet Dick?" When LaRosa said "Dick," he said it as if he had a pain in his cheek that forced him to grin and shut his eyes. "You tell the good citizen, Sweet Dick, that if he maintains his guilty plea he'll get a one-to-three. If he goes to bat and forces us to bring in the undercover to open court, he has *my* word he'll get banged with a seven-and-a-half-to-fifteen-year bit."

Ivan Jaeger looked around at the fish tanks, at the phony African artwork, then he glanced at the American flag behind Frank LaRosa's desk. "The man's innocent, Frank. Do you care about that? Does that matter to you?"

"Ivan, can I say something to you off the record?"

"Just don't tell me anything that can help Richard. Listen, Frank, on second thought don't tell me anything at all."

Ivan Jaeger got up from the couch and stretched. He looked like a man who had been fighting sleep and was now ready to roll over and call it quits. "I have twenty-four cases set for trial, another one more or less . . ." Jaeger's voice trailed off. He began clearing his throat. It was an announcement that he was ready to leave.

"Ivan, ya know what you can tell Sweet Dick?" LaRosa said, not looking up from his desk.

"I can tell him he's been fucked, that's what I can tell him."

"O.K., but after you tell him he's been fucked, you tell him he's gonna do a big nine months for a drug sale he may or may not have made. Tell him to consider all the crimes he's committed that he's never been caught for. Tell him to just think about the day Detective Lerner said he sold her heroin. Ask him if he didn't commit enough criminal acts on that day alone to compensate for the nine months. If the answer to that question is that he did not, then go to bat. I give you my word. You personally. If you're satisfied with Sweet Dick's response, and go to trial, and lose, he'll not do more than one to three." LaRosa felt that he did real well with that statement. He pushed himself back away from his desk and offered Ivan Jaeger his hand.

Ivan stared at LaRosa's hand for a long moment, then put both his hands in his pockets. "Frank," he said with his head bowed, "do you understand the implications of what you just said?"

"We're not talking implictaions here, Ivan, we're talking reality."

"You're telling me to advise my client to plead guilty to a crime he did not commit. And"—Ivan paused, then said with feigned overconcern, "he should consider all the crimes he's committed that he hasn't been charged with, not apprehended for. That's what you're telling me?"

"Right. The dirt bag probably commits twenty felonies a day," LaRosa said quickly.

"Do you know what you should do, Frank?"

"What?" LaRosa asked pleasantly.

"You should poison the guppies and get yourself some law books." Ivan began slowly, almost softly, but soon his voice rose. "You're a prosecutor, the people's voice in the courtroom. You're not a prosecutor in some third world happy-farm country. That Supreme Court building across the street is not a soccer stadium with gallows and shooting posts at midfield. Frank," he yelled, "this is the fucking United States of America. We have something called the Constitution. Defendants are presumed innocent until you, the state, prove that they are guilty. The Constitution, Frank, the Bill of Rights, Frank. The next time you get confused look behind your desk; that's the American flag, you schmuck."

As Ivan Jaeger turned and began walking from LaRosa's office, Frank spoke to his back. "I make sense; you talk Legal Aid missionary bullshit." Then Frank LaRosa got angry. "Guppies, guppies," he shouted, "these fucking Oscars cost me twenty bucks apiece. You're the schmuck, you can't even tell the difference between fifty-cent guppies and twenty-dollar Oscars."

Ivan Jaeger slammed LaRosa's door and a statue of a black man holding a spear toppled from his shelf. LaRosa smiled to himself. Jackie, you did the right thing, and now I've done the right thing. Everyone is better off for it. But now we're even.

21.

When Major Red Burke sank back in his seat, Bobby looked into his eyes for a clue. There was none.

He waited for the major to react, to say something, anything. But the red-headed man just slowly sipped his cup of tea and brandy. After a while he scratched his head, then he took a deep breath.

Bobby had told him the whole story. He'd left nothing out. He told him why his brother and the others had been killed. He told him about the Cold Spring Harbor Inn, about Detective Cruz and breakfast with the dwarf. He told him that he'd learned his partner had once been Doyle's bagman. Finally he told Major Burke that although he'd become a policeman as a lark, as a gesture to Cathy, he now loved the work. He'd lost Cathy, he said, he didn't want Doyle to take the job from him too. And that was the only time, during his hour's monologue, that he saw Major Red Burke smile. Then he showed him the book.

When the major had finished reading, he scratched his head again, closed the book, and handed it to Bobby.

"With the right publisher," Burke said, "this could be a bestseller."

It was amazing how explicit the book was. Bobby easily identified all the characters. He knew that this book could blow the lid right off the department. Who would gain? Who would enjoy seeing that happen?

"My partner once told me that he'd never take part in embarrassing the department. He said he had no need to make history. I agree with him. I just want to get Doyle."

"Well, if that's what you want, that book will do the job for you." The major's voice was both soothing and interesting. Bobby expected him to leap to his feet after reading the book. He expected Burke to scream for prison for every one of the book's characters. He didn't.

"I don't want to hurt the department. It's been good to me," Bobby said finally.

"Now that's your dilemma, isn't it?" And Red Burke was smiling. What a full, freckled boyish smile he had.

"I don't understand Doyle," Bobby said, "and to tell you the truth, I don't understand your brother either. I know that down deep these are not evil men. But, you'll forgive me, Major, the truth is, the captain was, and Doyle is, a criminal."

Red Burke bit the inside of his cheek and nodded his head.

"The truth is a wonderful thing, Bobby, but you can't understand the truth until you understand history."

I do understand history, Bobby thought, history is one of the few things I do understand.

The major got up from the table and walked over to the bar. He reached over and took a bottle of brandy.

The bartender said, "Just help yourself, Major." Red Burke looked at him, and the bartender smiled.

Now when he poured the tea into his cup it was only a touch. The major was a good listener. He could sit with his hands folded in his lap. He could smile reassuringly. But when Red Burke spoke his mind he spoke with missionary zeal. People listened.

"By the way, Major, I think I do understand history," Bobby said.

Bobby expected Jesuit fire, he got Christian-brother understanding. Even Red Burke it seemed, had a need to rationalize.

"Bobby," he said gently, "you don't understand what happened to your partner. You thought you knew him completely, but you didn't. You don't understand my brother and what happened to him. Chief Doyle,"—he paused—"no one understands him. I doubt if he understands himself. But I think it's about time you understand more about the world of the policeman. A world you've been part of, and still you seem to lack a real understanding."

Bobby poured himself a full cup of brandy. He took the teapot, he'd thought he'd add some tea. But there was no room in the cup. He put the pot down and smiled at the major.

"Take the police in New York," the major began, "and in Boston, and in Chicago, and in my own state. In Newark or Jersey City. As a matter of fact, take the police in any major city of this country. Take all those police officers, and put them on a line graph of one hundred. Do you know what you'll find?"

Bobby shrugged, and sipped his brandy.

"You'll find that five percent are criminals, and they would have been criminals had they not been police officers. Had they been insurance salesmen, bank tellers, or what have you, they would have been criminals. Do you understand what I'm saying, Bobby?"

Bobby nodded his head.

"Five percent on the other end of the graph are totally honest. They will be completely professional under any set of circumstances. The remaining ninety percent will go whichever way the peer pressure of their department is pushing."

"Are you saying, ninety-five percent of a police department has the potential for being dishonest?"

"Or honest," the major answered quickly. "The peer pressure of a department comes from the aura of that particular department. From the leadership, from the people in charge." Red Burke was beginning to raise his voice.

There were more people sitting around than Bobby would have liked. And as was his way, Major Burke drew attention. But he was totally oblivious to the salad munchers and beer drinkers. Now he was pointing at Bobby much the same way Mark did the day before he died.

"Police brutality, police abuse, police corruption exist only in those departments where the leadership accepts it. They show they condone it by doing nothing about it. When a young officer, just out of the academy, steps into a world where everything he deals with is perverted, where his sense of morality, integrity, is attacked the minute he hits the street, he will have a real problem unless he's supported by his supervisors and his peers."

Bobby's mind began to drift. The major brought him back quickly.

"You have to understand the institutions people are involved in and the historical forces that are brought to bear on them. How that combination affects people. If, in fact, a policeman is pressured by everyone around him to behave in ways that very well may be foreign to his nature, he has a serious problem. Most succumb, most join in, most lose sight of who and what they are. That's what happened to my brother. I know, I saw it happen, I saw the change."

"So you're answering my question. You think I should turn this book over to Roxbury. I should help him put Doyle in jail."

"That's not at all what I'm saying. First of all, that's a decision you'll have to make for yourself. I'm not going to make that decision for you. If what is described in this book were current, then I don't think you'd have a choice. But this information is ten years old. Institutions change. When institutions change, people change, and these people have changed now. Probably to a man, they're behaving very differently today."

"Doyle's not," Bobby said sharply.

"You're probably right." The major nodded his head and smiled. Bobby thought it was almost an admiring gesture. It annoyed him.

"But Doyle is a leader, a chief inspector, he's the guy who creates the aura you talked about," Bobby said quickly.

"Doyle is also a dinosaur. His day has passed. His police department no longer exists. Doyle's days are numbered."

"Why do you say that?" Bobby asked.

"You're the proof."

"How?"

"Tom Doyle, and my brother"—Red Burke spoke quietly now—"went into a police department that had a history of organized, systematic, institutionalized corruption. You either went along, and learned to live with it, or you got out. Now, I'm not saying you had to participate in the corruption, but you sure as hell had to go along with it or you were ostracized, you became an outsider. My brother wasn't built to be an outsider. And we both know Doyle. The police department you came into is not like that."

"I'm not sure I know what you mean."

"My point exactly. You'd know if those conditions still existed."

"Like what?" Bobby asked.

"Has anyone offered you money not to do your job?"

"No."

"Has anyone told you that if you wanted to work a certain tour, ride in a certain sector, walk a certain post, it'd cost *you* money?"

"Of course not."

"Did your sergeant give you a list at Christmas time of store owners to pick up money from?"

"Are you kidding?"

"No, I'm not kidding. Have you heard stories of other cops in the precinct taking money from known gamblers or other O.C. types?"

"No, no, I never heard about any of that."

"Well," Major Burke said, "like I said, times have changed. And Doyle, like it or not, his day is over."

"Major," Bobby said quietly, "you're not helping me!" Then he looked straight into the major's eyes and asked, "What would you do if you had this book?"

"Look," Burke said, "my brother, Doyle, and that whole crew that worked up on Harlem, your partner included, had something very special. They were bonded, not only by normal ties of policemen for policemen, but also by the fact that they needed to trust one another in a way only people involved in conspiracy can understand. Any one of them at any time could have brought down the rest of them. They all knew that, and still they continued doing what they were doing. Their trust and loyalty to each other was boundless. My brother, for example; Artie trusted Tom Doyle more than he trusted me. He went to Tom Doyle for advice and counsel before coming to me. Why? Because he believed Tom Doyle understood him better than I did. My brother was afraid that I would judge him harshly. Like your partner was afraid that you would judge

[250]

him harshly. Artie thought that what I would perceive as my duty would triumph over my love for him. You see, Bobby, I believe, and my brother knew it, that on some level duty does triumph over love and friendship. But my brother didn't know that I also believe that on other levels love and friendship triumph over duty. What my brother was doing, and what Tom Doyle did, happened within an environment where everyone was corrupt. We're not talking about violent crime."

"What would you do with the book, Major?" Bobby asked coolly.

Major Burke drained his cup, then stared at it for a long moment. "You once told me you were interested in sociology, right?"

"That's right." He's not going to answer me, Bobby thought. It's so much easier to direct the fire than it is to point the guns. Bobby was feeling depressed but he continued to listen.

"O.K., the problem with sociology and sociologists is that they live by, and believe in, a system of rules. They pin labels on things after the fact. You've been out in the street. That's not the way it works, is it? It's a case-by-case situation, isn't it? There is no adequate system. You have to go with what you think is right. Most times what you think is right can't be systematized, yet you know it's still right."

"Excuse me, Major. But with all due respect, I want you to answer my question. What would you do in my position if you had this book, this pad?"

"I don't have the book, Bobby. You do. You can destroy Doyle with that book. Just remember, that book is not a rifle with a telescopic sight. It's a machine gun. You'll take Doyle out all right, but you'll also drop twenty other people too. It's your decision, you're a bright guy. Go do what you think is right. Do the right thing."

When Cathy left she'd left behind the Volkswagen. That was reassuring; she'd have to come back for her car, he thought.

The little car was a blast to drive, and Bobby scooted along ten miles above the speed limit. The wind on the Verrazano Bridge made the VW dance. But Bobby didn't notice. He'd made his decision. He smiled when he thought that not even Major Red Burke of the Jersey state police knew what the "right thing" was.

First it was the siren, he looked in the mirror, then it was the whooper. He looked down at the speedometer. Bobby was doing seventy-miles an hour in a fifty-mile-an-hour zone. And he had no shield.

He pulled into a safety island and got out of the car. The operator of the blue-and-white met him halfway between the two cars.

"License and registration."

The cop was short, one of the new mini-cops. But he was in terrific shape, obviously a body builder; his short-sleeve shirt was cutting into his biceps.

"I'm sorry you had to chase me," Bobby said, then reached to his back pocket for his shield.

"Yeah," the cop said, "let me see your license."

"I'm on the job," Bobby said quietly.

"It figures, it's the end of the month and the only people I stop are cops and firemen."

The cop was waiting for him to show his shield and ID.

"I, ahh," Bobby touched his right, then his left back pocket. "I, ahh, don't have my tin."

"Ya got your ID or anything? . . . Whaddaya mean, you don't have your tin?" he added quickly.

"I'm under suspension. I was suspended about a week ago."

"Hey, my man, what's happening?" The cop's partner had gotten out of the car and now stood with his foot on the bumper.

"I said, what's happening?" he yelled.

"This guy says he's on the job. But he ain't got a shield or an ID. He *says* he's under suspension."

Bobby wondered if these two guys were steady partners.

The cop with his foot on the bumper nodded in sympathy, then walked over to join his partner.

As he approached, Bobby could tell this cop had been around a while. He had on one of those thousand-mission caps, the kind of hat generally worn by motorcycle cops, or old, sour hair bags. And he was at least ten years older than his partner. Mark's age, Bobby thought.

"Teddy, just look at this poor sucker and this ugly Volkswagen. If he ain't a cop, I ain't. Where'd you work?" the older cop asked.

"I was in the Twentieth for a while. Then in the bureau. I was suspended a week ago."

Bobby had noticed that the mini-cop with muscles had moved in closer. But he wouldn't say a word, the senior man would do all the talking.

"Ya see, Teddy, here's a guy, can't be much older than you. He's been in a precinct, been in the bureau, and been suspended. This guy's got an interesting career going. And what do you wanna do? You wanna chase speeders. The kid gets his rocks off playing with the whooper and the siren. Ahh, whaddaya gonna do, the whole job's going down the tubes."

Strange, Bobby felt more of a kinship with the older cop than the younger.

"Well, Evel, on my post we don't give other cops aggravation. This is one speeder you're gonna haveta let slide. Too bad, killer." The older cop winked at Bobby and patted his partner's shoulder. He said he called his partner Evel Knievel. "The guy terrifies me," he said. "I tell him don't chase nobody doin' over eighty. Every time I look up he's bouncing one-twenty."

"Young guys," Bobby said, "whaddaya gonna do? They give 'em all those toys; the car, the light, the siren."

"The fucking whooper," the older cop said.

"By the way, what's ya name?"

"Porterfield, Bobby Porterfield."

"Well, Bob, don't let 'em get ya down. Don't mean a thing. A little suspension don't mean shit. You oughta see my yellow sheet."

The older cop put his arm around the younger and walked him back to the blue-and-white. "I'm driving, Evel," he said. The young cop shrugged, then shook his head and got in on the recorder's side.

"Hey, Bob," the older cop called out. "Just do the right thing and fuck 'em if dey can't take a joke. Ya know what I mean?"

* * *

Bobby found himself staring out the window of District Attorney Roxbury's office. Red Burke had arranged it with one phone call.

How quickly things changed.

When the major called a few days after their meeting he seemed self-conscious, even contrite.

And Bobby had jumped at him.

"I have to do something!" He spoke to the major in a way he wouldn't have dared a few days ago. He believed that must mean something.

"Doyle's responsible for your brother's death! For my partner's death! Goddamnit, Major, you haven't helped me. I come to you for guidance and get sociological bullshit."

The major told him he was sorry. His concern for his brother's memory clouded his thinking. Tom Doyle's evaluation of him was essentially true. His purview was small. His problems far less complicated than his brother's and Doyle's.

Bobby barely listened. He was too angry.

"I have this book! I have this pad! I have Doyle right by the balls and I want to twist."

"Calm down," the major said. "The first thing you have to do is calm down." The major had a way of clearing his throat before he made one of his little speeches. "I want you to recognize the size of the task you're taking on. You're not going after Doyle. You're going to put yourself at odds with an entrenched system of doing business. And you're going to join forces with people who are just as entrenched. They have a way of doing business too, you know. They're politicians. You could be very disappointed."

"Are you telling me there's no answer?" Bobby asked coolly.

"I'm telling you I really don't know. But I'm also telling you to do what you think is right."

Then Major Burke told him that he had arranged, through a friendly prosecutor, for Bobby to meet with Roxbury. He hadn't mentioned the book. Turning that over remained Bobby's decision. In the end their conversation had been soft. In the end, Major Red Burke wished him luck.

District Attorney Roxbury's office inspired trust. Books, flags, and photos of law enforcement and city leaders found space on the D.A.'s wall. Nowhere did Bobby see a picture of a wife or children or even a friend. A photo of the mayor, signed and dated, along with a congratulatory letter, stood in a frame on his desk.

Roxbury had been on the phone for fifteen minutes. He was paying, it seemed, no attention whatsoever to Bobby.

Earlier, when Bobby arrived, there had been a quick greeting and a point to a chair. Then the phone rang. Two or three people had come into the office. Roxbury would look up and wave them out with a flicking backhand. Not Bobby's favorite gesture.

Now abruptly Roxbury put down the phone. He smiled and Bobby smiled back, and the phone rang again.

At the end of a surprisingly short conversation, Roxbury buzzed his secretary. After telling her to hold his calls, he turned to Bobby.

"Sooo," he said slyly, "you want to be a hero."

Bobby didn't flinch.

"I am a hero," he answered quickly.

Roxbury smiled again. And Bobby thought: How do you trust a guy who doesn't have eyebrows?

Then he wondered how all this would end.

Roxbury could have been as young as thirty-five or as old as fifty-five. He had one of those bodies and one of those faces that were ageless and ancient.

This guy didn't play for his high school football team. He was born thirty-five. And he looked like he hated the boys who laughed and played with the girls.

"Of course, of course," Roxbury said, nodding his head. His hair and skin were fair, and he had a puzzled look that made his face look fuzzy. Bobby disliked him immediately.

"You are a hero. I read all about it. As a matter of fact, I saw you on TV. I distinctly remember mentioning to a friend, now there's a cop with an education. I think you used the word 'perpetrator' only once or at the most twice. Not the normal half dozen times cops usually do."

And Roxbury was effective, very dramatic. He began pulling folders from a cabinet behind his desk. The files were ten years old, and they were all stamped "Sixth Division Investigation."

He displayed them on his desk, rubbed his hands together, and grinned.

"I almost had the strutting bastards ten years ago. I missed, but I'll get them this time. I love to watch their knees shake when I bring 'em in to the grand jury. They always make sure they wear all their medals. It really is funny."

The way Roxbury stood there, his stance, his body, and his grin, made Bobby's feet sweat. The big red-headed Irishman was right. The guy's a shit.

"Listen," Roxbury said, "I'm starting an official corruption unit. I have someone to run it who is absolutely terrific. He knows the street, and he knows the police department. I understand you had a run-in with Chief Doyle. He suspended you. Is that correct?"

Bobby nodded.

"Well, don't worry, I can handle that. I need a bright guy that knows Doyle. Knows him from the inside. From what I understand, you're eminently qualified."

Roxbury, it seemed, had a lot to say, but acted as though he had little time to say it. In a vague, abstract way, Roxbury reminded him of several people. He was a fan of none of them.

Roxbury spoke of policemen as if they were lesser people. And Bobby was experiencing feelings he had no control over. His mind, as it did when Cathy raved, took him away. It brought him to a place where he could rest; he could appear to listen, appear to understand. But he heard nothing. He watched Roxbury's face as he smiled and grinned. As he spoke the man contorted his nose like there was something foul in the room.

Mr. Roxbury, Bobby thought, you are not the answer. If I feel this way, he thought, then I belong to no one, to neither side. Not to Doyle, nor Burke, certainly not to Roxbury.

The phone rang; it was the intercom.

"Send him in," Roxbury said. "Oh, this is great. Send him right in."

Roxbury was doing a strange kind of dance behind his desk.

"You are going to meet the man I've chosen to head up my anti-corruption unit."

I can hardly wait, Bobby thought.

The door opened and Bobby was caught up in a sudden sense of panic. Phil, the dwarf's nephew, was in the room . . . no . . . it was just his cologne.

"Bobby Porterfield, I want you to meet Frank LaRosa, the newly appointed chief of my anti-corruption unit."

Bobby sat on a bench at his favorite spot on the Brooklyn Heights promenade. The book, Chief Doyle's cruise ticket for prison gray, was still in his pocket.

He was thinking about his meeting with Roxbury while leafing through the *New York Post*. Every so often he'd glance out at the river. Helicopters flew back and forth, brightly colored tugs and barges and a green-and-white Circle Line boat moved slowly against a mighty current. What an incredible city. There was nothing about this city that looked threatening from here.

Four predators, bent at the waist, hands cuffed behind their backs, looked up at a photographer on page two. They looked like beasts, animals from another planet. They'd been arrested for the stabbing murder of a fourteen-year-old high school student. They'd killed him for his radio. They'd stabbed him nine times, then danced on the subway platform. He was a good boy, the mother of the high school student had said. A quiet boy. He loved his radio. It was the only thing he could really call his own. And they danced, and they smiled at the photographer. And Roxbury enjoyed watching as cops' knees shook when he brought them in to the grand jury. They always wore their medals, he said. It was funny really, he said.

What could you expect from a guy with no eyebrows? Bobby thought.

And Frank LaRosa, head of the anti-corruption unit.

A police helicopter roared to a halt over Pier 3, its blades slapped the air. Bobby could almost see the pilot's face.

On page thirteen: "1B-a-Year Dope Ring Smashed." Three cops were smiling. One had his hand in the air, he was giving the world his own three-finger-and-circle sign.

He folded the *Post* and put it under his arm. He walked from the promenade down toward, then onto Willow Street.

Maybe he'd go up to Columbia and see if he could still

register for the fall semester. He thought about the four smiling predators in the *Post*. Let someone else be a social worker, he thought.

He'd heard that Cathy had gone out to L.A. Now that was a police department she could relate to. Maybe he'd go out to the Coast and find her. Cathy had never called him. She treated him as if he'd died with Mark, as if their years together never happened. Screw her, he thought. Let her marry an FBI agent and be happy. Cathy was gone, part of his past. He was growing up, building a history.

Maybe he'd call Jackie. Uhmmm, maybe he would call Jackie. Then he thought: Not now. Next week, maybe.

He stopped for a moment near a tightly covered trash can. He pulled off the lid, then opened the *Post* to the centerfold. He laid the paper on top of the garbage.

He dropped in the book, closed the paper over it, put back the lid, and walked home.

He felt relieved.

Maybe he'd call Red Burke.

That's it, he'd call Red Burke and sip Hennessy and tea, and listen to "Danny Boy" on a jukebox in New Jersey.